Pr

"a science fiction-fantasy thriller with an added dose of murder, mystery and mayhem ..." – Wendy, Goodreads

"funny, witty dialogues were enough comic relief in all the strange and sometimes scary crime scenes ... if the saying of starting with a blast is true, then this series is bound to become a hit!" – Lydia P., Goodreads Top Reviewer

"a very vivid imagination and I would definitely read another one of his books ..." – Angel S., Goodreads Best Reviewer

"the Black Dwarf takes what we expect from the fantasy genre and reforms it into something new and exciting. ..." – C. P. Bialois, Author of *The Sword and the Flame, Call of Poseidon,* and *Skeleton Key*

"a wonderful imagination in the life-and-death situations ..." – Erlinda C. N.

"a nonstop read. It took me three hours without putting it down to read from front to back! This book kept me flipping the pages wanting to know more!" – Misty A., Goodreads

~~~~~

~~~~~

Also by Dan Knight

Cretaceous Clay & the Black Dwarf
Book One of the Chronicles of Cretaceous Clay

Available from Amazon.com, CreateSpace.com, and other great retail outlets!

~~~~~

Coming Soon!

Cretaceous Clay & the Yellow Stone
Book Three of the Chronicles of Cretaceous Clay

~~~~~

Cretaceous Clay

& the

Ninth Ring

~~~~~

Dan Knight

~~~~~

Stonewald, LLC

Greenville, Texas

This book is a work of fiction. Names, characters, places and incidents are either the product of the author's imagination or are used fictitiously. Any resemblance to actual persons, living or dead, or to actual events or locales is entirely coincidental.

CRETACEOUS CLAY & THE NINTH RING

Published by Stonewald, LLC

Copyright © 2013 ALAN BROOKS.

All rights reserved.

No part of this text may be reproduced, transmitted, downloaded, decompiled, reverse engineered, or stored in or introduced into any information storage and retrieval system, in any form or by any means, whether electronic or mechanical without the express written permission of the author. The scanning, uploading, and distribution of this book via the Internet or via any other means without the permission of the publisher is illegal and punishable by law. Please purchase only authorized electronic editions and do not participate in or encourage electronic piracy of copyrighted materials.

This eBook is licensed for your personal enjoyment only. This eBook may not be re-sold for profit. If you cannot afford a copy: Please post a nice review. Thank you for respecting the hard work of the author.

Publisher's Acknowledgements:

Cover Designed by Stonewald, LLC

Cover Art: Copyright 01-06-13 © Constance Knox / iStockphoto.com / Standard License

Editor: Tina Musial

Maps of Nodlon and the Ninth Ring: Copyright © 2013 ALAN BROOKS.

Softcover Printed by CreateSpace, Charleston SC, an Amazon.com Company

Author's Website: BlackDwarves.com

~~~~~

ISBN-10: 0-9893861-1-2 (eBook – 1d)
ISBN-13: 978-0-9893861-1-1 (eBook – 1d)
ISBN-10: 0-9893861-3-9 (eBook – Dan Knight)
ISBN-13: 978-0-9893861-3-5 (eBook – Dan Knight)
ISBN-10: 0-9893861-4-7 (Paperback)
ISBN-13: 978-0-9893861-4-2 (Paperback)

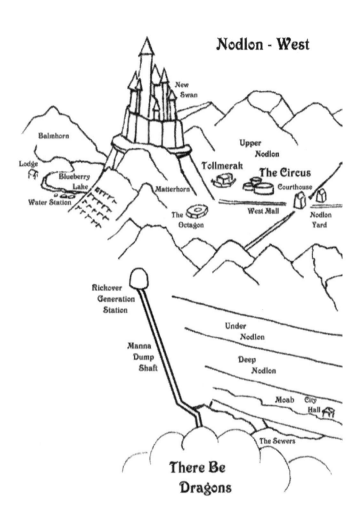

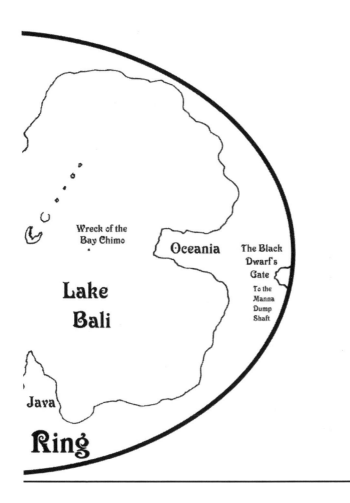

x

Contents

Sweet Dreams 1

No News is Good News 19

A Victim in the Sewer 23

Port of Moab 49

The Proconsul of Moab 73

Off the Case 85

Sacrifice of the First Born 93

Eldad and Medad 97

Beslan 101

Daisy 119

Mole Charity 129

Deprogramming 149

The First Born 159

None Dare Call It Conspiracy 169

Escape From Moab 183

Noddie 197

The Ninth Ring 213

Bora Bora 235

Intruder Alert 251

The Black Wharf 255

Port Royal 271

Castle Frankenstein 291

Blondie..323

The Emperor's Clothes..329

Orpheus 343

Flight of the Black Dwarf 363

Bouncy Balls 373

Epilogue: On the Beach 379

The Adventure Continues..383

Acknowledgements..393

Cretaceous Clay

& the

Ninth Ring

~~~~~

Dan Knight

~~~~~

Sweet Dreams

Count sheep, don't count sheep. What's the use? She rolled over. She rolled over again.

It was no use. She threw off her blanket and sat up.

Her bedroom glowed by the nightlight. Her room was pink, but it was too dark to see any colors. Ghostly shapes and dark shadows surrounded her.

Posters covered her walls. A bucket of kittens stared at her next to a pair of wide-eyed puppies. Above her vid was a poster of Cretaceous Clay bursting from a swirl of ballerinas. A star burst behind the magician.

The clock read the third hour. Half the night was gone, and she had hardly slept.

Her apartment was empty. *Oh, not completely empty.* She had a bathroom, a computer, a vid, and a sound system on which she could play the Rockhounds or a thousand other bands and a big closet full of clothes. *Comfy clothes.*

Yes, it's not empty, but it's not a home.

She had never had a home. *And this isn't it.*

Be grateful for what you have, said a little voice in her head.

"Shove it," she said. *They did that! They put voices in my head! It's just the programming! They programmed me so I won't feel bad.*

Letting go, she put her face in her hands and began to weep. She cried hot, bitter tears. "It's not fair!"

No, it isn't, said the voice.

"Shut up!" she yelled.

I'm only trying to help, said the voice, *it's not that bad. You're not sick, and you're not a monster. You're a healthy, beautiful young woman. They gave you that.*

"You're just an illusion they programmed into me."

You don't know that, Angela.

"I'm just a thing they cooked up in a lab! Bio-Soft mixed

up in a batch of dwarves and put me in an incubator for nine months. Three years in a crib, three years in a nursery, seven more years at Tollmerak, and they slap a chip on your forehead and you're done. All baked. And you've got a contract on your head that you'll never pay off unless you find some way to cheat death."

You're not dead.

"I'm not alive!"

You have so much to look forward to.

"To what? What? I'm nothing. There's nothing for me in Nodlon except work and this bedroom. If I killed somebody, I'd get the same darn bedroom."

On the moon.

"Is that a joke?"

No baby, it's not a joke. Think of what you've got instead of what you haven't got. You've got a day off, and then some. You have a chance. You can go to nursing school at Nodlon Tech. The agency will pay for it.

"Then what? I'll owe more than I do now."

You'll make more.

"I'll owe interest."

If Jack Clay succeeds with the Biots Are People Too campaign, there won't be any interest.

"What makes you think they're going to succeed? Biots are people too? No one cares about biots."

I care.

"No you don't. You're just a voice in my head to keep me stable. Where do they put you? Are you in my chip?"

No, but I know Jack Clay cares.

"Yeah, so what? Jack's a nice guy and all, but no one listens to him. He calls his blog *The Court Jester*. He's no better than the rest of us."

Would your chip know about Jack Clay?

She popped out of bed, and went to the bathroom. She turned on the cold water and splashed her face. Cool water soothed her eyes. She pressed the temple of her nose to make the soreness go away. Her eyes were black and blue.

She daubed her face with a clean towel, and looked at herself in the full-length mirror on her door. She was a black dwarf. Average intelligence, average height, average bones, and average athletic ability, added together to make one average female specimen of a biot dwarf.

In the mirror, she looked at her chip. By the nightlight, it was no more than a spot the size of a ping pong ball.

"If I could just rip you out…"

What would that accomplish?

"So I got your attention again, did I?"

I am not your chip.

"Then what are you? Are you me?" She sighed. "I'm nothing. They didn't even bother to make me pretty."

Baloney! You're very pretty. They gave you perfect skin tone, weight balance, and properly sized everything in all the right spots.

"I'm as ordinary as a cardboard box."

You're beautiful.

"What? They just don't want me to throw myself off a cliff."

No, no, baby. True, they want you to accept yourself. It's self-serving. It doesn't do to have dwarves implode mentally.

"I know, I know, they told me. We're perfectly balanced. No defects, no imperfections, nothing to complain about. We get a health bonus.

"So there's no reason to go postal, and shoot the designers. But there's nothing special either. Not enough altitude to get any respect. Not enough sweets to catch any guy with anything on the ball. So we're stuck. We're all alike."

You're special, Angela!

"I'm unique just like everyone? Stow it, Jiminy Cricket. I'm not buying your baloney. I couldn't pick myself out of a line up."

All dwarves have that problem.

"Yeah, I know I'm dwarf. Thanks for the info. I care about my fellow dwarves. I'm not heartless."

I know.

"But so what, what can I do for them? If I can't help myself, what do you expect me to do about them?" She knelt in front of the mirror, and closed her eyes. She wished she had a life. She wished she could go somewhere. She wished she could leave everything behind.

Go to the break room. Maybe Marple is there. She's up late, and she's always got a new joke.

"I don't want to go to the break room, or the kitchen or anywhere else. I want to get out of here. I want to marry a hunk, and live in a hut. He'll fish for our dinner. I'll fry it up over the fire, and we'll have lots of babies."

That's definitely an idea. You don't even know how to live without a bathroom.

"What's it to you? It's my dream."

It means a lot to me. I want you to be happy, but you've got to be practical. There are lots of nice boys here in Nodlon who would be proud to marry you. I bet they'd give an eye tooth to take you out, if you'd just give them a chance.

"They're geeks. Scrawny little pathetic losers with a contract just like mine or worse. Besides, the only ones that would want me are the schlubs. I don't want a dork."

What are you going to do?

"Kill myself. Then I won't have to listen to you."

Don't do that. What will we do without you?

"Who cares? What's Nodlon going to do with one less biot? What are you going to do about it? Tell on me?"

I can't. I told you. I care about you.

"Liar! You're just a program in my chip to feed me pablum!"

I'm not in your chip, and I don't work for your agency.

"So I'm crazy? Stuff it! Stuff yourself! Just go away."

"Thump," went the door. She started and held her breathe. Who would be knocking at this hour?

She stared at her front door. It was locked. The status indicator was red. She gripped her mirror. She knew she had heard the sound.

Just someone coming off the late shift, she breathed, *and he bumped my door. Probably tied on one too many.* She put hand over her heart, and willed herself to be calm. Her heart fluttered.

Health bonus? Her pulse slowed, and she stood up. *Yeah, right! Sometimes the designers make mistakes, and we die.*

It was almost four.

~~~~~

The next morning she dragged herself to work. She put her tea next to her workstation and leaned over the cup letting the steam rise into her head.

"Are you all right?" her boss asked.

She looked up from the computer.

Abrams looked concerned. He had big, blue eyes, and he smiled sympathetically.

"Yes, sir," she smiled to reassure him. "I had trouble sleeping."

"You look sick."

"No, I'm fine, sir. I just," she sucked in a breath. "I just can't sleep."

"Maybe you should see a doctor."

"I do, every day, right here."

"No, I mean a real doctor," he smiled. "Angela, you're special. I care about you."

A bittersweet longing beat in her breast. Dr. Abrams was much older than she was, and he was single. His wife had passed away, and he had never remarried. His work consumed him, and he rarely found time to leave the lab much less date.

She had dreamed of seducing him. But it was against the

rules, and it would ruin his career. She would not let it happen to him. He was the nicest, most decent human she knew.

She wanted no harm to come to him. But it would be so easy. He was so naïve, and he had so much money. More money than she could earn in three lifetimes.

"You just don't look so well. Is there anything I can do?"

"Really, doctor, I'm okay. I just need to sleep."

"I'd call the agency, but I don't want to get you into any trouble."

"I'll be all right, doctor."

"Take an early lunch, and get an hour's nap." He checked his watch. "I won't say anything, if you come back looking better. I feel like a heel, and I haven't even gotten out the whip yet." He grinned, trying to make light of the situation.

She hung her head. *He must think I'm a flake. He thinks I've been out all night bar hopping.* A tear welled in her eye. She wanted him to think well of her.

"Thank you, doctor. I'll do that. I'll take a nap in the lounge. If you need me, I'll be there after lunch."

"Good, then."

She locked her computer. Everything in the lab was hush, hush. She took her satchel and left.

In the washroom, she tried to cover up the black circles around her eyes. *No wonder he thinks you're a flake. And you haven't even got a headache to show for it.*

~~~~~

The rush had already started in the cafeteria. She waited for her turn at the lunch counter, and stared at her shoes. She picked up a turkey, lettuce and tomato on whole wheat, a side of coleslaw, and a cookie with a smiley face. To pay, she let the scanner run her chip.

As an Octagon employee, the Ministry of Manna bought her lunch. Lunch was free, but it was humiliating. If you tried hard enough, you could get along pretty well in Nodlon without scanning your chip. But not in the Octagon right in the heart of the Ministry's research facilities.

She stuffed the lunch in her satchel and left the counter. She dodged the lunch crowd pouring in.

"Angela," someone called.

Heaving a sigh, she knew who it was without looking. It was Steinem. The middle-aged crone had taken an attachment to her, though Angela had no idea why.

She thought for a second. Leaving was out of the question without an excuse. She could not let the old ditty have any reason to call on her.

"Hi, dear," she said. "Sorry, I'm really tired."

"Honey pot, you look like a truck hit you."

"I'm going to take a nap. The boss thought I looked so bad; he gave me an hour."

"You do that, sweetie, after you eat. Now sit down and let's eat together. I'm starved."

Trapped, she smiled, and sat down. At least Steinem agreed she needed a nap. The crone would have to let her go.

The older woman plowed into a roast beef submarine with obvious relish. Oblivious to the irony, she munched on the submarine with the gusto of a truck driver while holding it with delicately manicured nails each with its own frilly pattern.

"So why are you tired?" Steinem asked with her mouth full. "You look like you haven't slept a wink in days." Juice ran out of her mouth, and she quickly dabbed at it, smearing her lipstick.

"Can't sleep. I wake up in the middle of the night, and I just pull it together."

"Something troubling you?"

She glanced around. There were humans, dwarves, elves, goblins, and many other kinds of biots gathering in the cafeteria. Lunch was on now, and the rush had become a crush.

"It's all right, honey pot," said Steinem. "I've heard it all before. It's a boyfriend, or no boyfriend. You want to sleep with your boss, and he doesn't, or he made a move on you, and you said no. There's nothing really new under the sun." She winked. "It's not like you can get into trouble. One advantage of not belonging to yourself; you're not responsible."

"It's nothing like that. Not the way you mean. I guess you've heard it before. I just want a future. I want to be married. I'm only twenty-one, and I've worked here three years if you count my internship. I'm like every other dwarf. I have nothing to complain about, but then again I've got nothing to look forward to."

"Let your fairy godmother give you a piece of advice. Try gene therapy. Once you get enhanced, you can catch any man you want."

"But it's expensive. I can't afford it."

"No, sugar, it's not as much as you think. I know this new place where you can get the works. The whole shooting match. They take payments, and there's no interest." Steinem leaned forward and whispered, "And they give girls great discounts. Just for the asking. It's good for the business."

"I'm not sure. I'll be paying for years, and if the agency finds out they might not let me go to nursing school."

"Don't worry about it, sweetness. If anything goes wrong, and you decide you don't want a man, you can come see me, and I'll get you hooked up."

"But," she said.

"No, buts honey. Nothing tried, nothing gained."

"I don't know. I don't like taking chances."

"Look honey, after you get upgraded, no man can resist you! Before you know it, some guy will buy your contract. All you have to do is find the right man, and you're home free. Six months from now you can be living up on the mountain. Maybe even in New Swan itself. Nothing comes for free, but if you play your cards right, you'll find a decent guy who just wants babies and a good mother for his kids. Isn't that what you want? You'll get your own episode on *Nodlon Wives*!"

Nodlon Wives was the hottest afternoon show for women in the biot market. She watched their show at night since she was not a domestic. The producers told the story of a young biot maid finding what they called a situation. And it was not bad. Their show was about successful couples.

She started crying. Tears rolled down her cheeks and dropped on her sandwich. Love had happened many times before in Nodlon. But would it happen for her? Surely, if she were good enough, she could find Prince Charming with a log cabin on a lake.

The older woman took her hand gently, and caressed her fingers. "Sorry, I know it hurts. I didn't mean to be too pushy. What are you thinking of?"

"*Nodlon Wives*," she sat down her sandwich. "Did you see the latest show? An elf named Jenny married a businessman named Howell. They're taking their honeymoon on his yacht. They're sailing to the El Dorado Resort in Florida."

"Oh, how romantic," Steinem grinned like a cat with a mouse. "Just think sweetie that could be you."

"What if something happens? Remember the dwarf that disappeared? They found her in Blueberry Lake. I saw it on *Fuzz*."

"Now, now, honey pot, that girl has nothing to do with you. You know there are monsters crawling around Nodlon, right?"

"Yeah, and I don't want to meet any of 'em."

"What are the odds? Look honey, go through a dating service."

"How?"

"How? *Nodlon Wives* screens their men for everything. No deadbeat dads, no wife beaters, no drunks, and no bipolar mind games allowed. They're real careful. They even brain scan the human guys. Sure, you might meet a guy who's shy, or a little older, or has too much around the middle, but none of them are going to hurt you. Treat 'em right, and they'll take you places. Love 'em as much as they love you, and they'll worship you like a queen. Like I said, brain scans, background checks, blood tests."

"No, I mean how can I get enhanced? Gene therapy is like replacing my whole code. It's got to be expensive."

"No it ain't, sugar plums," Steinem grinned, and Angela felt a pit in her stomach. "New Gem has made it affordable." The woman reached into a huge purse with a psychedelic pattern and withdrew a card. "Here, take this card. Show it to them. Tell them I sent you, and you'll get another half off."

"But how can it be that cheap?"

"They're just repairing your code honey. They just put in the bits the designers left out to keep you humble. The designers cheated you to make sure you know your place. And they set your contract so high to make sure you can't buy your way out. They'd jack it up higher, but they want you to think you can pay it off. Then they add the interest to make sure you can't."

"Why then? Why would New Gem do it cheap?"

"Volume, sugar, volume," she smiled. "They keep the cost down, but sell ten times more treatments. So they actually make more than most chop shops."

Angela nodded, it made sense, and it rang true, but a doubt gnawed at her.

"What?" Steinem asked. "Is your stability program after you?"

"My what?" She was not sure she had heard right. "What did you say?"

"Your stability program, is it after you? I can tell you've got a strong one. It's eating you alive."

"Do you believe in stability programs?"

"Honey, don't you go buying into the propaganda put out by Bio-Soft or Cybernetics. Of course there are stability programs. They're built into your chip." Steinem made a long face. She rolled her eyes, and mocked the program. "Telling you right from wrong. Telling you, you're special just the way you are." Her eyes bounced back and forth, "Keeping you on the straight and narrow, and keeping you out of trouble. All for your own good of course." Then in her usual tone, she spat, "it's all rubbish. They just don't want you wandering off the reservation and living your own life."

Angela looked at the card and stuck it in her satchel. "Thank you, Stein. I'll think it over."

"You do that honey pot. You do that." With a wave, Steinem bussed her lunch box and left.

Don't do it, said the voice in her head, *please don't trust her*.

I said I'll think about it, she replied. *I'm just thinking. Can't you people at least let me alone in this little space in my head?*

~~~~~

Again, she tossed and turned that night. Sleep came in fits when it came at all.

She was running, and running, and running. Bristles caught her clothes, and thistles scratched her feet. *Where am I?* A ruin rose out of the brush. *The Pale! I must be in the Pale! I have to hide.* She ran into the ruin and around a corner. Beside a pile of stones she found a cedar. She darted behind the cedar hoping she would not be followed. A shadow fell on the dirt. The specter had found her. There was nowhere to run. She was trapped.

She awoke with a start. Sleep paralysis gripped her, and she could not move.

Nightmare, I was just having a nightmare.

She sat up in bed and cried. It was almost the third hour.

Beside her was her stuffed gingerbread man. She picked him up and hugged him. "I'm alone, Ginger." She said to the stuffie, "All alone."

Stop feeling sorry for yourself, said the voice. *Get over your pity party*.

She ignored him. "You're not the only one who's alone,"

she said to Ginger. "Don't answer him." She willed herself not to answer.

The card on her night stand caught her eye. She picked it up and looked at it. On the back was a schedule of times and vid channels. During the third hour, the channel read, "601." She sat the card down, and picked up her remote.

"Vid on," she said, and the screen brightened. A reality show was playing. Dwarves wearing funny costumes were trying to knock each other off of small boats floating in a pond. An elf explained the action and cracked a few lame jokes.

"Six, oh, one," she said, and the vid switched channels.

A muscle-bound jock appeared on the vid wearing nothing more than a loin cloth. He smiled, "Hungry? Angry? Lonely? Tired? Make it right, tonight!"

Angela, stop! The voice nagged her. *Be a good girl, and turn it off.*

The jock climbed a rock wall. He flexed his biceps and twisted to show off his rippling twelve pack abs. He shook his hips. "Don't be blue! All your dreams can come true!"

Turn it off, Angela, said the voice. *Please turn it off.*

She clutched her gingerbread man and breathed. The voice was silent.

This isn't for you, Angela. Please, I'll find you a boyfriend. It may take some time, but I promise you a good life, if you'll just turn it off.

"Sell it to Betsy. When I buy my contract, I'll get my chip removed, and that'll be the end of you."

I'm not in your chip.

"If you're not in my chip, why do you sound like a guy?"

Why not sound like a guy?

"Are you me?"

The voice did not answer.

"Look, if you're me, you should sound like a girl. But you sound like a guy because they set you up down in the control department and someone goofed and selected the male voice instead of the female."

The voice was silent.

"Right, so I guess I got your number."

A chimpanzee ran up to the jock. The hunk of masculinity picked up the ape, gave him a hug, and put him on his back. "Come one, come all," he cried.

One last time, Angela, don't do this. Save yourself.

"I am saving myself, silly. When I'm beautiful, I can have any guy I want."

"Come now! Come call!" The jock bellowed. He took hold of a green vine, and swung across the canyon into a magical forest of peppermint trees and lollipops.

If you call them, said the voice insistently, *your life will be over*.

"Rubbish, gene therapy is safe. I looked it up. It's more dangerous taking a robo-cab."

"Call me! Call now!" yelled the jungle jock. The jingle echoed off a candy cane canyon. "Call me! Call now!"

She put Ginger down, picked up the card and tapped New Gem's number into her caster.

"Call me! Call now! Call me now, if you want to feel alive!"

The call connected, and she heard music.

"Call me! Call now! Call me now, if you want to change your life!"

"Mute," she said, and the vid silenced the jungle man.

From her caster, a cello played a slow romantic solo by Rachmaninoff. She wondered how she knew that, but dismissed the thought. *All the brains you never wanted, and no place to use it.*

"New genes, New Gem!" said a goblin maiden. "How may I help you?"

"Hi, I'm Angela Christie and a friend of mine gave me your card."

"Oh, good," the goblin grinned. Her swarthy complexion

oozed youth and passion. "My name is Sally, and I just need some information."

Angela gave Sally her identification number, her debit card number, and answered a few questions.

"My friend mentioned a discount?" she asked.

"Oh yes, honey," said Sally. "You get half off the regular price to start. But don't mention it to the boys. That's the only catch. It's just for us girls. Since Steinem referred you, we'll give you half off again. She's a barker for us. So you'll only pay a quarter of the regular price. Usually that's as low as we go, but you can talk to the doctor. If he thinks you really can't afford it, he may take off a little more."

"Oh, good, good, thank you."

"Can you come in for an appointment tomorrow morning? I'm open from eight to nine-thirty. If you can't make that appointment, you'll have to wait until next Thursday."

"Oh, eight, I think. What with the rumors of war, we're all on alert. I don't think I can get a whole morning off."

"Great, eight it is," Sally beamed. "We'll see you then angel." The goblin closed the connection.

Angela put down her caster and the card. She picked up Ginger and hugged the stuffie. The jungle jock continued his silent dance on her vid.

Now you've done it, said the voice. *What will the agency say? If they find out you've gone and gotten genetically modified, they'll never let you go to nursing school.*

"Can it grasshopper. They'll never know about it. There's no reason to know."

They can find out by pulling your health record. All they have to do is get suspicious.

"So I don't let 'em get suspicious. What are you going to do? Tell?"

I told you. I don't work for them. Baby, please! It's not too late.

"Stow it! Quiet! I've got to sleep. Good grief, if you're

trying to keep me stable, you're not doing a good job."

I'm trying to save your life.

"What life? Living death you mean. And I haven't even killed anybody."

"Thump."

What was that? She clutched her stuffie, and glanced at her clock. It was half past three. *I would have sworn I heard a knock on the door.*

She rolled around and looked at the door. Her room was semi-dark. Only the nightlights and her vid held the shadows at bay. She stared at the security light on her door. *Did I lock the door?* The security light was green. *The door is open.*

"Thump."

It was the door.

She froze and her eyes darted around her room. She had no weapons, not even a knife. All she had were a few plastic knives she saved from the cafeteria. She used those for snacks, and they were not very useful for that.

Shaking, she felt waves of goose pimples run up her arms, and she shivered. *What do I do? I've got to do something!*

Quietly, she rolled down her blanket, and threw her legs off the bed. She picked up her caster, and set it to record to her friend-site. She pointed the caster at the door, and started filming. She reached the door and pressed the button on the lock box. The security status light turned red. A wave of relief swept over her. She put her hand on the door handle to test the lock.

"Thump." The handle trembled.

"Go away!" she shrieked. "Go away! I'm recording you!"

She shivered. She counted to ten. It seemed like an eternity, but when she looked at her caster, only seconds had past. She watched the seconds tick by, and still she waited. *This can't go on. It's just a drunk. He's lost and he thinks this is his apartment. He will go soon.*

She waited. *He's gone. It's been ten minutes.* She checked her clock. *Okay, it's been three minutes. I can't wait.*

"Yes you can wait," said the voice. *Leave it. Go to bed. Go to work early. Cancel your appointment at that chop shop, and forget it.*

She ignored the voice, and she pushed the handle down. The security light turned green, and she opened the door.

The lights were dimmed for the evening, but the hall was still well-lit.

Nothing stood in the hall. She stuck her caster out of the door and looked up and down the hall. She turned it quickly back and forth. She checked her neighbor's doors, the janitor's closet, and the lifts at the end of the hall in the viewfinder.

No one was there.

She twisted the caster the other way, and she stopped.

There was a shadow. She stared at the shadow, but nothing happened. She turned to see what might cast the shadow.

"Thump."

She jumped back into her apartment, and shut her eyes. She tried to scream, but nothing happened. She held her breathe and a cold breeze wafted over her. *This can't be happening!*

"Lights on," she said, and the bedroom lights rose.

She forced open her eyes. She looked around the room. She was alone. Nothing was there.

Forgetting caution, she charged the door, and slammed it shut. The security lock turned red, and for the first time since she had been assigned to the room she felt glad to be locked in.

She darted to her closet and threw open the door. It was empty.

She jogged to her bathroom, and opened its door. It was empty. She checked her shower, and no one was there.

She picked up Ginger, and hugged the little stuffie. Flipping open her caster, she fiddled with it and found the vid she had shot.

She raced through the vid of the door and the hall. On fast forward, the vid skipped the twist. The vid shook up and down as she jumped backwards.

Carefully she scrolled to the point just before she jumped. The shadow was tall. It had the head of a man. It had two eyes, which glowed. There were no other features.

She set her caster to record. "No one's going to believe this," she said. "I shot this vid just a few minutes ago. This creep was in the hall scaring me. He pounded on my door. I tried to catch him on vid, but all I got was his shadow. If anything happens to me, call security at Nodlon Biots. He's in the building, and he's got to be somebody who can get past security. Either he's an elf or a goblin. He's too tall for a dwarf." She posted the vid on her friend-site.

She sat on her bed, and leaned back on her pillow. The door lock was red. Her lights began to dim. She did not want to sleep in the dark. Not now. "Lights on, override," she said. The lights brightened, and she squeezed her stuffie.

Angela, they're after you, said the voice.

"Stuff it grasshopper."

The attack has only begun. Please quit now. I don't want to lose you.

"It's my life grasshopper, and I'm not going to lose it."

No News is Good News

Jack turned on his vid, and switched to the news channel. A smartly dressed elven maid stood before a map of Nodlon. Flashing her delightful eyes at the camera, she smiled as if she had just discovered a fresh litter of puppies on her doorstep.

"Our delegation to the peace conference on Elysium has walked out of negotiations for the third time. Through a statement issued yesterday, President Nogora accused Admiral MacArthur of blockading Titan. Baron Voltaire, Nodlon's Ambassador to Mars, withdrew from the negotiations after an Elysium moderator read the statement during an open session. We asked the Baron what these developments mean for peace in our time, and he said, 'No comment.' The Baron and his entourage returned to Nodlon in his personal low earth orbiter. Minerva Shaw for Mercury News; reporting to you from Elysium Station; back to you Bruce."

"Thank you, Minerva." The anchorman's smile melted away. A silhouette of a dwarf maiden filled the background.

"A shadow falls over all Nodlon tonight. All of us at Mercury News are gravely concerned about this epidemic of missing dwarves. Grim news in the Zodiac case; another dwarf maiden is missing. Angela Christie disappeared last night.

"None of us knows if Angela ran away, or if she was a victim of foul play. Since Nodlon Yard found Anna McCarthy on Blueberry Lake, our most intrepid investigative reporter has aggressively pursued the truth. Chesterton is on the scene with an update.

"Chesterton have you learned anything of interest that may explain this horrible crime?"

The scene switched to a middle-aged gentleman with a spray of white hair and a goatee.

"Bruce, I'm here at dorm forty-two in the Octagon where Angela Christie lived, and where she was last seen. Nodlon Biots runs this dorm for the Octagon, and a hundred young dwarf maidens call this dorm home.

"Nodlon Biots assigned Angela's contract to the Ministry of Manna where worked as a secretary in the Ministry's microbiot warfare lab. Her supervisor, Dr. Felix Abrams told us she was an exemplary employee. Rumor has it she once filled in for Princess Virginia's handmaiden.

"When Angela wasn't working, she enjoyed reading old science-fiction and fantasy novels, and she loved seeing Cretaceous Clay at the Circus.

"Tragically Bruce, everyone here feels a sense of foreboding. An eyewitness caught a glimpse of a horrific scene in Angela's dorm room. The constellation of Capricorn covers the missing girl's vid screen. Apparently it was drawn in the child's own blood. Our eyewitness wasn't sure what the sign of the Zodiac means, and the police are not talking."

"What else can you tell us about this case, Chesterton?"

"Bruce, a spokeswoman for Nodlon Yard confirmed the constellation of Capricorn matches the modus operandi of the villain in the Zodiac case. She refused to answer any further questions, though. For now, the police are treating this as a possible runaway situation. Some speculate an underground railroad offers sanctuary to distraught dwarves seeking a better life.

"Given the horror of recent events, I'm sure they are not ruling out foul play. It's a sad day here. None of us know what has become of Angela. All of us fear she may be in the hands of some monster preying on young dwarfs. Our thoughts and prayers go out to Angela tonight wherever she may be.

"If some beast prowls Nodlon seeking to ruin the lives of biots, we hope Nodlon Yard will catch the beast soon and end this nightmare. Our biots deserve better than to be preyed upon. Biots are people too.

"This is Chesterton, at Nodlon Biots' dorm forty-two signing off. Back to you Bruce."

The camera cut to the anchorman.

"Chesterton," Bruce's brow furrowed, "let everyone there know all of Nodlon shares their grief." The anchorman shook his head solemnly. "Nodlon Yard has their best homicide detective on the case. Inspector Lestrayed has never failed, and he's called in Jack Clay. All of Nodlon looks to them tonight. Watching. Waiting. Hoping they will end the nightmare soon. This is Bruce Ably saying biots are people too."

Pouring it on thick, hey Bruce?

The Black Dwarf has killed again. I can feel the pressure, and I know it in my heart. Is it my fault? Is it Gumshoe's? Was there something we didn't do? Have we missed a clue?

Jack turned off the vid and stepped out on to his patio. The stars twinkled over Babel Tower, and Nodlon's blue lights blazed in the valley below.

I'll be lucky to get any sleep tonight.

A Victim in the Sewer

Darn you Eddie! You just went up to Fisherman's wharf for lunch! Bet you tied one on and you called in sick!

It was dank, and the air felt cold.

I shouldn't be here alone! But he was alone tonight. He was the engineer on watch for any calls in the wee hours of the morning. Eddie was supposed to be his backup tonight. But Eddie had finked out on him.

Niles parked his cart in a substation's service bay. The service bay opened onto the oldest sewer main in Nodlon. The main was originally part of the mines, and the mines were older than Nodlon itself. The mines followed the coal seams, and so the main meandered more like an underground cavern than a pipe network.

Eddie should be here to watch my back! The only other tech on duty was Roxie. *Even if she wasn't handling dispatch, I couldn't send her alone. Not in the old sewer! Not down here! Not at this hour!* He swallowed. *Yeah, but I'd rather take her with me than come down here by myself.*

He slung his backpack over his shoulder, shook his torch to charge it, and took a deep breath. Though he had worked for Nodlon's Ministry of Sanitation for years, he had never quite accepted the idea of being alone in the sewers. *Yet here I am alone!*

He left his cart and walked to the end of the service bay. When he reached the main, he stepped over a trough, and glanced up at the flood gates. If the water rose, the flood gate would drop to protect the maintenance level. *An avalanche on the Balmhorn could do it.* An avalanche would set off a tidal wave, and millions of gallons of water would pour into the ventilation shafts. The flood gates would drop and shunt the water to the sewer.

Everyone in the sewer would drown! He imagined a wall of water coming down the sewer, and then tried to reassure himself.

These sewers have been here for three hundred years. Nothing like that has ever happened. He put it out of his mind and tried to focus on the task at hand.

The tunnel's faint lights broke the gloom, but they were little more than night lights. He waved his torch up and down the tunnel hoping he would not see anything unusual. The light of his torch faded into the gloom as the tunnel rounded a bend.

The main was a good ten yards across, and a small creek meandered along the floor. Puddles pockmarked the sand in the bed, and the creek trickled from puddle to puddle.

Are there Noddie holes here? He visualized the Mystery Map in the employee lounge. Push pins covered the map. Each color stood for something significant, but they called it the Mystery Map because the significance was only known to the insiders; red for smugglers, green for alligators, white for ghosts, black for strange shadows, and blue for Noddie holes. *And I think I saw a blue one up this way! I hope Noddie isn't hungry tonight.*

Oh, come on, no one's disappeared out this way in years. Was it years? He tried to recall, but he could not remember anyone disappearing out this way.

He checked his location on his caster. *This main runs up to the plant on Blueberry Lake.*

Thumbing his caster, he zoomed in and out, refreshing his memory of the tributaries and locks in the area. It wouldn't do for a senior engineer to get lost. *I'd never hear the end of it!*

Less than an hour ago, a hatch reported a signal malfunction deep in the ancient part of the system.

Now, I'm standing barely a hundred yards from the hatch. Normally, dispatch sent teams of two to check out any signals. Usually they found leaking manholes, drains blocked by rubbish, or sluice gates jammed with tree limbs. The inspection team noted anything interfering with the operation of the sewer, and they put in a work order. *Please let it be routine, perfunctory, ordinary, and normal.*

Yeah, but these aren't normal times what with evacuations, rumors of war, and missing dwarves. He was the only engineer left on duty so he had to go in alone.

After several more paces he glanced down at his caster. The map showed he was over halfway there. He glanced back, but the main had turned around a bend, and he could not see the bay or his cart. *Now I'm really alone!*

Steeling himself, he hurried forward. *The sooner I'm done, the sooner I can get out of here!*

Slowly, he approached the hatch, but when he neared it, he found what should not have been. A shadow leaned against the wall.

He froze. He trembled.

Good old Niles, why did you have to be here tonight? Before he completed the thought, the answer popped into his head. *Because you can read the ancient's runes and nobody else can! No one left in Nodlon anyway. All the rest have gone on to Iron Mountain.*

Fat lot of good that does! The runes in these parts are illegible. All the markings have worn off.

Afraid to go in and investigate, and afraid to leave, he mustered his courage. He stared at the shadow but it did not move.

Thinking his torch was playing tricks on him, he shook it to recharge the batteries. The light brightened, but the shadow still made no sense.

He forced his feet to edge slowly towards the hatch. Every nerve was on edge, and he heard flapping over his head. He turned quickly to catch whatever it was in his torchlight, but the light only darted up and down the sewer main. *Bats! Just bats fluttering their wings in the dark.*

He turned his torch upstream. He was so close now, the torch finally caught the shadow, and his mind solved the puzzle.

It was the hatch. The hatch that should have been closed stood wide open. Next to it, the sensor box was ripped from the wall. *Well, that explains the signal malfunction. How will I write this up? Found sensor box ripped from the wall? Cause unknown?*

Who could have opened the hatch? No one should be down here. No one was allowed down here unless they were with the department or on a tour. *Don't ask who! The question is what? No man ripped that box off the wall. Something pulled the box off the wall and opened that hatch!*

The air was still and cold. The hatch stood unmoving in the light of his torch.

Remember Goldilocks? He glanced over his shoulder. Nothing was behind him. *What if the thing is still here?!*

What of the unexplained stories of a creature waiting in the dark? Never reported, never seen. *Noddie!*

"Thump," he froze. *Was it behind him? Was it in the creek?*

Sometimes the tunnels spoke. Some said it was because the tunnels breathed. They creaked with the rise and fall of air pressure.

"Thump," he trembled. *Was it coming or going?*

Others claimed the sound was the phases of the moon. The tides twisted the mountain, and the rocks cried out. Still others spoke of cave men who for reasons rational or perverse, sought to separate themselves from the rest of human society.

Or it's a sea monster!

"Splash," he flinched. *That was close! It's in the tunnel!*

Is it Noddie? He held his breath. *Should I turn off my torch? Should I run?*

A small wave rolled down the creek. It fell over each puddle in turn and passed him by. Ripples reflected his torchlight.

The tunnel grew dark, and a shadow fell over the creek. Something blocked the lights upstream. Fear paralyzed him. He wanted to run, but he could not.

"Splash," the sound was just yards ahead. He switched off his torch and shut his eyes. *It's going to rip me to pieces!* He thought of his wife and his baby. *Goodbye! I love you!*

"Splash, splash, splash," the sound retreated. "Splash, splash, splash," the sound faded away.

The sound faded, and soon it disappeared altogether.

He opened his eyes. He was freezing and sweating all at the same time. He summoned his courage and switched his torch back on. He turned his torch up the bend, but the light simply faded into the gloom.

The main was as dark as ever. *It's gone.*

He cautiously advanced on the hatch, and peeked around it. He flashed his torch into the hatch and up the stairs. Nothing was there.

The hatch led up to the maintenance level on the Great River. He could have gone that way rather than walking up from the service bay, but it would have meant going a mile out of the way down corridors just as empty and just as old as the one he was in.

He lowered his torch and shined the light on the creek. *What am I looking for? Footprints? Any sign of Noddie?*

In his light, he saw a shape in the creek bed. It was a lump lying on a puddle. It looked vaguely like a tree stump.

Cautiously, slowly, he crept upstream towards the stump. He stepped down onto the creek bed and carefully closed in on the shape.

As he moved closer, he made out details and form. It was lumpy and it rose and fell and a branch stuck out. Hoping it was only a tree, he tried to cheer himself.

In his heart, though, he knew it was not a tree. Just yards from the stump, his light caught the branch and he stopped.

He studied the branch covered in mud and filth for several moments. He tried to make sense of it, but there was no mistaking it for anything else.

It was a dwarf. A desire to help overcame fear. He reached out, laid a hand on the dwarf, and rolled her over.

The maiden's open eyes met his, and he screamed. He

dropped his torch and jumped.

~~~~~

"Are crimes always committed in the wee hours?" asked Shotgun.

"Seems like it, doesn't it? Maybe crooks don't have an agency to negotiate their contract."

"What contract? My contract only gives you ten hours a day, and this ain't one of them."

"True, but you wouldn't miss this for the world."

Jack parked his Andromeda next to a police van. An officer guarded the entrance to the substation's service bay.

"Come to think of it, I'd rather tough out my own hours than owe my life to an agency." Shotgun shivered in the cool tunnel. "No coffee, and no breakfast."

"I asked, but you said we had to hurry. It's a matter of life and death."

"Yeah, yeah, being chivalrous is a pain."

Jack nodded his agreement, and the elf and the dwarf made for the crime scene.

Following the officer's directions, they crossed the bay. They gave the flood gates a nervous glance, and then turned upstream.

The crime scene was not hard to find. The number of fire fighters, police officers, and other responders going to and fro had pushed the technicians with the heavy instruments into the creek bed.

Portable lights brightened the sewer tunnel. Elves wearing the uniform of Nodlon's Fire Department hurried away with a litter bearing the unfortunate girl.

Gumshoe resembled a bloodhound in his trench coat and fedora. The usual huddle of technicians surrounded him, and they waited several minutes before the Inspector waved for them to join him.

"Thank you for coming down here." Gumshoe shook Jack's hand.

"Is it Angela Christie?" asked Jack. "I heard about the Capricorn on Mercury News."

"Yes, it's Angela," Gumshoe pushed his fedora back. "Pretty, too, she was, but she was not molested. She was covered with minor burns, but that didn't kill her. She didn't die of any natural causes. Her chip was ripped out, and she died of blood loss. All of her blood is missing. And the only exit wound is in her forehead. If it's not magic, I'll hand in my badge."

"Mercury News said a Capricorn was found in her dorm."

"Yeah, housekeeping found it." Gumshoe shook his head.

"What else do we know?" asked Jack.

"She worked in the Octagon."

"Yeah, I heard Nodlon Biots contracted her to the Ministry. She worked in a lab of some sort."

"Right, she was an administrative assistant for a scientist, Felix Abrams. He made the first report when she didn't come to work."

"Do you think he's a suspect?"

"No, Abrams is a widower and he lives alone. Rock solid alibi though. He works in the Octagon and lives in the Crown. His every move is on camera for the last two weeks."

"That's a change for the Zodiac case," Jack smiled. "Someone's on camera."

"Right you are, Jack. I checked into his report, though. Just wanted to see why we didn't follow up on it. Dwarves are reported every night now. In the last twenty-four hours, we took several reports. Dispatch gave Angela a low priority. It just didn't seem suspicious."

"What?!"

"Angela's been out sick several times over the last few weeks."

"Were they having an affair?"

"No, Jack, we have no reason to think so."

"So, why did Abrams call? If he's not having an affair, why worry about a biot?"

"She's always called in. She obtained passes to go to the doctor. Each time she's turned up or called before she missed work. This time she didn't call."

"Are you thinking what I'm thinking?"

"We dropped the ball, and she fell through the cracks." Gumshoe looked at his wingtips and kicked a stone.

"No, old man," said Jack. "Why she was sick? Maybe she went to a chop shop?"

The Inspector grinned, "You missed your calling Jack. She did go to a chop shop…"

"Let me guess," Shotgun interrupted. "Angela is a New Gem client, and Dr. Balaam is her doctor."

"Bingo," Gumshoe nodded. "If you boys decide to change careers, I'll make sure Nodlon Yard has openings. She started gene therapy about six weeks ago."

"What did she do for Abrams?" Jack glanced at the crime scene. "Is there any correlation with Anna McCarthy?"

"Nothing special about her work, it was just administrative stuff. She was Abrams secretary. She answered calls, entered a little data, and helped him write reports. Anna did much the same thing for Colonel Khan."

"I heard on the news she may have worked for the Princess."

"Yes, now there's a disturbing connection." Gumshoe poked his tablet with a stylus. "A few months back, she substituted for Virginia's handmaid, Nadia. Since then, Nadia disappeared. She was last seen just before the Princess visited you."

"That was Sunday," Jack sucked in a deep breathe. "Princess Virginia saw me Sunday. That's when I saw Anna."

"Yes, small world isn't it? Now, days later Anna's dead, Angela's dead, and Nadia's still missing."

"So, the Princess may be the connection." Jack grimaced

and shook a finger. "Has any other maiden been the Princess' handmaid?"

"Yes," Gumshoe shook his head. "Apparently, it's an honor. Virginia gave us a lengthy list. Two others are missing. Delilah and Blondie. We haven't found them yet. I'm not holding out much hope, but I've got my fingers crossed."

"Under that trench coat beats the heart of a softie," said Jack.

"Thanks, Jack," Gumshoe smiled. "I'm not sure though about Virginia being connected. By far most of the dwarves are not connected in any way to the Crown. And Evan Labe never worked for anyone in the royal household."

"He was a Bio-Soft engineer," said Jack. "An up and comer who earned enough to pay for his own apartment." Jack tapped chin. "Evan worked on Ministry projects."

"A lot of biot engineers work on Ministry projects, Jack. That's no news."

"Mercury News mentioned a micro-biot warfare lab," said Jack. "Any leads there?"

"They stonewalled us there." Gumshoe huffed. "Everything's top secret. I can make a few guesses. Abrams doesn't just work there. He's not the head cheese, but according to the staff, Abrams' the brains."

"So he designs bugs to kill us all?" Jack frowned. "Sounds like a mad scientist. Maybe, he moonlights as a mad man? Any chance he's Nodlon's version of Jekyll and Hyde?"

"Who knows what nightmares dwell in the hearts of men, Jack? I can't be sure, but I'm told he designs antidotes to known diseases. They don't build bio-weapons in that lab. At least that's the story they gave me. How would I know any different?"

"Now who is being naïve, old man?"

"Touché, Jack."

Shotgun quietly drifted away from the discussion. Ignoring the firemen, the technicians, and the police officers, he picked out the only person wearing the lime green overalls of the Nodlon Sanitation department.

The engineer sat perched on the utility ledge at the foot of the tunnel wall. Telecom cables, closed circuit vid cables, alarm systems, instrument cables, and a manna tube all ran along the wall just above the ledge.

"Hi, I'm Shotgun," he said.

"Niles," said the engineer. He doffed his cap. The dwarf sported a red chip on his forehead. "Don't you work for Cretaceous Clay?"

"Yes, I'm his butler."

Niles trembled beneath an olive drab blanket thrown over his shoulders.

"Are you all right?" Shotgun asked.

"Never better," he shivered again. "I just had a bit of a fright. Guess, I'm not quite over it yet."

Shotgun perched on the lip on the wall, and sat beside him. "She was pretty."

"Aye," Niles agreed. "Disgusting. How could anyone do it? No one deserves to go that way."

"What way?"

"Shot in the forehead, I reckon." Niles looked up. "Why should I talk to you, Shotgun? I'm sorry, but the police told me to say nothing."

"Inspector Lestrayed recruited Cretaceous Clay as a consultant for Nodlon Yard. We're working with the police."

The dwarf shaped an inaudible, "Oh." He hugged himself and looked down at the bricks. "I've taken the family to Mr. Clay's show more than once. The missus and I loved his dancing ice fairies, and we both miss the polar bear." Putting his hands on his knees, the engineer bounced once or twice. "Hey, since you work for him, maybe you know what happened to his bear?"

"She's fine. He gave her to the zoo. They call her Polly.

Everyone loved her except the crew. A half ton bear leaves an amazing amount of, uh, deposits."

Niles regained his composure. "Ah, yeah, I know plenty about deposits." He sniffed. "That Mr. Clay may be good, but the dancers are the best part." Niles leaned over conspiratorially. "Please don't tell the missus."

Shotgun flexed and deliberately imitated the engineer's bounce. "Not if you don't tell my fiancée." The dwarves bounced together, and shammed a silent belly laugh.

"What do you want to know?" asked Niles. "I'm not as much of a fool as I seem. I'll help you out if I can."

"Did you see or hear anything unusual? Anything the crime scene techs might miss or overlook? Any rumors, speculation, or unfounded suspicions? Anything no one can report?"

"Down here, we don't repeat stories or tales. Everyone's the same. Elves, goblins, dwarves, and even humans respect each other. Gossip might reach the wrong ears, if you know what I mean. Sanitation guys stick together."

"Mum's the word, Niles." Shotgun crossed his heart with his pinky. "Pinky swear. It's just for the investigation. Just to find Angela's killer. Nothing you say will be repeated officially. I'm not the police. I'm just Mr. Clay's butler, and I'm just trying to help him find a murderer before he kills again."

"No," Niles wrung his hands. "If I had anything to say, Shotgun, I'd say so. I don't want anyone getting killed.

"Niles, we need to stop the Black Dwarf" Shotgun tilted his head upstream towards the crime scene. "The scum has killed twice. He will kill again if we don't catch him."

"I saw that girl." Niles sucked in a deep breathe. "I'll never forget her face." He rubbed his face with his hands. "I've got a good job. I've paid my contract, married my girl, moved into a nice place, and I've got a baby." He mumbled through his palms. "I've got nothing more to say."

"Nothing? How do you know? Maybe you've got a clue that can help us work out what happened?"

"Nothing is on the cameras. I know, I checked." Niles shivered again. "I'm not risking it all on a trick of my imagination. They'd investigate me. I'd have to admit I was scared. Then, they will say I was seeing things."

"Gotcha," Shotgun filled in the pieces. "If you say you heard a bump in the night, they might demote you." Niles nodded and for a moment they sat in silence.

Niles shivered and glanced upstream.

Shotgun followed Nile's glance, and pushed, "Niles, can you tell me anything?"

"Yeah, the kind of stuff you don't report."

"But it wasn't the killer?" Shotgun pressed. "Surely, whatever you saw was related?"

"No, I don't think so. No one can get in or out without being caught on camera. The scum know that." He looked Shotgun in the eye, "It wasn't the killer anyway."

"How do you know it wasn't the killer?"

"I just know." Niles paused. "I've worked down here a long time. You learn things. You know things. What I saw – what I think I saw was big. It wasn't anything that can wander around Nodlon without attracting attention. Especially nothing going topside where the hoity-toity live. If Upper Nodlonder's saw this thing, bet their bubble would pop faster than a bottle of champagne."

Shotgun leaned over the engineer. "Was it Noddie?"

Niles looked away and then back at Shotgun. "I don't know. No one's seen her. All I heard was thump, thump. It was big and moving away from me, if it was anything at all and not my imagination."

"Bumps in the night?"

"Yeah, only these happen when you're wide awake. And you can't say anything cause there's nothing on camera."

"If a camera can't catch anything, it's not an animal." Shotgun scoffed, but he searched the dim sewer main trying to reassure himself there was nothing in the shadows.

"Oh, yes it can be an animal," Niles began. "Accidents happen. Ten years ago, a gator escaped from the zoo. Terrified the old hand who found him, but no one got hurt. That gator wandered around down here for weeks before we caught him. When they tried to figure out what went wrong with security, they found the gator on just a few fuzzy frames here and there. He was on-camera all the time, but we didn't see him at all. He looked like a log."

"Help me out, Niles. Noddie is too big to be mistaken for a log, right? If no one gets in or out of here without being on camera, how can Noddie do it?"

"She makes her own holes."

"Stands to reason," said Shotgun timing his words. "Mythical monsters never appear on security cameras."

"Exactly," snapped Niles. "I'm not gonna be the one to argue with the cameras. We've all heard noises. We've all seen shadows. You know what I mean?"

"It's okay, Niles. I won't say anything. I've got kids too." He put his hand on Niles' shoulder. "If it's not Noddie maybe there's another explanation."

"The older guys say Nodlon Yard found several dead dwarves down here years ago. According to the rumor mill, they were all black dwarves." Niles tapped his forehead. "Guess red dwarves must have more sense, huh?"

"We dwarves tend to be naïve," said Shotgun. "We can be hoodwinked pretty easily."

"You said it." Niles gave Shotgun a gentle push.

"You said years," Shotgun rolled the idea around in his head. "So it's happened before? When was that?"

"Thirty years ago," said Niles. "They say a dwarf killed several black dwarves."

"Why do the gossips have to blame the dwarves? If black dwarves were the victims, that doesn't mean dwarves were the killers."

"Not dwarves, just one black dwarf. Nodlon Yard

discovered this dwarf was a witch doctor. He led a coven of witches who practiced black magic. He turned some of his followers into zombies so they would follow him mindlessly. The Yard tried to arrest him. It turned out to not be so easy. They all went out in a blaze of glory. After the firefight, the Yard didn't find the killer. They never found his body. After that, the murders stopped so the police figured they got their dwarf. The black dwarf just disappeared."

"Whoa, that's a story I haven't heard before. Can you back this up?"

"No, it's all gossip. The Yard buried the story. They didn't want anyone knowing what happened. It's supposed to be one of Nodlon Yard's most closely guarded secrets."

"Understandable. If Nodlon's citizens knew a dwarf might become a killer, the city would erupt in pandemonium. Dwarves may not show up for work once in a while, or get depressed, but they don't murder or steal."

"Right, they couldn't afford to let this get out."

"If that's what happened, I wonder if there's any link between those crimes and the ones we're investigating."

"There's that," Niles stuck his thumb at the wall above them. "There's a bunch of spots on the wall there. I told the techs, and they got pretty excited about it."

Shotgun stood up, and turned to look at the wall.

The dwarf tugged on Shotgun's sleeve. They stepped off the sidewalk and backed into the creek bed. Niles pointed at the wall.

Anyone unfamiliar with the tunnels might have overlooked the spots. They appeared to be no more than dirt on the brick.

"Capricorn," said Shotgun. "It's the stars of Capricorn."

"The constellation or the sign of the Zodiac?"

"What's the difference, Niles?"

"One's a sign foretelling one's future, and the other is a group of stars."

Shotgun shrugged in defeat, and mentally noted the

observation.

Niles drew close, and clasped his arm. "I've got two more items to add to your notes." He pulled the butler towards the maintenance hatch. The hatch stood open the way he had found it. Next to it a lifeless box dangled from a tangle of wires.

"Whatever went through that hatch, Shotgun, it went up to the access corridor. And it didn't come down again. You can report this. I told the police techs, but I don't know if they get it."

"I'm not sure I get it," Shotgun said. "What's the point? So someone went up? Isn't that the way they came down?"

"Whatever came down here, it didn't come that way." Niles pointed to the hatch, "When it left, it went up."

"Up?" asked Shotgun again, "I'm missing it. What's the significance?"

"Yeah, that's why I'm making the point. Don't you mistake it for nothing just cause I don't know what it means. It means something. See the alarm dangling off the wall." Niles' whole body wobbled.

"Help me out, Niles. I'm pretty sharp on a computer, but I'm not picking up what you're laying down."

"Above us are the access corridors. All of Nodlon's utilities use some of the right of way up there. We use them for the lights and the power to the valves and the gates. The fastest way to get anywhere from the substations is the way we came today. Go through the service bays and up the mains.

"So if I need to work on a light, I drive out here and go up a hatch. During a flood, I can't do that. I'm not a fish, right? I have to take a lift and drive through the corridors. It's slow going. There're lots of turns. It's easy to get lost. It's tight." He tapped his head. "I've been whacked more times than I can count. A hard hat can protect you, but you can still get clocked." Niles paused. "When we're not using the hatches, they're always locked. We can't have flooding in the corridors. What a mess?

"What brought me here was a 'no-response' signal from the

hatch. Imagine my surprise when I found the hatch open. If someone had gone through the hatch, we would have logged an open hatch." He pointed to the hatch. "The alarm box was ripped out. That's what opened the hatch. If they had come down, they would've forced the hatch to get it open." Pleased with himself, the dwarf smiled.

"If they didn't come down this way," mused Shotgun, "how did they get here?"

"The next service bay is my guess. It's a few hundred yards upstream."

"Why?" Shotgun rubbed his ear. "Why leave the body here?"

"They were just dumping her. It's out of the way, and no one is likely to notice. If they hadn't triggered the alarm, I would never have found her."

"Right, if they wanted to dispose of her quietly, why did they give away her position by setting off the alarm? Niles, did you go through the service bay or come through the hatch?"

"I got here the same way you did. I parked my cart at the service bay and walked upstream to the hatch. Instead of taking the level-ways, of course, I used the connectors between the substations to reach the service bay."

"Did you see anything in the connecters?"

The hairs lifted on the engineer's head. The dwarf put his hand over his mouth, and shook his head.

"Thank you Niles."

"One more thing I need to tell you."

"Yes?" Shotgun gave the engineer his full attention.

"Whatever pulled the alarm box off the wall; it must have been in a hurry or scared."

"Scared? What would scare a murderer? Would it have been you?"

Wide-eyed the dwarf blew a low whistle. "Scared of me, that's a laugh!" Bursting with excitement, the dwarf bounced on his toes.

"Niles, do you know what he saw?"

"What he saw? No, no, I don't know, but he ripped that panel off the wall, and he ran up those steps." Niles flew one hand up the other in a flying motion. "He was scared!"

"Maybe he saw what you heard?"

Niles shrugged, "Maybe."

"Thanks Niles," Shotgun pressed Clay's card into the dwarf's hand. "Call us if you think of anything. I owe you one. I can get tickets for you and your family when normalcy resumes."

"Glad to be of help." For a moment, Niles studied the technicians working several yards upstream. "Sorry I couldn't help you more. I hope you and Mr. Clay catch this monster before he kills again."

"Me too, Niles, me too."

~~~~~

Jack and the Inspector faced the Capricorn. Niles was nowhere to be seen.

"Real bricks, the sewer here is very old." Gumshoe picked at one of the stars. He tried prying a stone out of the melted clay.

Shotgun sidled up to his employer to listen in.

"Glass," Gumshoe tapped one of the stars. The bubbles make it look like dirt."

"Something melted the clay," said Jack. "It was hotter than a kiln. Clay doesn't melt in a kiln."

The Inspector nodded, "Right, a kiln isn't hot enough to make these marks."

"Could a blaster do it?" Shotgun asked.

"No," the policeman sighed. "Not that I know. That's just the preliminary assessment by the forensic team. A blaster is hot enough, but it doesn't spit out enough energy. Our resident physicist, Dr. Maiman, said it would require an industrial laser."

"But it's not magic," said Jack.

"Are you sure?"

"No, but I don't think I can do it. If it is magic, I'd hate to run into this guy down here."

"You can conjure lightning," Shotgun chimed in again. "Isn't lightning hot enough?"

"I suppose. I don't know how I create lightning anyway. I haven't spent much time trying to figure out how to use magic as a weapon. I conjured up that lightning in a life or death moment. I think I can do it again, but I'm not sure."

"Yes," Gumshoe said. "If you can control it, is it hot enough?"

"I don't know," Jack held out his hands. "I'll test it when I get a chance."

"Then we've hit a brick wall," said Shotgun. "No pun intended."

"Shotgun, I saw you talking to Niles," said Gumshoe. "Have you learned anything?"

"Yes, I think so Inspector." Quickly, Shotgun reprised his conversation with the engineer.

"What do you make of his story?"

"He was credible and sincere even if some parts of his tale seem incredible."

"That was my guess too." Gumshoe nodded. "He could be mistaken. Dwarves are naïve as you pointed out. Did you get anything else out of him?"

"No, but he was emphatic. He didn't want us to overlook the hatch. Whatever scared the killer, he risked exposure to escape up the hatch."

"So we know the killer left through the access corridor," said Gumshoe.

"But he entered the sewer through service bay upstream," said Shotgun.

"Yes, and he probably went back to the local substation to return to his vehicle. If he came from downstream, Niles would have run into him."

"In that case, we'd have two bodies instead of one," Jack finished.

"Yep," Gumshoe sighed. "My men will search the corridors and the sewer tunnels. I'll have to call in more men. If we can believe Niles, the Black Dwarf and his men entered the sewer nearby. He intended to return the way he came, but something interrupted him. We'll search the other lifts and hatches in the area and see if we can find traces of them."

"What are we looking for?" asked Shotgun. "It's been hours, he's got to have gone into hiding."

"Anything suspicious," said Jack. "Something clean, something dropped, or footprints.

"Are you sure you don't want my job?" Gumshoe tapped Jack with his tablet.

"Sorry, old man, just speaking my mind." Jack shrugged, "But it's obvious isn't it."

"Speak away, Jack. You're doing all right."

"If it's all right with you, Shotgun and I will go up the tunnel and see what we can find while your men check the area."

"Knock yourselves out," Gumshoe turned away. "There's plenty to do."

The mage set out at a stiff pace and headed upstream. Taking Jack's confidence as bravado, Shotgun straggled behind his employer. The tunnel curved until the crime scene disappeared around a bend.

"Boss, what will we do if we meet the Black Dwarf?" Shotgun glanced about furtively. "Worse, what if we meet Noddie?"

"Worry not my good man, I'm sure whatever startled the killer is no longer there. If it was Noddie, she won't be back until after we leave."

"How do you know?"

"Classic mythical monster behavior, my good man," Jack grinned. "Sea monsters never appear when you're looking for them."

"Is Noddie a dragon or a sea monster?"

"All the old folk tales claim Noddie is a sea monster. She lives in the mines. We Noddie lovers believe she feeds in the Great River. She comes to the sewers to drop the bones. She's not a real sea monster though. If she exists, she's a synthetic leviathan."

Shotgun searched the dim light thrown off by the sewer's lamps.

"Fear not, Shotgun. Remember you're traveling with an all-powerful magician with genetically manufactured command of the forces of nature." Jack pretended to conjure a spell. "Abracadabra," he wiggled his fingers. "Open say's ah me."

"Fine lot of good that'll be if a sea monster eats you first," said Shotgun.

Jack's flippant attitude irritated his dogsbody, and his irritation merely goaded the mage.

"Shotgun, this is a great opportunity to see if there's a cave or some other opening nearby. It isn't every day you're invited to explore a restricted area. It's a chance to find out how the killer entered the sewer without being seen, and we might discover another crypto-zoological creature. Come on!"

Jack spun on his heels, and walked down the dimly lit tunnel. "We are far below Nodlon. Below us are the old mines. If we can find a shaft or breach in the tunnel, it might lead to the mines below or Moab above if doesn't run up to Rickover Station."

The dim lights in the tunnel barely lit the walk. They watched their footing by torchlight. From time to time, they passed tributaries. Weirs originally carried the sidewalk over the tributaries, and connected one side of the tunnel to the other. Time and water had dislodged many stones. They tested each stone to find the solid ones, and then stepped carefully over the weirs.

"Whoa," cried Shotgun. A stone turned under his foot, and he fell. He flailed at the air, and tried to steady himself. In a panic, he braced himself for the cold splash into the murky pool.

An invisible hand caught him. The hand lifted him into the air and set him down on the walk.

"Watch your step," said Jack. "I'm not always around to levitate you."

"Whew," Shotgun caught his breath. "Thank you, boss, I thought I was going for a swim."

"No problem," Jack grinned, "I just didn't want to pay for drying cleaning your tuxedo."

"Right, you probably just didn't want to have to clean the Andromeda. I wonder what it would take to get the smell out of the leather."

"Nonsense, if you fall in you'll walk home." Jack chuckled. "Ha, for that matter if I fall in, we'll send the Andromeda home on autopilot, and I will walk home."

"I knew it." Shotgun mocked his employer. "You care more for that over-priced piece of junk than you care for yourself."

"True," said Jack, but he gave the dwarf's shoulder a quick squeeze, and kept walking.

After a few hundred yards they saw the end. Making their way slowly down the tunnel, they approached the terminal of the sewer they were in. Thirty yards from the tunnel's end, it opened up and broadened out.

The roof ended. They looked up into a square vault. At the back of the vault a chimney rose some stories above them and disappeared in the dark. It bespoke of ancient engineering. The chimney's throat opened onto a shallow landing. The landing spread outward from the throat and resembled a hearth.

Two tubes were bored into the mountain on either side of the throat. The tubes rose sharply into the mountain. Between the tubes was a hole cut in the chimney's throat. Brick and stone from the wound in the chimney's throat fanned out over the landing where the pieces fell. The mound covered most of the landing.

A muddy delta surrounded the landing. In the middle of the

delta was a shallow pond. Little waterfalls fell from the tubes and splattered over the mound of bricks. Tiny brooklets emerged from the jumble of stones, bricks, and mortar. The brooklets flowed off the landing and into the delta. They wove across the delta and flowed into the pond. A tiny creek drained the pond into the sewer.

Shotgun strained to see in the dark. "Doesn't that beat all?"

"Yeah," Jack agreed.

They followed the walk along the wall. The sidewalk dipped at the end and sloped down to the landing. The ancient brickwork curved up to the gaping wound.

Stepping carefully, Jack picked a path between the brooklets towards the fan of bricks.

Shotgun hesitated before taking after the mage. *Guess he hasn't had any thoughts of breakfast.* Shotgun climbed taking his time.

Finding a purchase on the bricks, Jack climbed. To his satisfaction, the fallen brickwork held its position for the most part and he soon reached the top. He avoided the waterfalls on either side of the mound.

Standing atop the brick jumble, he chided his man-servant. "Can't a dwarf climb as fast as an elf?"

"Better to let the elf test the stability of a fallen pile, than to risk a dwarf. Besides, I'm not sure you can carry me."

"Touché," said Jack. He surveyed the area from his vantage atop the mound. A pattern stood out on the muddy delta.

Blinking, he refocused his eyes. Holding up his torch, he flipped the switch and flooded the muddy floor with light. The torch blazed vanquishing the shadows in the terminal; reminding Jack how very dim were the lamps. On the floor was a footprint.

A tingle surged up his back, and Jack swung the torchlight into the cavern behind him. He saw nothing save a cave. Grateful, he lowered the torch as Shotgun reached his side.

"See something?" Shotgun whispered, perhaps more cautious than his magically armed employer.

"Yeah, look at the rivulets in the mud," Jack lighted up the footprint with his torch. "Is that what it looks like, or is my imagination working overtime?"

"Holy cow, that's big. But there's only one. If it really was what it looked like there should be a track, and we should have passed more of tracks coming up the tunnel."

"Yes," Jack ran a hand through his hair. "And we didn't see any other Noddie holes," he sighed. "This hole runs back into the mountain, and it's been here a long time." He shined the torch into the cavern. "See," he waved the torch around, "nothing but stalactites and stalagmites."

"Are we going up it, or try finding some breakfast?"

Jack switched off his torch, and slid it back into his cloak. Letting his eyes adjust to the dim, he stood still for a moment.

"Breakfast, then check with your maintenance friend. They must know about this cave. If not, I'm not sure I want to explore a dangerous, unknown cavern on an empty stomach, and without backup."

Carefully, the pair retraced their steps down the mound and over the little delta. On the landing, they wiped the mud off their shoes until they felt less slippery. Walking faster on a path once trod, they returned to the crime scene in half the time.

Only police tape and Gumshoe waited at the scene.

"Sorry Gumshoe, I hadn't expected you to be waiting."

"Turns out there aren't as many entrances to check as I feared."

"Have you learned anything?"

"We found the lift they used, and the spot where they parked their airship. We went up the access corridor the way the dwarf suggested. We found nothing at all until we reached the first lift upstream along this trunk, not a hundred yards from here. At the lift, we found three sets of footprints. The lift ran back to the service bay upstream. They must have used a small airship. We found one print of a landing pad."

"Sounds like you found quite a few clues while we enjoyed

a pleasant walk."

"No great feat of magic, Jack. Just basic police work."

"Was the mud from the sewer here?"

"Probably, but forensics will test it just to be sure. We think Niles guessed right. They came here to dump the body. They hoped the victim would wash downstream. Whatever Niles heard, it startled them. They ripped the alarm box off the wall, and beat a hasty retreat up the hatch. They forgot to wipe their shoes, and they unintentionally alerted Sanitation to the location of their victim's body."

"Do you still think Angela was murdered at the Ritz?"

"Yes," Gumshoe frowned. "We'll know for sure when we get the blood samples back from the lab. But there's plenty to connect the two. Obviously, we have two Capricorns. We have three suspects at both scenes. The landing pad print in the service bay matches the ones at the hotel. To top it off, no one was caught on the cameras."

"If they wanted to hide the body, why scorch the walls with the Capricorn?" said Shotgun.

"Easy," said Jack. "It's a signature. The killer is proud of his crime and wants to take credit for it. They're self-absorbed narcissists. You don't murder someone like this if you care about others. All criminals are selfish, but these guys are cold-blooded. They wanted to hide the body to avoid being caught, but they wanted everyone to mark this place as theirs. Think of a vicious dog pack. The pack leader always marks his territory. He probably thinks his victim deserved to die and he deserves to consume her life."

"Thanks for the analysis, Jack. Want to write my report for me?"

"No way Gumshoe, I'll leave the bureaucracy to you."

~~~~~

When Jack and Shotgun returned to Babel Tower, they

found the remains of dinner on his dining table.

Shotgun cleared the table, "I'll make us some breakfast." He walked into the kitchen, and called out, "I've got a message, boss. Jazz, Goldie and my girls reached Iron Mountain."

"Great! All the girls are safe. That's a relief."

"Yeah, you'll love this next bit."

"What? Is it good? Let me see."

"Somebody tried diverting all the biots to a tent city in the salt mines."

"What? There's plenty of room in the barracks there. That place was built to hold three times the population of Nodlon!"

"Wait for it, boss. Jazz moved Goldie and the girls into her place, and some pinhead with the Evacuation Coordination Office turned them in. Jazz called Princess Virginia, and the Princess called Marshall Arnold."

"That's my girl; taking charge and pulling strings."

Butter knives and forks, and spoons appeared.

"It worked. Nodlon Memorial picked up Goldie's contract. The hospital gave them an apartment, and Goldie's enrolled Faith and Hope in a daycare. So they won't even have to stay in the barracks.

"It's good to have friends in high places."

"Yeah, and it gets better. Look." Shotgun twisted the screen.

"Ha! Virginia shut down those nuts in the E. C. O. All the biots get the same rooms in the barracks. Biots are people too!"

"Are the barracks better than the mines?" Shotgun covered plates with toast, jelly and pats of butter.

"It's not exactly home, but millions lived in those barracks during the Regressive Wars. I don't know how anyone can live in the mines."

"They did good then?" Shotgun filled two bowls with oatmeal.

"Yes, they all did. I'm glad Goldie went with Jazz. I'm proud of Jazz for putting up a fuss, and I'm impressed with

Virginia. It's good to see real leadership out of a teenager. She's not some wimp going to a conference to listen to some dried up old witches."

"Yeah, I'm looking forward to meeting her. She seems special. If I were in her shoes, I think I'd spend all my time partying in Bermuda."

"We all would. We're very lucky to have Virginia as our Princess. We might have been stuck with a dumb fluke."

"Perhaps, and perhaps our higher power has graced us."

"I don't know about that, but I hope it's true." Jack shrugged, "Any news from Korman? I want to know if my road show has arrived."

"No," Shotgun tapped the screen. "Jazz sent the message. Only priority communication's relays are allowed. So she used the hospital's line."

"Sneaky," Jack said. "But I'm glad for any news. We'd better catch a nap before Gumshoe calls again. Thank you for breakfast."

"It's what you pay me for."

Port of Moab

Traffic was heavy for a Thursday morning. Gumshoe's emergency lights parted the traffic. Most people had fled to Iron Mountain. Still, many remained in the city and most of those were in the streets trying to evacuate. Weaving through the frightened crowds, they descended to the level-way, and turned east towards the port of Moab.

As the cruiser ramped up to speed, the Inspector brought them up to date. "A longshoreman found the body of a dwarf girl in the Great River about an hour ago. He called the Moab Surete, and they're searching the port now. So it's back to Moab we go."

Gumshoe checked the autopilot, and let the cruiser slip into the fast lanes. "They've recovered three bodies so far." The autopilot changed lanes. "Lord knows what else they're going to find. Constable Wiggles is in charge of the investigation. We're going to meet him at the upper docks."

"Are they related to our other cases?" asked Jack. "Mercury News is on the warpath. They seem to think these are part of the Zodiac case, but you haven't said anything."

"Can't say over an open channel," the Inspector grumbled. "The hysteria level is too high. All of the police feeds are being monitored. Even the secure feeds are streaming on the net."

"How are they connected?"

"By their microchips, the killer ripped their chips out and drained their blood somehow. It's not much to go on, but at the moment, the only killer on the loose with that M.O. is the Black Dwarf."

Shotgun said something inaudible, and Jack bit his lip.

"Could they have been killed at the Ritz?" asked Shotgun. "The ballroom was a mess, and they must have killed, what, two people? Maybe there were more?"

"If both of the girls were murdered there," Jack asked, "why was one disposed of in the sewer, and another in Blueberry

Lake?"

"No, I don't think so, gentlemen." Gumshoe held up a finger. "We found the blood of two victims in the ballroom. The blood in the Capricorn on the wall was Anna McCarthy's. Anna was probably murdered there. We haven't identified the other victim, but he was a human male."

"Was he murdered?" asked Jack.

"Maybe, but we can't be sure. We found only traces of his blood to be sure." Gumshoe tapped the wheel. "Angela must have been killed elsewhere. Maybe she was killed in the fiend's lair."

"What about the business manager, Jezebel Steele?" Jack pushed the bloody scene to the back of his mind. "She was slaughtered where she stood and her body left where they killed her. They didn't take her blood."

"She didn't have a microchip," said Gumshoe. "She was human and they couldn't use her in their army of mesmerized dwarves."

"Why didn't they want her blood?" asked Shotgun. "Nothing was wrong with it."

"Don't try to be too rational," Jack shook his head. "We're dealing with a sociopath. The Black Dwarf performed some kind of bizarre ritual in the ballroom. He used a dwarf maiden and a man. Maybe it was some sort of bizarre human sacrifice."

"Why sacrifice Anna, then?" asked Shotgun, "And not Jezebel."

"Maybe they wanted a virgin. Anna probably was, and Jezebel almost certainly wasn't. Who knows? But if Angela was murdered as a virgin sacrifice, my theory of a pagan cult trying to summon an ancient demon may be panning out."

"Maybe, Jack," Gumshoe said. "It's still only a theory. They may have murdered Jezebel when they realized she knew too much. She was a loose end they had forgotten."

Shotgun leaned forward and added his two cents, "I disagree, Inspector. She wasn't forgotten. The Black Dwarf is pretty brazen. Anyone who will blow up an interplanetary supertanker isn't going to have a hard time murdering someone in broad daylight."

"Go ahead Shotgun, butter up the old man," said Jack. "But you've got a point. The Black Dwarf flaunts his power. He enjoys our inability to stop him. I don't think this guy is planning to retire on Bora Bora." Jack thought a moment. "Maybe we're looking at this the wrong way. Maybe he wants us to know what he's doing. He walked into Jezebel's office with his pet monster and ripped her apart. No one noticed and we caught nothing on camera. Then, he ambushed us on a city street with a military grade lightning cannon. He controls what we know and what we don't know about his crimes. Maybe he's only sneaky to throw us off track or waste our time while he sows fear and panic."

"If you're right, Jack, he's doing a good job."

"All of the missing dwarves sought gene therapy at New Gem," Shotgun chimed in. "They all worked for the Crown, the Octagon, and the Ministry of Manna. What does it add up to?"

"Not sure yet," Gumshoe sighed. "Maybe we'll find some answers in Moab."

Leaving the level-way, the cruiser slid through the Halls of Industry and into the Strand district. *Halls of industry: No great mystery there. When Thornmocker ran out of names he liked, he simply named places for what they were.* The Strand separated the Halls from the Harbor of Industry by a few blocks.

Here on the Strand, Moab stirred with life. Shops, mills, and wholesale houses bustled. Shipping still flowed up the Great River from the Great Lakes, the Appalachian Mountains, and from the old kingdoms across the sea.

Molemen, goblins, and dwarves pushed carts full of rags, bolts of cloth, and pallets of handicrafts. The cruiser yielded the right of way to tourists and workmen alike. Jack watched a pair of dwarves struggle with a rack of carpet. *It's nothing like the empty halls of broken dreams and shattered illusions in Deep*

Nodlon.

The cruiser turned off the Strand. A sign welcomed them to the Harbor of Industry. *How original?* A security guard waved them through.

Gumshoe disengaged the autopilot, and drove carefully down the boardwalk. He turned upriver, and headed towards a collection of emergency vehicles parked in a semi-circle at the end of the boardwalk.

Overhead hoses vacuumed up rice and barley. The hoses rocked and swayed as the bulk cargo flowed into the grain elevators. High above the harbor, a stevedore conducted the activity on the docks from a control room mounted on the dome.

Heavily laden barges rode low in the dark waters. Longshoremen offloaded pallets. Forklifts and levi-trucks choked the piers. They stacked the pallets on the dock in a rough order.

Gumshoe wove through the longshoremen and the chaos. He dodged forklifts and pallets. A motley group of green and blue ambulances, police cruisers, and fire trucks clogged nearly every available space. "We'll just have to park out here and hope they don't drop a pallet on my cruiser."

The Inspector squeezed the cruiser in to a space next to a police cruiser marked with the seal of the Moab Surete. "We're in luck, Wiggles is here."

They stepped out of the cruiser and into the cool, crisp air. Jack drew his cloak and followed Gumshoe towards a knot of investigators at the end of the boardwalk.

A longshoreman broke away from his co-workers and turned his forklift at the mage, the Inspector, and the dwarf. The forklift bore down on the trio.

Gumshoe held up a hand. "Halt police!"

The driver waved and turned aside. He stopped the forklift and jumped off. His heavy boots slapped the pavement. Grease and oil blackened his coveralls. He was shorter than the other molemen, but broader.

Gumshoe rubbed his hands, and cracked his knuckles in the cool air. "What can I do you for, sir?"

The longshoreman saluted. "Hello, Inspector. My name's Hoffer." Hoffer took in the mage and the dwarf and straightened his careworn coveralls. "How do ya' do, Mr. Clay? And you must be Mr. Shotgun. I've seen y'all on the vid."

Drawing a dirty rag from his back pocket, he shook it out. Briefly, he wiped his hands in a vain attempt to clean them. He made a decision, and clutched the rag, "Forgive me, Inspector Lestrayed, I'd like to shake your hand, but uh..." he broke off.

"Well, sir, how can we help you?"

"Aye, you're a gentleman, Inspector, but I ain't no sir. A workin' man am I, and a workin' man I'll be." The longshoreman's eyes searched the dock. "Ah, you're time is valuable, I understand, so I'll say my piece quick.

"I found the first girl, just a child really. She was on the boat ramp at the end of the dock. After we found her, we scoured the piers. Call it a hunch, but we had a feeling there would be more. The second one washed up against Pier Six. Then, we found another and then another." He waved at the emergency vehicles. "Horrible, I've never seen anything like that. A cave crab was riding on one of them girls, and I tossed him back. The little bugger wasn't gonna get a ride here."

"Have you made a statement, my good man?" asked Gumshoe.

"Aye, I gave a full account to Constable Wiggles, a full account." He swayed side to side, and flexed his toes. "Yeah, ya' can read it if ya' like, though, it'll do ya' little good. I pulled the child from the river and laid her mortal remains upon the stones at the end of the boardwalk. Me mates watched over her to keep off the birds, and we called for the cops.

"We were back at work when Crazy Martin found another one on the fisherman's wharf side." Hoffer hooked his thumb at the piers on the opposite shore. "One was bad enough, but so many." His eye grew misty. The honest lug paused for a moment to regain his composure. "Nothin' else for me to tell; nothin' that is for your report."

Gumshoe sighed deeply, took off his fedora, and pinched the brow before setting it back on his head. "So, is there something else you want to tell us? Something you'd rather not have on the record? Some speculation or a hunch, you'd like to share, which may help?" He frowned, and his jowls stiffened.

"Go ahead, Mr. Hoffer. If it's material, we will have to add it to our report. If it's speculation, I'll hear what you have to say, but you must understand I cannot rely on it officially."

The moleman thought a moment, sizing up the Inspector. His face tried to work out a conclusion. Was the pressure to speak worth the risk of rejection or ridicule? He rubbed his chin, and then made a decision. "Yes sir, I understand. Chalk it up to speculation or a hunch if ya' will, but I tell ya' I've a powerful intuition all is not right here in Nodlon tonight."

Hoffer focused his gaze on the faraway, and he recited a verse from a poem. "When the Moon rises and Capricorn is high, the old wives say a dragon will fall from heaven. He will send out his beast, and the world will end." His gaze fell on Jack, and he mopped his hair to console an inner demon. "They will take away the true believers. The rest of us they leave to ruin.

"A dragon? Do you mean Noddie?"

"Nay, sir," he said. He cleared his throat, and added a bit of gloom. "No, it ain't Noddie of whom I speak. It's a dragon of a kind less physical than myth, and yet as real as my fist. The dragon and his servants will come on the cusp of Capricorn."

"Why Capricorn, Hoffer?" asked Jack. "Do you have any ideas?"

"It's the time," said Hoffer. "All the signs have passed. Nothing is left for the prophecies to fulfill. We are out of time. If you don't defeat this enemy, we are all doomed."

"Come on, you old gaffer," said Jack. "What prophecy are you talking about? Dozens of prophecies fit your story."

"Mock me if you wish, Mr. Clay. The dragon will con the dwarves. They will place their hope in a paradise on Earth. He'll mesmerize his followers, and he'll demand they put their faith in him. Once ensnared, the true believers will obey like zombies. They will live as if undead until someone breaks the spell and releases their souls. Unless that happens, they will die rather than give up their faith."

"Rather gloomy prophecy, Hoffer," said Gumshoe. "How do you know all this?"

"I've read all the old books."

"Uh, huh," Gumshoe shot a glance at Jack.

"Don't look at me." Jack held up his palms. "I've heard a dozen variations of the same prophecy. He could mean any one of them."

"All right," said Gumshoe. "Hoffer, tell it to me straight without the mumbo jumbo. Are you a true believer?"

Hoffer cocked his head, and his brow crinkled. "Do I look like a zombie?" Holding his hands out palms down, he opened his mouth slack jaw and addled side to side. He mimed a movie version of the undead. "True believers are dupes. I said, he'll mesmerize them he will."

"Enough of the histrionics, Hoffer, do you have anything else to offer?"

"Scoff, if ya' like, Inspector." The longshoreman examined his boot. "The signs are in the heavens. While he marks the innocent, Nodlon will ignore the warnings as others have. The Zodiac turns while you dither. It's been thirty years since the last killings, and this isn't going to stop until you close the gate."

"Hoffer, there was a series of murders thirty years ago, but we kept it hush-hush. What do know about those murders?"

"I'm not blind Inspector. It's happening the same way it did then. One of the victims washed out of the river and into the port. Somehow it stopped, but there were rumors of more victims."

"Dumping a victim in the river doesn't require a

supernatural explanation, Hoffer. What makes you think those murders thirty years ago are linked to these?"

"I've studied the prophecies." He touched one eye, and he waved towards the knot gathered round the victims at the end of the boardwalk. "He consumes these children to further his purposes. They're expendable. Besides, you just told me they're linked."

"Hoffer," Gumshoe reddened.

The old geezer grinned and gave him a wink. "Aye, Inspector, you'd not have admitted to knowing about the murders if you hadn't been thinking the same thing yourself. In those days, I was no older than the boys that went missing. Black dwarves they was then too. Nary a word since then. Like some kind of superstition. Everyone acting as if not talking about it will keep him away. The only way to stop him is to keep the faith. Nodlon has to remain true to Colonel Justin's promises."

"Biots are people too, Hoffer," said Jack. "I believe it, but Colonel Justin promised freedom to the molemen and they have it."

"Aye, Mr. Clay, Moab is free. Any green man can hold his head up just like a human, but that's only if he hasn't got a contract on his head to begin with."

"True, Hoffer," said Gumshoe. "And it's a darned shame too. But the House of Justin has done far more than most politicians; I don't see that they could do much more than they are. What's that got to do with the murders?"

A faraway gleam appeared in the longshoreman's eye, and he straightened his stocky frame. Slowly, he took in each of them. The man, the elf, and the dwarf pondered the moleman for a split second.

"Happiness, Inspector. As long as a man's got a soul, he's gotta dream. And as long as he dreams, the dragon can press his advantage. That's his window. That's how he poisons men's hearts, and how he traps his victims. If a man's soul can't find its way, he can't be happy. If a man is trapped, he can be tempted to believe lies. If his soul is dark, he'll join the dragon willingly. If not, he'll become a victim."

"I'm afraid you've lost me, Hoffer," said Gumshoe. "And we really must be going. If we don't catch these monsters, the whole city will explode."

"Nodlon will explode anyway, Inspector. Biots have souls too. As long as the biots live hopeless lives of unfulfilled dreams, the dragon will find many followers and many victims.

"Poppycock, Hoffer," said Jack. "Biots dream. I know, I'm half-biot and I dream all the time. Biots are people too. I agree with you there, man. Few of us have a family, and even fewer have a home. I know I'm one of the lucky few, but I grew up in an agency's dorm and I know what every biot in the city faces. It's not fair, and it isn't pretty. I'll grant you that. But if your theory was correct, Nodlon would be burning now."

"To be sure, Mr. Clay very few biots would willingly give the dragon their lives. Very few would kill for him. But they don't know any better. No man knows what he'll do when he's at the end of his rope. He panics. He sees things. Maybe, he goes mad. He knows no more what he does than a stag in the woods." Hoffer's tone dropped, "Nevertheless, Nodlon will pay for what happens to the biots. As long as their dreams are squashed, there will be some who answer the dragon's call. That's why they say it takes faith. Nodlon has to let the biots go or face the consequences. You can destroy a man's dreams, but you can't destroy his soul. That's the source of the dragon's power."

"No one in Nodlon has a soul." Jack scoffed, "No one has a soul because there's no such thing as souls. If biots runaway and fall prey to the Black Dwarf, it's because of discontent. It certainly has nothing to do with souls. Of all the people in Nodlon, I don't blame them. I'm a biot too, and Princess Virginia has tasked me to help her free them. I will do everything I can as soon as I get a chance. If we can stop this Black Dwarf fiend, maybe I will get that chance. But there's no such thing as souls, Hoffer, and if all of the biots in Nodlon were freed tomorrow, there would still be malcontents. If the dragon gets his jollies murdering malcontents, we will have to learn to live it. Life isn't fair, and yet life goes on. What else can anyone do about it?"

Hoffer pursed his lips, and looked down at his boots. "I don't blame ya' at all for thinking that. Right ya' are not only by your lights but by the facts plain as day. You're right that the dragon can always count on the malcontents. There's always exceptions too when the wrong people cross his path. What I'm saying is this: Nodlon is under attack! Nodlon's forgotten what it owes the biots! Oh, I don't mean Nodlon's people individually. I mean the power Nodlon has collectively to take the lives of biots and grind them into dust." Hoffer shook his head sadly, "Oh, many will not cave in to the dragon. They will accept their lot and go on against all odds, and they'll hope there's some reason for it. Somehow, they will do what's right. They can't explain why. They only know a flame burns in their own hearts. Still many will go into the dark. The dragon has that power over their minds."

"Hoffer, I'm sorry," said Jack. "I'm sure you mean well, and generally I agree with you. Nodlon owes it to the biots to treat them like they're human beings. I just don't think this has anything to do with the murders or catching the Black Dwarf."

Hoffer grabbed a rail on his forklift, and climbed up its side with surprising grace and agility for one so large. "Good day to ya' sirs, then," He put two fingers to his temple, and saluted in his odd way. "I can see you'll not be needing any more of my advice. Got to be goin' about my work."

"If I have any questions," Gumshoe asked, "where can I find you?"

"Always here, Inspector, and if I'm not, Lucky will know how to reach me. He's the foreman." Hoffer drove his forklift away.

Jack and Shotgun huddled around Gumshoe. "What was

that about?" asked Jack.

"All is not right here in Nodlon tonight," mocked Shotgun. "Go figure, dozens of dead black dwarves, and five murdered girls? Where does he think we've been, under a rock?"

"Keep an open mind," said Gumshoe. "Either he's a crackpot, or he's letting on more than he's telling."

"Another crackpot," Shotgun asked. "How many will we run into on this case?"

"Crackpots follow me wherever I go," said Jack. "They're a paranormal phenomenon common to a supernatural life. Happily, they're mostly harmless."

"Every case has its share of crackpots baying at the moon," added Gumshoe. "With the vid coverage of the murders, it's no surprise we've had more than our share. Bound to be more of them trying to read our palms or divine our future before we're through."

"And don't forget that detail about snaring them with temptation and then mesmerizing them." Shotgun sniffed, "Yeah that made sense."

"The ambush was all over the news," said Jack. "Bet he saw it all on the net. All the black dwarves were zombies before we restored them."

"All the victims were tempted by hope," said Shotgun. "That part makes sense. The hope of a better life tempted them to go to New Gem. There they were shanghaied. The rest of his story sounds like gibberish. It's got nothing to do with the heavens."

"What of the inane babble about prophecy?" Jack said, "A dragon will destroy the world, signs in the heavens, the Zodiac turns, and the undead walk. Sounds like mumbo-jumbo out of a cheap, horror flick."

"Who is the dragon he kept on about?" asked Shotgun. "We're looking for a black dwarf aren't we?"

"Could be any of a dozen myths," said Jack. "Around the world since the dawn of the time, dragons are always villains. It wasn't until recently they became sensitive, friendly creatures in our popular culture."

"Shotgun, check the net." Gumshoe threw back his trench coat, and scratched his chin. "Have there been any leaks? No one should know about New Gem."

"I can look into it." Shotgun tapped his laptop.

"Thanks, Shotgun. Please do."

"Somehow he knows a lot about the old murders," said Jack. "How did he know about those murders thirty years ago?"

"Intuition perhaps," said Gumshoe. "Can't be sure, I was a greenhorn on traffic. All I heard was rumors, but I think the bodies were dumped here too. Maybe he found one and he's trying to make sense of it."

"Intuition?" asked Jack. "Finding the girls may have jogged his memory. Maybe he can't remember the full story, but he can fill in the blanks with rumor and an overactive imagination."

"Whatever he remembers," said Gumshoe. "He's conflated what he's read, and what he's seen in the news. He may be on to something, if not for solving the case, then certainly for his peace of mind. He wasn't as upset as most of us because he has a theory that makes sense to him."

"Do you think he's involved?"

"No," snorted the Inspector. "He just has a hunch." Gumshoe struck the pose of an ever-vigilant watch dog. "We'll have to keep an eye on Hoffer now, though."

"Inspector," said Shotgun. "There's nothing on New Gem. The ambush is all over the net, but there's nothing about the dwarves being mesmerized or the stunned dwarves recovering. I'm sure our secret isn't out there unless it's on the rumor mill no one's posted the gossip."

"Rather hard to believe," said Jack. "The Surete knows and the hospital staff. Yet no one has leaked it? Incredible."

"Miracles never cease," said Gumshoe.

They approached the crime scene without a challenge. No one had bothered to run a tape yet. Techs and investigators hovered around the gurneys with their macabre loads.

A moleman liveried in green greeted them with a friendly wave. "Good to see you, Gumshoe."

"Magnum Wiggles," said Gumshoe, "the finest policeman in all of Moab."

"All of Nodlon," Wiggles corrected him with a wink. He thrust out his hand, "Good to see you, Mr. Clay."

"Call me Jack, Constable," said Jack smiling.

"Sergeant York told me all about your narrow escape from the Marie Celeste."

"Yes," said Jack. "I'm glad we all survived. The Black Dwarf nearly eighty-sixed us. I hope our next encounter will be more productive."

"It's an honor, Jack." The rotund moleman swelled. His belly threatened to pop the buttons on his green coat. "Round here, you're famous. My missus and all the kiddos saw your show couple of years back." His wave took in the port. "Welcome to the Strand, Mr. Clay. You too, Mr. Shotgun, I do wish we had met under better circumstances."

"Thank you sir," said Shotgun.

"Call me Wiggles," said Wiggles "Biots are people too."

"Biots are people too," said Jack. "I'm glad the Surete takes these murders seriously."

"We're all biots in Moab," Wiggles winked.

"Our job is to prevent people from assuming room temperature," said Gumshoe. "I don't care who their parents were or if they had any at all."

"I'd love to let our firefighters have a go at this Black Dwarf of yours." Wiggles frowned. "To do what he did! Polite words won't work for it."

A gaggle of curious on-lookers surrounded the crime

scene's investigators. "Follow me chaps," Wiggles said. "Let's meet the victims."

The Constable parted the crowd, and they all plowed into his wake. They stepped lively to keep up with the moleman. They wove through the crowd to reach the stretchers bearing the victim's mortal remains. Soon they reached the end of the boardwalk.

Shotgun spotted a technician in the crowd. He had to skip a bit to pull alongside Wiggles. "Constable, may I cross-check our records on the victims?"

"Yes," Wiggles hesitated, "but please share your findings."

"Certainly," Shotgun dropped back to find the technician.

"Can you fill us in, Wiggles?" Gumshoe asked.

"Five female dwarves have been recovered so far." Wiggles choked up. "All maidens, all maidens, tragic, really tragic." The Constable coughed. "We have identified three of them. All the victims were pulled from the river, and we're still searching. A fishing boat returning from Stevedore Lake found one maiden floating in the harbor. Two more bodies were found under the Fisherman's Wharf." Wiggles pointed across the harbor to the wharf on the other side.

The Constable barked an order, and the crowd parted to offer a view across the jetty to the end of the wharf. He pointed at a pair of fishing boats working a string of buoys blocking the mouth of the Great River. "Volunteers ran fish nets across the mouth of the river to catch anyone floating into the harbor."

Ripples spread quietly over the harbor. The ripples sparkled under the warm, yellow lamps of Moab. "We've sent officers and volunteers downriver to search for more victims." The portly moleman frowned. "I hope we won't find any more bodies, but I don't want to leave any of these young women behind."

"Did you get my report, Wig?" said Gumshoe.

"Are you always a harbinger of doom old man?"

"I could ask you the same question, Wig. Every time I

come down to see you, all you have for me is a full meat locker and a load of bad news."

"Very bad news," said Wiggles. "Same modus operandi as in your report I'm afraid, very bad. Could have used it the day before yesterday, old man."

"Sorry, Wig. Didn't intend to leave Moab out of the loop, but the Black Dwarf is full of surprises. Having a supertanker fall on us left me a bit rattled."

"No matter, old man," the rotund police officer patted his ample girth. "One never knows the facts until they're discovered, right?"

"What about the cause of death, Wiggles?"

"The same," the jolly policeman turned dour. "Their microchips were ripped out of their foreheads as if they exploded from within. The killer drained their blood. They have minor burns over their bodies. Their clothes were intact for the most part. They weren't molested as near as we can tell from the initial scans. So I can agree it's sadistic, but it's not obvious why they were murdered. Any questions?" the Constable studied their faces to assess the impact on his guests.

"No," said Gumshoe, "but let me update you on the girl we just found in the sewer." Quickly, he summarized what they knew.

"We need to share this information with headquarters," said Wiggles. "Just give me a moment to wrap up here, and we'll go down to City Hall." He collected his reports from his technicians.

"Gumshoe," said Jack. "We've got to stop these murders before we run out of biots."

"Now, this isn't a joking matter Jack."

"No jokes, this is bigger than we thought. This is more than a murder. This is a massacre. We have to expect more victims. The Crown must warn all the dwarves in the city! Whether or not they're synthetic they feel and suffer."

"All right Jack," Gumshoe waved down the elf. "Now I

follow you, and I agree. I'll do everything I can. I'll tell Barfly to issue a warning."

"You need to shut down New Gem," said Jack. "The Black Dwarf is targeting dwarf maidens because he can lure the hopeless into his web."

"How Jack?" Gumshoe sniffed and put his fists on his hips. "I can't even pull a warrant on them. Our evidence is only as good as the judge thinks it is. If I push hard enough, I've got a feeling I'll be the one under the microscope."

"We've still got to warn them. Biots are people too."

"Weren't you the one just saying they don't have any souls?" Gumshoe lifted an eyebrow. "The lady doth protest too much."

"I've researched everything supernatural, old man," said Jack. "I've found no evidence for souls, and I don't know why it would matter to the Black Dwarf. The Black Dwarf is a psycho. Maybe he gets his jollies sacrificing young women to his idols. I don't know. All I know is that people are special."

"People are special," said Gumshoe. "I can't prove souls exist, Jack, but I do believe there is a world inside each of us. Simply because we can't explain it doesn't mean it doesn't exist. When we figure that one out, I think we will find the evidence for your missing souls."

Their dwarf walked up swiftly and rejoined them. "Bad news, Inspector" said Shotgun. "A yacht put in with another victim aboard."

"God save the King! Was it another maiden?"

"Yes Inspector. Her chip was ripped out the same as the others."

"Dagnabbit, I'd better go collect Wiggles." The Inspector spun on his wingtips and strode off into the crowd. A knot of technicians and molemen engulfed him, and he disappeared.

~~~~~

A boat motored out of the Great River's mouth. The fishermen lowered their net, and the boat drifted across the harbor. Jack watched its wake lap the piers.

"Since we have a moment, boss, I'd like you to meet one of the techs. He said something I'd like you to hear."

"Sure, let's hear what he has to say."

His butler disappeared in the busy crime scene, and returned with a dwarf in the blue coveralls of Nodlon Yard. The tech carried his equipment and sample cases in neatly organized bags.

He put a boot on a black pier and leaned on his knee. He appraised the two dwarves. The technician carried a pathology scanner, sample cases, and a backpack. On his shoulder was the insignia of a senior technician.

"Boss, this is Martin Fields."

Lines of stress creased Martin's face and betrayed his maturity. Dwarves enjoyed an extended youth. It was a consolation prize of sorts for the curse of synthetic genes. Nonetheless, Martin's wrinkles bore witness to the tell-tale signs of age.

"Good to meet you, Mr. Clay. My daughter and I saw your show a few years back. Good show, good times." He fell silent and gazed out over the harbor. "She won't take me with her any more. She thinks she's an adult now."

"Thank you Martin. My shows are for kids of all ages. I aspire to inspired silliness. If you have a good time, we've done our job. If we can make you forget your own troubles for a while that's icing on the cake. Under the circumstances, I assume you didn't want ask for my autograph."

"No sir, I'm not looking for an autograph. I've noticed a spooky clue. A clue I'm afraid may go unnoticed. Maybe it will help, and maybe not, but I wanted to bring it to your attention."

"Why me, Martin?" Jack asked. "I'm just an amateur sleuth. I'm sure your supervisor or Inspector Lestrayed will listen to anything you have to say. You must have been doing this for some time. I believe your experience beats mine hands down."

"Thank you, sir. I've worked crime scenes for over thirty years."

"Wow, I'm impressed. That's longer than I've been alive."

Martin smiled sadly and nodded. "That's why I know this clue isn't going to be given any weight. My supervisor's a good man, and the Inspector is too. But our reports are thick, and they don't have time to consider everything. I may put a clue in my report, but it may be overlooked."

"Fair enough, but why would I think it's important?"

"You know biots are people too, Mr. Clay. I'm a Claynet subscriber and I've been following your campaign. You understand the cause better than most. Better than any of us maybe. I know you'll hear me out, and keep an open mind."

"I'll hear you out Martin, though I can't promise anything."

"I've run the neural scans on all the victims. As I'm sure you know, their microchips were blasted out of their foreheads. All of their blood was drained from their bodies. The neural scans all match and the machines don't lie. The Christie girl, the McCarthy girl, and now we know these girls were all alive when the perpetrator ripped out their chips."

Jack took his elbow off his knee and looked at Martin.

"Were the chips off?" Jack knew the answer, but he had to hear it.

"No," said Martin, and a grim shadow fell over him. "When the chips were fired, the victims were alive and awake." The dwarf's gave them a hard stare and a stiff frown.

"Are you sure?"

"Positive. I ran the scans myself. When a chipped biot dies, their chip retracts, but these chips came out before retracting. The wiring was still in place. It interfered with my scans. That means the girls were alive and awake, so they must have known they were about to die – or worse."

"As if the killer wanted to intentionally inflict emotional

distress on his victims?"

"Exactly, Mr. Clay, he wanted to torment them. The agony must have been terrible in the moments before the chips were ripped out. Ripping these chips out lobotomized the girls. The wiring shredded their frontal lobes. If they had survived, they'd be little more than zombies."

"Disgusting," spat Shotgun.

"How does this help us, Martin?" Jack felt his pulse race, and he sucked in a breath. "We already know we're looking for a monster."

"Most of us biots are chipped all the time. Humans don't understand. An unauthorized removal is unimaginable ..."

"Meaning," said Jack, "we're dealing with a madman who gets his jollies hurting maidens."

"Maybe he wanted to destroy their souls," said Martin.

"Souls, souls, souls," Jack looked back at the knot of technicians and onlookers surrounding the stretchers. "What is it about souls? Why does everyone keep bringing it up? No one even knows what a soul is. Souls may be anything. Philosophers and sages make all sorts of wild claims. Whatever we think souls are, there are no souls. Souls are always magical elements separating humans from animals. Bio-technology destroyed that idea. Biots are manufactured from human, animal, and synthetic genes. Yet biots are self-aware. So there's nothing special about humans and there's nothing magical in our heads. Now there's nowhere left for the soul to hide."

"Yes, sir, I know," said Martin. The dwarf seemed pained. "In my business, I am well aware of the latest advances in neurology and especially the analysis of neural output. It's strange though to hear that from you, Mr. Clay. Of all the people who would believe in magic, I thought it would be you."

"Sorry, Martin," Jack smiled and tried to soften the impact of his sharp words. "I believe in magic." As if on cue, a buoy lying on the jetty lifted itself off the deck and floated mysteriously for several feet. "My magic is just in the genes. I'm sorry, Martin, because I'm angry. I want to catch the Black Dwarf and stop the killing. I don't want to waste time chasing rabbits."

"Mr. Clay maybe your Black Dwarf is only a madman. Even so, I think he's a madman who believes biots have souls."

"What does having a soul have to do with this, Martin? Animals have no souls, and we slaughter animals. If a madman thought biots had souls wouldn't he be more respectful?"

"Sorry, sir, I don't mean to disagree," Martin bounced the way dwarves do. "The Black Dwarf hurts biots as if there's a soul inside his victims. Whether or not his victims have a soul doesn't really matter. He enjoys destroying their world inside."

"Why?" Jack huffed. "I don't see the point."

"Well sir," Martin hesitated, "In my downtime I enjoy reading, and I've been reading something called Black Dwarf."

"Oh?" Jack seemed genuinely puzzled. "Every time we turn around, why are we always turning back to a black dwarf?"

"Black Dwarf is an old science fiction-fantasy series about a black dwarf. Everyone tries to destroy him, because they think he is evil." Martin trailed off and glanced at Shotgun.

"Go on Martin," whispered Shotgun. "It's safe. Mr. Clay won't report you for what you read on your own time. He believes in life. Remember, biots are people, too."

Encouraged, the technician cleared his throat. "Mind you, Mr. Clay, the stories are fantasy. In the books biots have souls. The kicker is the villains believe everyone has a soul. They believe destroying souls creates magical power and saving souls weakens your magical power."

"Rubbish, Martin," Jack doffed his hunter's cap and played with his feather. "Magic has nothing to do with souls, and souls have nothing to do with magic. Magic is a force, and souls are just a fantasy. When I discovered my magical powers, everyone wanted to know why. The Octagon drafted me and sent me to their bioresearch lab out in Area 51. After I showed up, they all joked that I was from outer space. They probed me, and tested me. They sequenced my genes, and just generally made me miserable for a year. They found nothing supernatural, and they didn't find my soul. And I didn't see any aliens there either."

"Yes sir, I meant no offense. I know it's far-fetched, but what if the Black Dwarf believed it? This is important. Might a madman who believes souls create magical power try killing biots to gain magical power? Those girls are the same age as my daughters, and they all wear black chips." Martin touched the black chip on his forehead.

"Martin, it is important," Jack sighed. "I understand. I'm sorry if I sound dismissive. My mother was a biot. My fiancé is a biot. Almost all of my friends are biots. Anyone who would pull a biot's chip while she's alive deserves every punishment we can mete out. I'm going to catch the Black Dwarf or die trying. I don't know how, and I don't know when, but I'm not letting him go."

Martin's shoulders drooped.

"I'm sorry, Martin." Jack patted the dwarf on the back. "Your idea is not all that far-fetched. I just don't see how your clue will help. As I already said, we know we're after a monster."

Looking over the harbor, Martin watched the fishermen check their nets. He shrugged, and his voice dropped. "Thank you for listening, Mr. Clay."

"My pleasure, Martin," said Jack. "Thank you for letting us know the girls were alive when the Black Dwarf took their chips. I do think that's important, and I won't forget it."

"Thank you, sir," said Martin with a hint of skepticism. He shouldered his sample cases and his equipment, and he headed for one of Nodlon Yard's vans.

"Sorry boss, I thought it made more sense when I first heard it."

"No problem," Jack frowned. "We weren't busy, and he needed to get this soul business off his chest." He studied his boots, and then sighed. "I should have let him say his peace without arguing with him. I don't disagree with him. Not entirely anyway. If it fits in the puzzle, we'll use it. But we know we're chasing a monster. What if he believes in souls, or chakras, or reincarnation? Who cares? What's the difference?"

"Should we read the book he recommended to find out?"

"We don't have time, Shotgun."

"Maybe this will be more useful," Shotgun reached into his pack. "Martin gave me an update on the Yard's files on the victims."

"The Inspector needs to see that," said Jack.

"I've sent him my analysis."

"He's an old coot. Make sure he gets the message, Shotgun."

"Will do, boss."

~~~~~

The Inspector scribbled furiously on his tablet as he absorbed the technician's reports. Eventually, he finished with the last one. The knot of onlookers dissipated. The last of the investigators packed up their gear. Gumshoe broke away from the group and meandered towards the jetty where Jack and Shotgun waited. He answered questions and gave directions along the way.

"Gentlemen," said Gumshoe. "What have you got for me?"

"Inspector," Shotgun handed his tablet to Gumshoe. "All of the victims visited New Gem within the last couple of months. I've highlighted the updates. I've also sent you a copy for the record."

"New Gem," spat Gumshoe. He curled the brim of his fedora. "The chop shop must be their recruiter." Nonplussed, the Inspector's expression clouded over. "Why would the Black Dwarf slaughter sexually-repressed, synthetic servants?"

"Gene therapy defies the gods, Inspector," said Shotgun. "They sell hope to the hopeless, and offer pipe dreams to the desperate. When they have a likely victim, they mesmerize them and turn them into zombies."

"He's nailed it, old man," said Jack. "The Black Dwarf and his gang prey upon the lonely, naïve, and very, very shy. Their victims come to them. They minimize their exposure to witnesses. Biots have few if any friends, and often no relations. They can easily screen the synthetic from the naturally born."

"Few dare tell anyone they're going to a chop shop," said Shotgun. "Humiliation is a powerful emotion. Fear of derision ensures silence."

"Yes," Gumshoe said. "You're right. It's a perfect front. Let's go. I've got to get out of here. Plenty of work to do, and my missus is probably already wondering where I am. We'll round up Wiggles and get down to East Moab Station."

The Proconsul of Moab

Gumshoe engaged the autopilot and set the destination to east Moab. The cruiser followed Wiggle's green and white, and they left the harbor. They passed through the Strand, and the cruiser took them into the Halls of Industry.

"I hope we're not ambushed," muttered Shotgun.

"Does give one a sense of déjà vu," Jack said.

Terrified citizens fleeing the city lined Moab's tunnels with moving vans. The cruisers crawled up an entrance ramp to the level-way.

"Should have anticipated this," muttered Gumshoe. "Maybe we'll have to take the surface streets home."

On the level-way, they moved slowly. The driver of a cargo truck honked at a red ground-car. The offended driver stuck his arm out of the window and waved angrily. Gumshoe tapped his siren, and flashed the emergency lights. The whoop reverberated down the level-way. Cowed, the drivers fell silent and stewed in their private resentment.

"Stress will drive people crazy." Gumshoe cut his emergency lights.

"When they reach Iron Mountain," said Jack, "they'll calm down."

"Nice thought," said Gumshoe. "Keep on thinking like that. We need optimists."

~~~~~

The Surete's eastern stationhouse was a beehive. More people were leaving than arriving. Those leaving carried stuffed bags, backpacks, and briefcases. And those arriving pushed hand trucks loaded with empty boxes.

"We're below Lower Nodlon, Under Nodlon, and Deep Nodlon. Imagine, the edge of the Pale is just a few blocks east of us, and a hundred floors straight up." Gumshoe cut the air with a hand. "Incredible engineering the ancients did. Knowing we're so far below the surface and yet not far at all gives me the creeps. Always feel a bit claustrophobic here in Moab, though I never feel it anywhere else."

A moleman pushed a cart loaded with boxes out of a service lift. He crossed the sky bridge towards the garage. Wiggles dodged the cart. He flashed his badge at the security guard and called out, "Hi, George."

The guard waved amiably, "Afternoon Constable." George leaned back in his chair, oblivious to the commotion.

"Never seen it like this," said Wiggles. "Everyone is pulling out of Moab, and so is the Surete. I'd be on my way too if we hadn't found those maid's swimming in the river."

A lift discharged its passengers, and Wiggles held the door as they boarded. Near the top, they stepped out into a lobby. Around them in all directions partitions subdivided a cubicle maze. Police officers and detectives packed their desks.

"Where do they keep the cheese?"

"In the break area," said Wiggles. "When we're good, they bring us donuts too. This way."

Wiggles led them down a wide aisle in single file. They darted past officers carrying boxes and dodging moving carts. In the flurry of activity only a few waved at Wiggles as they strode by.

After a few turns, they reached Wiggle's desk. They waited in the corridor while the portly moleman dropped his notepad on a stack of paperwork. The Constable pulled out a disk, shoved it into his computer, and stabbed his keyboard.

A uniformed officer rushed down the corridor. He jumped over a box, and stood between the mage and his dwarf. "Scuse me, gents," he said. He blocked the Constable's cubicle. "Hallo Wiggles, glad to see ya back."

"Yes, Jenkins, what is it?"

"Captain Willoughby wants to see ya now," said Jenkins. "Don't know what's it's about, but it's not hard to guess. Your dwarf maidens are all over the news. The higher ups are breathing down his neck."

"Thanks Jenkins," said Wiggles. "Tell the Captain I'm on my way, and keep your guesses to yourself. Loose lips sink ships."

"Mum's the word, Constable." The officer left with a wave.

"Gentlemen, the Captain has called for old Wiggles, so something is amiss. Better come with me."

Again they followed the portly moleman through the maze, maneuvering around stacks of boxes and dodging fleeing officers.

The Captain's cubicle sat against the building's core. It had high partitions and an office door, which stood open. Wiggles stopped in the doorway, and knocked.

"You wanted to see me, Cap?"

Willoughby sat behind a pile of clutter. He continued typing on his workstation without looking up.

"Magnum, come in. The Zodiac case is all over the news. Mole News started a brouhaha that's reached the top. They spotted Inspector Lestrayed and Cretaceous Clay at the scene this afternoon. The vultures are in the Proconsul's office now asking if there's any connection between the Zodiac case and the poor girls in the river. They want to know who's in charge of the investigation, and if we've abdicated our jurisdiction to Nodlon. They want to know if Cretaceous Clay is consulting with us or with the Nodlon Yard."

Willoughby sounded tired, but not irritated.

Gumshoe and Jack exchanged looks, and the Inspector shrugged.

"We need to get a statement for the Information Office," said Willoughby. "Nodlon Yard is working with us on the case of the dwarf maidens found in the Port of Moab, and we're working with Nodlon Yard on their Zodiac case. Got it? Get Inspector Lestrayed and Mr. Clay on the blower and ask them to go along. Mr. Clay has to be working with Lestrayed.

Gumshoe's the only one on the ball up there."

Wiggles chuckled, and his belly jiggled like a bowl full of jelly. "Cap," he said, "I've got them right here."

"Why didn't you say so, Magnum?" Willoughby stood up.

Wiggles backed out of the doorway to make way for a slightly heavier version of himself. The heavy-set police captain could have been Wiggles' twin.

"Speak of the devil," he took Gumshoe's hand in his massive paw. "Good of you to come, old man." Willoughby patted his girth, and he beamed at his visitors.

"Glad to help, Cap. We really should get together more often than once upon a crisis."

"So true, Gumshoe," said Willoughby. "Let's drink a few pints at the Green Mole when we solve this case."

"As I recall, Cap, I owe you a few pints."

"Bet you still can't hold your liquor, old man." Willoughby grinned and tucked his thumbs under his suspenders. "You've got no padding."

"In your dreams, Cap," Gumshoe scoffed. "When I have a chance, I'll give you a call, and we'll see what that tub of yours can hold."

"You're on, Gumshoe." Cap nodded at the mage and his dogsbody. "Mr. Clay, Mr. Shotgun, thank you for coming." The personable molemen jerked his thumb at Gumshoe. "Good to see you're helping out the old bloodhound." He tapped his nose, "Gumshoe would get lost without a keeper."

Everyone except Gumshoe chuckled, and Jack slapped him on the back, "Your reputation precedes you, old man."

"It comes with the trench coat, Jack." Gumshoe said, "Let me introduce Captain Willoughby, Moab Homicide. He's as honest as the day is long." Gumshoe winked at Jack and Shotgun, "That's what you say, boys, about a man who solves cases by accident."

"The pot calls the kettle black," Willoughby chortled.

"Cap," said Gumshoe. "Jack Clay and his man-servant,

Patrick 'Shotgun' Morgan, are consulting with Nodlon Yard. Jack is my specialist on the occult, and Shotgun is my computer consultant. If you have any secrets you want to keep, don't let Shotgun near your computers."

Jack stepped back to share the stage with his butler, and the dwarf beamed with pride.

"Mr. Morgan," said Cap, "I'm glad to meet you. Are you the Ministry of Manna hacker? It's what they say in the news, but I never trust them."

"That I am, Captain Willoughby. I was trying to do some genealogy. Fortunately, Gumshoe helped me out of the pickle I got myself in."

"Aha," said Cap. "Any friend of Gumshoe's is a friend of mine. Call me, Cap. Glad you're on our team." Cap patted his girth again. "Sorry about your genealogy project. Too bad we have no influence over Nodlon Yard's human paranoids." Cap winked at Gumshoe.

"Quite all right, Cap," said Gumshoe. "Nodlon Yard's in the same boat. If we had any influence with Parliament, biots wouldn't be deprived of their genetic history."

An Italian opera burst from the Captain's desk caster.

"Gentlemen, that will be the Proconsul's office," said Cap, ducking back into his cubicle. He answered his caster. "On my way," he said.

"The Proconsul wants to see us," said Cap. "I took the liberty of agreeing for us all. I hope no one objects."

"Full steam ahead, Cap," said Gumshoe. "Nodlon Yard is always happy to support the Surete of Moab."

Cap put on his coat, and assumed an air of importance out of keeping for his appearance. His girth made it impossible for him to button his coat. The brass buttons and his medals completed the picture of a Burgermeister in a Teutonic village.

Cap led the way to a conference room. "Vid on," he said. Soon the vid displayed the seal of Moab. A steel ring encircled an industrious mole in field of green. The mole wore a miner's cap, and he carried a welding torch and a shovel. He stood proudly on a mound of coal, and gave them a toothy grin.

Cap punched the screen, and a matronly mole woman in a neat business suit appeared.

"Hello," she said, "Proconsul's office."

"Hello, Wendy."

"Captain Willoughby," she said. "They've been asking for you. Are you ready?"

"Yes, Wendy. We're all here, including my man Wiggles. Inspector Lestrayed of Nodlon Yard and his consultants, Mr. Clay and Mr. Morgan, have joined us."

"Good, I'll let the Proconsul know you're ready."

The matron pressed a screen in front of her, and she muted the vid and walked off camera.

"Proconsul Agatha Miner is an elected official," said Cap. "We show deference for her office, but she's not royalty. Please follow my lead."

"She's popular isn't she?" Gumshoe asked.

"Yes, she is," said Cap. "She's cleaned house, and she's made quite a few enemies. Moab has recovered under her leadership. The People's Party emptied the treasury. I'm grateful for all the bonuses they gave us, but no one can explain where most of the money went. She's in her last year, and she's running for reelection. No one knows who will replace her. Her chief lieutenant, William of Green, was the odds on favorite, but there's rumors going about. Seems he's been taking bribes from the Solar Monetary Fund."

"Aren't they a front for the Nodlon banking cartel?" asked Jack.

Gumshoe snorted, and the molemen guffawed in unison.

"Nodlon's banking cartel is a front for Warburg," said Gumshoe. "A lackey for the Baron runs the Solar Monetary Fund, and the Baron works for Warburg."

Wendy reappeared on the vid. "Gentlemen, you will be addressing the Proconsul, her cabinet, and several special advisors." She leaned forward, and added, "Good luck." Then she pressed a button, and the screen dissolved.

Another conference room appeared on the vid. The Proconsul sat in the middle of a long table facing them. She was a striking mole woman in her middle years. Her advisors surrounded her on either side. On her right sat the Commissioner of the Moab Surete. Next to the Commissioner sat a goblin with the Nodlon Defense Force.

Mimicking Captain Willoughby, they all bowed slightly.

"Madam Proconsul," said Cap, "Constable Wiggles is our man working on the case of the dwarf maidens." He stepped aside. "This is Inspector Lestrayed and his consultants, Cretaceous Clay and Patrick Morgan. Inspector Lestrayed is in charge of the Zodiac Case."

"Thank you all for joining us," said the Proconsul. "Mr. Clay, your fame precedes you. My family caught your winter show when it opened last December. We bought all of your tee shirts."

"Yes I remember," said Jack. "Please say 'hi' to Ashley and Zoë for me."

Wiggles and Cap exchanged glances, and then they looked at Gumshoe. They all glanced at Shotgun who simply shrugged.

"We're sure you understand the gravity of the situation, Mr. Clay, and we can count on your discretion."

"Madam Proconsul," said Jack, adding a slight bow. "Mr. Morgan and I have seen those poor girls with our own eyes. If our efforts can stop these murders, we will do everything we can. We consider it a duty and an honor to serve Nodlon and Moab. Anything we can do to stop the Black Dwarf, and help our fellow citizens, we are proud to do."

"Very well then," said the Proconsul. "On behalf of Moab and Nodlon, we accept your services, and we look forward to your success. I am sure you are aware of the severity of the crisis." The Proconsul paused and looked at the Commissioner who nodded. "When a killer dumps a young dwarf maiden in a sewer, it is a tragedy. It warrants a police investigation, and every possible resource must be brought to bear to find the murderer. When a spacecraft explodes, it is not an accident. It is no longer an ordinary crime. Add six more innocent maidens floating in the Great River, and people are alarmed.

"The newsmen are obsessed with these horrible crimes. Rumors of war fill the news. Talk of Mars attacking fills the air. Moab is falling apart. Just minutes ago, there was a near riot at Molly-mart when they ran out of bottle water. Panic is upon us. You can cut the fear with a knife.

"Every newsman in Nodlon is standing in the lobby outside my office. The ones that can't squeeze into the lobby are in the pressroom downstairs. I need answers and I need them now.

"Gentlemen, we have got to do something. Do you have any leads or suspects? Is there any hope you can give me? Anything at all?"

"Madam, if I may be so bold," Gumshoe twirled his fedora. "We have learned something about the perpetrators of these crimes. We are looking for a gang led by a Black Dwarf. This dwarf styles himself a warlock and he leads a gang of some sort.

"Speaking for Nodlon Yard, we will not rest until we stop these crimes and bring these fiends to justice. I'm sure Captain Willoughby and Constable Wiggles and the Surete agree. We are working together on solving these crimes."

"Thank you Inspector," she said. "You have my full confidence, and the resources of our department are at your disposal."

"We're working on coordination now," said Cap. "No serial killer has ever struck like this before. The scope of these crimes is without precedent."

"Perhaps it is without criminal precedent," said the Proconsul. She held out her hand. "Commissioner Warden, would you introduce our guest?" The Commissioner rose.

"Thank you, Madam Proconsul," said the Commissioner. "Our guest is Chief Warrant Officer Ferrell. Chief Ferrell is with

NOSS, the Nodlon Defense Force's Office of Strategic Security. He has joined us today to share the Octagon's perspective.

"Chief Ferrell is an expert in asymmetrical warfare, and he has devised a more radical theory. Chief would you explain?" The Commissioner sat down and offered the floor to the goblin.

Chief Ferrell bowed briefly, and launched into his presentation. He clipped his words in the crisp manner of a graduate of Nodlon's Military Academy.

"We believe espionage accounts for these murders. Earlier this afternoon, my office issued a notice to the Crown advising the King of our findings and urging him to turn over the police investigation to the NDF. By order of the King, what the press calls the Zodiac case is now the responsibility of my office. With all due respect to Chief Inspector Lestrayed, we believe the police are outgunned and outmatched.

"I am here to persuade Moab to cooperate. As you know, the Surete is under no obligation to turn over their investigation to us. However, Madam Proconsul, I believe you may be persuaded, if I may proceed?"

"By all means, Chief Ferrell," she said. "If the Octagon will take over this case, we will be glad for their help. Who knows what this monster will do next? He may bomb Rickover Station or start murdering our school children."

"Thank you, Madam," he bowed again. "The information I am sharing with you is classified. I expect the utmost discretion on your part. Only the King, his Chief of Staff, and the Octagon's General Staff know of this. Nothing must be said, and no action taken that may alert Mars that we have any knowledge of their plans.

"Mr. Clay and Mr. Morgan; as civilians you are not officially bound by an oath of office to secrecy. Will you agree to be so bound?" Together, they agreed to the goblin's terms, and swore an oath to secrecy in this matter.

"So be it." Chief Ferrell clasped his hands behind his back and stepped away from the conference table.

"Mars is bent on war and their diplomats parry with ours rather than parlaying for settlement. They wheedle down our patience hoping for us to either resign ourselves to the inevitable or succumb to frustration and lash out. Whatever their tactics, they are stalling for time while the pressure builds on the Crown.

"Random, senseless violence against helpless and innocent targets foments fear in the populace, sows doubt in Nodlon's leadership, and incites rebellion among the disaffected. The strategy undermines the targeted community, and leaves the victims without a clear target for their fear and frustration. Injustices multiply and the civilian population divides itself into warring tribes.

"For weeks we evaluated the possibility of just such a tactical strike against the morale of the people of Nodlon. A series of asymmetrical attacks would increase the pressure on our diplomats to sue for peace, and ironically play into the Martian's plans for war. Now, we think the Martians have deployed just such an espionage team.

"Recently, a group of black dwarfs ambushed Chief Inspector Lestrayed, Mr. Clay and Mr. Morgan. When the black dwarves attacked Inspector Lestrayed's cruiser, they brought a military grade lightning cannon. At once we were convinced Martian spies were behind the attack. Fortunately, Inspector Lestrayed and his consultants survived. Mysteriously, the Inspector defeated the black dwarves and destroyed the cannon armed solely with a lightning pistol.

"We immediately reviewed the reports filed by Inspector Lestrayed and his consultants concerning the Zodiac case. We focused on the murder of one Jezebel Steele, a sometime trade show coordinator with no prior record. Although the Inspector drew no conclusions, we felt his report suggests the use of an advanced technology we do not yet possess.

"At the same time, we searched for the source of the lightning cannon used in the attack and discovered that the serial numbers matched those of a cannon missing from a secret stockpile several hundred miles north of Nodlon. The commanding officer reported the cannon missing and presumably stolen several weeks ago. An inquiry into possible court-martial proceedings against the commander and his staff had been underway since the report. Upon review of Inspector Lestrayed's reports, we have temporarily suspended those proceedings.

"While investigating a lead at an abandoned space dock belonging to Thornmocker Industries, the Inspector and several other witnesses encountered a suspect who identified himself as the Black Dwarf. After a brief, inconclusive gun battle, the Marie Celeste, a supertanker registered with Warburg Munitions was destroyed. Apparently, the attack was another attempt on the life of the Chief Inspector and his investigation team including his occult specialist, Mr. Clay.

"Inspector Lestrayed believes this Black Dwarf is responsible for the missing dwarves, the murder of the dwarf maidens in the Zodiac case, and the military scale attempts on his life.

"NOSS is inclined to agree.

"Setting aside fanciful theories, we believe the Martian War Maker has penetrated Nodlon with an espionage team for the purpose of destroying morale. We believe the Black Dwarf is a spy sent as an advance guard to reconnoiter our defenses, probe our weaknesses, and undermine our resolve through sabotage.

"The black dwarves in league with the Black Dwarf may be duped or they may under the influence of drugs developed by the Martian War Maker. Whatever their motives, they work for the Martians, and they cannot be stopped using police methods.

"We intend to find the Black Dwarf using every means at our disposal. When we do, we will treat him as an enemy military asset, and we will terminate him with extreme prejudice. We have the resources and the training to do so, and we intend to do just that.

"While we have great respect for the Inspector's abilities as a homicide detective, Nodlon Yard is unprepared for this threat. If our assessment is correct, and the Black Dwarf is the leader of an espionage team sent by Mars, we very much doubt the Inspector's capacity to make an arrest. The Black Dwarf is no ordinary criminal.

"Nodlon Yard has already been advised, and I believe the investigation of the Zodiac case has been handed over to the Nodlon Defense Force. I'm sorry if this comes as news to you Chief Inspector. If you contact your superiors, they will confirm the change. No one holds you or your consultants responsible for the sabotage of the Marie Celeste at the Thornmocker space yard. Such an event is inconceivable for any ordinary criminal. Still, we cannot allow another such incident to take place."

"Madam," Chief Ferrell bowed, and resumed his seat.

"Thank you, Chief Ferrell," said the Proconsul. "These are no ordinary murderers. Moab lacks Nodlon's resources, and the secrets available to the Octagon. Please share everything you have with NOSS. Give them your full cooperation. If you locate their hideout, I expect you to notify Chief Ferrell immediately. Captain Willoughby, you and your men are so directed. Is that understood?"

"Absolutely, madam," Cap said. "We have no desire to tangle with spies."

"Thank you Captain," she said. "By no means is this a reflection on the Surete. Inspector Lestrayed, how will Nodlon Yard handle this news?"

"Officially I can't speak for the Yard, but I assure you, madam, the Octagon will have our full cooperation. If we stumble upon the nest of these vipers, the first call we make will be to Chief Ferrell."

They exchanged salutations and completed their business. Wiggles showed them out. They bid the portly moleman a somber goodbye and took their leave of the Moab Surete.

Off the Case

Normally, Nodlon Yard would be quiet at this hour. The day shift was over, and the evening shift had begun. Today though, movers labored with loaded carts, and police officers carried boxes out of their offices. Gumshoe dodged the pedestrians and bound into the building. In the lobby, he waved at the security guard, and took a lift.

Stepping off the lift, old friends and colleagues waved. Many packed their belongings and personal effects. Others hurried to wrap up projects. Hardened veterans and rookies alike worried about the move to Iron Mountain. He wove through the hubbub.

The division clerk had manned her desk admirably for years. She was a pretty white dwarf, but she rarely offered him good news.

Before he reached the sanctuary of his office, she called, "Gumshoe!"

He sighed, and made excuses, "Not now Nikki, I know my timesheet's not ready, my paperwork hasn't been done, and I'm late for dinner." For emphasis, he waved his hands sadly.

"Afraid not Gumshoe. Captain Barfly wants to see you." She smiled wryly in that way she had of warning someone of really bad news. "And before you ask why, he's probably taking you off the case."

"What?" Gumshoe groused. Ferrell had wasted no time. He had just heard about it in Moab, and now the scuttlebutt was in the rumor mill. It was no good. He would have to talk Barfly into going along. He had done it before, but bucking the city attorney's office was not on par with bucking the Octagon.

"Sorry, old-timer, I had nothing to do with it." Nikki smiled sympathetically and he felt genuine compassion radiate from her. "I'm really sorry, Gumshoe. I know you're trying to save lives."

"Later, Nikki," he spun around and shot back to the lifts as fast as the crowd allowed.

Officers loading moving boxes clogged the aisles. Respect for his grey hair parted his way, but the aisles were still an obstacle course. Rank had its privileges, but there was nowhere for the crowd to go. Gumshoe ducked into a stairwell.

He launched himself up the stairs into an oncoming mob of tired paper pushers. He fought the press of bureaucrats seeking a faster route to the exit. He clambered up the stairs and onto the next floor. He pushed his way across the lobby and reached the cubicle bay. It was a small victory over the traffic. He weaved to Captain Barfly's door and arrived breathing heavily. He knocked once, and opened the door without waiting for an invitation.

"Come in," called Barfly. "Oh, good it's you Gumshoe! Thank you for coming. What's the latest on the Zodiac murders?"

"Barfly, are you thinking of removing me from this case? "

"No, old man, calm down, I wasn't thinking anything of the sort. It's completely out of my hands. As of this afternoon, the Zodiac case belongs to a special operations team out of the Octagon. The whole kit and caboodle is their responsibility. The murdered girls, the missing dwarves, and especially the lightning cannon all belong to the boys at the Octagon now."

"But I have leads! We know their leader is a black dwarf, who styles himself a magician of sorts, and they're using a gene therapy clinic called New Gem."

"Think man, you were nearly barbequed a few days ago. By your own account, if Jack Clay hadn't been there, I'd have had to call Betty and tell her she's a widow." Barfly waved his hands. "This Black Dwarf thing is beyond us. If he's the Zodiac killer, he's left more bodies in the tunnels of Nodlon than your whole caseload last year. We need the military's help."

"Those Octagon types will get a bunch of innocent dwarves killed," said Gumshoe. The policeman's jowls worked furiously. "The Black Dwarf turned innocent dwarves into some sort of zombies. His henchmen are under the influence of something.

Jack doesn't think it is magic, but I'm not so sure."

Barfly's eyebrow shot up. "Shouldn't Jack know if it's magic?"

"Jack's good, but he's conflicted or I'm not a cop. He thinks he's the only magical person in the Solar System. Jack's convinced he's a mutation and he's unique. He thinks the Black Dwarf is using a mind-altering drug or a mind-control technology. I think the killer weed's using magic."

"Jack Clay is the only magician in the Solar System. Come on, old man, what makes you think the Black Dwarf is using magic?"

"If an elf can be magical, Barfly, why not a dwarf? When we stunned the dwarves they returned normal. They don't remember disappearing or committing any crimes. We can't explain it. If Ferrell and his boys don't use stun settings, they'll murder plenty of innocent dwarves."

"Well, true Gumshoe, true. We'll let them know your concerns. I'm sure we can get them to use stun once we can explain."

"Regulars yes, but those pinheads out of the Octagon think they're Earth's gift to Nodlon. We heard Chief Ferrell speak in Moab. He struck me as one of those pompous know-it-alls they pump out at the Academy. The Octagon's gung-ho operations teams will just shoot them all."

"Gumshoe, I understand." His old friend smiled sympathetically, and patted him on the back. "But it's beyond me I tell you. The Commissioner called me himself. He wants you off this case before you get killed. The higher ups came down on him – came down hard, I think. They think we've underestimated the problem, and they're taking it out of our hands. It's the military's problem now."

"They're not detectives, Barfly. Yes, the Black Dwarf is a dangerous character, but where is his lair? What's his motive? Is he working for Mars, or is he a free radical? If we're going to save anyone we need answers."

"Martians, Gumshoe. That's what the Octagon thinks anyway, and the Crown agrees. Give it a rest, old man. Homicide detectives have better things to do than becoming cannon fodder. It's a miracle you're alive."

"What? Invent new forms for the uniforms to fill out? Locate missing pets? If you want a cat out of a tree, call the fire department." Gumshoe heard the desperation in his own voice. "I'm getting old, but I'm not drooling."

"What was your last case, old man? Wasn't it a domestic?"

"Yes, it was a drunken elf who smacked his maid after she told him he had knocked her up." He struggled with himself to control his temper. "Did you tell the Commissioner I've handled every last homicide in the city for over a decade, and I've solved every case for the last three years?"

"Yes, I did old man," said Barfly. "But the Commissioner reads your reports, too. On your last homicide, you caught the boy literally red-handed. He killed his girlfriend in another elf's bed after she dumped him. You found blood on his nails, and he confessed. Not exactly the stuff of legend, Hercule Poirot."

"Criminals are stupid. You have to be stupid to hurt others." Gumshoe snapped his suspenders, and pushed his fedora back. "For the first time in my career we have a super-villain on the loose right out of the late night vids, and I'm off the case? I've spent my life preparing for this case! And I'm off the case?"

Barfly put his arm around Gumshoe's shoulders. "Face it Gumshoe, they're not going to let you have the Zodiac case. The Black Dwarf belongs to the Octagon. Don't let your blood pressure get too high, old man, or you'll pop a gasket."

"What about the Lovelace case? Or the case of the Lonely Vampire?" asked Gumshoe. "I solved those."

"Very good police work those were. But we have a vicious black dwarf on the loose murdering dwarf maidens. He's not afraid to ambush police officers driving an armored cruiser. And in addition to those criminal accomplishments, he's got access to military-grade lightning cannons. It's just no good, old man.

We're on the brink of war, and this madman is adding to the tension. The whole city might explode."

Gumshoe took off his fedora, and combed his hair with his hand. "I can solve this case."

"Yes, I agree with you. You've got all the experience. You wrote half our training manuals. Yet they just don't want you. They're afraid the city will panic unless the military blows something up."

"Barfly, I came up here to ask for you to warn Nodlon. I want authorization to issue an alert. The agencies need to escort their female dwarves to and from work. When they're not working, they have to keep their dorms locked until we catch the Black Dwarf."

"You really care don't you? Taking those girl's lives is beyond words. I know, I'm not blind, old man," Barfly said. "Biots are people too." He dropped his eyes to a memo on his desk. "Orders are orders." He stabbed the memo with a finger. "To avoid a panic, the Crown issued a gag-order on the Zodiac case." He wagged a finger at Gumshoe. "We've got our orders, Jacques, the case must be turned over to the Octagon, and there's to be a complete blackout to the news media."

"Orders?" Gumshoe choked in dismay. "All of those maidens were younger than my boys. The Black Dwarf ripped their chips out, and drained their blood! You know what that means!"

"Yes, I do, old man. Those maidens were no older than my son either. I don't think their lives are worth any less. I'm sorry Gumshoe. Likely as not you're right, but there's nothing we can do."

Gumshoe flopped into a chair. Putting his satchel and his notepad on his lap, he put his face in his hands.

Barfly patted him on the back again. "If it makes you feel better," he said, "your Black Dwarf will keep on killing whether we warn anyone or not."

"It doesn't make me feel better," said Gumshoe. "We have

to stop these murders before anyone else is killed."

"The Crown agrees with you. The Commissioner and I agree with you." Barfly shuffled trying to relieve tension. "We only disagree as to the means. The Octagon has far more resources than we do. They're probably flooding the sewers with troops as we speak."

"Those girls deserve justice, Barfly. They had hopes and dreams. The Black Dwarf destroyed their world and we can't let him get away with it."

"Can't work long in our line without seeing the good and the bad. The biots endure without hope. Their worlds matter to you, do they?" Barfly sighed. "Too often the synthetics are better people than the natural-born are. If Nodlon can't give them justice in life, at least the Yard can find them justice in death. The Black Dwarf won't get away with it much longer. The Octagon will find him and terminate him."

"If it's all the same to you, I think the Yard needs to keep its hand in. I may be off the case, but the Octagon needs our crime labs, and our forensics teams. I can be a liaison."

Barfly assumed his usual posture for asserting his authority or issuing a reprimand.

Gumshoe's eyes narrowed, and he gripped the chair.

The captain slouched and sighed. He looked at the memo, and then back at Gumshoe. "All right, old man, you've got it. You're the Yard's observer. But, play it straight and no leaks."

"You've got a deal, Barfly. I'll be the soul of discretion."

"Come Gumshoe, let's go to O'Malley's." Barfly dragged him out of the chair. I'll walk you down. Drop off your things in your office and call Betty. Blame me. I'll call Greta and blame you."

"Why do I feel like I've sold my soul?" Gumshoe donned his fedora. "What'll we do about the Black Dwarf?"

"Tomorrow we will turn the case over to the Octagon, and they can deal with it." Barfly stood in his doorway. He shrugged and threw his cloak over one arm. "Whatever you do, I'll stand by you." He hooked Gumshoe by the elbow and ushered the detective out. "Your hunches are better than most people's facts, but feel free to change your mind. I've got a backlog of missing pets."

In the twilight, the sky was purple, and clouds were tinged with pink. O'Malley's overlooked the south mall. They dodged traffic, passed the Courthouse, and entered the park. They crossed another street, and approached the Irish pub. A robot in a tuxedo opened the door.

"Don't worry, old man, you'll feel better when I pour you out of a robo-cab three sheets to the wind."

Sacrifice of the First Born

Nimrod faced his master. His crystal ball projected the Dragon Lord's disembodied head into his lair. Forgotten trays of snacks surrounded him. His dwarves prostrated towards the dragon.

He poised on the edge of his turntable and waited for his master to speak. He held his tongue lest he spark a display of the dragon's cosmic powers with an ill-timed remark.

"Very well, Nimrod, I trust you have bad news to report?" The dragon smirked with a twist of his deadly fangs.

"Good, my lord, the wheels turn. The Proconsul of Moab steps into my trap. The dwarves failed us, and the mage cost us a squad of zombies. To pay for this, I shall take a baker's dozen of Moab's first born."

"Make it so, Nimrod."

"Yes, my lord, shall I stick to the plan or attack the mage?"

"Stick to the plan. Step up the terror. Drive our enemies to desperate measures. Fear is their weakness. Divide them and set them against each other. When our spy launches the big lie, his friends will abandon him. Keep Phaedra's son busy, and if he survives, he will come to you and meet his end."

"What of the mage, my lord?" Nimrod bowed. "Can we not turn him through his dreams?"

The Dragon's lip curled into a frown, and his whiskers twitched.

"Cretaceous Clay is under protection. The enemy cloaks his spirit. None of my servants see his dreams. They know him only through the dreams of others. We cannot follow him when he is alone, nor read his true thoughts when he speaks."

"What weakness then can we exploit, my lord? If he is Phaedra's son, how shall we defeat him?"

"Fear not Nimrod, you are greater. He has no idea what he is, and he has no one to train him. The days of the Nephilim passed away in the last age and none of the ancient masters survive to show him the way. Had he a master to teach him the arts and drive him to his limits, still he would not be greater than you. Soon, you shall meet him in mortal combat, and you shall defeat him. As the days of men are numbered, so are his days. As the triumphs of the Black Dwarf are counted, so his defeat shall be your triumph."

"As you command," Nimrod bowed low.

The crystal ball darkened, and the dragon vanished. He retied the sash of his bathrobe and stepped off his turntable. He kicked his servants, and they hurried back to work. Running and scrambling to resume their duties, their ankle bells jingled. He smirked with delight. Mesmerized by the ancient magic, their glassy eyes betrayed their imprisoned souls.

He waved, and his patio door slid wide. He stepped into the cool night, leaned over his parapet, and gazed upon his domain. His lair occupied the topmost suite of Devil's Tower. He savored the irony.

From the tower, he enjoyed a view of the whole of the Ninth Ring. Lake Bali shimmered in the light of the Moon. Waves broke on the barrier reef at the edge of his lagoon. The surf crashed on the beach, and the sound soothed his nerves. In the distant jungle, the cries of werewolves drifted on the wind.

A dwarf dressed in an Amazon costume waited at his side. He flagged her, and the wench approached.

"Bring my caster," he said.

She bowed, and trotted off, and her bells jingled as she bounced. When she returned, his caster snuggled between the grapes and slices of Muenster.

"Sargon," he said.

A black dwarf appeared on the caster's vid screen. He sported a Captain's cap with scrambled eggs on the brim.

"Master Nimrod," Sargon answered.

"We need more sacrifices to fuel our plans. Those dwarf maidens opened the gate, but not for long. We need not just innocent souls, but the first fruits. We need to sacrifice first born."

"Yes my lord."

"Ready my airship, and tell Helter and Skelter to meet me at the airport at my usual hour."

"As you command, master."

Eldad and Medad

"Goodnight, Shotgun. Leave the mess. Get some rest. I have a feeling Gumshoe isn't through with us, and we need some sleep. I'm so tired I could sleep through a hurricane."

Jack headed for the master suite. He changed into his pajamas. He caught sight of himself in the mirror. His corporate logo was embroidered on his bathrobe. A pang of guilt for his vanity struck him, and he returned the robe to its hanger. Lying on his bed, he closed his eyes.

How can I relax when the Black Dwarf is still on the loose? Dwarf maidens are losing their lives, and I'm just lying here. He tossed and turned. He tried to relax and let his mind go blank.

~~~~~

For some reason, he was in a robo-cab terminal in Deep Nodlon. The streetlights were dimmed for the evening, though he was sure it was morning. His hands were grimy, and when he rubbed them on his overalls they were only greasier.

He had to wash his hands. He ducked into a men's washroom. Trash brimmed over a can inside the door overflowing onto the floor.

Beside the trash can was a mirror. In the mirror was an elf wearing the overalls of a flyer mechanic. On his breast was a nametag but he could not read it. Around the corner, men came and went to the lavatory going in and out of an unseen entrance.

He tried to use a sink, but a hobo wearing a dingy sport coat and torn slacks butted him aside. Another man left a sink, and he tried to reach it first, but a toothless old man in a blue blazer beat him to it. Yielding, he backed away. Four men bathed in all four sinks.

"Excuse me," he said.

None of the men heard, and they continued to wash.

The toothless old man finished washing, but he blocked

Jack and let another old man in a sport coat use the sink. The toothless derelict walked away, and he followed.

Despite a limp, the derelict quickly led him through a door to a dwarf dressed in a black suit and shiny loafers. On the dwarf's forehead was a black spot, and in his hands was a bowl of water.

The dwarf faced the terminal full of empty robo-cabs waiting for a fare. He stood with his back to a wall covered by a poster of a woman.

Though the woman covered the wall, Jack could not make out who it was.

Each derelict knelt in front of the dwarf and he poured a little water on his head. After the dwarf watered the head of the toothless one, the derelict went back into the washroom. Jack followed the derelict back to the sink and again tried to wash his hands.

A goblin dressed for a tennis match entered the washroom, and Jack wondered what he wanted to do.

The goblin walked directly up to him. "Would you like to wash your hands, Jack?"

"Yes," he said. His voice echoed off the washroom walls.

"Then follow me," said the goblin. Following the goblin out of the washroom, he found himself in an old fashioned movie theatre instead of the robo-cab terminal.

A burgundy curtain hung over the vid screen. Rows of scarlet seats with black leather armrests sat empty save for another goblin sitting in a middle row near the aisle.

He followed his host into the theatre. Amber nightlights guided them down the aisle. They stopped, and Jack saw that the other goblin was also dressed for a tennis match.

"My partner told me you want to wash your hands," said the second goblin. "Is this true, Jack?"

"Yes," he said.

The second goblin held out a clean white washrag. "This is for you," he said. "Take it back to the washroom, and use it once. Leave it for the others. When you come back here, your movie will begin."

Hating to get the washrag dirty, he picked it up between the tip of his index finger and his thumb.

Urgently, he walked swiftly up the aisle. When he pushed on the door to the lobby, he stepped back into the washroom.

Again, four men bathed in the four sinks. He held out his washrag, which reflected in the mirrors. A young man sporting a familiar blue blazer stepped aside and waved for him to take his turn.

He turned on the cold water and soaked his hands. He lathered them with a frothy mix, and rinsed them. Taking his washrag, he dried his clean hands.

~~~~~

He was in his bedroom again. *It was a dream.* When he was a child he had dreamed of losing his teeth, and battling monsters, but somehow this dream was different. *It was no ordinary dream.*

Swinging his feet off the bed, the sun was high and its rays filled his bedroom through the patio door.

Beslan

The Black Dwarf's airship cruised over the busy streets of Moab. Moving vans and trailer tractors and rental flyers lined the normally quiet streets. Fearful molemen packed their belongings into whatever transport they could afford.

They turned into an alley between a cobbler's warehouse and a tailor's shop. At the end of the warehouse, the alley broadened into a loading dock. Bays for airships ran the length of the warehouse and rose above the street.

Narrow alleys led away to other buildings. They turned into another alley and landed.

A burly dwarf and a gangly dwarf emerged from the cab. Both wore black uniforms, and baseball caps.

The burly dwarf opened a passenger door and stood at attention.

Nimrod stepped from his ship. His hood obscured his features, and gloves covered his hands. He flicked his hood off, and he admired his reflection in the airship's black polish. His robe glittered, his boots gleamed, and his hair was perfect.

"Skelter, bring my staff."

The gangly dwarf retrieved his staff from its compartment. "Your staff, sir," said the gangly dwarf as he offered it to his master.

Nimrod twisted the staff, and power surged through the staff's filigree. "Raw power is my favorite medium of exchange." The staff hummed as it drew manna across the differential between the living world and the other side. The runes on his robe flickered. "Who needs cash when misery will do?" He chuckled softly, and he's eyes narrowed.

"Come Helter," he said, and turned to the back of his airship.

"Yes, sir," said Helter. The burly dwarf closed the airship's door, and followed the warlock.

"Don't forget your backpack, Skelter," he called.

"Got it, sir," the gangly dwarf slung a pack over his shoulder. He fell in behind his heavy set colleague.

The warlock led the way, and marched up the alley. He stepped over trash and dodged the puddles to keep his boots clean.

An elderly goblin curled up in a doorway as they approached. He hunkered down and feigned sleep. He watched them pass through narrow slits.

At the alley's end, Nimrod strode into the crowd bustling along a busy sidewalk.

Skelter drew alongside Helter, and the three dwarves carved a path through the pedestrians.

Commuters rushed to their jobs. Today fearful molemen joined the usual bustle. The crowds swirled around the dwarves. They hardly noticed the dwarves' presence.

Drivers struggling to get out of the city jammed the streets. Ground cars crawled along in the traffic.

The warlock plunged into the street with his minions on his heels. The dwarves wove a path through the cars, trucks and vans. Drivers blinked as the dwarves passed. They wondered if they had seen a trio of ghosts.

Rental flyers and moving airships clogged the streets. Every vehicle was pressed into the service of moving.

Balding molemen struggled with levitators hauling heavy loads. All carried packages, briefcases, suitcases, or backpacks. It was hard to tell if they were off to help their employers pack or heading out of the city to sanctuary.

The warlock turned into a stream of pedestrians, and the odd trio deliberately marched against the flow. They forced many molemen to jaywalk or be toppled.

Bewildered, irritated molemen glared. Then, stoic and taciturn, they forgot about the dwarves and continued on their way.

The warlock tapped a traffic signal with his staff, and the lights changed. Brakes screeched, horns honked, and the traffic halted. The warlock and his dwarves crossed the street and entered a park.

The warm yellow light of Moab bathed the park. Miniature trees sheltered little paths of pebbled stone meandering through the park. Ignoring the paths, the warlock and his minions marched through the park. On the other side, he stopped on a grassy knoll and pondered his objective.

They faced a school. It occupied the block opposite the park, and it rose from the busy sidewalk to an ornate crown supporting the dome over the park. A broad staircase led up to three sets of double doors. A stone arch over the doors bore the school's name.

Nimrod studied the school. Overwhelmed with déjà vu, he tried to remember something long forgotten. "I've been here before," he mumbled.

"Master Nimrod?" Helter asked.

"Nothing, Helter, go back to not doing anything."

"Yes sir."

Nimrod twisted his staff, and the lights changed. Again, the traffic stopped. They crossed the street, and climbed the steps. The warlock snapped his fingers and the doors opened.

In the quiet hall, their boots clicked. A security guard sat in a small kiosk and watched a vid. Under Nimrod's spell, he was oblivious to their presence. They passed the security guard.

Teachers lectured behind closed doors. The sound of grammar and arithmetic floated into the hall through the transom windows.

They marched to the principal's office at the end of the hall. To the left, a hallway led to more classrooms. To the right, the hall opened into a lobby with several lifts, and it ended at a broad staircase.

"Helter and Skelter, wait for me here."

"Yes sir," they said in unison, and they each took a post beside the principal's door.

Nimrod snapped his fingers and the principal's door

opened.

A matronly mole woman worked on a small desk surrounded by stacks of files. A small couch in front of her desk awaited unruly students. Filing cabinets jammed the remainder of her office.

The intruder startled her, and she stood up. His garish costume exuded a disturbing aura of malice. She eyed the staff, and wiped a hand on her frumpy dress nervously.

"May I help you sir?" She was taller than the black dwarf, but he still made her feel uncomfortable.

"Yes, I'd like to see the principal."

"Visitors need to make an appointment. Principal Chapel is very busy. We're short staffed and she's making arrangements for the evacuation. She cannot see anyone until we move to Iron Mountain."

"Ah," sighed Nimrod. "It is precisely these circumstances, which are the reason for my visit. Once she has heard what I have to offer, she will no longer have trouble making arrangements for an evacuation. Indeed, I believe she won't need an evacuation at all."

"Sir, you'll have to make an appointment. Whatever you're selling, I'm sure she will be willing to talk to you after we have relocated with the other refugees."

"Schoolmarm's are all alike," he sighed. "You never listen."

Gazing into her eyes, he snapped his fingers, and the woman froze. He sucked the will out of her soul and emptied her mind. *That was quick.*

"Dear me, isn't that better?" He smirked. "Now, I think I have an appointment with the principal."

The matron waddled away from her desk. Carefully she squeezed between her stacks of files and the text books jammed into her bookcase. Without knocking, she opened the door and held it open for him.

"Master is here to see you, mum."

"Margaret, I told you I'm not taking visitors or appointments today," said the principal.

The matron stood frozen staring into blank space. Not looking at the principal, or acknowledging her, the dazed woman said nothing.

"Margaret, what's wrong with you?"

Nimrod pushed the matron aside and walked into the principal's office. He thrust his staff at her with a flourish. He played with his staff melodramatically, and then glared at the principal.

The Principal shot out of her chair and glared back at the warlock. She was a handsome woman who cut a figure of crisp professionalism. She wore a business suit cut in viridian, and the friendly frog on the school's crest was embroidered over her heart.

For a moment, the two adversaries stared at each other in a battle of wills. A friendly frog sitting on a lily pad smiled down upon Nimrod from a poster on her wall. The lilies on which the frog sat formed the words, *Education for the greater good.*

"Margaret, please escort this gentleman out."

Nimrod smirked.

"Margaret?" She frowned at the Black Dwarf. Her sense of unease grew, and a tingle ran up her back.

"She's mesmerized. Look it up if you can. I suggest you try the real dictionary, the one you keep in the closet. It's the name of an ancient magician."

"Who are you and what are you doing here?"

"I'm here to offer you a magic show. My show will take all of your troubles away."

"We're short staffed and under-manned. I'm trying to make arrangements to evacuate. We have no time for magic shows."

"Not even one by Cretaceous Clay?"

"You sir are not Cretaceous Clay. Many of my students saw his show only last week, and you are not Jack Clay. What do you do? Birthday parties?!"

"Ah, wit," he snarled. "You cut me to the quick."

"Whatever you are, sir, you are not welcome today. We are preparing for evacuation. All of the students with families have been sent home. We're only open for the orphans who have no one to take them."

"Oh good, orphans are the best kind for my purpose. Only the most innocent and vulnerable children are suitable." He smirked again.

"Get out!" She raised her voice, "Get out!"

"And just when we were starting to have fun!"

He snapped his fingers, and the principal froze. "Gaze into my eyes and you shall be mine."

She struggled, but her will was no match for his. Quickly, she fell under his spell as he bound her to his will.

"Order all of the staff and children to the gymnasium. Tell them Cretaceous Clay will do a public service announcement on obeying your teachers."

Principal Chapel tapped the happy frog on her intercom, and the frog dissolved.

"Good morning everyone, I have a special announcement. Cretaceous Clay will honor us with a show. Mr. Clay will present a public service announcement on obeying your teachers. All teachers shall escort their children to the gymnasium."

"Good Principal Chapel," said Nimrod. "Shall we?" The warlock spun about, and darted out of the office with his new zombies in tow.

In the hall, the classroom doors opened and the teachers and their pupils poured out. The mole women stood by as their charges lined up. Little girls and boys stood in line beside their teachers. The happy frog beamed from their shirts.

Spying the bank of lifts, the warlock led his small entourage to the nearest one. He waved a finger and the doors opened.

"After you my dears," he said, "All aboard."

In a trance, the mole women entered the lift and his goons followed them. On the top floor, they stepped into a hall running the width of the school. They faced the gymnasium. Next to the lifts was the physical education office. On the other side was the swimming pool. Locker rooms for girls and boys were on either side of the pool entrance.

The warlock walked into the gym. Lamps hung from the gym's rafters. Open bleachers blocked the windows facing the street.

Nimrod stood on the half-court line as the students mounted the bleachers. A holographic baseball cage was on one side, and a traditional volleyball court was on the other. The principal and the receptionist stood behind him, and his minions stood behind them. He watched with approval as the little groups of children filed in. Slowly they filled the lower rows of bleachers, and sat down. As the stragglers appeared and joined them, they barely filled the lowest bleacher.

"My, oh, my, we have so few today. Just the ones left behind. No matter. You will all soon be part of a much larger plan." He flipped off his hood and revealed his pallid complexion and elegantly coiffed locks.

"Welcome to childhood's end. I'm afraid Cretaceous Clay was not able to make it today. He sent me instead."

~~~~~

One small girl dawdled in the hall. She was late again. If she walked across the gym everyone would stare at her. The dwarf in the funny robe might call her out and make fun of her.

They might say, "Late again, Daisy? Why can't you be on time?" Or worse, she might even get detention. "We'll teach you this time, Daisy. You'll have to help Miss Dewey file books for a week."

Miss Dewey is a sourpuss. She shivered at the thought of working in the library for Miss Dewey.

She peeked into the gymnasium. Everyone stared at the dwarf wearing the sorcerer's robe. *He's a wicked warlock*, she thought. *Is he going to a Halloween party?*

She hugged herself, and backed away. The walls of the hall jogged around the massive columns supporting the cavern over their heads. Daisy snuck behind a column where she could hear and not be seen. *I can hear everything here. I'll know what they say if Miss Heartburn asks.* Satisfied with her hiding spot, she strained to listen. *When they leave the gym, I'll catch up with my class.* If Heartburn caught her, she would say she had to powder her nose.

~~~~~

Nimrod twirled his staff and chanted an incantation. A fire ball appeared over his head. Flames shot from the ball. The ball drew a pentagram over his head. The children stared at the pentagram and oohed and ahhed. A few exchanged whispers and others ribbed their friends.

"Your new mascot is not a silly frog," said Nimrod.

He lifted his staff, and pointed its foot at the one free wall and mumbled an incantation.

White fire flared in the staff's stone and flashed down the shaft. A ray shot from the end of his staff and scored the wall. The ray scorched the paint. In seconds, the ray marked the sign of the Capricorn.

"Can you all hear me?" There were nods all around. "Look at the pretty drawing, and listen to my voice."

He pointed the staff at the assembled students and teachers, and mumbled another incantation. Their faces went slack and their eyes glazed over.

"All of the first born stand up," said Nimrod. Almost all of the children and the teachers stood up.

"A plentitude of riches," he muttered. With a few commands, he culled the students. He selected thirteen boys not quite old enough to shave.

"Helter shall be your new teacher. Line up boys."

Unable to disobey, the boys clambered over their classmates. They jogged up to Helter and queued up in front of the fat dwarf. They formed a single line as they were taught to do. Pleased with himself, he assessed the group. *Good of you to volunteer.*

Nimrod slammed the floor with his staff, and puffed out his chest. "Skelter, I think we're done here."

"What will we do with the others, master?" Skelter waved at the assembled students and teachers.

Why is it so difficult to get good henchmen these days? Nimrod hung his head. "Skelter, did you bring those gas canisters I told you to bring?"

"Yes master, I've got them right here." He patted his backpack.

"Oh good, Skelter, I was afraid I was going to have to send you back to my airship to get them. What do you think the canisters are for?"

"I don't know master."

"What's in them, Skelter? Laughing gas? Perfume? Smoke bombs designed by the special effects department for use when the director needs to hide a trap door?"

"The canisters have magical poison in them, master."

"Ah, good," sighed Nimrod. "Now we're getting somewhere."

The warlock gripped his staff, and struggled to control his temper. "We're going to leave now. You wait. When we've gone, set the timers on the canisters to three minutes. Leave the canisters here. They're marked with the emblems of the Martian War Maker to cast blame on Mars. Return to the airship. If you get lost, you will have to walk back to the lair. Do you understand?"

"Yes, Master."

Nimrod strutted out of the gymnasium. Falling in behind

his master, the heavy dwarf followed the warlock. Obediently the boys trailed after the malevolent Pied Piper.

~~~~~

Daisy peeked into the hall. The warlock entered a lift. The fat dwarf and the boys took another lift. She scrunched back into the corner so she would not be seen. *The warlock said, "Magical poison!"*

Anyone can be brave! She remembered what Heartburn said. *All we have to do is try!* The lift closed, and she snuck another peek. No one was in the hall.

She tip toed across the hall, and tried not to make a sound. She kept an eye on the center door of the gymnasium but she saw no one coming out.

She made for the lifts. She pressed the button, and looked around at the doors to the gym.

A lift chimed. Startled, she turned. The door opened. The lift was empty, and she darted inside. She turned around and peeked out to see if anyone had seen her.

The gangly dwarf appeared in the door of the gym. *Oh no, did he see me?* She jumped to the side and froze. The control panel was above her head.

"Oh, good, there's a lift I can catch," said the gangly dwarf.

Her blood raced. *Close the door!* She punched the button, and the door started to close.

The dwarf's footfalls sped up. "Aw, now I gotta catch another one," he said, and the lift door closed.

Frozen, she held her breath.

The lift was dark and quiet, but it did not move. *What's wrong? Why aren't we moving?* A thought came to her. *Press the button!* She did, and the lift moved. She breathed and sighed with relief. She wanted to cry, but she knew now was not the time.

What am I going to do? As the lift slowly sank, the floor

indicator blinked four and a bell chimed. *Will they go out the front or the back?* Either way, they would have to go through the lobby unless they left through the basement. *Why didn't George stop them?* The bell chimed as she passed the third floor. *Can I run? Where? Can I hide? Where?*

She touched her forehead. The green microchip on her forehead was cool. She had always felt secure knowing she would never be lost. *They can find me! They know where I am!* Now she wondered. *Will they look for me?*

The lift passed the second floor and the bell chimed. The dwarf in the Halloween costume wanted to poison everyone in the gym. All of her teachers, all of her friends, how could she help them? *I'm a little girl.*

What can I do? She hated Dirk. He sprayed her with cold water when they played with water pistols. *What if he dies?* It was not fair, someone needed to save him, but why should it be her?

When she was sick and she threw up on her floor, the nurse called her a cur. *She doesn't deserve to die!*

Heartburn is my teacher. Mike, Wallaby, Mona, and Diane are my friends! And all the others! I can't just leave them! What can I do?

The lift door opened. She peeked out of the lift. No one was there.

I can get help! She put her foot in the door holding it open and stuck her head out of the door to look around. The main hall was only a few yards away.

The bells chimed and she heard the lift next to her open. Jumping backwards, she hid in her lift. The dwarf got off his lift. She recognized the footfall of his boots.

The door of her lift started to close. The dwarf stopped. She heard his boots squeak on the marble floor, and come closer. Clinching her fists and squeezing her eyes shut, she hoped the dwarf would go away.

"Crazy lifts," said the dwarf, "got a mind of their own."

The door of her lift shut. She waited. She had no idea how long to wait. If she opened the door too soon, the dwarf would hear, and if she waited too long she would be too late. Her friends would be poisoned.

Daisy raised her finger to the button to open the door. She hesitated, uncertain what to do.

Then she counted to twelve. Twelve was a good number. Going by thousands, she counted from one to twelve, and pressed the button.

The lift door opened. She put her foot in the door again, and leaned forward. She peered out.

In her mind, Dirk waited for her behind the door with a water pistol. She flinched, and then looked again.

No one was outside the lifts. She tip toed across the lobby, and she stopped at the corner.

Remember how Dirk plays water pistols. She sidled up to the corner and peeked into the main hall.

The gangly dwarf walked nonchalantly towards George. The security guard paid no attention to the dwarf's approach. *Why can't George see him? Is he blind? Can he hear him? Will he stop him?* She wanted to scream, but she gritted her teeth.

He stopped in front of the guard and read the guard's nameplate.

"George? That's your name? Can't see me can you, George?" The dwarf made faces at the security guard. He stuck his tongue out at him, and waved his hands in the guard's face. "Can't hear me either, hey George? You're such a George, George!"

Laughing, the gangly dwarf slapped the kiosk. He turned and burst out the door. He crossed the landing and went down the steps as the door swung shut.

Daisy rounded the corner and ran down the hall. "George!" she yelled.

The security guard slowly rolled around in his chair, and said lazily, "Hi Daisy, what can I do for you?"

"You gotta come with me! We've gotta go to the gym or everybody's gonna die!"

"Now, now, honey, it's not right making up stories to fool old George."

"No sir, I'm not making up a story! We have to save everyone! It's full of magical poison! They're all gonna die!"

"Magic poison, hey?" George chuckled. "That's a new one."

She recalled a cartoon. *If only you had done more.* She imagined all her friends dead. *No!*

Recalling some instinct long forgotten, Daisy knew what to do. She cried.

"Daisy, don't cry," he tried to console the child.

Tears welled up, and she balled.

"We've got to save them George!" She wailed. Tears rolled down her cheeks Grabbing the moleman's pant leg, she tugged at him. Then, she turned and ran. "Come on George! Come save everyone!"

"Please don't cry, Daisy," he frowned and slowly rose from his chair. He knew it was a trick.

That troublemaker, Dirk, had once told him there were rats in the basement. When he found nothing but a couple of old socks stuffed with construction paper, they had laughed and called him, 'Gumball.'

The little green girl cried. Daisy was upset. He tried to console her, but the tears only flowed all the more. "Please don't cry, Daisy," he repeated. He had to do something.

Sighing, he patted his belly and adjusted his utility belt. "All right, Daisy. Leave it to George. We'll go find out what this is about?" Striding down the hall, his boots landed hard as he waddled after the child.

"Hurry up!" She ran ahead, and turned the corner to the lifts. "Please George!"

He knew this was where the trick would happen. He braced himself for a water balloon, and turned the corner expecting a dozen laughing children. He told himself not to blush.

Secretly, he reminded himself not to cry.

There was no one there except Daisy holding the lift. "Please George! Hurry! We have to go up now!" Tears ran down her cheeks, and she bounced.

He stepped into the lift and she pressed the button to the top floor. "We only have three minutes! You have to get everyone out!" The bells chimed as they rode the lift.

"Now, little lady, if this is a trick, I'm going to be mighty mad! I'll ask Principal Chapel to give you detention."

"Give me all the detention you want George," she said, startling him. "Save everyone! That's all you have to do!"

What kind of trick was this?

Kids had put glue on his chair and gum in his hat.

The sixth grade once threw him a surprise birthday party. The students had bought him a gift card from the bowling alley with ten games. He liked that.

The lift door opened. Cautiously, he stepped out.

"Go on George! Go save them!" Daisy wailed.

The little girl pushed him. She tried to shove him forward. His bulk was too great for her to move, and her shoes slipped on the floor.

"All right, little lady. I'm going, I'm going."

The eerie quiet alerted him. Principal Chapel had called an assembly in the gym, but he expected nothing special. It was not his birthday, and there was no reason to expect a trick now. There was no sound. No children played, no whistles blew. Usually, he heard the sound of running. The weight room was empty. Normally, the clacking of weights echoed in the hall.

"Wait here, Daisy," He held her back, and he peeked into the gym.

"Go on, please hurry up!" Daisy cried.

Hesitating, he peered into the gym. Everyone was frozen. The boys and girls, and their teachers all stared into space. Principal Chapel and Margaret stood paralyzed in front of the assembly.

"Principal Chapel?" He called.

As he walked up to her, he saw two aluminum cylinders on the half-court line. The canisters were the size of a small fire extinguisher. Each canister had a valve connected to a dispersion cone, and a timer. The timer counted down, and only seconds remained.

George's eyes grew round.

All of his life flashed before his eyes. In all his years, he had held many jobs. He landed a job with the sanitation department, and collected trash. He met a girl he loved, and he married her. He retired, and his wife passed away. His only friends were on his bowling team. Alone, he had to find something to do in his spare time. *Was it fate?* He was lucky to land a job with the school. For all his complaints, he loved the school. The children greeted him and waved to him. They showed him their homework. They were his friends and they gave him pictures they had drawn themselves. *They're just kids!*

He knew what he had to do. He ran across the basketball court. His bulk pounded on the court, and his boots marred the glossy floor. He ran past coach Merry, and she never even flinched.

The students and teachers all sat frozen. They were oblivious to the fat moleman huffing and puffing across the gym. He was out of shape. The blood in his ears pounded, and his lungs burned. But his massive hands were still strong after decades of loading trash.

He grabbed a canister. The canister was as light as a feather. He wheezed. The seconds ticked away. He jogged to the other canister and picked it up.

Principal Chapel stared into space. Her eyes were glazed over. Her pupils were dilated and she was oblivious to his presence.

"Get out!" he croaked. He tried to call out, but his lungs refused. She just stood there.

Cursing his body, he ran for the exit. His boots pounded away.

An idea popped into his head. Maybe it was a distant memory from his military service or a vid he had seen. He ran for the swimming pool. The water might drown the timer or the gas might react with the water and neutralize the poison.

Airlocks isolated the pool from the children's locker rooms for privacy. Maybe the locks would stop the gas. From years of working in the sanitation department, he knew the pool's vents led to the city's exhaust system, and the exhaust went through incinerators before it was released on the surface.

If the gas escapes, it will have to pass through the incinerators. It's all I can do. I can't do any more.

Daisy cried in the hall. She was shouting, but he could not hear her. His heartbeat pounded in his eardrums.

Stuffing a canister under his arm, he pulled his mobile caster from his utility belt, and tossed it at the girl.

He sucked in air, and croaked, "Run Daisy, call for help."

He jogged to the boys' locker room. He twisted and slammed the door with his back. He rolled into the locker room and shuffled towards the pool.

One of the canisters beeped. He pointed it away from his face and charged the door to the pool. He held his breath. The beeping canister hissed, and a white mist shot from the dispersion cone. He kicked the door and it flew open. Gas trailed from the canister as he ran to the pool.

Momentum carried him through the door. The pool glittered. A pebbled walk surrounded the pool. A diving platform sat on one end. Competition lanes marked the bottom. The other end was shallow for small children learning to swim. Slides dropped into a lagoon on the far wall.

The other canister beeped. George ran to the pool. He heaved the canisters into the deep end.

Gas blocked his way back to boy's airlock. Gas wafted from the pool. He looked for a way out. *The girl's locker!* He had never seen the girls' locker room before. *No one will object today!* He headed for the girls' airlock and ran from the gas.

Grasping his chest, his mouth opened. His lungs screamed. He willed himself not to breath.

He fell beside the pool. His flash light popped off his utility belt and rolled to the edge of the pool, bounced over the lip, and rolled into the pool. His key ring skittered on the floor.

Gas escaping from the canisters roiled the water in the pool. Brown smog floated over the spot where the canisters had sunk. The thick smog drifted lazily towards the exhaust vents.

Gently, the cloud thinned.

Daisy

Shotgun stuck his head in the open door, "Lunch, boss."

He sat up and rubbed his temples, and pushed the dreams from his mind. "Be right there."

Joining his butler at the dining room table, he found a spread of pate and creamed cheeses, cold cuts and toasted bread.

"I had a strange dream. That makes two this week."

"You're cracking up." Shotgun filled two crystal goblets with sparkling water. "Do you recall any of it?"

Jack recounted as much as he could remember. He told him of the four derelicts being washed by the dwarf and the two tennis players with one clean washrag between them.

"Good thing you didn't need a shower," said Shotgun.

Heavy metal music interrupted them. He stopped in his tracks, and scrambled to open his caster.

Gumshoe appeared on the caster's screen in his fedora and trench coat. Whiskers speckled his face, and purple flaps sagged below bloodshot eyes.

"Morning Gumshoe," said Jack. "Were you up all night? You look like a levi-truck ran over you."

"Barfly and I hit O'Malley's last night." He stroked his chin. "Half my brain is still swimming with mermaids."

"Ha, old-man, aren't you getting a bit old for that?"

"Jack," said Gumshoe. "Good cops are like fine wine and cheese. We only improve with age."

"What did you tell Betty, old man?"

"She's up at Iron Mountain. So I called her from the office and made excuses." The inspector winked. "Jazz still has you wrapped around her finger, but you'll learn how to manage."

"You're getting too old to stay up all night, old man." Jack yawned. "What's up? You didn't call to tell me about your hangover."

"Do you know where Beslan is?"

"No, what is it?"

"It's an elementary school in Moab. Get down here as soon as you can. Expect to be here a while. I'll explain when you get here."

"Be there in ten."

"Thanks," Gumshoe flipped his caster and closed the connection.

"Now it's a school," said Jack. "This can't be good! We've got to get down there."

"Right behind you, boss."

~~~~~

Pandemonium reigned at the Beslan School.

Jack and Shotgun squeezed through the onlookers and passed a pack of reporters. The reporters threw a barrage of questions at him.

"Sorry no, we cannot answer any questions." He evaded the questions. "No comment. We do not speak for the police. We're not at liberty to say. Didn't I say, no comment?"

A policeman held back the crowd. "We're consultants with the Nodlon Yard."

"Go on in sir," said the officer. "We were told to expect you Mr. Clay."

They ducked under the police tape and scrambled up the school's steps. A policewoman directed traffic into a classroom. A few middle-aged mole women stoically waited for news. A husband comforted his wife.

Outside the principal's office was a portable table. A knot of officers and technicians blocked the office.

"Mr. Clay," a police matron waved at them. "Constable Wiggles and Inspector Lestrayed are upstairs. They're in the gym on the top floor."

~~~~~

They stepped off the lift into a scene of controlled chaos. Two of Moab's crime scene technicians scanned the hall. Another disappeared into the boys' locker room.

They walked into the open gymnasium. Medics hovered over little green girls and boys. Emergency responders carried off stretchers bearing the victims. The children stared into space as if dead. Only the rise and fall of their chests told him they were not dead. Jack's stomach turned. *I've got to stop this!*

A technician scanned the bleachers, and another scanned the floor. Gumshoe watched over the scene from the volleyball court.

"Jack, Shotgun, good to see you." Gumshoe waved them over. "Welcome to the party." The Inspector was unshaven and his eyes were bloodshot. If anything, he appeared worse in person than he had on Jack's caster.

"We heard the news." Jack surveyed the scene and frowned. "No one was killed, and the Surete sent the survivors to Moab Charity."

"Don't jump to conclusions," said Gumshoe. "We're still piecing it together. Moab got an automated emergency call from the security guard's caster. The uniforms found the teachers and the children here in the gymnasium. They were comatose, so the officers called for backup. Wiggles called me after he got the report. Now, look behind you."

Jack and Shotgun followed the Inspector's gaze. Scorch marks covered the wall.

"Capricorn," Jack swallowed. "That's not good. It's burnt into the wall, isn't it?"

"Yes, the heat was intense."

"Thank our lucky stars," sighed Jack. "It's not the children's blood."

Constable Wiggles broke free of the knot of technicians.

"Unfortunately," said Gumshoe, "that's not the whole story. Here comes Wiggles."

The portly policeman waddled over. "Good to see you,

gentlemen," said Wiggles. "My uniforms found the security guard next to the swimming pool. A little girl had the security guard's mobile. She must have sent the emergency call. The officers who found the girl and the guard began feeling sick, and we sent them to Moab Charity. I'm not taking any chances."

"What happened to them?" asked Jack.

"Poison," said Wiggles. "Gas, we think. We're still working it out, but we found canisters in the pool. We've got a hazmat unit in there now fishing out the canisters."

"Can it get any worse?" asked Jack.

"We're all frustrated," Gumshoe thumbed his holster straps. "The best men in Moab are working on it. I called you boys out here in case we can use your talents."

"Thanks for the vote of confidence," said Jack, "but I'm not sure what we can do."

Medics took vital signs, recorded observations, and cared for the comatose. Other officers struggled to move the victims on stretchers.

"Excuse me," said Wiggles, "back to work."

"We'll be in the physical education office," said Gumshoe.

The Inspector squeezed Jack's elbow. "Can I talk to you alone for a minute? Shotgun, come along." Letting go of his elbow, the Inspector headed out of the gymnasium.

"Wiggles has other business," said Gumshoe. "He doesn't need to hear this again."

"You look like you haven't slept in a week."

"Let's say Barfly and I had a meeting of the mind's last night. We sailed to Tahiti seeing things differently and we sailed back seeing eye to eye."

"Remember that Octagon paper pusher?" Gumshoe took off his fedora, and combed his thin hair.

"Ferrell," said Jack. "I remember. He's the one who thinks the Black Dwarf committed the Zodiac murders to destabilize Nodlon, right?"

"Yeah, and he thinks the Black Dwarf ambushed us twice,"

sighed Gumshoe. "And he thinks the dwarf works for Mars. I'm inclined to agree. Barfly thinks so too. Wiggles' men found Martian War Maker marks on the canisters."

"Is he sure? Why would the Martian's want to murder children? I can't imagine President Nogora stooping so low."

"Not our problem. Not mine anyway. Officially, I'm off the Zodiac case. The higher-ups ordered Barfly to take me off it. The Black Dwarf belongs to Ferrell now. Barfly's afraid of losing his retirement and, frankly, so am I."

"If you're off the case, what are we doing here?"

"Unofficially, I'm a liaison for Nodlon Yard. Barfly knows this is too important to leave to the military. We have every confidence in the military's ability to destroy things, but they're not policemen. We're going to keep looking for the Black Dwarf until someone catches him."

"What does that make us, gate crashers?"

"Technically, we're all here as civilian consultants with the Surete. Don't let it bother you two. Wiggles is a good moleman and the best detective in Nodlon. Present company excluded of course. He insisted we stay on the case and continue chasing any leads. If I am pulled off, I hope you will both keep working with him."

"We'll see this case through to the end," said Jack. "I think we've seen enough dwarf girls murdered, and now mole children! What do you say, Shotgun? Are you in?"

"You can count on me too, boss," said Shotgun, "I'll help any way I can."

"Thanks, you're good men, both of you."

"Changing the subject, old man," said Jack, "what about warning Nodlon's biots? The Black Dwarf and New Gem targeted dwarves. We need to shut down New Gem and warn the dwarves."

"No warning," Gumshoe grimaced. "They won't warn the biots. They nixed it at the top. Warning the biots now will create panic. That's what they say anyway."

"That's a lie," Jack spat. "The city's already in a panic. How can a warning make it worse?"

"You're right, but it's probably Warlord Arnold's doing. He doesn't rub shoulders with many biots if you get my drift. And if anyone goes after New Gem, it has to be Ferrell. Besides, everyone's already been ordered to leave the city. That should disrupt their plans for now."

"What happens when they set up shop in Iron Mountain, and the murders continue there?"

"That's why we need to stop them now, before they can move," said Gumshoe. "Why do you think I'm here? Barfly figured it out for himself. We can't trust the military to stop New Gem especially on the evidence we have. What else can a policeman do?"

"What can a magician do that the police cannot do?" asked Jack. "How can Barfly do that? The police are here to protect us. My fiancée is synthetic. My mother was synthetic. I'm half synthetic. Biots laugh just as loud at my shows as any human, why should their lives and dreams count any less?"

"Faith and Hope are my children," spat Shotgun. "They look like children, sound like children, and play like children. Even a regressive can see they're children. Why should it matter their parents are synthetic? If the Black Dwarf was after human girls, they'd issue a warning!"

"Now boys, I wouldn't be so sure," Gumshoe consoled the mage and his dogsbody. "Jack! Shotgun! Charity, please friends! Why should high and mighty pinheads care anymore for common humans than for biots? Whatever the motive, right or wrong, it's not about biots. They don't give a penny about the world inside. They're sociopaths. It's got nothing to do with the victim's DNA!"

"No dignity in life," muttered Shotgun bitterly, "None in death!" A scowl fell over the typically optimistic dwarf, and worry lines bundled the skin around his chip.

Not for the first time, a pang of remorse struck Jack.

"Biots are people too," said Gumshoe. "If I didn't believe it I wouldn't spend my time looking for their killers. What can I do? I'm only a glorified police officer. I'm not an aristocrat and no one gave me a silver spoon." Gumshoe slowly wagged his head.

"I'm sorry old man," said Jack. "I didn't mean it that way. I don't even know a human who thinks less of a biot. Even Princess Virginia thinks biots are people. It's just outrageous. Who would gag the truth? Who would lie to kids? Lying to children, it's sick."

"Tell me something I don't know," said Gumshoe. "Look this isn't about people's prejudices. If they put it to a vote, everyone in the city would vote for equality. It's about Baron Voltaire, the Nodlon Banking Cartel, and the mob families running Deep Nodlon. If Parliament had any chutzpah, the Yard would arrest them in twenty-four hours and we'd put an end to the curse. No one has done it because no one has tried. If you talk about it, you disappear. Remember the Right Honorable Hoffa? He was up to his eyeballs in a trafficking ring. When he came clean, he disappeared. He's probably orbiting Pluto now."

"We have to stop this before more people die," Jack reddened. "We were lucky no one died here today."

"We don't know that, Jack," Gumshoe shook his head, and looked Jack in the eye. "Some of the children may be missing. The technicians are double-checking the records." The detective worked his jowls.

Jack's shoulders drooped, and he squeezed his temples. He gulped, and tried not to be angry. More dwarves were dead, and now mole children were missing. *Gumshoe's doing his best! If the old man worries any harder, he'll blow a gasket!* For as long as Jack had known him, Gumshoe always presented himself as a curmudgeon. The gruff exterior protected an old softie.

Wiggles tapped on the window. "They're through cross checking downstairs," he said. "We've got a problem." The constable waddled off. "A baker's dozen are missing."

Forgetting their conversation, they chased the constable to the lift.

"Bad business," said Wiggles, "bad business."

"Maybe they were replacing the dwarves they lost in the ambush?" Jack suggested.

"Maybe Jack," said Wiggles. "Back at the farm, my techs are almost through with their reports. The hazmat team is finished on the top floor. They think the area is clear, but they've got it sealed off as a precaution. Our chemical boys have taken the canisters to the crime lab."

The lift opened. Wiggles waddled towards a policewoman. The knot had moved on. Two other technicians worked on their laptops.

"Maureen," Wiggles asked, "what have you found?"

"We've got thirteen missing children – all boys."

"Are you sure?"

"We had trouble figuring out who was supposed to be here today. The children and staff were given leave due to the evacuation. Only a skeleton crew was here today to stay with the orphans. We had to locate the student's attendance records and the time clock record for the staff. We compared the security records to the chips on the victims. All of the staff are accounted for, but thirteen of the students are missing."

"So we've got a baker's dozen missing - all young men?"

"All boys," she said, "just boys." She dropped just a hint of bitterness.

"Can you get me a list?"

"I'm printing one out now."

"I'd better find out who to notify. Who do they belong to?"

"There shouldn't be that many calls. Half the boys belonged to Big Bee – Moab Biot Management. Five were with Moab Replacement Services, and two were in foster homes. Would you like me to place the calls?"

"No, thank you Maury, I'll take care of it. Especially Moab Replacement, I don't want them thinking they can investigate us for losing their little darlings. They abuse the younger children, let the tweens run in gangs, and blame us when they grow up to be hooligans."

"My sister worked for Moab Replacement when she was still under contract." Maureen leaned back in her chair. "If a brat gets out of line, they treat him like royalty. But if a quiet kid makes a peep about being bullied by anyone in a gang, he gets detention and sensitivity training. I think there's something wrong with those people. They're anti-mole."

"Must be hell growing up in a place like that," said Jack.

"It is," said Maureen, "and everyone knows it. It's no kindness to be kind to the bullies and the aggressive and never shed a tear or share a hug with the kids who follow the rules. The place ought to be shut down and turned over to Big Bee."

"I'll give you no argument there," said Wiggles. "I'm Big Bee. I still have my honey jacket."

"Big Bee is different," Maureen handed Wiggles a list. "A Big Bee kid hits the jackpot of life."

"Yeah, we've never had to pick up a Big Bee kid in all my days," Wiggles rapped on the table, and wagged his finger. "They make fine upstanding members of the community. Take myself for example, and they make it easy to pay off your contract. No interest." Wiggles seemed a bit misty to Jack.

Maureen looked up from her paperwork. "Do I detect a hint of pride there Constable?"

"If you didn't have any parents, Maury, wouldn't you be glad to be a Big Bee?"

"I have to agree with you, Constable. A happy family is the only better place to grow up. If I didn't have parents, I'd want to be a Big Bee." Maureen lifted her tablet. "Back to the here and now, Wig. I've sent all the friends and relatives to Moab Charity per your instructions. What else do you want us to do?"

"Friends and relatives?" asked Shotgun. "Weren't they all orphans?"

A pall settled over the hall.

"Staff," said Jack. "All of the teachers had families. And I'm sure the agencies sent someone."

"Yes, that's right," said Maureen. "And the nannies were right upset. Not every mole is as callous as a bureaucrat." She glanced at Wiggles. "Is there anything else, Constable?"

"Keep the place locked down, Maury. No comments and no statements. I'll talk to Willoughby and see what we need to say. We don't want any reporters snooping around especially on the top floor. I don't want Chesterton or that Shaw woman getting poisoned. I'll try to put out something this evening before their late night broadcast. And get some rest. I have a hunch we'll be busy tomorrow."

"Yes sir," said Maureen. "What about you sir? Are you going to get a nap?"

"I'm going to Moab Charity. If any of the victims come around, I want to be there to question them. It'll be a long night." Wiggles looked at his companions. "Gentlemen, care to join me?"

Mole Charity

A knock on her door woke her. "Dr. Norman?" A rumpled blanket and two squashed pillows littered her couch. Fly away locks made her look haggard. Hastily, she tied her hair, clipped it, and opened the door.

"Welcome to Moab Charity," said Norman.

"Evening, ma'am," Wiggles introduced them. "Dr. Norman is the assistant director here at Moab Charity. I'm afraid the Black Dwarf is taking a toll on her. I believe you know everyone."

"Yes, Constable," she said. "I've seen all of you on the vid. I take it you've had no luck at all finding your man." Norman glared at him.

"None, I'm afraid." Wiggles sounded contrite. He turned to the others as a guilty schoolboy would for support from his mates. "How are the patients from Beslan, doctor?"

"They'd be better off if they hadn't been attacked." She huffed. "We moved them to the psych ward. It's the only wing with personnel trained to accommodate the comatose. They are unresponsive. Scans show no brain function above that required for cardiopulmonary function and basic metabolic activities. We've tried stimulants, smelling salts, and even mild shocks without avail."

"Can't you do anything to help?"

"We don't know what's wrong, Constable. There's nothing wrong with them according to our scanners and tests. It's as though their voluntary nervous system stopped functioning for no good reason. I'd say they're brain dead, but they're not. We searched for traces of known neurotoxins, and found nothing. The lab boys haven't given us anything either. We haven't found any chemical trace of a poison. The tests we've completed are negative."

"So you haven't made any progress," Wiggles shook his head.

"Thanks for your professional assessment, Constable," said Norman. "Would you like me to grade your progress? But no, the prognosis isn't good. We're still in the dark, but I haven't given up."

"Sorry, doctor," said Wiggles. "Pardon my bedside manner. Please don't take it as criticism. We're just desperate."

"No need to apologize. Everyone's on my back. They're accusing me and my staff of everything from incompetence to complicity in a conspiracy theory." She rubbed her temples. "The way they carry on, you'd think we poisoned the children. I've contacted Nodlon Memorial for advice. I've called everyone I can think of. We've put out a medical advisory alert to the whole planet. So far, no one has any new suggestions. If anyone has any new ideas, I'd like to hear it."

"I'm sure you're doing your best, doctor," said Wiggles. "How are the security guard and the girl?"

"They're still in intensive care," said Norman. "The little girl is hanging on. She's strong. The security guard isn't doing nearly so well."

"Is there anything we can do to help?" Wiggles flashed a smile. "Anyone we can lean on?"

"Lean on the Moab crime lab," she said. "Pauling runs the lab. He's a friend of mine, and he runs a tight ship. I know they're working around the clock. I'm sure they'll let us know as soon as they find anything. But they won't return my calls. The silence is deafening. I assume it means they've run into dead ends so far, but it would be good to know if they've made any progress."

"Yes, doctor. I know Pauling too. I'm sure it's just pandemonium over there. The lab's been evacuated to Iron Mountain. Half the staff was mobilized. I'd bet Pauling is in a panic, but I'll put in a word."

"Fine Constable, it's good to know we're not alone, but it's just frustrating being left in the dark. I'll call him later and see if we can shake the tree."

"Can we see the patients?" asked Wiggles.

"You'll have to wait. I'll contact you immediately if there are any developments."

"Doctor, the killers tried to murder seventy orphans and their teachers. We got lucky this time. But they're still on the loose, and they've kidnapped a dozen boys. If we don't stop them, I'm afraid those children may die. I can't afford to miss a clue."

The doctor's eyebrow shot up, and her shoulders straightened. "Constable, I'm well aware of the seriousness of the situation. I can't let you speak to patients who are in no condition to answer questions."

"What about my men?"

"We moved your officers to a recovery ward. They must not have received a full dose. They weren't comatose like they others. They've recovered sufficiently to have visitors. You can see them."

"Yes, thank you doctor," said Wiggles. "We'll start there."

They all feared for the patients, but the Black Dwarf had a dozen hostages. Wiggles frowned. *Little green biots! They're just boys.*

"Good," said the doctor. "I'll have a nurse show you the way." She pressed a call button.

A spritely mole woman with a gentle smile peered around the door and said, "Yes mum?"

"Show these gentlemen to the recovery ward. They're here to see the policemen from Beslan." She glanced at her divan. "If you need me. I'll be here all night."

The nurse led them through the hospital's maze of corridors, walkways, and passed labs to a ward for recovering patients.

"Where are the officers who came in from Beslan?" she asked at the nurses' station.

Jack missed the answer, but she led them to an inconspicuous room like any other and walked in. "If you need anything, the charge nurse here is Misty. She can help you." Turning on her heel, the nurse departed.

Both officers watched the news on the vid.

When Wiggles came through the door, they turned off the vid, and saluted. "Sorry, sir," the older one said, "but we're all hooked up." He waved at the tubes and cables.

"At ease Jones," said Wiggles. "Gentlemen, I give you, Adam and Jones. I understand you two are lucky to be alive."

"Yes sir," said Jones, "After finding the guard by the pool we took ill and I passed out. Adam managed to call for help before he lost it."

Quietly, Gumshoe took a seat in the other visitor's chair. Shotgun made an advantage of his size and sat on the room's trash can. Jack leaned against a wall, and folded his arms.

Wiggles maneuvered around the patient's wardrobe, and wedged his bulk into a visitor's chair. "Let's have a quick debriefing, if you're up to it. I want to know what happened. What can you tell us, Jones?"

"We found the children and staff in the gym staring into space."

"Worse than stoners," added Adam.

"That's when we called in the medical disaster code" said Jones. "We were trying so hard to get their attention we forgot to look around. We hadn't even noticed the Zodiac sign."

"Spooky, it was like they were zombies."

"The lights were on, but no one was home."

"Did you try to rouse them?" asked Wiggles.

"Yeah," said Jones, "we shouted at them, poked them, and gave them a whiff of the smelling salts from our first aid kit."

"We couldn't think of anything else to try," said Adam.

"Lives were on the line," Wiggles said. "You did the right thing."

"So we started searching the floor," said Jones. We saw the Zodiac, and that chilled us to the bone."

"After we saw it," said Adam, "we called you. Big trouble

in little Moab."

"We found the guard face-down next to the pool. The two canisters were on the bottom of the pool."

"How did you know it was gas?" asked Wiggles.

"We smelled an odor," said Adam. "Jones thought it was gas right off."

"It smelled like pine trees," said Jones. "The cylinders on the bottom of the pool looked like thermos bottles. Maybe a terrorist used the bottles to mix the components of a gas the way kids do in chemistry class."

"Good thinking, I'll mention that in my report," said Wiggles. "What did you do next?"

"Not much we could do sir," said Adam. "We left our gas masks in the boot. I held my breath, but it was no good. I had to breathe. I was closer to the girls' locker room door, and I ran that way. My head spun and I got sick to my stomach. I tripped on the kid, and I almost passed out there. I reached the hall, and I called dispatch and warned them of the gas. Then I passed out."

"We heard on the news they got our warning," said Jones. "Lucky for us, Adam doesn't need to breathe like most folks."

"I'm in better shape than you are," said Adam. "I work out more."

"Those with less upstairs," countered Jones, "need less air than the rest of us."

"You two sound like you're married," said Shotgun.

"Hey, they're announcing something on the vid," said Jones. "Turn up the sound Adam."

"Put it on Adam," Wiggles shrugged. "We'd better all hear it."

Adam stabbed a button, and the anchorwoman's voice filled the hospital room. "Good evening, Nodlon," she said. "I'm Minerva Shaw, we will hear from Warlord Arnold in the wake of the horrific attack on the Beslan School in Moab. The Warlord will speak to us from the Octagon's pressroom. Now please stand by."

A middle-aged elf made his way to a podium standing in front of Nodlon's blue flag.

"Citizens of Nodlon, friends and visitors, I come to you tonight with a heavy heart. We have been attacked again by vicious terrorists. Last week, we thought these fiends were ordinary murderers, but a few days ago they destroyed a supertanker. Fortunately, the only casualties were among their own.

"Yesterday, they attacked innocent dwarf girls.

"Today, they attacked mole children. By the narrowest stroke of luck, the bravery of a security guard spared us from a greater tragedy. The victims lie in a psychiatric unit of Moab Charity Hospital.

"Even now, a dozen mole boys remain missing. All of Nodlon has seen the news. These may be biots, but biots are people too. Make no mistake, agents of Mars are behind these attacks. The Martian War Maker created the poison used in the latest attack. We don't know what it was, but we suspect an advanced military neurotoxin. All Nodlon grieves tonight.

"We have advised the King of all the information available at this time. No doubts remain. King Justin and his advisors are considering the matter now. I am certain they will reach the right conclusion and take the only proper course of action.

"I pledge by my sacred honor to find the missing mole children, and bring this filth to extreme justice. Thank you for your attention. May Mother Earth cover your bones."

Reporters called out questions, but he only raised his hand, "Later, ladies and gentlemen."

Finished, the elf parted a curtain and strode off the stage.

Adam muted the vid and for a moment the room sat in stunned silence.

"Well that cuts it," said Gumshoe. "Arnold's advised them to go to war, and he's hoping they'll do so immediately. Now that he's blamed the War Maker's for the poison, the Council has no choice, and King Justin must agree or risk becoming irrelevant."

"If Mars wants a war," growled Shotgun. "Shouldn't we let them have it?"

"On their terms?" asked Gumshoe. "The Martian war mongers have stoked this war for twelve years while we sat on our hands. When President Nogora replaced Director Goodenuf, and executed him for executing terrorists, we said nothing. When they threw their own in the prisons in the crater of Hellas, we said nothing. When they took Ceres station, we said nothing. What choices do we have left?"

~~~~~

A nurse knocked on the open door. "Constable, the little girl woke up. Director Norman told me to let you see her if she's up to it. Do you want to speak with her?"

"Yes, we'll be right with you," said Wiggles. He turned to Adam and Jones, "No loitering allowed on this job, I need you two back on the street." With a wave to his men, they took off after the nurse.

"Yes sir," the officers said.

"We're moving her out now. No visitors are allowed in the unit. We've got a recovery room near the unit where you can visit with her. I'm Katie the duty nurse. Feel free to ask me any questions."

"Thank you, Katie," Wiggles said.

Katie led the way, and the portly detective waddled out of the room with his consultants. Going through a wide door, they reached the recovery room. She waved a hand and invited them in.

"Nurse Fanny will be staying with you to watch over the girl. If you need me, my station is right through the double doors. If you need anything else, Fanny can probably help you."

Wiggles thanked Katie, and popped into the room. "Hello,"

he said to a comely mole maid puttering about the girl's bed.

"Hi, I'm Fanny, and this is Daisy."

They all gathered around the girl. Her eyes were closed, and she clutched a green teddy bear. She was a small mole child whose green complexion and dark green hair contrasted sharply against the white sheets.

"Is she sleeping?" whispered Wiggles.

In answer to his question, the nurse touched the girl, "Daisy, you have some visitors."

Daisy opened her eyes and pulled her bear closer. Her eyes widened in surprise, and her lips quivered. "Hi," said Daisy.

"Hello Daisy," Wiggles patted his girth and his belly jiggled. "Are you feeling better?"

The girl nodded, and her eyes widened. Then she pulled on the nurse's sleeve. Fanny leaned over Daisy, and the girl grabbed her and pulled her down. Fanny let Daisy whisper in her ear.

Fanny stifled a giggle, and looked up at Jack. "Sir," said Fanny, "Daisy wants to know if you're Cretaceous Clay."

Jack's spirits lifted, and he forgot the horrors he had witnessed. He put on his best theatrical face, and beamed at the child. "Yes, Daisy I am Cretaceous Clay. Can I show you some magic?"

Daisy visibly brightened, and she nodded.

He signaled the others to back away, and threw back his cloak with dramatic flair. He held out his arms and fluttered his fingers. "The key to magic is a positive attitude." Summoning his magic, he started a routine for small children. From his sleeve, he pulled a bouquet, "Daisies for Daisy."

Daisy smiled.

"Flowers need a vase," and Jack created the illusion of a vase full of water on the stand next to her bed. He tossed the flowers through the air and they landed in the vase with a plop. For good measure, he added a few droplets of water to sell the illusion of the splash. She was delighted.

"Do you like bunnies?" The girl smiled and nodded. Jack cast a white bunny rabbit with a pink bow. Everyone oohed and ahhed. The bunny bounced, and Daisy reached out to pet the bunny. Her hand passed through the illusion.

"Bunnies can multiply. Can you?"

Daisy said, "Yes I know all my times tables."

"That's great sugar," Jack smiled. "Can you do six times seven?" Five white bunnies joined the one on her bed, and seven black bunnies appeared on the dresser under the vid.

"Forty-two," cried Daisy. With jabs of his fingers, Jack created forty-two black and white bunnies. He put bunnies in the sink, and on the chairs, and on the medicine counter, and one on the intravenous fluids pump. He parked a bunny on Gumshoe's head.

Daisy laughed, "You look silly."

"I always look silly, Daisy," said Gumshoe.

"Would you like to see my whole show?" Jack asked.

"Yes, please."

"As soon as you're well, I'd like you and your friends to come to my show. All of you are invited."

"What if my friends don't wake up?"

"The doctors will figure out how to wake them up, Daisy," said Jack. "Don't you worry about it now, sugar plums."

"Are you sure?" Daisy looked at him, and he hesitated.

"Yes," said Jack, "They're doing everything they can."

Jack pulled the portly policeman closer to the bed. "This is Constable Wiggles. He's a policeman and a friend of mine. He has to ask you a few questions. Can you help him, Daisy?"

"Yes, I'll try."

Wiggles assumed his best bedside manner. He beamed at the little girl.

"Hello Daisy, were you the one who called us?"

"Yes sir, I pressed the emergency button. Mr. George told me to, so I did."

"You saved many lives, Daisy," said Wiggles. "You're our

little heroine." He squeezed the girl's hand. "Daisy, can you tell us what happened?"

"Principal Chapel told us to go to the gym. She said Cretaceous Clay was doing a magic show."

"Did you see Mr. Clay? Think hard."

She shook her head again. "No sir, but a dwarf in a Halloween costume said Cretaceous Clay couldn't be there, so he came instead."

"What kind of Halloween costume honey?"

"It was a robe. It had silver drawings on it. He looked like a magician."

"Was he carrying a staff?" Wiggles held out a hand. "A long pole about this high with a stone on top. It might look like a walking stick."

"Yes, yes, he was."

Sitting back, Wiggles turned to the others. "Sounds like your Black Dwarf, gentlemen. What do you think?"

"It's the Black Dwarf all right," said Gumshoe. "The fiend's expanded his repertoire."

Wiggles nodded. "Did you see the magician dwarf's face, honey?"

"No, he had a hood."

"What about the other two, can you describe them?"

"One was fat. I've never seen a fat dwarf before. The other one was skinny." She pointed at Shotgun. "He looked like him. All dwarves look alike."

"Out of the mouths of babes," muttered Shotgun behind Jack's back.

"They had Halloween make-up," said Daisy.

"What kind of make-up?" Wiggles asked.

"Zombie make-up," she said. "They had black eyes, and their faces were white like ghosts. Were they pretending to be dead?"

"I don't know, honey," Wiggles glanced at Jack.

"Drugs maybe," Jack said. "It sounds like zombie

possession, but I can't be sure Constable. I've never tried anything like it. I'm not in the habit of mesmerizing people."

A frown flittered across Wiggles' lips, and he nodded. He sucked in a breath, and then smiled again. "Why didn't you go into the gym, honey?"

The little girl's eyes narrowed. "You promise not to tell?" she asked.

"Cross my heart, honey." The constable crossed his heart with his pinky. "I won't tell a soul."

"Promise you won't tell." Daisy looked around the room.

"Scout's honor," said Jack. They all crossed their hearts and promised.

"I was thirsty. When Miss Heartburn wasn't looking I went into the locker room to use the water fountain. I took a drink. When I came out everyone was in the gym. I was late, so I hid in the corner."

"Could you see from where you were hiding?"

"No, but I could hear. The magician dwarf told them all to look at something. Then a red light came out of the doors. There was a loud noise and a snap. Then, there was a flash. The magician dwarf started asking questions."

Wiggles nodded, "That's good, honey. What happened next?"

"He told his friends to use magic poison."

"Did he say why?"

"No sir, I don't think so."

"Okay, go on honey. Then, what happened?"

"They took the boys. The magician dwarf and the fat one got into a lift and left with the boys. I was so scared I didn't know what to do. But I followed them."

"What about the skinny dwarf?"

"I snuck past the doors," said Daisy. "The skinny dwarf was looking the other way. He didn't see me."

"Did you see anything in the gym?" Wiggles asked.

"They were all staring."

"Staring at what?"

"I don't know," Daisy shook her head. "I just wanted to get away. I took the lift downstairs. The skinny one almost saw me, but I hid. I learned that playing water guns."

"Daisy, I need some more help," said Wiggles, "Why didn't George stop the dwarves, honey?"

"He didn't see them. The skinny one walked right up to him. The dwarf made funny faces and he called him names. Mr. George couldn't see him or hear him at all. It was like magic."

All eyes shot to Jack, but the mage shrugged. "Selective invisibility? No way. I have no idea how to do that."

"If George didn't see him, how did George rescue everyone?" asked Wiggles.

Daisy rolled her eyes. "I told you silly. I made him do it. I ran down the hall. I made Mr. George go upstairs. He didn't want to. He thought I was playing a trick on him, but I cried so he went upstairs. He picked up the poison cans, and he ran to the swimming pool. He threw me his caster in the hall and he yelled at me. 'Call for help,' he said. Then, he got sick."

"Thanks Daisy." Wiggles squeezed her hand, "Last question. Why were you in the girls' locker room?"

"Mr. George ran into the boy's locker room with the cans. I called for help." She moaned. "I waited for Mr. George to come out. But he didn't come out. I wondered what happened. I can't go in the boy's locker room, so I ran into the girl's locker room."

She made the sort of face one makes when your jaw tingles when you're eating hard candy. "I opened the door to the swimming pool, and George was lying on the floor. There was an icky cloud over him. I was so scared I tried to run, but I felt sick, and I fell down."

She stopped.

"Daisy, what's the matter?" Wiggles' brow furrowed. "What's the matter then?"

"Is Mr. George well?" She choked up and began crying.

Taking her hand, the policeman bent over the child's bed. *If she was my daughter, what would I say?*

"George is very sick," he said. "Whatever happens, Daisy, remember you gave George the greatest gift a little girl can give to an old man. Do you know what that is?"

Tears rolled down her cheeks, and she sniffled. "What gift?"

"Thanks to you, George is a hero. If you hadn't made him go up the lift, everyone would have died. He saved everyone's life. He did what he had to do, and he did what he wanted to do. He was supposed to protect the school, but he was drinking coffee and eating donuts. If you hadn't told him, he wouldn't have known, and he wouldn't have saved anyone. The Black Dwarf pulled the wool over his eyes. You gave George the chance to prove how important his job was. Now everyone in the Solar System will know George was tested, and he passed. Do you understand?"

Daisy looked bewildered and not at all sure. She searched Fanny's face.

"Mr. George is our big hero," said Fanny, "and you're our little hero." Fanny daubed Daisy's eyes. "Blow your nose, Daisy."

"So, Mr. George wanted to be a hero, and he got his wish?"

"Yes, honey, that's right. Now, remember George wants you to live, and he wants you to be happy. He gave you a life, and it's a gift, all right?"

More tears flowed, and the little green girl wept.

"Thank you, honey, you're our little heroine. You did a great job. You helped George save the life of everyone in the gym. I'm going to make sure everyone knows it too."

Daisy held up her arms, and the Constable gave her a hug.

"Fanny, thank you," said Wiggles. "Please take good care of her."

"I will sir," she said, and tucked Daisy under the sheets.

Wiggles walked out of the intensive care unit. Katie sat at the nurse's desk.

"Any news on the security guard?"

Katie shook her head, and looked downcast.

The Constable started to turn away.

"Constable," she said.

He stopped and looked back.

"Sorry," said Katie. "I meant it's too late. The guard passed away while you were with Daisy. I'm sorry."

"From what Daisy told us, he made a good end of himself. He's the reason they're not all dead." Wiggles tapped the counter. Turning, he walked away.

Gumshoe sized up the look on Wiggles' face. "I take it the security guard didn't make it."

"Yeah," said Wiggles. "He's gone."

"If the body count goes any higher," muttered Shotgun. "They'll make a video game out of the Zodiac murders."

"Can we take a look at the other patients?" asked Jack.

"Why not?" sighed Wiggles. The portly constable patted his girth. "We don't have an escort, and there's no one stopping us."

~~~~~

They made a few false turns before they found the psychiatric unit. An unattended nurses' station guarded two wards. Locked double doors barred the way.

"I pressed the call button," Wiggles said. "Can you see anyone in the corridor?"

Jack peered through the windows of the locked doors.

Green children stared at the ceiling with unblinking eyes from beds lining the halls. An orderly shuffled between the patients with eye drops. He waved, but the orderly turned away.

"The children look dead," Jack said. "I saw an orderly, but he didn't see me. Is there anyone in charge here?"

Walking around the nurses' station, Jack checked the other doors. "More children, but I see a nurse coming our way."

The nurse tapped a code into a keypad, and the doors swung open. She was as green as grass and wore a crisp white uniform. With a stern look, she sized up each of them. "May I help you gentlemen?"

"I'm Constable Wiggles," he waved, "and these are my consultants. We'd like to see the patients from Beslan."

"Only Doctor Norman can authorize you to see patients in the psychiatric ward." The nurse answered in a tone sharp enough to cut a treble cleft. "Not that it would help."

"This is police business." Wiggles never missed a beat. "If you want authorization, get Doctor Norman on your intercom and get it now."

Pursing her lips, the nurse strode to her station and tapped on her desk caster. The caster buzzed softly.

"Norman here, what's going on up there? Has there been a change?"

"Sorry to bother you doctor," said the nurse, "but I have a policeman, a man, an elf, and a dwarf at the nurses' station. If we had a troll we could hold a renaissance faire. They want access to the psych ward to see the patients."

"Has there been any change in their condition?"

"No ma'am, they're in awful shape. They're dehydrated, and I've run out of intravenous fluid pumps. I've got Scott working on finding me another thirty pumps."

"Good work, Hatchet. Put the fat cop on the caster and let me speak to him."

Nurse Hatchet glared at Wiggles, and waved, "She wants to speak to you, I believe."

Going around the counter, Wiggles squeezed his bulk between the nurse and her desk, and sat down.

Norman was disheveled. She still wore her white coat.

"Doc, you need some rest," said Wiggles. "You look like you haven't slept in days."

"I've had four hours sleep since you brought the last victims in for autopsies. We're trying to evacuate and my pathologist looks worse than I do. If you would get out there and do your job, I might get a few winks to prepare for the next disaster you haven't prevented."

"Doctor that's a bit harsh," Wiggles chided her. "I appreciate your position, but I am keenly aware of my responsibilities. As such, I insist on seeing the patients from Beslan. It should only take a few minutes. As you say, I must be on my way to prevent the next disaster. If need be, I will serve you with a warrant. I, too, am aware of the urgency, and I see no reason to delay while I wake up a justice of the peace."

The doctor slumped and shook her head. "Very well Wiggles, but don't get in the way of my staff. And don't harm any of my patients," she sighed. "Nurse Hatchet, are you there?"

"Here mum," said Hatchet.

"Show the constable and his friends around, quickly. Don't let him waste too much of your time. Thanks."

"Yes mum." The caster darkened. Hatchet glared at Wiggles.

"Follow me, gentlemen." They dutifully let Hatchet lead them. "The scans show they are comatose," she said. "I've got the aides working full time just caring for them. We even have to apply drops to their eyes because they won't blink."

Jack brought up the rear.

"Have you tried stimulants?" asked Wiggles.

"We've tried olfactory shock with salts, electroshock, optical strobes, trans-cranial magnetic fields, and a host of psychotropic medicines. We've used enough Afterlife to bring zombies back to life."

Hatchet led them through a bay full of patients to a private room where a mole woman stared at the ceiling. "Principal Chapel is typical." She pointed to the monitors. "The scanners indicate she's in a coma. She's catatonic."

"Why are her eyes open?" Shotgun asked.

"No idea," said Hatchet. "And we can't close them, and don't tell me that doesn't fit the symptomology. We know that." Hatchet checked Chapel's pulse. "We shot Principal Chapel up with enough Afterlife to raise Caesar's ghost. No response on the scanners. No brain function; nothing, absolutely nothing." She let go of Chapel's wrist. "Not even her heart fluttered. She reacted as if we had shot her up with water."

"Nurse Hatchet," Jack said. "Would you be willing to entertain a hare-brained idea?"

"A hare-brained idea? If it even sounds half-baked, I'll hear you out. What have they got to lose? If it won't kill them, I'll try it."

"What are you thinking, Jack?" asked Gumshoe.

"Remember when we stunned the dwarves who ambushed us? After we stunned Billy, he came to. Just minutes before he had tried to kill me with a lightning gun, and then he was back to normal. He thought he had a pass."

"Possible," said Wiggles, "but he could be faking. He's in a lot of trouble. We haven't had time to probe him and his buddies, and verify their story. If we can't verify the truth of his statements, he'll spend the rest of his days on the Moon watching re-runs."

"Look at the Principal," said Jack. "What is the risk? If stun works on these patients, it will save their lives. If not, how can it hurt?"

"What's the difference between a stun and an electric shock treatment?" asked Hatchet.

"The shock treatments you administer affect only small portions of the brain," said Gumshoe. "Modern electro-shock stimulators operate on a principle similar to medical neural stimulators. They target selected neurons, and stimulate those neurons to fire." Parting his trench coat, Gumshoe flashed his lightning pistol, and patted the weapon. "Lightning weapons are completely different. They fire an electro-motive pulse. A weak pulse triggers all the neurons simultaneously causing momentary paralysis."

All eyes turned to Gumshoe. Everyone expected him to go on.

"What?" Gumshoe asked. "I'm no expert on weaponry. Weapons are just a professional interest." He glanced at Wiggles for support, "Basic stuff right?"

"Yeah," said Wiggles. "Do you read Tech Blaster or Solar Security?"

"Oh, I like both, but Tech Blaster tests everything in live simulations."

"Excuse me, gentlemen," Hatchet cleared her throat. "This isn't a convention for gun nuts. I can't believe I'm even saying this, but we need to know if it's safe to stun a patient. If we don't find a solution soon, my patients may suffer permanent side effects of this pseudo-catatonia, and they may even die."

"Stun rarely harms healthy people," said Gumshoe. "Stun victims are usually sick or under the influence of drugs. All of us with military training have been stunned." He smiled. "Some would say that's what's wrong with us, but it doesn't seem to have done me any harm."

"It wasn't fun," said Jack, "but no one was harmed in our cycle."

"We can't be sure it's safe on the patients," said Gumshoe. "Occasionally we've lost suspects stunned in the course of a pursuit or during a fight. Usually they are under the heavy influence of narcotics, and they suffer a heart attack."

"Let me call Doctor Norman again," said Hatchet. "She won't be happy, but we're desperate." She pulled out her caster.

~~~~~

"What is it?" snapped Norman. "Oh, it's you Hatchet. Have our guests left or created some new controversy?"

"The latter I'm afraid, Jean," said Hatchet. "I think you ought to hear this." She handed her caster to Gumshoe, "Go ahead and explain your idea."

"We've had brainstorm," Gumshoe cleared his throat. "If I may make a suggestion, maybe we might try stunning a patient. A stun might snap the kids out of their coma."

The doctor put her head in her hands. "You want me to shoot children with stun guns? Inspector, are you out of your mind?"

"You've seen the results. We were ambushed by a number of dwarves. The dwarves were sent here for treatment. Before they were stunned they tried to kill us, but afterwards they were normal, harmless dwarves. Maybe it will work on the victims."

"We've tried shock treatments, Inspector, and it hasn't worked."

"Stun guns operate differently than anything you've got here at the hospital," Gumshoe pushed back his fedora. "Every nerve cell is temporarily disrupted."

"I know I'm tired, and I know I'm desperate, but I must be out of mind for listening to this." The doctor rubbed her temples, "Is it even safe?"

Briefly Gumshoe explained the operation of stun guns and what he knew about the side effects of stunning suspects under different conditions. "I think it's worth a try. I'm not a weapons expert, but I know more than most laymen. Stunning is generally safe for healthy people. I've been stunned in training. It wasn't pleasant, but I'm none the worse for wear. If something goes wrong, we are in a hospital. You can deal with it."

The doctor rubbed her temples, "Hand me back to Hatchet." He passed the caster to Hatchet.

"What do you think, Jean?" The thought visibly rattled Hatchet.

"I'm going to try it Lizzy. Don't let them shoot anybody yet, though. Get Forest on the blower and tell him to prepare a trauma room. I want all his techs and nurses on standby. We'll use their neural scanner to see if we get any brain wave activity." The doctor rubbed her neck, and rolled her head. "Mobilize every available nurse, and find a volunteer. Check with the relatives and friends, and find someone who will volunteer one of the adult staff for the first trial. I'm not experimenting on any of the kids until we know if it works."

"Leave it to me, doctor," said Hatchet. "Get some more rest. I'll come by when I've got a volunteer, and we're set up in emergency."

"Thanks Lizzy."

Hatchet closed the caster, and looked at the Constable and his consultants with grim determination. "I think we're done here. If you go down to emergency, I'll see you there with our first volunteer."

Deprogramming

The emergency bay buzzed. Nurse Hatchet held up a hand and stopped the detectives and the amateur sleuths. "You'll just have to wait in the break room," she said.

They retreated to the break room. Fortunately, someone had brought in a stack of boxed lunches for the emergency. "Just what I need," said Wiggles, "I'm starving."

"No wonder, we haven't had a bite to eat since yesterday," said Gumshoe.

They were still picking out meals when Doctor Norman arrived. Norman considered the motley crew of investigators, and shook her head. "I must be crazy, I've practiced medicine for over thirty years in this hospital and this is the wackiest thing I've ever done. I expect all of you to testify to temporary insanity at my malpractice hearing."

"We'll both testify," said Gumshoe, "if we can get out on probation. If this doesn't work, I'll be lucky if I'm sleeping in an alley in Deep Nodlon."

"Who's volunteering their weapon?" asked the doctor.

Wiggles drew his weapon. "My case and my jurisdiction, and if they try taking my pension, I'll hire Dershowitz to sue the Proconsul." The portly moleman tossed his lunch on a counter, and waddled to the door. "I'll do the stunning. There's an art to stunning a suspect and we don't want to injure them."

"Very well, let's get this over with." Norman disappeared out the door and made a beeline for a busy trauma bay guarded by Nurse Hatchet.

Wiggles chased Norman down the hall waddling like a locomotive. "Okay, doctor, who are we experimenting on?"

Norman glared at him. "Principal Chapel volunteered," she said. "Her husband gave permission and signed a waiver on her behalf." Norman passed the hardcore nurse with Wiggles trailing after her.

"We're ready, doctor, except for a stun gun." As Wiggles

caught up, Hatchet lifted her nose and looked down upon him.

Nurses, paramedics, and doctors filled the bay. Norman's eyes rested on Forest. "Constable Wiggles will stun the patient," she said. "If anything goes wrong, I'm the only one here. Are we clear?" A row of heads nodded. "Constable, it's up to you now. Do your stuff."

~~~~~

In the break room, the minutes passed in tense silence. The tired sleuths munched on their meals, and listened for activity.

"Whoop!" Someone broke the quiet. Shouts joined the first voice, and soon a chorus of yells echoed down the hall.

Dropping his sandwich, Jack scooted the chair out from under him and sprang to his feet. He ran to the break room door with Shotgun on his heels, and the Inspector brought up the rear.

Hearing more cries, Jack ran down the hall toward the commotion. His long legs out paced the dwarf and the human detective.

He reached the trauma room, and Hatchet stopped him. Jack leaned over the stern mole woman and peeked into the bay, "What's happened?" Seeing Doctors Forest and Norman, and Wiggles, he called out again. "What's happened?"

"We have normal brain function on the scans," said Forest. "She's alive again. Wiggles, how long should we wait?"

"Best to let her sleep a few winks before you try rousing her. That's what they say for suspects. Then you can question them until they get tired again. Usually all you get is a few minutes before they have to rest."

"We'll let her sleep, and then see if we can wake her. Everyone stay on your toes. I want her monitored until we wake her." Forest identified who needed to stay and sent the others back to their regular duties.

Norman sent Hatchet to inform the Principal's husband, and then collapsed in a chair. She propped her head on her fists and closed her eyes. "Gentlemen, please wait outside. We'll call you when she wakes up."

Jack and the detectives pressed Wiggles for details.

"Chapel took the bolt and she went limp," said Wiggles. "She closed her eyes and looked like she'd fallen asleep. Her vital signs hardly blinked. None of the alarms on those monitors went off. Then their brain scanner picked up a few bleeps. I'm not sure what it means, but they were happy, so I'm happy. If you'll excuse me, I'm starving." The portly moleman returned to his lunch.

An orderly burst into the breakroom. "Constable Wiggles! Doctor Norman wants you. Principal Chapel is awake."

"Yes son!" said Wiggles. "I'm on my way." He dropped his sandwich. "Gentlemen, you're welcome to come too." With that, he waddled after the orderly as quickly as his bulk allowed.

~~~~~

Doctor Norman hovered over Chapel like a nervous hen. The principal was a pasty green and her lips were dry. Her eyes were bloodshot from long hours frozen in an unblinking stare.

"Mrs. Chapel, this is Constable Wiggles. He is in charge of the police investigation in the attack on Beslan. He can explain the situation to you. Excuse me; I'll be back in a few minutes."

Norman stopped at the door next to Wiggles and lowered her voice. "Keep it short. If she exhibits any sign of distress alert the nurses immediately. I'm going up to the psych ward. We're scanning everyone's heart. I don't want anyone having a heart attack."

"Doctor, by this afternoon, you'll be a heroine."

"The credit belongs to the police and your magician. I would never have thought of stunning my patients. And if you repeat that, I'll deny the charges."

"No, no, that won't do," Wiggles' eyes widened. "Not sure how I can explain it. You'll have to come up with something."

"Constable, just ask your questions. Let me worry about explaining it." With that, the doctor strode away to set her plans in motion.

The portly policeman waddled to the educator's bedside. Wiggles noted her skin was the pallid shade of a soybean rather than the healthy green of a shamrock.

"Principal Chapel, I'm Constable Wiggles, and I hope you're feeling better. Are you up to a few questions?"

"Yes, anything I can do to help. The doctor told me the school was attacked. She must be crazy."

"Mrs. Chapel, can you tell me what you remember?"

"A black dwarf wearing a magician's robe barged into my office without an appointment. He wanted to perform a magic show. I told him I was busy, and we argued. He carried a large staff, which he twirled. He thrust his staff in my face. It was very intimidating. He called himself Cretaceous Clay as if I was supposed to believe such a cockamamie story. He wasn't even an elf."

"Did you see Cretaceous Clay?"

"No, Constable," a puzzled expression crossed her face. "I assure you, Cretaceous Clay wasn't there. Why do you ask?"

"Just for clarification when I write my report. We think Jack Clay was with Inspector Lestrayed of Nodlon Yard at the time of the attack. Where the magician is concerned though I want all the evidence I can put my hands on."

"Attack?" Chapel glared the policeman. "What is this nonsense?"

"After the Black Dwarf offered you a magical performance, what do you recall next?"

"Next?" She looked around the trauma bay. "Next, I woke up here. That doctor asked me a bunch of silly questions. There's nothing more to tell. Can you tell me what's going on?"

"The Black Dwarf is the primary suspect in the Zodiac murders."

"The Zodiac murders," Chapel gasped. "But the victims are

all dwarf maidens?"

"No, ma'am, not anymore, just a few days ago, the Black Dwarf sabotaged a Galaxy class star freighter, the Marie Celeste, in an attempt to kill Cretaceous Clay. Only providence and Jack's magic saved himself and several police officers."

"Why are you telling me this?" The incredulous educator looked at the ceiling for answers. "What does that have to do with my school? I don't remember any attack that's for sure. Can you just tell me what happened at my school?"

"Maybe later I'll know more. What I can tell you is that the Black Dwarf mesmerized you by some unknown means. He compelled you to call an assembly in the gymnasium. He mesmerized your staff and your students. And he tried to poison them."

"Mesmerized? Poison!" Chapel sat up in alarm. "What's happened to my children? Where are my children? Where are my teachers?"

"The children and your staff are safe. They're upstairs in the psychiatric ward. They're still mesmerized, but Dr. Norman discovered a solution."

The principal put a hand on her cheek. Her face flushed, and she shook her head, "What? You're kidding. Why would you make up nonsense like this? Are you a xenophobe? No one can mesmerize people. Magic is supernatural, and the supernatural is imaginary. There's no such thing as magic."

"It's black magic to be precise," said Wiggles. "If it's magic. Cretaceous Clay thinks it's some new form of advanced technology. And his magic is real."

"At least Mr. Clay has the good sense to offer a logical explanation. Can't you do any better?"

"The Black Dwarf tried to kill you, your staff, and some seventy children with a poisonous gas."

"Surely, you're mistaken?" The principal flushed and pulled herself up to sit. "People make up stories like that to sow fear and frighten people. Fear and lies make people believe the unbelievable. Like those fools on the news who claim Mars wants a war."

Wiggles straightened his back and adjusted his lapel. He noticed a piece of lettuce on his jacket and picked it off.

"Principal Chapel, I am a chief homicide detective of the Moab Sureté. I'm not in the habit of fabricating stories."

"Well, that's good to hear, Constable. I'm glad you're on the job even if you don't make any sense. But who would try murdering over eighty children? And why? Why would anyone murder children?"

"Ma'am, I'm not trying to argue with you. If you'll allow me to finish, I'll tell you the rest of what we know."

"Go ahead, as if it means anything, but you've already discredited yourself. You said this black dwarf tried murdering seventy children as if I don't know how many children I have. Ignorance causes fear, and education is the cure. If we had more education, no one would be afraid. You can't even get your numbers right. My degree is in mathematics, and I happen to know we had eighty-three children at Beslan today. They were the orphans. I sent the others home to be evacuated."

"I'm afraid it's worse than you think." He softened his tone. "My arithmetic is not out of order. The Black Dwarf kidnapped thirteen children. All of them are boys under the age of fourteen."

"What?" Her eyebrows rose, and tears welled in Chapel's eyes. "Oh no, tell me the rest."

"After you called the assembly, a little girl named Daisy slipped away to get some water. When she caught up, she saw what was happening and she used her head. She alerted your security guard George, and George saved your lives."

Chapel's eyes widened, and she covered her mouth. She blinked and looked away. "Daisy's always been bright, but she's never been social. She belongs to Moab Replacement Services. I think she's been abused, but she clams up when we ask her." Chapel's shoulders slumped. "I wish I could help those children, but those bureaucrats won't listen. To them every biot is a case number, not a baby."

"Daisy would love Big Bee, and they would love her."

"Constable?" said Chapel, brightening. "Do I detect a hint of pride?"

"Be a Bee, class of 329." Wiggles held out his hand and wiggled his fingers.

"Well, I'll be a Bee," said Chapel, finally breaking a smile. She wiggled her fingers. "Class of 344, Constable," She relaxed again and sighed. "I'm sorry for snapping at you. It's just hard to believe. After this maybe I can force Moab Replacement to let me find a family for Daisy. She's a good child. Many families would take her, and if not, there's always Big Bee."

"Big Bee takes everyone today. Did you know Bio-Soft modeled their latest nursery program on Big Bee's Baby Day Plan?"

"No, but I'm not surprised. Bio-Soft doesn't want biots running amok."

Wiggles fingered his cap. "Speaking of biots running amok brings me back to the Black Dwarf. George found two canisters of poison gas, and he threw those canisters in the swimming pool. He gave his caster to Daisy, and she called us. If it wasn't for Daisy and George, you all would be dead. They saved your life along with everyone else."

"Can you tell George I want to see him? I'll want to recognize him for this and see he gets a raise."

"No, Mrs. Chapel. He caught a whiff of the gas." He let her absorb the news. "I'm sorry. He passed away here in the hospital not an hour ago. You're going to have to honor George posthumously."

The principal's eyes widened again, and her jaw dropped. Tears welled in her eyes, and ran down her cheeks. She started to say something, and then she shook her head. Chapel closed her eyes, and rubbed her temples.

"Thank you for your help, Principal Chapel." Wiggles took

her hand. "Your husband is here. We'll get a nurse to find him for you."

The principal nodded and mumbled. He heard her weeping softly as he left the bay.

~~~~~

He collected Gumshoe and the amateur sleuths from the break room.

"Will you help me interview the witnesses?" asked Wiggles.

"Yes," said Jack. "Anyway, it's better to do something than wait."

"We'd better get some rest while we still have a few minutes," Gumshoe yawned. "It's going to be a long night."

"How can we sleep knowing there's a child killer on the loose?" Shotgun asked.

"You get used to it," said Gumshoe. "Life goes on. I'm in no hurry though. The missus has taken a room in Iron Mountain already. Without her, there's nothing to go home to."

"I feel the same way," added Jack. "With Jazz missing it's just too depressing."

"No kidding," Shotgun said. "Without Goldie my better half is gone."

"Did they go to Iron Mountain?" asked Gumshoe.

"Yes," said Jack. "We sent them ahead with the Clay Players. With my shows cancelled, Jazz is working for Nodlon Memorial's mobile hospital. Goldie volunteered too. With the risk of an attack by Mars, there's no reason for anyone to stay here."

"Take my advice," said Gumshoe, "and don't postpone your weddings."

"Thanks for the advice," said Shotgun.

Doctor Norman interrupted them. "We'll be ready to start in about an hour. We have no code for 'stunning' patients. Don't use that word when you speak to the press, the patients, any relatives, or the public. Better yet, just don't use that word at all. For the record, we will call this procedure a general electro-neural stimulation."

"It's genius," said Shotgun. Everyone looked at him, "Just making up an acronym folks."

"Thanks, Shotgun," said Gumshoe. "But if we value our pensions, I think we'd all rather keep this to ourselves."

"If you and your team want to rest before we get started," said Norman, "you can use my office. I'll send an orderly when we need you."

"Thank you doc," said Wiggles. "We'll take you up on that offer. A short nap is better than none."

All too soon an orderly appeared.

Wiggles led the way. He deputized Jack and Shotgun, and then joined Norman.

Slowly, as the Constable stunned one victim after another, the investigators took statements from the bewildered teachers and students.

The First Born

In the third hour, only a few night owls reveled in the last open tavern. Distant laughter came from the tavern as the ever optimistic celebrated the coming of tomorrow.

Artificial twilight covered the marina. Half the berths were empty. No light came from the cloud lamps. Chinese lamps lit the fisherman's wharf on the other side of the harbor. Dimmed streetlights lit the Strand.

A lone longshoreman with wide shoulders and greasy overalls paced up and down the boardwalk. Fighting insomnia and a sense of unease, he walked up and down the piers. When his dreams haunted him, and he became philosophical, he left his room at the Union Hall, and wandered the Strand. Usually, he stayed on the boardwalk, but tonight he crossed the foot bridge to the fisherman's wharf and back again. Time and again, he repeated the circuit as the night wore on. He had done so for many nights and for many years.

Hoffer had worked here all of his life. When he felt down he always consoled himself by crossing over to fisherman's wharf and cleaning out a pot at the crawfish boils. Love had eluded him, and he had never paid off his contract.

Though he knew now he had no other hope in this life, yet he believed there was more to life than the part he had lived. He had decided it was not a bad life. He wanted to dream again. He wanted to fall in love. He wanted so much, but his time had passed. *No going back!*

"Don't feel sorry for yourself," he said to himself. "If you feel sorry now, you'll be sorry when the time comes to do it all again."

Occasionally, fish disturbed the water. "Hoffer, you've enjoyed good times and you've seen the sights." he whispered to the fish. Often he dreamed of fishing and writing a book.

At the end of each pier, he stopped and contemplated the waters of the port. A feeling of foreboding grew. He tried to escape it, but his anxiety mounted. Gentle ripples shook the reflections on the placid surface.

A tingle ran up his spine, and he caught a shadow out of the corner of his eye. Spinning slowly he stared at the shadows between the pools of light. *Nothing!* Listening, he heard the revelers in the nearest tavern raise their glasses in another toast. They celebrated the night as others passed away. Time crushed dreams, and the waters swept away their hopes.

Again, a shadow flitted out of the corner of his eye, and he tried to catch the elusive figure. Looking at the cargo, nothing moved. Goosebumps ran up and down his arms.

Flexing his muscles, he felt no fear of the living, but what of the dead? *No fist stops a ghost.*

The old salts told tales of ghosts in the night. One favorite was the mariner who called to yachtsman along the Great River. He offered to work his passage, and then disappeared before they reached Stevedore Point. Another tale told of the maid who had died at the hands of a faithless suitor. She haunted the old road that ran along the river below Outfall. *Hogwash! Don't scare yourself with old wives' tales, Hoffer!*

Then, the water rippled, and he twisted. A gentle wake lapped the pier's posts. He backed away from the pier's end. His eye's searched in vain for the boat that caused the wake. Another wake lapped at the posts under the pier. He walked back to the boardwalk, and stared into the dark water beyond the boat ramp. He watched the wake turn. He looked over the lake and saw no launch, no catamaran, and no yacht.

"Aye Hoffer," he said, trying to calm his nerves. "There's a sight ya' ain't never seen. Don't ya' worry none about Noddie. She ain't never ate no one in the port, and she ain't never done in a man doin' his job neither."

"Go on back to the Hall, Hoffer." Curiosity tugged at him, but he picked up his pace. Reaching the boardwalk, he started jogging back to his room. "It's no good Hoffer. You've got to see." He slowed to a halt. "If it's Noddie, you just have to take that chance." He argued with himself. "Yeah and what if it's a gator living in the sewer all these years. Maybe she's come up the river looking for an easy meal?" He swayed back and forth. He started to walk back.

"Hoffer where's your common sense. Doggone it." He started to walk away. "You're gonna go and leave a beauty of a mystery when she's gone and offered you a shot." He stopped, and turned around. "Yeah what if she goes and carries you off to a watery grave?" He shook his head. "Aw, Hoffer you can't go now."

Choosing his fate, he ran to the end of the boardwalk. On the pier, he watched the ripples in the water. The water was quiet, placid and dark in the shadows of the harbor's cranes. Only a few streetlights illuminated the pier, and he struggled to see where the pier ended and the water began.

Edging back to the boardwalk, he looked down the pier onto the boat ramp. The ramp sank into the water and vanished in the dark shadows where light of the lamps could not go. At the boundary between the land and the lake, the water of the port looked as it always had on his midnight strolls. *Is that a pale patch?* The water was as smooth as glass. The pale patch was out of place, but it was real.

"Nay Hoffer, don't ya' go down there. It's a bit of trash, and if it ain't then it's a gator. And if it ain't a gator it's a ghost." From the top of the boat ramp, it looked like a buoy dropped overboard by a negligent yachtsman. Spellbound by curiosity, he circled the pier where the police had collected the dwarf girls and faced the boat ramp.

He looked away and blinked. Then he checked the water, and saw the patch. "It's a buoy Hoffer. It's gotta be." Keeping his eye on the water, he walked down the ramp. As he approached the patch, a fear grew in his mind. Chills ran up and down his spine and his flesh pimpled.

A shadow flitted by, and he started. "Hoffer, you nervous Nellie, it's just a ghost ship." A wake rippled across the port in the opposite direction this time. "Nothing to worry your wee brain about."

Turning back to the object of his curiosity, he stared at the buoy trying to discern what was in the water. Only yards separated him from the buoy. *If it's a buoy!* The streetlights cast the shadow of the pier over the ramp. In the dark of night there was too little light to see. The ripples lapped the ramp, and the buoy bobbed in the water. The hair on the nape of his neck tingled, and he reminded himself again of his purpose.

"You're no fair weather fairy Hoffer." He cheered himself on. "You'd break up a bar fight with any twelve molemen."

Ashamed of himself for fearing the dark, he straightened his back and strode towards the patch. He was angry for feeling ashamed.

"Yeah," he argued, "but you've no more power against a spirit better than a babe in a cradle."

He summoned his courage. "Nay Hoffer, ain't no spirit in that water. If it ain't a buoy, it's just a bit o' trash some human folk threw into the storm sewer."

His boot slipped on a patch of moss and flew out from under him. He slid towards the water. Momentum sent his other boot out after the first, and he landed on his rear. He slammed into the ramp and pain shot up his back. He slapped the moss and saved his head from cracking open on the concrete. He clawed at the ramp, but the moss slipped through his fingers. He kicked at the moss and struggled to stop.

He slipped into the water. He imagined a gator making lunch of him and scrambled and flapped about in the water. He kicked the buoy and it bounced in the water. It floated away and twirled around. It twisted, and he saw two long skinny balloons attached to the buoy. *It's an overturned cooler with a handle bar.* He told himself that, but he did not believe it.

The mysterious object drifted away from the ramp. If he failed to act the buoy or whatever it was would drift out of reach.

"You'll have to find a launch Hoffer, or go swimming for

it. Just what ya' wanna do in the dark with a gator lookin' for a fat moleman for breakfast."

Cringing, he plunged into the water.

Cold water poured into his boots and soaked his overalls. If he slipped now, he would swim for sure. He shoved his fist into the water and grabbed the nearest balloon.

For a longshoreman of his years, the object was no heavier than a ball of cotton candy. He pulled the balloon, and the buoy came out of the water.

It was no buoy. Even in the dim twilight, the streetlights dispelled wishful thinking. His heart raced, and the blood pounded in his ears. He wanted to shut his eyes, but he had to look. Fear melted with the certainty of knowing.

His fist held a small arm connected to a pale green boy. The boy's head rolled, and he stared into the boy's face. Black eye sockets and a gaping mouth stared back at him.

"Argh," he yelled. "Oh no! Not this Hoffer! Not again!"

Trembling, he held the boy by one hand at arm's length. The boy wore only his underpants, and his hair was short and matted down.

Carefully, he drew his burden from the water. His animal brain screamed to let go. He overruled his horror, and commanded his fist to tighten the grip.

"Hoffer will not let ya' go laddie, not today."

Hardened by long years on the dock, he held the boy in a grip of iron. His lungs complained and his back ached. He choked and gulped.

"No dignity in life, none in death. Boy, Hoffer will give ya' your dignity. You should'a been someone's baby but I bet ya' had no one. For a little while ya' got ol' Hoffer to take care of ya'." Cautious, he sidled up the slippery slope. With each step, he carved the slime out of the ridges with his heels. He made sure the heel of his boot caught the small lip of the traction ridges ground in the ramp.

He reached the top of the ramp, and laid the boy on the

dock. He put his hands on his chest. "You're getting' too old for this Hoffer." He tried to close the boy's eyes, but the lids were tight.

"They'll not cremate ya' without a eulogy if I can help it."

He knelt beside the boy. "Hoffer, ya' should've read more poetry. You've got no words fit for the death of a child."

On the boy's forehead was a hole where his chip should have been. His skin dangled from his brow. Hoffer looked away and shuddered. He sucked in a deep breath.

"Old Hoffer is not a man of words, but I'll see ya' through."

He cleared his throat and summoned his best diction.

"In times of old our fathers sacrificed their sons for riches now corroded and forgotten. Today, our babies perish for the crimes of their makers. You lived for nothin' more than whatever life they gave you. And now that's gone too. Remember man thou art mortal. And there will be justice in the next world, and there will be justice for the forgotten man.

"I've no idea who you were, or what world you lived in, but if your world was half the size of mine it must have been a grand place indeed. They made their plans to use you, boy, and the only thing they forgot was you. Fear not, wherever your spirit is. There's no place for you to go, except it's a good place. You'll not be forgotten boy, so set your sails for the seas of paradise and the shores of the Elysian Fields."

Stifling a tear, he pulled his handkerchief from his back pocket and blew his nose. Then, he stuffed the hanky back in his pocket. "I'll make sure they take proper care of your remains…"

He caught a shadow out of the corner of his eye. He looked up, and the shadow flitted away. A wake broke the water with no sign of a boat or a gator. Ripples ran across the water, and lapped the posts under the piers. Waves rolled up the ramp and broke on the cave moss.

As he watched, the wake tacked. It turned around the end of the pier and headed for the ramp.

"Ghost ship!"

The wake broke over the ramp, and he saw a pale object floating on the crest. This time he knew it was no buoy. The breaker crashed, and the wave washed a child onto the moss.

Overcoming fear he ran to the edge of the ramp and gave the ghost a piece of his mind. "Come out and take your medicine you coward!" He shouted at the water.

A wave slapped the body, and the child rolled over. The child's arm flopped with a squishy sound. Searing anger welled up inside him, and he shook his fist at the ghost, and yelled again, "Show yourself, ya' baby killer! What are you doin'?"

A knot of inebriated sailors stumbled from the tavern. A pair of salts dragged along a third. One said something he could not hear. Turning away he heard a reply, "Yeah, it's a mad sot yelling. Four sheets to the wind, he is." The drunken sailors laughed.

He hung his head, and felt sick. He wanted to throw up.

Cursing, he wrung his fist at the water, and shouted again, "Are you afraid of little old Hoffer? Face me like a man."

The dark waters shook, and another wake turned around the pier. Fear quelled his anger. He stepped back and shivered. The wake came towards him. The waves broke over the child and washed up the ramp.

Dumbstruck, he wished he had thought before shouting at the water. *Should've held your tongue Hoffer!*

The wake grew, and became a waterfall. Water rained down on the body of the child and ran back into the lake.

Spines shot from the wave, and the head of a dragon stared at him. Red fire burned in her dragon's eyes. Water dripped from her fangs.

"Noddie," he gasped, backing away.

The dragon growled, and the rumble shook the dock. Her whiskers twitched, and her eyes narrowed. Her ears bent in his direction and her spines clicked.

Standing his ground, he stifled his fear. "Are ya' killin'

these kids? If you're the one, ya' gotta stop!" He yelled at the beast.

The dragon growled again, and smoke wafted from her nostrils. The noise echoed around the port. She glared at him with her angry, red eyes.

A thought stunned him. His idea was as improbable as the idea of a mythical monster murdering children.

"Noddie? What are you telling ol' Hoffer?" He sucked in a breath. "Are ya' bringin' the babes in for Hoffer, right? Is that what you're doin'?"

Mollified, the dragon's snarl faded. Slowly, the dragon withdrew and she slid back into the water.

"Sorry, Noddie, I get it." He waved, and let out a whoosh. He put his hands on his knees and sucked in more air.

The dragon snorted a puff of steam, and slipped into the lake with a plop. The water swirled into a tiny whirlpool and she disappeared.

The longshoreman gritted his teeth, and carefully sidled down the ramp.

Snatching up the child's arm, he lifted the boy from the water as he had the first. He was smaller, and Hoffer ground his teeth as he made his way back to the top of the ramp.

Gently, he laid the new boy beside the first. Like the other, there were no marks on him save for the hole in his forehead.

Tears welled in his eyes and he pursed his lips in a tense grimace. Blood pounded in his head, and he rubbed his temples. Looking down at the boys, he recalled a love long unrequited, and of dreams of children unfulfilled.

Love stabbed his heart. He wished he had had a boy. He imagined building models, playing ball in the park, and fishing for swordfish in the gulf. Squeezing his eyes shut, he tried to stop the tears.

"Yeah, none of us will ever see that on this side. Fear not babe. Go into the light, and you'll find the fishin's good on the other side."

Waves slapped the pier again, and he cursed. *Dagnabbit!* The wave rounded the pier, and the tell-tale pale patch appeared in the trough. *When will it end!* As before the wave broke, and it tossed another child upon the ramp.

Rage flooded him and wracked his muscles. Tears ran down his face, and he curled his fists and ground his teeth. For him the pale blue light of the night turned red. He bent over and tried to control his feelings.

He dug into his overalls and pulled out his caster. He flipped it open, and pressed the emergency call button.

"State the nature of your emergency," said the dispatcher.

He recalled a prophecy.

"A dragon fell from heaven, and he's here to collect his harvest. Hoffer's gonna need your help to care for our dead."

"Sir, I don't speak in riddles."

None Dare Call It Conspiracy

Heavy metal wracked the quiet of the ward and jarred his nerves. Guitar riffs ripped the air in the lobby of the psych ward, and he fumbled with the folds searching for the right pocket.

"Shut that off," snapped Hatchet. She worked at her desk completing her reports.

"For the love of Mother Earth," Gumshoe groaned. "Can't you silence that thing?"

"I picked a tune that gets your attention."

From her station, the nurse shot him a glare full of icicles.

Shotgun rolled his head and popped his neck. Gumshoe muttered something about the failure of elves to learn common courtesy.

He pulled the caster from his cloak and the sound of the rhythmic accident escalated.

"Jack," he croaked.

"Wiggles here, is Gumshoe with you? He's not answering his caster."

"Yeah, I'll let you talk to him." Handing his caster to Gumshoe, he said, "Wiggles wants you."

"Oh, this can't be good," said Gumshoe, taking the caster. "What's up Wig?"

"Where have you been old man?"

"Taking a nap in the psycho ward. There's only so many we can do at a time apparently. Sorry, I missed your call. My caster's on silent."

"Sorry, I interrupted your break old man. I know you haven't gotten any beauty sleep, but I need you to find Doctor Norman and cover for me. I tried calling her, but her butler said she's still at the hospital. She's about to get busy again."

"Mother Earth!" Gumshoe rubbed his temples. "Norman is here somewhere."

"I'll get her," said Jack, "I saw her just a minute ago." He found the doctor, and they returned to the nurse's station and huddled around his caster.

"Wiggles, we're all here," said Jack.

The moleman still wore the same disheveled uniform in which he had left the hospital.

"Spit it out, Wig," said Gumshoe. "We'll all hear it."

"Brace your selves," said Wiggles. "It isn't pretty. I'm down at the Strand. Remember the philosophical longshoreman who told you about some myths and prophecies?"

"Yeah," said Gumshoe. "The crackpot seemed like a good enough chap, but he didn't need any drink to help him chase albatrosses."

"Right, his name's Hoffer." The portly detective grimaced. "He found the missing Beslan boys."

Jack felt a pit in his stomach, and Norman gasped. He glanced at Hatchet and Shotgun. The veteran nurse looked ready to spit bullets, and his butler looked sick.

"Don't say it Wiggles," groaned Gumshoe. "Don't tell me it's the same modus operandi."

"Afraid so old man," said Wiggles. "The techs are just setting up now, but I've looked at the bodies myself. Your Black Dwarf ripped out their chips. I can't tell, but I'd bet a paycheck they have no blood."

"How many?" Gumshoe asked. "Have you found all of them?" He combed his thin hair with a hand.

"All thirteen," the moleman drooped. "He found them all on the boat ramp."

"Thirteen autopsies," interrupted Norman, "Mother Earth! Do you expect us to handle them all?"

"Right doc," said Wiggles. "I'm sending all of the boys to Moab Charity."

"And you'll want us to follow homicide protocol for the autopsies?

"Yes doc. And we need them done A-sap."

Norman shook her head. She turned away. "Hatchet, get on your blower and let Forest know." She pulled her caster. "I'll get pathology out of bed."

Gumshoe stuck his nose up to Jack's caster. "Were the boys dumped on the ramp?"

"No old man," said Wiggles. "They were dumped elsewhere. But that isn't the craziest thing about it."

"What?"

"Wait for it," said Wiggles. "You're not going to believe it."

"We're all ears," said Gumshoe.

"He saw Noddie. She pushed the bodies up to the ramp. He thinks she found the bodies in the sewers and brought them up to the river. He said she knew he would say a few words for them."

Reaching up to his forehead, Gumshoe felt for his fedora and grabbed a few locks of his hair instead. Lacking a hat to throw, he pulled on his bangs. "Do you believe that cockamamie story?"

"You've met Hoffer and you know this case," said Wiggles. "What do you think?"

Gumshoe stretched and groaned. "I believe he thinks he saw Noddie. He wouldn't make this stuff up. But how do we know he's not hallucinating?"

"He's not tweaking if that's what you mean. I've already asked him to take a truth scan and a drug screen. But I know the answer. He's cleaner and more honest than I am."

"How are you holding up Wiggles?" asked Norman. "I take it you didn't get any sleep."

"Oh, I got home, and I tried to crash on the couch. Just got my shoes off when the caster rang."

"Are you holding up, though?" asked the doctor. "I can prescribe something if you need it."

"Thanks doc, but I'll hold up." The portly constable lifted his cap and rubbed his hair. Carefully, he placed his cap back on his head.

"You look terrible," said Jack. "Let the doctor give you something."

"Spare me, Jack, I'm a grown-up. It's just that times like these make me wish for the good old days. In the old days, I'd have to call these boys next of kin, and console their mothers. Now, I have to fill out a breach of contract report. Before it's over, I'll have to explain how these boys died to a small army of pencil pushers. It doesn't sit well with me."

"Gotcha, Constable," said Jack. "Biots are people too."

"I'll see you later at the autopsies. Got to go now," The Constable broke the connection.

"Wait here and I'll send an orderly when we're ready," said Norman. The doctor rubbed her neck. "This is a nightmare, and I need one of you to wake me up."

"Sorry, doctor," said Jack, "I'm afraid you're already awake."

Norman smiled, "Thanks, Mr. Clay."

Shotgun rolled his eyes and put his face in his hands.

The Inspector worked on his tablet. Jack supposed he was updating his endless paperwork.

"Gumshoe," asked Jack, "why do I feel like I failed those kids? Do you always feel like this?"

"There's nothing you could have done, Jack. We still have no idea where the Black Dwarf is hiding. Until we find him, there's not much we can do." Gumshoe stretched. "I need coffee."

"I'll get it," said Shotgun, "Anyone else?" A chorus of assent rose from the little group of investigators.

"All we can do is hope we find a clue" said Gumshoe. "We could tap New Gem's com channels, but Ferrell probably has the place staked out. If the beast could be tracked on security cameras, we'd have found something by now. But this guy has magic or some really advanced technology."

"Advanced technology or magic?" Jack frowned. "I could stop him if I really understood magic."

"What makes you think you can stop him, Jack?"

"Just a hunch, I can feel it. Maybe it's a clue I'm

overlooking. Daisy's story of the invisible dwarf is hard to explain."

"Get some rest, Jack. Maybe it'll come to you."

No dignity in life, no dignity in death. The faces of the dead spun in Jack's head. The girl in Blueberry Lake, the girl in the sewer, and the girls in the port haunted him. He closed his eyes and tried to shut off the memories.

Now thirteen mole boys were dead. *They're just orphans. They'll be cremated and forgotten. No one loved them in life, and no one will miss them.*

That's not true, Jack Clay! He remembered Princess Virginia. She reminded him of his promise. *'You care! I know you do! I read Clay-net too!' she said.* He felt the ring on his finger. The princess was right. *Biots are people too!* Anger boiled in him, and he rubbed his arms.

Clutching his face, he forced the angry thoughts from his mind. *Peace! Rest! You're no good to anyone if you can't think straight!*

~~~~~

"Inspector Lestrayed?" an orderly asked.

Gumshoe rose to his feet. "That's me, son."

"Doctor Norman told me to take you to the morgue," said the orderly. "She's gotten our pathologist out of bed. He's prepping right now."

"Come along, gentlemen," said the Inspector.

Shotgun picked up his satchel. "For once, I'm glad I'm not a doctor."

The orderly led them through the hospital's labyrinth of corridors. "You can watch the autopsies from the pathology lab's observation room."

"Are all police officers ghouls?" asked Shotgun.

"No," said Gumshoe, "but a sense of macabre humor helps."

They passed the coroner's office and entered the pathology lab. They turned into an auditorium. Leather seats faced a wall vid. The orderly stopped at a small podium in the middle of the front row of seats and tapped the tablet. The vid lit up and displayed an autopsy room. A mole boy lay on a table, and a sheet covered him.

"I don't think I can handle this," said Shotgun.

"Wait outside Shotgun," said Gumshoe. "Normally we don't watch these. I've only seen one once, and that was during a forensic science class. We're desperate though."

"Shotgun," said Jack, "go get some more shut-eye. I'll join you if we don't learn anything new from the first autopsy." Shotgun started towards the exit when the door opened.

Wiggles walked in and stopped Shotgun.

"Gentlemen, we've got a problem," Wiggles tapped the controls on the podium. The chilling image of the boy lying on the autopsy table dissolved. "Willoughby called me. Agatha Miner is making an announcement about the Beslan children."

The Proconsul of Moab appeared on the vid. She spoke in a professional monotone. "And the victims of this horrendous act were taken to Moab Charity where through the diligence and courageous action of the staff and physicians, the survivors have been restored."

Agatha's bangs glittered in the spotlights. On her forehead was an emerald spot.

Was the Proconsul chipped? Thinking hard, Jack tried to recall.

"Unfortunately, we have received grave news," Agatha continued. "Only a few hours ago, thirteen orphans kidnapped from Beslan were found dead in the port of Moab." She paused.

"Just yesterday, these boys were in school with their friends awaiting transportation to evacuate Moab. They were innocent school boys who were no threat to anyone." Agatha paused dramatically and sucked in a deep breath.

"Before now, the police were unable to stop these crimes.

But now, the victims have identified the perpetrator of this heinous crime. Now we know the name of the perpetrator and his accomplice." Agatha waved at the crowd melodramatically.

Startled, Gumshoe popped out of his chair. "Freeze that Wig."

Wiggles froze the transmission, "What old man?"

"None of us have spoken to the Proconsul, have we?" Gumshoe looked around the room. Jack shook his head, and Shotgun shrugged.

"You haven't spoken to anyone?" Gumshoe asked.

"Only Willoughby," said Wiggles, "I told him all the victims said it was the Black Dwarf."

"Let's hear what she has to say," said Jack, "maybe she's just describing the three dwarves."

Wiggles tapped the controls, and the broadcast resumed.

"Molemen, Nodlons, and Terrans, hear me," said Agatha. "The perpetrator of this horrific crime is a Martian agent. He is a magician who walked into the Beslan School under the auspices of his good name. The fiend travels with a black dwarf who serves him and aids him in his nefarious plans."

"What is she talking about?" blurted Jack. "None of the witnesses heard the Black Dwarf say his name. No one knows his name, and he has two sidekicks."

"There," said the Proconsul, "this agent of Mars kidnapped thirteen mole orphans. He attempted to poison the children with gas to destroy all of the witnesses to his crimes. The heroic action of the school's security guard spoiled his plan." Again, she paused.

A commotion stirred the reporters. They asked questions, and muttered to each other.

The Proconsul waved and silenced the reporters. "This villain, this blackguard, this devil, this miscreant is an unrepentant scoundrel who traveled to Mars where he was friendly with their people. He will never turn himself in, and he will never confess to his crimes. The criminal is none other than

Cretaceous Clay."

Jack and Shotgun exchanged glances with the homicide detectives.

"Clay's accomplice is Patrick Morgan. Morgan is a known hacker. He goes by the alias, Sidekick. I am hereby ordering all police, law enforcement officers, and citizens to arrest Cretaceous Clay and Morgan on sight. They must be considered armed and dangerous. You must report him on the emergency channel if you have no weapons to defend yourself. If he offers the least resistance, kill the monster."

"Is she crazy?" Shotgun asked. "She didn't even get my nickname right!"

Stunned, Jack fell into one of the leather chairs, "What are we going to do?"

Wiggles stabbed the controls and muted the Proconsul.

Jack popped out of his chair, and faced Wiggles. "Constable, we were with Gumshoe all day! We couldn't possibly have kidnapped the boys or murdered them without cloning ourselves."

Whistling, Gumshoe shoved his fedora back, "Wiggles, this is a frame job. Did Willoughby have a clue?"

"No, I don't think so," said Wiggles, "All Willoughby told me was this would affect the case. The commissioner got the word from City Hall so he could watch, and he called Willoughby. The Captain passed it on to me. I'm sure he had no idea what it was about."

"None of the victims identified Jack or Shotgun," said Gumshoe. "No one told her Jack was responsible. None of the victims saw Jack until he was interviewing them."

"What about that pinhead from the Octagon?" Shotgun asked, "Chief Ferrell, the guy who took us off the Zodiac case."

"No," said Gumshoe. "I can't believe he'd stoop to a lie that low."

"Principal Chapel spoke to the Black Dwarf," said Wiggles. "She was certain it wasn't Jack."

"Wiggles," said Jack, "does the Proconsul have a chip?" He pointed at the vid. "She didn't have a chip two days ago, did she?"

Wiggles studied the vid screen, and his eyes widened. He tapped the controls, and he zoomed in on the image. "She's got a chip now." On the Proconsul's forehead was an emerald green chip. "That's a chip on her forehead all right." Wiggles brow furrowed. "I don't know what's going on. Mole women under contract are not eligible for office. Yet now she's got a chip."

"Ferrell can't chip the Proconsul," said Jack.

"Forced into it by duress or trickery," Gumshoe said. He paced the auditorium and put a finger to his lip. "Agatha Miner is successful, beautiful, and powerful. She would no sooner take a chip than any free citizen in Moab."

Jack paced the floor and shook his head. "What are we going to do?! Chip or no chip, she fingered Shotgun and I for murdering a bunch of children! Orphans! Who cares if they're biots?! No words fit this!" Jack threw out his hands. "It's a big lie!"

Wiggles and Gumshoe joined the elf and paced back and forth. The two detectives were momentarily lost in thought. Worried, Shotgun paced up the aisle and dodged the elf and the detectives.

"Jack has to hide," said Gumshoe. "If he's important enough to frame, he's too important to lose."

"Hiding!" said Jack, "I'm one of the most well recognized elves in Nodlon! I've been on the home page of Personality's website dozens of times, and I've made their list of the top ten most influential biots in Nodlon every year since we started playing the Circus!"

"He's right," said Wiggles. "We've got to hide him. There's no other way." Wiggles turned to Jack, "I'll put you and Shotgun into our witness protection program as soon as I can speak to Willoughby."

"Look on the bright side, boss," Shotgun pointed to Jack's

cloak. "You're dressed for the part."

"Dressed? I didn't know a flamboyant costume with a velour cloak and suede boots makes a good disguise for a fugitive on the lam."

"Oh, I think you've got great taste. Robin Hood would shoot an apple off the Sheriff of Nottingham's head for the name of your tailor."

"What about you? If you're going as Will Scarlet, we need to get you some green spandex."

"I'm already dressed as your sidekick, and I've got a nickname to match. Besides, my hands are registered as lethal weapons on twelve outworlds." Hamming it up, Shotgun demonstrated with a judo chop.

Wiggles stopped pacing. "We don't have time to discuss fashion or martial arts." He came to a decision. "Jack, you and Shotgun are fugitives as of right now. The Proconsul is wearing a chip. She makes no sense. We can't follow procedure and take you into custody. Someone will kill you and Shotgun before we can clear you."

"How can we get out of Moab when we're wanted?" asked Jack.

"The Proconsul is compromised," said Wiggles. "I'll put out the word. We cannot trust her. We've got to get you out of here. I'll call Willoughby."

"Wiggles," Jack sighed. "You and Gumshoe aren't safe. If the Black Dwarf can chip the Proconsul, you two may be our next accomplices."

"We're old detectives," said Gumshoe. "We've got friends in low places."

"Come on, Gumshoe," Wiggles squeezed Jack's elbow, "let's give these boys a police escort." The Constable led Jack through the exit, and down the hall. Shotgun allowed Gumshoe to take his arm, and they fell in behind Wiggles and Jack.

The nurses and orderlies stared at them as they passed. Jack felt everyone's eyes on him. He wondered how they could be fooled so easily.

Wiggles flipped open his caster, and set it to audio. After a short ditty played, Jack heard Captain Willoughby answer.

"Shut up Wiggles. Listen carefully, I know what you're going to say and I don't want to hear it. The Proconsul has publicly offered a reward to private citizens for their help in chasing the pooch and the fox. She's ordered us to find them, and terminate them on sight. The lead dog sent a smoke signal to the chief. The trail is clear for now. The cowboys will stampede the herd in twenty minutes. Got that?"

"Got it, the sled dogs are chasing the pooch now." Wiggles closed his caster and slipped it into his jacket.

"Pooches and smoke signals? What's that mean?"

"Navajo code, in case we're under surveillance. I don't know what's going on, but we can't trust the higher ups. They've got a kill order on you, so you're not safe anywhere in Moab for now. The Captain's put out the word. We're clearing a path for you to get out of Moab."

"Oh, great," muttered Shotgun. "Now we're wanted for mass murder and the police are supposed to shoot to kill."

"Looks like it, son," said Gumshoe. "They've gotten to the Proconsul. We all saw the chip. Don't blame Jack. There's no way any of us could have foreseen this move."

Going around a corner, they nearly bowled into a harried Norman. The doctor's hair flew in all directions.

"Oh, there you are Wiggles," said Norman. "You can't arrest Jack and Shotgun! The Proconsul's lost her mind! She's ordered the police to kill them."

"I'm not at liberty to discuss it doctor," said Wiggles. He winked.

"Do you have a tic Constable?"

"Out of my way, doctor," said Wiggles. He winked again, and Norman blinked. "I'm taking a dangerous suspect into custody for his own protection."

"Oh," she said. The doctor shielded her face from the

security camera. "Good luck," she whispered.

"Thanks doctor," whispered Jack, "call Chesterton for us. We need public support."

~~~~~

The Andromeda sat where he had left it. Jack had never felt so grateful to see his flyer.

"If this doesn't work out, we're going to be out our pensions," muttered Wiggles.

"At this point, I don't think it matters, Wig. If we don't save Nodlon and Moab from whoever chipped the Proconsul, I don't think there will be any pensions to save."

"You're probably right, old man."

"What about us?" asked Shotgun. "What will we do?"

"We'll get you out of it," said Gumshoe. "There's an answer. There always is."

"The way is clear for the next few minutes," said Wiggles. "Get out of Moab. Head for the mines. There's no way anyone can find you there. Call me in about two hours. If you can't raise me, call Gumshoe. By then, we can get you into our witness protection program. Not even the Proconsul will know where you are."

"What are you going to do?" asked Jack.

"Don't know," grumbled Wiggles. "It's a coup. The Proconsul's not in her right mind. She isn't the kind to assassinate a person for mere suspicion. I'll just have to find out who I can trust. Good luck to you boys."

"Good luck Jack," said Gumshoe.

Jack looked back at the detective. "Luck to you too, old-timer." The flyer beeped as he fingered the remote. The Andromeda's hatches opened. "Good luck to you, Wiggles," he said. "I've got a feeling we're all going to need it."

Jack and Shotgun climbed into the Andromeda and buckled their harnesses.

"Please get us out of this," said Shotgun. "I want to see my girls again."

"We're on it," said Wiggles.

"Don't you boys worry about a thing," said Gumshoe. He stepped aside and threw back his trench coat.

Jack fired up the Andromeda and the hatches closed. He disabled the autopilot, switched the navigation system off, and cut off the inboard caster. He waved at the detectives. He set the levitators on ground effect, and sped towards the exit.

Escape From Moab

"Good thing, we're in an unmarked vehicle." Shotgun pointed to Jack's logo on the Andromeda's hood.

"What?!" Jack mocked the dwarf with twinkle in his eye. "A luxury flyer with my corporate logo on all sides isn't inconspicuous enough for you?"

He steered the Andromeda out of the parking garage, and put her in flight mode. The Andromeda rose over the traffic. No one on the ground stared or pointed. Perhaps the word had not yet reached everyone.

"No, we need a racing flyer covered with the Major Manna logo and decked out with bling lights. Really, we might be better off stealing a moving van."

"If they weren't all taken by evacuees, I might agree with you. As it happens, families need all the moving vans to flee Nodlon." He waved at the crowd of molemen on the street below. Women and children scurried to and fro helping their husbands and fathers loading their family's belongings. "We're not actually criminals though we stand accused. So we can't go stealing vans when others need them."

"Yeah, boss, we can just be chivalrous and get killed."

"I wouldn't be so concerned," said Jack. "But I don't understand how the Black Dwarf chipped the Proconsul!"

"However he did it," said Shotgun. "It's done. She can't violate the chip's programming. I can pretty much do what I want because Biot Staffing has my chip set to nothing more than monitoring and tracking. How safe are we if the Black Dwarf controls our leaders?"

"Speaking of it, can they use your chip to find us?"

"Yeah, they can track me if we're within the reception distance of a telecom station. But who cares? They can track us with our casters. For that matter, if they wise up, they can track the Andromeda. The flyer is registered to you. Putting her in manual simply takes us off the optimization board. Flight control can still track us."

"Thanks for the technical analysis. How long do we have before they're on to us?"

"If Wiggles and Willoughby can give us a diversion, we might have time get out of range. Who knows? Until someone wakes up and tries to track us manually, we're safe enough. If they don't check, they can't find us."

"What if they check?"

"In that case, they'll know. Our casters are on the board even when they're off. They'll call Biot Staffing, and the agency will finger me."

"Maybe we can get some help. Put a denial on Claynet. Say the Proconsul is mistaken. She's been duped by Martian sympathizers, but don't call her a liar. The bad guy can never complain, even if it's the truth."

"I'm on it," Shotgun pulled his laptop out of his backpack. "Boss!" A police van blocked the street. "Road block!"

"I see it." Jack rounded the corner. He drove slowly over a convoy of moving vans pulling out of the hospital's loading docks. A police van pulled in front of them.

"There's another one! Are all the streets blocked?" Jack turned again. Suppressing his worry, he turned again in search of a clear direction. Studying the traffic, he wondered if he could find a way to run one of the road blocks. Slowing, he checked the next street leading away from the hospital.

"No road block." Jack pushed the flyer down the street two stories over the road.

"It's an ambush. They left this one free. They'll shoot us when we try to escape."

"Optimist," quipped Jack. He gunned the flyer through an intersection.

"Moab police! They're on both sides!" The Moab Surete cruisers lit their emergency lights and their sirens. "They're following us."

"Thanks Shotgun. I've got that one figured out. They're in

front of us too."

"Oh boy, what will we do?"

"Stop and hope they don't shoot us." Slowing down, he set the flyer in the only clear spot on the street. He powered down the Andromeda, and set it to standby to keep the manna generator warm. Opening the doors, Jack unbuckled his harness and climbed out of the flyer. Shotgun followed suit.

They walked to the front of the flyer and put up their hands. Moab police cruisers, interceptors, vans, and riot police wagons surrounded the flyer.

Moab policemen leapt from the vans, but they showed no signs of enthusiasm. Leisurely, the officers began setting up a perimeter. An athletic moleman approached them.

"Lieutenant Wobbly at your service," said the commander. "I'm your sled dog. Please keep your hands up for the cameras while I commandeer a building here." He checked his tablet and made a decision.

Wobbly led them to a tired office not far away. Two officers fell in behind. "Guard the door until I call for you." The officers saluted and stood guard on the front.

The entrance opened for Wobbly and his detainees, and they walked into a wide hall. Offices faced the long hall. A directory listed accountants and an advertising firm. Their footfalls echoed down the corridor.

"Willoughby put out the word. Someone chipped the Proconsul."

"It's a coup," said Jack. "What are you going to do?"

"Don't know. I've been a cop for eleven years and I've never seen anything like this. The Surete is in disarray. The Proconsul declared martial law just minutes ago. Commissioner Warden ordered us to handle only priority calls. We're to assist evacuees and maintain order, but we're to shoot looters and rioters on sight. Regardless, the Proconsul's orders are unlawful. She has no authority with a chip in her head."

"Thank you lieutenant," said Jack. "Accusing innocent

citizens of kidnapping children and attempting mass murder without proof is certainly unlawful. Putting out a bounty on heads and threatening our lives is beyond the pale. I've met Agatha before. She would never agree to such a thing."

"Agreed, someone forced her to take the chip."

"The Black Dwarf kidnapped those children from Beslan," Jack complained. "Wiggles and Gumshoe know it. We were with them at Moab Charity when the Black Dwarf murdered those boys. We don't know where he's hiding, but we have to find him before more people get hurt."

"I gathered the situation was along those lines," said Wobbly. "Moab's situation is dire when our chief elected official cannot tell friend from foe."

"What next, Lieutenant? Wiggles suggested we lay low, but I'm not keen to be a fugitive from the law."

"For now Mr. Clay, you need to make for the mines. I'm sorry I can't give you any better advice, but we're going to need a few hours to determine what to do."

"Wobbly," said Jack. "The children and staff mesmerized by the Black Dwarf at Beslan recovered after they were stunned. Maybe the Proconsul's mind will return once she's been stunned. Set all your weapons to stun. Don't forget that."

"Can't believe I'm hearing this, but that's good to know. I won't forget it. We live in strange times."

"We do indeed Wobbly. Now, how do we get out of here?"

The lieutenant flicked his tablet, and showed it to Jack. "Here's the floor plan for this building. This office connects to the next one and you can exit there. That will allow us to create a diversion. I assume you can handle it from there?"

"Thanks," said Jack studying the floor plan. "I think we can handle it."

"How much time do you need?" Wobbly closed his tablet.

"Seconds, if you're not shooting at us."

"We'll let you have fifteen minutes at least." Wobbly winked and gave Jack a thumb up. "Go," he said. He left them and barked a few orders. Molemen began running and shouting.

Jack and Shotgun jogged down the hall.

Jack opened the rear door and peeked out. There was a flight of stairs. No one was about. He held the door for Shotgun, "Carpe diem." Jack filled the hall behind them with an illusion of smoke and plunged down the steps.

At the bottom, they reversed their direction and doubled back.

Again, Jack cast a smoke screen to delay pursuit. They ran up a short flight of stairs and burst into a hall identical to the one they had just left. A moleman in a business suit glanced at them nervously, and stepped into a lift.

Calmly, Jack strode through a set of double doors. Below them was the street. Traffic crawled. Police vehicles jammed all but one lane. A pair of officers directed traffic. Other officers waved furiously at the onlookers and tried to maintain order.

Mole women and children watched the excitement from their windows. A crowd loitered around the scene. They milled about the police tape. Young and old alike strained to see.

The Andromeda was hardly visible. But she glittered in the warm yellow light of Moab. A crowd swirled on the street, and drab police vans surrounded the sporty flyer.

"She looks ready to go," said Jack. "There's no boots on her levitators."

"Any ideas, boss?"

"Yeah, we need the right moment."

Wobbly appeared on the landing of the office next to them. He whispered to one of the guards, and they reacted immediately. They whistled and shouted.

True to the Lieutenant's word, troops flowed up the stairs into the office. Officers ran to and fro generating a scene of chaos. More officers ran into the alley to cut off the fugitives' escape route.

Two officers gave them a friendly wave as they passed by. They darted into an alley not twenty feet from where the fugitives stood.

He glanced at Shotgun. "Good to have friends in high places."

"Jack Clay has left the building," Shotgun muttered.

A consummate performer, Jack watched for the right moment to distract the crowd. When all the officers had left the vicinity except those directing traffic, Jack stepped forward. He cast a fog spell over the street. Fog filled the air. As the crowd lost sight of the police officers, nervous cries erupted.

Someone shouted, "Run for your lives." The street broke into pandemonium.

"Now," Jack gently squeezed Shotgun's arm. Down the steps they ran. They dodged molemen and passed vehicles in the fog.

He tripped on the curb, and a truck broke his fall. Inside the truck, a dog barked.

"Where is she?" Shotgun cried.

"Around here somewhere," Jack shot back. "She is white you know." He reached into his pocket and searched for his remote.

In the distance, officers shouted all around them, "Get him!" and "There he is!" Molemen ran to and fro, and many boots slapped the pavement, but he saw no one in his magical fog.

A frightened baby started crying. *It'll be all right, kid.* Jack forgot his own panic *It will or my name isn't Jack Clay.*

"Boss, where are you?"

"Over here, Shotgun." He found his remote and pressed the lock button. The flyer beeped behind him, and he realized he had passed it.

Molemen and women shouted and cried. Fear and tension pressed him.

"It's behind us, Shotgun." He pressed the button again. The flyer beeped. "Go for the beeps."

"Found it, boss! Hurry up!"

They hopped in. Jack switched to instruments, and his head's up display flashed. A schematic of everything casting a radar reflection appeared on his windshield.

Seeing nothing in their way, Jack fired up his flyer and lifted off into the thick fog. Thinking only of a diversion, he cast an illusion. Bright flashes startled passersby. Thunder cracked over the street, and the crowd dispersed.

"Hope no one gets hurt," Jack said.

"Can't be any worse than when your shows sell out."

Shotgun's quip reassured him. He suppressed his fear of hitting a bird or a sign, and shoved the flyer's joystick forward. Manna saturated the levitators, and the flyer gunned down the street.

"Warning, restricted zone!" Andromeda's console lit up and a pretty young elf wagged a finger at him from the dash. "Use ground effect in residential tunnels. If you need assistance, say 'Auto-pilot' and I will assume control…"

Shotgun stabbed the override and shut her off. "Thank God, you're rich. Hate to try getting away in a Cloud Nine."

"Money still has some privileges."

Still fearing an abrupt end to their escape, he steered the flyer out of his fog. He checked his rearview mirror. There was no pursuit.

"We won't have long. We're breaking every traffic law in Moab."

Watching the artificial clouds on the tunnel ceiling flash by, Shotgun gripped the scream bars and his knuckles whitened. "One good thing about flying, if anything goes wrong we may be killed outright. No long, lingering death."

"Yes that would spare us the trouble of saving Nodlon."

"Not bad for a day's work. Now you've reduced us from celebrities to notorious public enemies on the lam."

"Chin up, Shotgun. I suppose I should have foreseen this. No good deed goes unpunished."

"Maybe I can turn you in for the reward or time off for …"

Jack twisted the joystick, and the flyer rolled. They dove into another tunnel. He pulled on the stick and threw them against their harnesses.

"Where did you get your license?" Shotgun gripped his scream bar.

"There's always a silver lining even if we don't see it at the moment."

"I hope the girls are all right."

"Me too, Shotgun, me too."

The ceiling lights whipped by. He wove a path through the tunnel to avoid signs and cables.

"Where are we going?" Shotgun's grip slipped.

"Down," said Jack. "There's nowhere left. Remember the hole we found in the sewer? It's the only thing we've found out of place. It has to be an answer to a mystery." He dipped under a laundry line. The line twirled, and clothes flew into the air.

"Sure boss, but which mystery?"

They floated in their seats as they lunged passed an advertising banner.

"I don't know which mystery, but I'll take any answers right now." He grinned. "I need to cross something off my list to satisfy my latent neuroses."

"I've got all the mystery I need. We're looking for a Black Dwarf who murders dwarf girls. What more can you want? What if we find Noddie?"

"Sticking to your bright side, Shotgun," Jack chuckled. "We'll be famous for finding Noddie. I can see it now. They'll welcome home the great adventurers who discovered the lake monster of deepest Nodlon. They'll call our show *Mysterious Nodlon*. They'll air it every Friday night during the creature feature hour."

He rolled the flyer to avoid a high load. The hard roll threw them against their harnesses again.

"We can get Dick Mackey to narrate," said Jack. He lowered his voice and imitated the famous narrator. "'Go with us as we plunge fearlessly into the mysteries of Nodlon. Explore long forgotten ancient sites in search of ghosts, mysteries, and crypto-zoological creatures. Tonight, we present the discovery of Noddie.'"

"I beg to differ, my short-sighted supervisor. How will we make a vid if a ravenous sea-going reptile eats us? Noddie's holed up in Nodlon's underbelly for who knows how long? Who knows when she last ate? Maybe she's starving. Explaining mysteries has no appeal when you're the meal! Hey that rhymes!"

"Not to fear, my poet laureate. If Noddie tries eating us, I'll stun her with a brilliant display of magic, illusion, and thespian performance never before seen in the sewers of Nodlon!" He slid the flyer under a level-way, and turned up Southlake Boulevard.

"Never seen again you mean."

He dived under a grocery sign. "No one's in pursuit."

"An apt assessment, my humble knave," Jack slid the flyer off the boulevard and onto Harbor road. "Let's try going through the port, it's only a block."

"At this speed, we'll never dodge a boat mast!"

He checked his instrument panel. All alarms were silenced. "Our radar will give us a heads up." Thumbing the controls, he flipped the collision warning on. He flew over the Strand, over the Marina gate, and over the port of Moab.

The flyer roared into the port, and whipped up a whirlwind around the dome. The wind blew towels off the startled bathers on the south shore. The wind tossed drinks off tables and sent tourists running for cover. He pulled up to miss the boat masts, and rolled the flyer to miss the cranes. He dove into the Great River's tunnel and vanished upstream. Boats rocked as sails fluttered in his wake.

"Call our sewer buddy," he said.

Shotgun fumbled briefly with his caster, and the device hummed and buzzed. "Let me guess, you want to know how to get into the sewers?"

"Wow, you read my mind."

"Easy enough, you're so predictable."

"Ah, but I'm smart enough to hire you!"

A black dwarf woman appeared on the caster's little vid screen. "Hello, may I help you?" A baby fussed in the background.

"Is Niles there?"

"May I say whose calling?"

"Shotgun, and tell him it's urgent please."

"Oh, yes sir. He told me all about you. He was so excited." In the background, they heard the baby crying. "Oh, I'm sorry, I'll go get him." A door opened and closed, and they heard a call. "Honey, the cast is for you. It's Shotgun and Mr. Clay."

The screen brightened and the sanitation engineer beamed at them.

"Hi Shotgun, you and your boss are all over the news."

"Don't believe a word of it, Niles," said Shotgun. "We have an iron clad alibi. We think our chief suspect is controlling the Proconsul mind. She's been chipped. Don't believe anything she says."

"Don't worry my brother from another mother, I don't believe lies." Niles tapped the black chip on his forehead, "Everyone knows someone chipped the Proconsul. It's all over Mercury News. Chesterton said she's got no authority. He called her allegations poppycock.

"Chesterton said high level officials in Moab and Nodlon Yard know you two were helping the police at the time of the crimes

"Princess Virginia said she supports you, and promised her father will look into it. I haven't been to Clay-net yet, but I bet Mr. Clay's popularity has never been higher."

"Thanks Niles. That's great news."

"How can I help?"

"We're flying up the prime tunnel. We're looking for a way to reach the sewer terminus where you found the girl."

"Easy," Niles said. "Where're you at now?"

"We just passed Turtle Creek, the next waterfront is Riverwalk."

"Good, stay in the prime tunnel. It's easy. Follow the cloud lamps. Tributaries have ordinary overhead street lamps and look like a level-way with water. The river will fork a number of times. Simply veer left each time the prime tunnel forks. Just follow it to the end."

Flying over a white yacht at speed, they startled an elderly couple sailing down the river. Jack hugged the ceiling and rolled the flyer.

"The Great River is the city's water supply, and the sewer is the drain." Niles narrated their journey, as though giving a lesson to school children. "The two connect only at the headwaters of each tributary. Blueberry Lake feeds the southernmost tributary. Go up to the end and you will see boat locks and an aeration chute. Flyers can't go up the locks. Fly up the chute.

"At the top is the Snow Water plant. Go over the plant with the lake on your right. You're looking for a ventilation shaft just beyond the sediment traps. Just fly down it. The hole is at the bottom of the shaft. Be careful not to fly through the waterfall, it's been disinfected but it's not drinkable," Niles paused. "Anything else I can do for you?"

"Niles, do you know anything about the hole?"

"Yes, Mr. Clay. Officially, the hole is an Oversized Structural Breach of Unknown Cause, but we call them Noddie holes. Wall one up, and another one appears. There's always several open at any one time."

"Has anyone tried exploring them?"

"Oh sure, lots of times," Niles grinned, pleased to help. "They always end at a ventilation shaft. The shafts run straight down for miles all the way to the mines."

"If the holes always run to the ventilation shafts, why hasn't anyone seen anything?"

"No mystery there. Since Good Queen Henrietta gave Moab its independence, Moab controls the mines. They mine gold, copper, iron, and manna down there, and they don't want anyone stealing ore. No one explores the mines without authorization. Prospecting teams go in, but it's hush, hush. Only tightlipped geologists allowed. If you're not a rock hound, you can forget it."

"But there are tales," said Shotgun. "Some of those rock hounds must talk."

"Claim jumpers, you mean. Unauthorized prospectors explore the abandoned mines and poach ore. I know a few of them. They hang out at the wharf when they're not in the Blues District. They go down there to poach ore. Some come back with strange tales. Some don't come back at all."

"Any theories on what causes the holes, Niles?"

"Oh yeah," Niles chuckled. "Anyone who asks will be told water seeps cause the holes. Hydraulic pressure builds up and the walls burst outward."

"Sounds plausible, Niles, doesn't that explain the hole mystery? Pun not intended."

"No way," Niles blew off the suggestion. "Miners sank the ventilation shafts away from the aquifer. Where the shafts run through groundwater, it's shunted to the river. The holes always run from a mine shaft to the sewer. The holes never pass through the aquifer."

"What then causes the holes?"

"Noddie. Don't forget, when a tunnel fails, groundwater and mud floods the tunnel, and the Earth behind the hole collapses. Tunnel failures are rare, and they hit all levels. It's a disaster, and people die. Any engineer responsible for a tunnel collapse will wind up on the street crew collecting garbage.

"Noddie holes are clean, neat almost; and they're always in places where people won't get hurt – at least not by accident. No sanitation worker has ever been hurt near a hole, in a hole, or inspecting a hole. Nobody loses his job. No engineer pays for a hole, no matter how many times we patch it. Think about it."

A waterfall appeared at the end of the tunnel. "Thanks, Niles," said Shotgun. "I think we're here."

"Good luck." Niles signed off.

Noddie

The aeration chute and the boat locks matched Nile's description. Water cascaded down a wide series of terraces before falling into a pool large enough to allow two yachts to pass.

A fish ladder separated the waterfall from two boat locks. An engraving above the unnatural headwaters memorialized a forgotten dignitary. Hawks fished the ladder.

Designed for form and function, the locks unmistakably resembled a pair of lifts. As if to demonstrate, a lock slid open as the flyer entered the chamber.

A small schooner sailed into the pool. It's mast and yardarms were lashed down. An elderly yachtsman manned the helm.

Jack jerked the joystick, and the Andromeda heeled. Levitators hummed and the manna core surged as he swerved to avoid a collision. The weekend mariner ducked.

Thank you for stowing your mast old timer.

Blue sky appeared above the lip of the waterfall. He pushed the flyer up the chute. The manna generator purred. The levitators twisted the bonds of space. The overpowered playboy toy flew up the chute and over the waterfall.

The flyer shot out of the chute. Their shadow flitted across the lake.

Nodlon's elite bathed on the lakeshore in the pleasant spring weather. Interrupted from their work, hired sailors looked up. Bathers grabbed their towels and children shrieked and pointed.

The levitators kicked up a mist. The geyser blew over the lake and sprayed a hawk. Water sparkled in the mid-afternoon sun. The sun cast rainbows onto the locks.

He wheeled over Blueberry Lake and glimpsed a magnificent view of the Balmhorn.

"There's the shaft, boss."

"Yep, let's go."

He rolled the flyer and the levitators roared. And they dove into the shaft.

Momentarily blinded, he slowed to a hover. He let his vision adjust. Then, he gently released the stick, and they dropped slowly into the darkness.

They hung from their harnesses. Sensing the failing light, the headlamps flooded the shaft and the beams disappeared into the void. His heads-up display dimmed. Faint graphics depicted a rectangular point of perspective. Nodlon's original builders spared no limit on their imagination of her public spaces. But the vent reminded Jack of his parking garage without the comfort of pavement to set the flyer in ground mode.

Their ears popped.

A concrete floor appeared in his headlamps. He leveled off the flyer. The beams flashed off a little pond at the bottom of the terminus, spread across the wall, and filled the cavern with light. He swiveled the flyer and splashed his headlights over the brick mound and into the Noddie hole.

Jack studied his instruments. "It's a tight squeeze."

"Can't stay here boss, and we can't go down the mine shaft without Andromeda."

"Desperation is the mother of simplifying choices," said Jack. He guided the flyer over the mound of bricks, and eased her into the mouth of the hole. He hoped nothing would scratch the flyer. The cave rose for several yards and then dipped into the dark. He drove the flyer up the hole.

"Danger!" cried the flyer, "Collision imminent!" Shotgun jabbed the flyer's mute button.

As the cave dipped, Jack overcorrected and scraped the floor. "That'll cost."

Over the rise, the cave widened, and the floor smoothed out.

"Niles wasn't kidding," said Shotgun. "This is no accidental cave."

For a hundred yards the cave ran nearly straight. It fell gently towards the root of the mountain. He let the flyer slide down the cave in ground effect, and avoided scratching the flyer. They passed a fork, and the slope dipped. The cave wove a twist and a turn, and they passed a few intersections.

"Not as straight as I thought. If we run into Noddie, I'm not sure how to get out of this place."

"Don't look at me, boss, I'll just be screaming."

The cave ended in an inky black shaft. They had not expected light in Noddie's cave, but never before had they seen a man-made shaft missing the blue light of Nodlon. Even in the sewers, Nodlon's blue lights cast a reassuring glow, but the darkness in the shaft was unexpected.

Sliding to the edge of the precipice, the beams illuminated a chimney of impressive proportions. Forty yards from where they sat, the beams barely reflected off the rock. Above and below them, the glow of the headlamps vanished.

"It's darker here than in the sewer's ventilation shaft," said Shotgun. "I've never seen anything this black. There's no light at all."

"Yeah, I don't think this is an ordinary vent shaft." He lifted the flyer into the air, and they soared into empty space.

The instrument flight graphics broke into a puzzling scatter.

"What the heck?" He fiddled with the controls. "Everything's gone haywire."

Shotgun tapped on the menu and checked the settings. "Technically, it's working. There must be a field interfering with the radar."

"We'll have to fly by sight then." Jack twisted the stick and tipped the flyer.

They stared into the shaft. Scattered points of lights danced across his windshield. "Shotgun, I don't think this is a ventilation shaft."

"Yeah, I think you're right."

He adjusted his display and tried to clear the static.

"Nothing, it's no use." He dimmed the display and brightened his exterior lights.

The beams reflected the dust in the gloom. The eerie swirls reminded Jack of deep ocean water. He pointed their nose into the chimney, and dropped into the pit.

An uncomfortable pang of fear ran down his back. *Steady Jack, you're a magical elf.* He checked the tension of his harness for reassurance. The flyer fell slowly, and the engine purred.

"Is there anything you can do with the radar?" he asked.

Shotgun fiddled with the controls, and slapped the dash, "Nothing but static boss."

The flyer dropped into the shaft. A hush fell over the mage and his dwarf.

"Deeper than I expected, boss, how far down can this go?"

"How far have we dropped?" Jack tapped the altimeter, "I'm reading zero, and we have no radar."

Shotgun fidgeted with the weather panel. "Using pressure, I'm guessing we're over a mile below Nodlon."

"There has to be a bottom somewhere. The ancients mined the roots of the mountains. We're not going straight down. The shaft is deviating. Maybe we will level off."

The beams bounced off a dull grey object.

"Something down there."

"Yes, I see it," Jack switched the heads-up display back on. Pixels raced over his windshield and blinded him. He flipped the device off. "No depth perception, I can't tell how far it is."

Shotgun muttered something he did not hear clearly, but he was sure he shared the thought.

The reflection flickered. "Did you see that? There! What was it?" Shotgun flinched, and gripped the scream bars. He shoved the floorboards and rocked the flyer. The latches on his harness jingled.

"Shotgun!" Jack popped the stick, and the flyer jerked to a stop.

"I saw something!"

Sweat beaded on his forehead. His pulse raced, and it warned him not to panic. He checked his instruments. Nothing seemed amiss other than the radar and the navigation displays.

"Peace, Shotgun, peace! It's just a trick of the light. There's nothing down there. We're pouring enough light down this shaft to illuminate the moon. If anything was down there, we'd see it."

"I'm not worried about anything. I'm worried about Noddie! She's a sixty foot long, flying sea-monster!"

"Yeah, but we don't know if Noddie is dangerous. She probably eats fish."

"Great! Newsflash, boss! You can play a crypto-zoology expert on late-night audio feeds! But I know you're not a biologist. For all you know, Noddie eats dwarves!"

"True, Shotgun," Jack chuckled, "but Noddie might eat magicians too! All I know is what I've read. Until there's more information we can't lose our heads."

Shotgun clinched the scream bars. He breathed deeply a few times and released his grip. "Sorry boss, I think I've got it now."

"No problem," he said. *Stay with me Shotgun! If you panic, I'm right behind you!*

Holding the joystick carefully, he released his death grip. He flexed his fingers until he felt blood flow. Then he wiped his palms on his breeches.

"No worries Shotgun." He affected a bright mood. *Just between me, myself, and I, an emotional outburst is just what we needed. The rush woke me up. No more sleepy head. Let the tension go.* He missed his morning coffee, and Shotgun's raspberry tarts.

He pushed the joystick and descended into the shaft. The reflection grew in his headlights. First without form, the reflection took on shape as they approached. Across the shaft's throat lay a concrete bowl tipped half over. The bowl resembled an overturned punch bowl with a melon in place of a base. Ribs ran from the melon to the shaft walls. Rubble littered over the bowl spoke of long, deferred maintenance.

"See Shotgun, it was only moving shadows. The headlights reflected off this structure and the shadows moved." Jack studied the structure. He tried to make sense of the shape without success. "Any ideas what it is?"

"No," Shotgun relaxed and let go of the scream bars. "I've never seen anything like it."

Jack spun the flyer, and panned his lights over the bowl and the chimney. Between each rib was a tunnel. Clouds of dust swirled in the tunnels forming wavy patterns. He had an uneasy fear.

"Why is there so much dust?"

"It's a draft? What else? Air must move around down here as the weather changes."

"Yeah maybe," scoffed Shotgun. "Maybe Noddie stirred up the dust."

Jack shivered. He aimed the flyer towards the main shaft, "We've got no radar, and I don't want to scratch my baby in the smaller tunnels."

They sailed over the bowl's ribs, tipped over the lip of the bowl, and dipped into the gloom. The shaft fell eastward at a steep angle. The shaft was nearly the same diameter as the chimney. The shallower angle was a relief. Jack pushed on the floorboard and relieved some of the tension on his harness.

"This way, Shotgun, let's stick to the main tunnel."

Any floor at all helped him focus on his speed and direction. Light reflected off the rock, and he edged the nose towards the shaft.

"Don't want to get lost down here either boss. We've got no mapping without the system."

"We'll have to make do."

They resumed their descent, and flew for a few hundred yards. The sharp angle of the wall curved, and became a steep floor. Stalactites hung from the ceiling and walls. Crystals with hard edges and sharp corners decorated the tunnels walls. The steep floor was covered with rounded stones.

"Look boss, there's no stalagmites on the floor."

"Erosion, it's just water from the occasional rain over the mountain."

"Down here, boss?" Shotgun shook his head, and squeezed the scream bars.

Hanging from his harness reminded him of parasailing. He tugged his harness. On a trip to the Bermuda Triangle he had parasailed with Korman. His director was thrilled, but he failed to see the point. Korman had reminded him that most people cannot fly. *Keep our home fires burning buddy and stay safe.*

The tunnel was still steep, but not quite as much. He doubted he could land. Only a few rounded stones protruded randomly from the floor. No ledges, ridges, nor escarpments offered a purchase to aid a climber or to slow his descent. Once in motion, anyone falling down the shaft would slide until he reached the bottom, if there was one.

Farther down, the shaft broadened into a cavern with three forks. The forks dropped into the darkness and turned away in shallow curves. Light reflected from hard rock and glittered off the crystals. The headlight beams faded into the murky dark.

"Which way, Shotgun? Want to flip a coin?"

"Perhaps we can cast lots?"

"Yeah, or I can make a command decision." He pushed the joystick gently towards the central shaft. "Let's try the middle route. If it worked for Goldilocks, maybe it'll work for us." They crept into the intersection, over the ribs, and into the central shaft. He nosed the flyer into the shaft's maw.

The headlamps caught a red swirl around the shaft.

"Noddie!" yelped Shotgun.

He jerked on the joystick. Automatically, the rear lights flashed, illuminating a rock face on the rearview monitor. Moving fast, the flyer rammed the rock. The abrupt halt jolted them. They sank into their seats, and then bounced off the overstuffed leather. The impact crushed the back end and doused the rear lights. The rearview monitor blinked and went black.

The flyer bounced forward. He gripped the joystick with both hands and tried to steady the flyer. The levitators responded to his command, and whirred. The engine growled, and the flyer stopped.

An eerie quiet saturated the cockpit. Only the purr of the generator broke the silence.

The dragon filled the shaft. Her underbelly blocked their way, and her tail disappeared down the shaft and vanished into the dark. Orange ridges on her underbelly filled the flyer's windshield. The dragon filled every window. Red scales tipped with gold covered her in an armor of knives. Dorsal spines rippled along her serpentine form.

She stared at them, and they stared back.

Jack relaxed. "On the bright side, Shotgun, we've found Noddie."

"No late-night audio shows for you," said Shotgun, "if she eats us tonight!"

Perhaps Noddie understood and took offense. She snapped up the flyer, and her forepaw flashed. Red armor covered the top. The golden tips sparkled in the flyer's high beams.

The beast's claw spanned the flyer. The sole pressed the moon roof. Foot long nails slaked the windows. Scales scratched the metal.

Pressing hard, her nails pierced the windshield. Glass cracked into starbursts. The claw pierced the hood and tore the sheet metal. Only the flyer's instrument panel lit the cockpit. The dragon flexed her claw and glass burst. Bits of aviation glass showered them.

The beast threw the flyer. Suddenly weightless, Jack's stomach leapt. "Hang on, Shotgun!"

"What do you think I'm doing?"

Air blew through the shattered windows. The rollercoaster ride lasted an eternity.

Jack grabbed his scream bar.

The Andromeda slammed into the shaft floor, and they came to a gut wrenching stop.

The engine died. Glass rattled on metal. Plastic moldings shattered. The moon roof burst and showered them with more glass. The shock threw them against the harnesses. His harness bit him.

Lights went out, and darkness blinded them once again.

Sheet metal snapped. The dragon's hook popped the hood. She scratched the flyer's side, and then the dragon lifted her weight off the flyer. The roll bar groaned in metallic relief. The claw withdrew into the dark.

The flyer's shattered body slipped on the steep floor. Air blew through the windshield frame and threw glass and dirt into their faces.

They slid down the shaft into the dark. *We'll fall into the abyss!*

The dragon's scales scraped the walls.

Recovering, he cast a telekinetic anchor to stop their descent. He poured all his effort into stopping their slide. The machine hit a ledge and rolled. They were catapulted against the ceiling, bounced off and hit the floor. *The Andromeda slid faster. I can't stop it, we've got to get out.*

A slithering sound filled the tunnel. Stones rolled down the shaft. Pebbles clattered against the flyer. Sand slid past the flyer and more stones smacked each other. A claw slammed the flyer into the floor, and the flyer jerked. They stopped.

The dragon scrambled up the shaft. Her scales scraped the shaft, and she slithered away.

Stunned, Jack braced for a strike. He breathed, and tried to think. He cast a shield around the flyer.

A jet of fire shot over the flyer. The blast illuminated the shaft, and was gone.

Noddie shouted, "Beware the dragon!" The throaty shout rumbled down the shaft and echoed off the walls. "Go away!" The hoarse roar made him cringe.

The dragon scrambled up the shaft, and falling rock added to the racket.

The shaft was quiet. Miles below Nodlon, he sat in darkness in his dead flyer. *She's totaled! She'll never fly again!* He waited, not daring to move for fear of falling. *Discretion is the better part of valor old man.*

He restored his perspective. They were alive, and he was still magical. *If I have to, I can levitate us out of the mines.* The thought reassured him. *Good!*

"Shotgun," he whispered. Blind in the dark, he touched his face. He could not see his fingers. "Shotgun?" Resisting panic, he felt for his friend. Slumped over, Shotgun dangled from his harness. *Can I risk a bit of light?*

He shook the little dwarf gently. Again, he shook a little harder. "Shotgun, wake up, buddy," *Wake up, buddy! Wake up, dagnabbit!* "No dying on the job!"

Risking a light, he cast a blue ball of cool flame. The ball of magically created light was the basis of all his illusions. It was one of his simplest and oldest tricks. He put the ball over the dashboard and attended to his dwarf. *Where is the first aid kit? Did I ask you to pack it?*

He clutched the dwarf's harness. He hoped the clasps held. If Shotgun fell, the jolt might plunge the Andromeda into the abyss and take them with it.

He felt a breath. He looked up, and sighed in relief. Softly he patted the dwarf's cheeks. Shotgun moaned, and slumped farther over. Jack struggled awkwardly trying to hold him upright. To get a better purchase, he levitated the dwarf.

He released the latches on his harness. He steadied himself with a foot pressed against the flyer's floor. With both hands free, he adjusted the dwarf's position. He levitated the dwarf to relieve the pressure on his lungs. "Breathe friend, breathe!"

The dwarf's spirit returned, "Did she eat us?"

"No," Jack whispered. He hoped the dragon was not waiting in ambush. "No, we're still in the shaft."

"Where is she?"

"Up the shaft."

"She threw us down the hole then?"

"She caught us." Jack paused. He thought about the encounter. "My anchor wasn't strong enough. We slid forward. We could've slid into the abyss. Noddie saved us. She stopped us here."

"Saved us for later? Maybe she didn't want to chase her dinner to the bottom of the shaft."

"She hasn't eaten us yet. She threw a bolt of flame over us and warned us to go away. If she wanted us for dinner, she could have roasted us alive."

"She spoke?"

"Yeah, she said, 'Beware the dragon.' Maybe she thinks we're trespassing.'"

"Everything happens to you doesn't it?"

"What?"

Shotgun rolled his eyes, "Boss, you found Noddie, and she spoke to you! Don't you get it?"

"She's synthetic and intelligent," Jack thought about it. "I guess that should be surprising, but I was too busy trying to think of ways to stay alive."

"Oh brother, most of us would just count ourselves lucky to see Noddie. You talk to her and just blow it off."

"Give me a break, dude, we weren't exactly having tea and crumpets."

"And I thought I was the comic relief."

"Don't worry, Shotgun, you have to deliver a straight line once in a while. Can't have a laugh without a foil."

"What'll we do now?"

"Would you like to go back and interview a crypto-zoological monster? It'll be fantastic for our creature feature show, and I'll definitely make all the late-night audio shows."

"Boss, be serious, we're fugitives on the lam. An angry dragon suffering from PMS destroyed the Andromeda. We're stranded so far below Nodlon I wouldn't be surprised if Beelzebub popped out of the next hole. And you're cutting up the crowd. Look I'm not laughing."

"Look on the bright side of life, Shotgun! We've met Noddie and survived! It can't get any worse. If we run into a ghost, we'll just tell him we've had a bad day, and he can go haunt someone else."

"Have you lost your mind? Are you seeing Moonbats? How are we gonna get outta here?"

"Levitate, Shotgun. I can still fly. Of course, if you'd rather wait here, I can send Gumshoe back for you with a rescue team."

"Are you loony, boss? If something happens to you, I don't even have a torch."

"Good point, my intrepid companion. Let's look, I think I've got a torch in the boot. And you might put the first aid kit in your satchel."

"All right," he said, looking in the dashboard compartments. "Found it."

"Cheer up, Shotgun, we'll make it."

"Sorry boss."

"No problem, let's try getting the Andromeda running. She's in bad shape. If we can start her, we can fly her. And you won't have to worry about bats in my belfry."

He brushed pebbles of glass off his cloak. He was thankful the rounded glass had no sharp edges or he would have suffered a thousand cuts on the slivers. Dusting the dash and the instrument panel he cleared aside more glass. Finding the ignition panel, he picked glass out of the cracks of its keypad.

Without expecting anything, he pressed the start button. Nothing happened. Thinking, he tried to remember the passcode. *Jasmine's birthday!* He punched in the seven digit birthday code number. Again, nothing happened.

Glancing over his shoulder, Shotgun deadpanned. "It's a long walk from here."

"Maybe if we start the engine, we can get power to the

levitators. I just need the joystick to control the flyer."

"Yeah, boss."

He flipped the manual switch on his hatch door first, and it hissed and gurgled. The hatch jiggled and fell back into place.

"Guess, we'll just have to climb out." He grasped the roll bar and pulled. Balancing carefully on the seat, he climbed through the moon roof. Glass in the gasket seals fell on his seat and the floorboard.

Astride the broken moon roof, he cast another blue ball to illuminate the shaft. The tunnel ran down hill into the dark. The shaft was too steep to stand on comfortably. His heart ached seeing the broken flyer. He sighed. *Mom always said, 'Never love anything that cannot love you back.'*

He jumped into the air and levitated to the shaft floor. He slid on the sand and levitated to avoid falling. Righting himself on the slippery slope, he faced uphill and climbed. "Shotgun, be careful, the slope is slippery."

The dwarf gazed up the tunnel. Caution overcame his usual spunky nature, and he climbed carefully out of the flyer. "See any sign of the dragon?" He danced on a sandy patch, and waved his arms to steady himself.

"No," Jack glanced up the shaft. He would not be caught unaware twice in one evening.

Wobbling shakily on the sand, he assessed the damage. All of his lights were shattered. Hitting the wall had almost totaled the flight controls. The vertical stabilizer was intact and the rudder was in good condition. The starboard flaps dangled from wires, and the portside flaps were cracked. The ground effect lift was shoved neatly under the bumper. The engine hood was buckled.

Shotgun scrambled up the slope. Crawling in the sand, he examined the levitators. "Can I get some light?"

"What?" Jack cast a blue ball, "Can't you see in the dark, Shotgun?"

"Can't see much even with the light. Starboard levitators

appear to be intact." He struggled to climb up the slope, and Jack helped him with a little levitation.

"Oh, don't worry," Jack replied. "We can fly out of here on magic."

"Yeah, two miles straight up past Noddie." Not waiting for an answer, Shotgun staggered to the portside. He sat on the floor and slid down to look at the portside levitators. "Don't give me any baloney, boss. You can't levitate us two miles straight up."

"Puncture my bubble, why don't you?"

"This isn't the Circus, Jack Clay. You're not superman. I've seen you sweating after a show." Unsteadily Shotgun got to his feet and tried to climb back. He slipped on the sand, and dropped a couple of feet.

Jack levitated the dwarf. "Steady on, Shotgun."

"Think Noddie has insurance?" Shotgun twisted side to side and stretched his back.

"Ha, afraid you're out of luck there."

"Will she fly?"

"She's a wreck, but we need only its levitators to fly. The flight controls simply gave it a sporty look and a touch of maneuverability in the air."

"Do you think the levitators will work?"

"If we can get her to start, maybe, let's see if we can get the hood off."

"Bet the starboard hood won't give." The hood was folded into an origami omelet.

"We'll try the portside," Shotgun released the hood's latches and tugged hard. The hood's hydraulic lifts gurgled. "It won't budge."

"Stand back, I'll magic it off."

Shotgun climbed upslope several feet, and Jack rolled up his sleeves.

The magician struck a dramatic pose. He waved his arms melodramatically and hammed up his performance.

"Boss, no one's watching except me." Shotgun crossed his

arms, "and Noddie and the ghosts.

"Oh, ye of little humor," said Jack.

He cast a telekinetic burst and pried the hood off. The buckle popped. The pressure blew the hood off the flyer and launched it across the shaft. The hood twirled end over end and it sailed in an arc. The little hunk of metal flipped over, and briefly floated above them. The hood struck a wall and rolled. It bounced off a rock and hit the flyer.

"Whoa!"

"Oh, no!"

The flyer shuddered, and then slipped. It slid through Jack's blue ball, and down the shaft. An avalanche of sand and stones fell after the flyer.

Shotgun momentarily forgot the futility of a dwarf trying to stop the flyer. He flung himself after the flyer.

"Boss!" Shotgun leapt into the air. The dwarf flailed at the flyer, and caught only air. He sailed over the dropping floor before gravity reasserted itself. The dwarf slapped the floor in a belly flop.

"Shotgun!" Too late to stop Shotgun's headlong flight, Jack levitated the dwarf. He reeled the dwarf in before he slid off after the flyer. "Careful, Shotgun, you can't catch a two ton machine!"

"What now?!"

"I'll catch her!"

He cast a light ray down the tunnel.

An avalanche of rocks and stones chased the flyer. A cloud of dust rose from its wake. The flyer plunged into the dust, and disappeared. The rumble echoed up the shaft.

Catch it! He cast a telekinetic tether. The tether caught the flyer. He felt magic drain out of him, but the machine hardly slowed down.

Desperate, he poured every thought into slowing the flyer. *Heavier objects take more effort! Concentrate! Conserve energy!* He renewed the spell.

The force snagged him, and he jerked forward. He cast a shield to protect himself, and he flopped on the floor. He shot headlong down the shaft. He passed Shotgun, and flew into the dust cloud.

Let go! The flyer dragged him face first through the sand. *No! Hang onto her!*

On his magical cushion, he bounced on the rounded stones. *It's like snowboarding on the Balmhorn!* Dust blew into his face, and he ate dirt. He tumbled. *Snowboarding towards a bottomless pit!*

He strained to slow the flyer. His energy drained, and the flyer accelerated into the abyss. Sweat stung his eyes.

Seeing a rock ahead, he kicked it. The jolt twisted him around, and he slid feet first.

If the shaft levels off, I might save her. He shoved his feet into the dirt, kicking up still more sand and a dust cloud. *You're too tired!* His heels plowed furrows in the floor. *If she drops into a pit, I'll fall too!* He redoubled his effort.

Dust billowed in front of him. Sand blasted his face. The cloud blotted out his view, and he shut his eyes.

He hit a rock and somersaulted head over heels. He belly flopped into the sand and his chest collapsed. The blow knocked the wind out of him, and his tether snapped.

The weight of the flyer was gone. He flipped over. He threw out his arms, and he landed on his back again.

He rolled to a stop.

The avalanche of dirt slowed to a halt.

Air defied him. His chest burned. He fought for a breath. His lungs screamed. All his strength turned to breathing. He sucked in air and gasped.

Darkness surrounded him. *Am I up or down!* He cast a blue ray again and the soft glow illuminated the thick dust.

All he saw was dust. He breathed slowly and tried to relieve the searing pain in his chest.

The sound of the flyer was gone. *Gone! It's gone!*

The Ninth Ring

Cool, dank, and dusty the air in the shaft tasted as sweet as a pure mountain breeze. He struggled to breath. He savored the air. His lungs still burned. His feet and hands felt clammy.

Gone! It fell!

Dirt caked his eyes, but he forced them open. The blue light of his ray danced off the settling dust. The dust floated eerily. The cloud swirled.

An avalanche of sand and stones struck him. Pebbles clattered on stones. Gravel rolled by.

"Watch out!" Shotgun somersaulted past him.

A cloud of fresh dust engulfed him. Reacting with a start, he levitated Shotgun to check the dwarf's fall.

Shotgun jerked to a halt. "Whoa!"

The magical tether dislodged him, and he slid after the dwarf. His energy spent, the magic vanished, and he dropped the dwarf.

Shotgun hit the floor. He slid a few feet on the loose sand, slapped a wall, and twisted around.

Sliding on the sand, he ran into the dwarf and they spun around. He jammed his boots in the sand and stopped.

"Ouch!"

"Sorry buddy!"

Shotgun caught his breath. "No worries, boss, it's what I do."

Hesitating, lest he resume his harrowing slide, Shotgun carefully crawled around Jack and sat next to him. "Are you all right?"

Silent, he thought about the question.

"Jack?" Shotgun asked, "are you with me?"

He nodded. He patted his chest. "Wind," he wheezed. Together, they watched the cloud settle. The dust billowed. "Better," he croaked. "Now, I feel better."

"Is the flyer gone, boss?"

"Don't know. I can't see anything. My tether broke when the air was knocked out of me." He waved at the grey cloud of dust. "After that the sound stopped. I'm hoping she's still in one piece."

"Maybe she fell into a bottomless pit." Shotgun cleared his throat.

"I haven't heard a crash."

"Maybe she's still falling."

"Shotgun!" he scoffed, "Ever optimistic!"

"One of us has to be." Shotgun poked him. "You're too introverted."

"Ha," Jack chuckled. "The pot calls the kettle black. When we get out of here, I'll hire an analyst. He can solve our neurotic tendencies."

"Right now, I'd just settle for getting out of here. And a mad dragon guards our only way out."

"I can still fly. I just need a few minutes to recharge."

"You're exhausted. Face it, boss, she's gone. We'll have to climb out of here."

"Maybe," he sucked in a deep breath and summoned up his strength. "I think I've got power again. Let's clear the air."

He cast a breeze, and blew the dust away.

The shaft reappeared as the dust settled. Out of the haze, the flyer emerged from the cloud. It appeared no worse for its journey down the shaft.

"Look at that!" Shotgun pointed.

Jack's blue ray ran the length of the shaft and ended on a cliff. The dust dropped into a pit. As the dust sank into the hole, it swallowed the glow from his magical light.

"Good grief," Jack's eyes widened. The flyer rested on the lip of the pit.

"Saved by a stroke of heaven above," Shotgun whistled.

"What no faith in your employer, Shotgun?"

"We've just gone from beloved celebrities to wanted outlaws on the lam, and you want me to have faith?" Shotgun mocked him, "At this point, I'd just as soon settle for a plea bargain. I'll claim I didn't do it, and blame you for all the crimes." He ribbed Jack.

"Thanks for the vote of confidence, friend," Jack chuckled, "I'll put your Christmas bonus in a postcard from the Moon."

"I'll take gold. I've got a feeling I'll need a solid currency after the war with Mars."

"Yeah, well, before I can exonerate you of aiding and abetting me, I have to figure out what my crimes are first."

"No problem there boss. If we're guilty of Beslan, I'm sure we're guilty of sabotaging the Marie Celeste, and the murders. They'll blame us for all of the Black Dwarf's future crimes too."

"Unfortunately, you're right, and we can't stop him." Jack put his head in his hands. "We're certainly not going to find him down here. Gumshoe and Wiggles are on their own, and the Black Dwarf can do anything he wants with impunity."

"On a positive note, boss," said the dwarf. "How are we going to get down there? Slide?"

"If we slide down and kick up an avalanche, we might send her into the pit."

"Can you levitate us?"

"Maybe," Jack stood up slowly, and balanced in the furrows gouged by his heels. He tried to levitate, and the magic failed. The shaft went dark.

"Boss?!"

He felt a pit in his stomach, and he slipped on the sand. He rolled a few yards. An avalanche of sand and gravel slewed around him. Pebbles pelted the flyer. The little stones clinked against the sheet metal. He held his breath. *Don't fall!*

"Boss," called Shotgun. "Jack! Jack! Are you there?" The dwarf's voice quivered.

"Here, I'm okay," he sighed. For the first time in years he remembered what it was like to be unable to fly.

"What happened?"

"I just ran out of magic." He took a breath. "I'm tired. I've run out before, but it's been years. Trying to save the Andromeda drained me."

"Great! What happens if you run out of magic while you're flying?"

"Same thing that happens to cows when the space aliens drop them."

"Remind me not to fly with Jack Air."

"Thanks, Shotgun," he laughed. "I need someone to keep my feet on the ground." Laughing made him feel better. He cast a blue ray, and a dim light filled the shaft.

"There you go, Shotgun. I just needed a little rest. And I think the joke helped too."

"Any time, boss, that's what I'm here for."

Dust billowed from where the avalanche had come to rest.

"So what do we do now? I don't want to be stuck here forever, and I don't want the Black Dwarf to get away."

"Magic, Shotgun, I need time to recharge, but I feel the magic coming back."

Jack cast a shelf under the flyer. He put a magical bridge across the pit to brace the shelf, and he added a wedge to keep the flyer on the shelf. He jammed the magical wedge under the flyer's nose.

"What do you think, Shotgun?"

"Great, if it holds. A moment ago, you couldn't even fly."

"Optimism, Shotgun, optimism," he grinned. "I'm feeling better now."

"I'd be more optimistic, if I knew how much energy you've got in your manna can."

"Trust me, Shotgun, I'm here to help."

"Last time I checked, boss, punch lines were my job." The dwarf grinned, "You stick to magic and leave the comic relief to me."

"Ah, but you should do more straight lines, Shotgun," Jack wagged a finger in the air. "Often, the straight lines are more important. Remember Abbott? He was the great Atlantis comedian who left his monastery and joined the musician Costello to become a comedy team like no other of their age? Abbott was a very funny comedian, but he played the straight man in their partnership."

"Here's a straight line, then, my elven superego," Shotgun put his hands on his hips. "Have you got enough magic to fly and hold the shelf?"

"Not sure," he studied the slope. "Let's take a page out of mountain climbing." He reversed his stance, and faced upslope. Shotgun was several yards above him.

"Do as I do," he said to the dwarf. He leaned into the slope, and found a hand hold. Each step triggered a tiny rush of sand and pebbles. Slowly, he made his way to the flyer on all fours. He kicked himself mentally. He should have tried this first.

Taking his cue, Shotgun climbed after him.

~~~~~

With Shotgun beside him, Jack cast a light over the engine compartment, and they examined the generator.

"Any ideas, Shotgun?"

"No not really," the dwarf reached into his satchel and pulled out his caster and a short cable. "If I can talk to her, maybe she'll tell me what's wrong." He plugged the cable into his caster.

Shotgun bent over the engine compartment and searched for a port. He spotted a likely port between the generator and the firewall. He inserted the cable. The caster blinked, and he studied the screen.

"Found her, boss," he announced with satisfaction. "I'm in the ignition system." He studied the data, "She's alive! Her battery is dead, and there are hundreds of error codes. I'm not sure if they're critical. If we give her some juice, I bet she'll start. After that, we'll have to take our chances."

"Juice?" Jack held up his hands. "Where are the jumper

cables? I'll just make some lightning." He leaned over the dwarf and peered into the engine compartment.

Shotgun pointed to the battery. "Light her up, boss."

Jack took hold of the battery cables. "Ready?"

"Careful, lightning will fry everything in the system. A hint of juice is all we need."

"Not to worry."

"Go ahead," Shotgun fingered his caster. "Give her some juice."

Sparks flared off his fingertips, and his fingers tingled. "Anything?"

"Nothing yet, give her a little more."

Jack made a little more effort, and sparks shot off the cables.

A metallic screech startled him. His concentration broke, and the generator stopped and the turbine stalled. "Sorry, she almost started."

"One more time, boss," said Shotgun. "Do that again and I can start her. Just don't fry her brains."

Jack nodded, "Ready." He repeated the spell, and sparks flew off the cables.

The turbine fired up with a roar. The generator jolted back to life, and the flyer shuddered.

"It's alive!" said Jack.

"Was there ever any doubt?" Shotgun unplugged the cables and stowed his caster. He waved a hand, "Best hacker in the business. Now, I can add hotwiring flyers to my list of skills."

"That will come in handy the next time we need to steal a flyer." Jack levitated up to the moon roof. He kept a hand on the roll bar, and climbed in. He buckled his harness, and grinned at his dwarf.

Shotgun grimaced, "Will she fly?"

"One way to find out, let's fire up the levitators and see if she'll whirl," said Jack. "Want a lift getting in?"

"No, thanks, I'll climb. I don't want you to drop me."

Shotgun climbed up the flyer and slipped through the moon roof.

The instrument panel was black. Only the glow of his ray lit the console.

Jack pressed a few switches. A few dials and indicators lit up.

"That's an improvement," Jack tapped the console. "No flight instruments." He gripped the joystick. He flicked the flyer into flight mode. "Brace yourself!"

He pressed the accelerator, and the levitators hummed. The dials stubbornly refused to move. He trusted his ears, and pulled back on the joystick. The hum rose and the flyer vibrated. The nose lifted, and the flyer took off and hovered over his shelf.

He waited for the other shoe to drop, and he enjoyed a second of peace. The dead instruments were of little use. He shut off his autopilot, and killed the warning systems.

"Now, where are we, Shotgun?"

"Back in business, boss." He held up a hand and Shotgun slapped it.

"Right you are, Shotgun. What were we doing when Noddie so rudely interrupted us?"

"Searching for the Black Dwarf!"

"Do dwarves understand rhetorical devices, or are they always black and white?"

"We're very literal."

"Thought so," said Jack. "Let's find out where this hole goes. If we find the Black Dwarf, we can end his reign of terror. If not, at least I've satisfied my curiosity."

He goosed the engine and pushed the flyer into the dark pit.

"No headlights, I'll have to make my own." He cast blue balls into the headlamps.

"If we find the Black Dwarf, he'll kill us."

"Optimist!"

"It's my blood type."

"Nonsense, dwarves are type A."

"Boss, you're such an elf."

"Guess I asked for that one." He pushed the joystick, and eased forward. In the hole, he tilted the battered flyer for a better view. The well plunged into the dark. His makeshift headlights vanished into the bottomless well.

Gently, he let the flyer descend. He flew by sight, and he listened to the flyer's hum.

Occasionally, they passed side tunnels. A cool breeze rushed through the vacant windshield. Despite the breeze and the cool temperature, sweat beaded his forehead.

"There's the bottom," said Shotgun.

Haze swirled in his magical headlights. "It's hard to see."

"It's the dust you blew into this pit, remember?"

"Yeah," Jack smiled. "Thanks for the reminder."

He hovered and slowly spun the flyer. They discovered a tunnel. Turning, they found another, and then more. They searched the openings.

A faint white ball appeared in a tunnel, and it quickly vanished.

"Stop, boss," Shotgun hissed. "I see something."

"I'll turn off our lights." He cut the magic and they were plunged into the dark. False colors flashed in his eyes. He blinked, and he looked away. He let his eyes adjust to the dark, and then he looked back. He searched the tunnel.

The white ball appeared again, and then vanished.

"Did you see that?" Shotgun asked.

"Yeah, I saw it!"

"Is it a light, boss?"

"Don't know, Shotgun, but I saw it too."

The ball appeared a third time and vanished just as quickly as before.

"Whoa," Shotgun jumped. "Is it a ghost?"

"Maybe," Jack shrugged. "Maybe it's a prospector carrying a torch."

"If it's not a ghost," said Shotgun. "I hope it's not a dragon. I have no wish to meet any of Noddie's relatives."

"This must be the way to go," Jack said. He restored his magical headlamps, and drove into the tunnel. They descended at a low angle for a hundred yards or more.

A reflection caught his eye.

"What's that, boss?"

"I'm not sure, but it's not a ghost."

Something metallic glinted in the tunnel ahead.

"Let's light it up." Jack cast a blue ray.

The ray bounced off the metallic object.

"Whatever it is," Shotgun sighed. "It's not a dragon."

"Yeah, but what is it?" He pushed the flyer forward.

"It looks like the shell of an insect."

"No insect can be that big. They can't breathe." Jack closed the distance, and a mechanical monster loomed in the haze.

"It's a mining ship."

"From the rust, I'd say it's been here awhile." Jack landed the flyer. The derelict blocked the tunnel. "Let's check it out and see if we can get around it."

Jack unbuckled his harness, and climbed out of the flyer. He looked into the bucket. It was empty.

Shotgun joined him, "It's bigger than a garbage scow."

"Much bigger, and there's no markings. She's probably a claim jumper."

"Independent or one of Guggenheim's ships?" asked Shotgun.

"Indie," said Jack. "Guggenheim would never leave her here. She's a million quid if she's a farthing."

"If she's an indie, where's her rock hound? He must have forgotten where he parked."

"Maybe he had an accident."

"Yeah, but what we need to know is if we can get around her. My side is as tight as penguin's tuxedo."

"Try my side, Shotgun. This way," he walked around the ship, and stopped at the levitators. The coils towered over him. "Wow, those are big."

Shotgun passed him and went ahead. "The passage widens out." He called back. "Can you give me some more light?"

Jack cast a light ray.

"I can see the front," said Shotgun. "Let's go." The dwarf led the way. They walked the length of the mysterious ship and examined the passage.

"No outcrops block the way," said Jack. "I can fly sideways and get through."

"If we can get her generators started, maybe we can move this rust bucket."

"Why would a prospector abandon an operating ship?" asked Jack.

"The Marie Celeste operated until the Black Dwarf blew her up."

"She wasn't abandoned," he said. "I don't know how she wound up sitting in the old Thornmocker space dock, but someone parked her there. This rust bucket's not parked. It's been here for years."

"Think it's haunted?"

"Why not?" asked Jack. "Ghosts can't hurt us, Shotgun. If she's the Flying Dutchman of claim jumpers, we've got another episode of *Mysterious Nodlon*."

"Admit it, boss. You're obsessed with late-night vid."

"What's wrong with a good ghost story? Here's the cab. I'll check it out. Maybe I can find out who this ship belongs to."

He climbed up to the driver's hatch. Rust covered his hands. He pulled, but the hatch did not budge. "It's rusty. I'll magic it off."

"No, it's not worth the effort." Shotgun stepped back.

"It's no effort."

"Great!" Shotgun backed up some more, "Like it worked so well the last time."

"Silence in the peanut gallery. The Flying Dutchman isn't going to fall into a bottomless pit."

"Nothing would surprise me now, boss."

"Here goes nothing."

Jack cast a magical push on the hatch. The handle cracked and the hatch flew open. He lost his balance, and he grabbed a rung on the ladder. The rung broke.

Startled, he flailed at the air. He levitated and grabbed the hatch handle. Swinging on the ladder, he reached out to steady himself. His sleeve caught on a piece of cloth on the driver's seat.

Dislodged, the cloth flew off the seat. He looked at what he had caught. *It's the driver's coveralls!* He tried to push the coveralls back into the cab. Loosed from the driver's seat, the coveralls rolled out of the cab.

Bones rolled down him and caught between his foot and the ladder. He tried to catch the coveralls, but bones spilled out of the sleeves and legs. The driver's hip slipped out, and shattered on the tunnel floor. The coveralls rolled over onto his chest, and the driver's skull landed on his chest. He stared. The skull stared back. *It's the driver!*

"Whoa!" he shouted. He jerked, and the rusty ladder broke loose from the cab.

The ladder swung away, and swayed side to side. The driver's legs flipped out of his coveralls. Bones bounced off the ship's fenders. Bones thudded as they hit the dirt. Rocking dislodged the driver's skull, and it rolled off. Frantic, he levitated the skull.

"Oh, boy!" yelped the dwarf. He dodged the shower of bones. The skull floated over Shotgun's head, and the dwarf jumped back a few feet.

"Sorry," Jack apologized. "I didn't want all of him to shatter."

"Oh, boy!" Shotgun put his hands on his knees and bent over. His chest heaved. "When I asked if it was haunted, I was joking."

"So was I."

Gently, Jack lowered the skull to the floor. Taking the

sleeves and legs, he hoisted the coveralls, and freed his foot from the gruesome catch. He formed a sack containing the remains of the driver's broken body. He levitated the sack, lowered it to the floor, and put the bones next to their owner's skull.

He levitated up to the cab, took hold of the hatch, and looked in. The driver's boots had toppled under the joystick. He levitated the boots, and added them to the pile of the driver's remains.

On the passenger's side, a pile of soda bottles and disposable coffee cups rose to the glove compartment and spilled onto the seat. The driver's log hung from a loop on the ship's console. He took the log and slipped it into his pocket.

He risked using a bit more magic and levitated to the floor.

Shotgun was pale. "Are we having fun yet?"

"Great fun," said Jack. "We all need more excitement in our lives."

He pulled the log out of his pocket and handed it to Shotgun. "Do you think you can make this work? The log might tell us what happened."

The dwarf fiddled with the log. "Power's dead." He stuffed the log in his satchel. "Drive's probably unreadable anyway. We need an expert who can dismantle it and scan the drive."

"We can let Nodlon Yard handle it then."

Shotgun glanced at the bones. "What will we do with the driver?"

"Consign him to the rear bucket. He doesn't need to be embalmed. For now, we'll put a few stones over his bones, and ask Mother Earth to protect him." Jack looked back at the mining ship. "We'll let Wiggles know where he is. They'll send a recovery team. I'm sure Moab will give him a decent burial. That's about all we can do"

"What happened?" Shotgun asked. "He couldn't have been lost."

"He wasn't lost," Jack shook his head. "He was probably a

claim jumper prospecting without a permit. His transponder was off so no one could pick him up or follow him. Something went wrong."

"Something went wrong?"

"A heart attack, perhaps," Jack tapped his chest. "Ticker went out. We're over two miles down. Without relays to retransmit a signal, no one would know."

"Maybe," Shotgun frowned. "Noddie scared him and he popped his gaskets."

"It's possible."

Carefully, they piled the bones into the prospector's coveralls and tied the ends. Jack levitated his bones and boots, and piled them into the ship's bucket.

Jack doffed his cap, "Can you think of anything to say?"

"No, I don't believe in mumbo jumbo. I'd like to. Ever since Faith was born, I've believed there's more to life than struggling and dying. But I can't get into any of Nodlon's cults. If they don't ask you to leave your brain at the door, they want you to leave your heart behind."

"What, Shotgun?" Jack scoffed. "I didn't know. I figured you believed in a higher power and life after death. After all, you named your daughters Faith and Hope."

"Oh, I do believe in a higher power," Shotgun straightened his tux. He leaned back on his heels. "Goldie and the girls convinced me of that. Faith is believing life is good even when it's obviously not." Shotgun shrugged and bounced on his toes. He rocked on his heels. "I just don't buy into Nodlon's cults. That's all." He dropped his eyes to his boots.

"Very sensible, Shotgun," said Jack. "Reject charlatans both silly and dangerous, but keep hope alive. I wish I could share your notions, but my heart isn't in it."

"Boss," his butler choked up. "Jack, you of all people should believe in something. You're magical. I don't know how that happened, but it's no accident. I know you don't believe in anything. I know it's gotten worse since Phaedra passed away.

Jazz and I have talked about it. You put on a great show face, but you're heart's darker than ever. You've seen Phaedra. You know she's alive, and still you don't see, or you don't want to see." The little man fell silent and squeezed his elbow gently.

He put a hand on the dwarf's shoulder. "Thanks, Shotgun." He grimaced and fought back against a tear. "Thanks for trying, but I know the truth. As for magic, I'm just a freak of nature. Yes, I've seen Phaedra walk in the night because I'm just an incurable neurotic. When I wake up from a nightmare, I hallucinate and I see my mother."

"You're too hard, Jack. You know so much that just isn't true, and you think you know things no one can know. Let go of the trash, and the cream will rise to the top. It won't be any easier to believe nonsense, but it will be easier to disbelief what isn't true."

"After Phaedra died, I was in danger of believing in something. I wanted to believe in a higher power, but I thought, 'If this is what he's like,' I'd be better off if I stopped believing.'"

"Unbelief is just one more cult, Jack. I stopped believing in it the moment I held my daughter. I'm not telling you what's happening because I don't know, but I'm sure the universe is good. And I'm sure you'll see Phaedra again."

"I try to respect the beliefs of others, Shotgun, but my visions of Phaedra are hallucinations. Maybe I'm distraught, or maybe it's just the gravy." He turned away from the mining ship. He patted the rust on his breeches and then tried to brush it off. He only succeeded in spreading the stains. "We'll send someone back for the poor devil. When life returns to normal, the Surete will send a recovery team." He started to walk back to the flyer. "Shall we try flying around the ship?"

Shotgun stopped in front of him. "Look," he hissed, pointing up the tunnel. "Did you see it?"

"What?" He peered into the darkness. A ball of light floated across the tunnel. "I see it." He cast a ray, and lit the tunnel. The tunnel twisted and curved upward.

"Nothing, Shotgun, it's just our imagination."

"We both saw it! It's the same light we saw when we chose this tunnel."

"Now you're scaring me. Only one of us can be an incurable neurotic, and I've got that position covered. Your position is level-headed sidekick. Now get in, and we'll finish exploring this tunnel."

"Thought I was the comic relief, boss."

~~~~~

Glass stuck to their hands as they climbed back into the flyer.

Good thing this stuff is safety glass. He brushed it off, and buckled his harness. He revved the engine, and the turbine purred. He pulled on the joystick. The levitators hummed, and they lifted off. He twisted the joystick and slipped into the narrow gap between the derelict and the tunnel sideways.

He kept a sharp eye on the abandoned miner. Drills, grinders, and footpads threatened to catch the damaged flyer.

"Stop!" Shotgun flinched.

They struck an outcrop, and bounced off the stone and hit the mining vessel.

"That'll cost." He jerked on the joystick, and stopped the flyer.

"Back up, boss, we're caught. A chain's wrapped itself around the flap."

"Yeah," he backed up.

The chain tightened, and jerked the flyer to a halt. A panel flipped out of the ship's side with a metallic pop. A hoist unfolded from the miner and hammered the tunnel wall. Sand showered them.

"Physics," Jack cursed.

"Watch your language, boss, kids might hear you."

"Why is reality suspended when you make a mistake?"

The hoist shuddered. "Boss!" It rolled away from the miner and clattered against the wall.

The hoist blocked their path, and the machine's stabilizer unfolded over their heads. Shotgun's eyes widened. A double pair of crampons, each with a set of metallic claws and sharp teeth threatened them. "Do something, Jack!"

"I'll magic it back into place." He held out a hand and cast a kinetic spell. The stabilizer rose, and folded back into a pocket on the hoist. "There. Now, I'll put that thingamabob back." He levitated the hoist and flipped it back into its compartment with a clang.

The ship quivered. The hoist shuddered. Dirt scraped from the wall fell on them. The ship listed and the hoist fell again. It hit the wall with a thud, and the stabilizer fell. The crampons slapped the flyer.

"No!" Shotgun ducked and the flyer crumpled. Steel teeth went through his window. The teeth slashed the dwarf's seat. The steel slapped him.

"Shotgun! Are you all right?"

"Yeah," Shotgun rubbed his arm and blinked. "That was close! It didn't cut me. What is that thing?"

"I'm not sure. I guess it's designed to keep the hoist from flopping under a load."

"What about flopping on a load?"

Shotgun pushed on the crampon. "Can you magic it off? It's too heavy for me." The ship shuddered, and the stabilizer dropped again. Shotgun ducked again, "Get it off!"

"I'm trying!" He levitated the crampons back into their seats, threw the stabilizer against the hoist, and pushed the contraption back into place. "I've got it! I'm holding it!" He hesitated a moment, and then let go. The hoist remained in place.

"Okay, we're clear!"

"Go boss, get us out of here!"

The mining vessel shuddered again. It shook, and began

sinking.

"That's not good!"

"Where's it going?" The miner sank steadily.

"Quicksand?"

The ship rocked and tossed a chain out of its compartment. The chain slammed the flyer and wrapped itself around a flap.

"The chain! The chain! It's got us, boss!"

The ship plunged into a growing hole. The chain went taut, and the flyer jerked. He rolled the flyer and tried to lose the chain. The ship disappeared in a whirlpool of dirt.

"Whoa!" He twisted the flyer, and pushed the manna generator to full power. The chain dragged them into the hole.

"Get us loose!"

"I'm trying!" He froze the metal hoping to shear the links. Then, a distant thud rolled up the hole. The chain shot into the quicksand. His levitators whirred, and they plunged into the hole.

Everything went dark. Dirt and sand poured on top of them. The ship threw them into their seats, and they fell. They shot down the hole.

A ring of light outlined the mining ship. "Light!" Shotgun gripped his scream bar. "Free us!"

"Light at the end of the tunnel!"

"It's a lava pit! We're gonna fry!"

"No!" Jack froze the flap. He jerked on the joystick, and the flyer flipped. They bounced against the tunnel wall. The flap snapped. He fought the joystick to control the flyer. The levitators whirred and the engine howled.

The mining ship dropped away and disappeared in the light.

They dropped out of the hole and into the light. He rolled the flyer and righted their ship. Reflections dazzled them, and then their vision cleared. He slowed to a halt and hovered nose down.

~~~~~

"It's the Ninth Ring!"

The ship fell towards a blue lagoon. It toppled slowly end over end and splashed into the lagoon. It sank in the clear water. It hit the bottom and disappear in a cloud of white sand.

A vast dome soared over a lake. An artificial sky played a rerun of a summer day from long ago. The sun shared the dome with a distant thunderstorm. They marveled at the Caribbean paradise.

Stalactites ran along a grid of reinforced arches. The frozen stone interrupted the projection. A massive stalactite through a thundercloud broke the illusion.

"They've deferred the maintenance too long," said Shotgun.

"Ha, yes! Still, it's impressive. The sky looks real and the stalactites look like the rusty remains of the circus."

"Now we know what that prospector was looking for," said Jack.

"Did he find it?"

"Yes, I'm sure of it. He found a seismic anomaly. He drilled a well there. When he saw what he'd found, he bored it out to get in."

"Why bore a hole big enough to swallow your ship and park over it?"

"He wasn't parked there. He was drilling. The ship was there for years. See the stalactites. When he punched through the dome, the support rusted out. After that the well eroded. That ship needed just a tap to sink her."

"Why was he in the driver's seat? Was he trying to get in, or trying to escape?"

"Who knows?" Jack shook his head. "I'd hoped we'd figure that out when the coroner examined him. Now he's entombed on the bottom of the lake. Our first guess is as good as any though. Maybe he had a heart attack, and that's as far as he got."

Jack steered the flyer lower. The lake teemed with life. The lagoons shimmered in the artificial sun. "It's a shamrock shaped lake."

"It's Lake Bali," said Shotgun. "Each lagoon is a different resort. Four lagoons, four resorts: Oceania, Bora Bora, Java, and the Black Wharf."

"Awesome," Jack circled the flyer to take in the view, "a Caribbean resort built in the heart of a mountain in Wyoming. What a feat!"

"Thornmocker built it to survive an interplanetary war."

"No one's seen the Ninth Ring since the Madrid quake! How do you know such trivia, Shotgun?"

"It's online."

"Dwarves," Jack sighed. "Shotgun, I meant why. Why do you know this stuff?"

"Goldie loves old vids," the dwarf shrugged. "So I became an old vid buff to woo her."

"Aha, a motive!" said Jack. "I remember that. They shot vids here during the Regressive Wars. How many vids were shot here?"

"Dozens, maybe hundreds," said Shotgun. "We'll never know. Not many copies of the great vids survived the wars."

"Remember our history rather than trivia. Read your Gibbon, Shotgun. A resort for the Captains and Kings to hide from the war they started. They refused to let a silly thing like an interplanetary war ruin their vacations. Ironically, it may have saved Nodlon. The children of the elite on both sides lived here. Those human shields protected Nodlon from the ultimate weapons. What with their children learning how to protest and feel superior down here, Nodlon was safe."

"Always too busy to read my Gibbon, boss," Shotgun chuckled. "I have to keep up my Biot Staffing lifestyle."

"Touché, Shotgun," Jack smiled, "but I hope it's not too much trouble keeping me in raspberry tarts."

"You're hardly a slave driver. I know – What?"

Sunrays flared off the flyer's hood, and he blinked. Dark storm clouds boiled out of the east. Lightning crawled across the dome. Low thunder rolled over the lake. Lightning flashed and outlined a tower. A gothic castle stood on a stony peninsula. A massive tower on the end of a peninsula faced the lake. Torches burned on the parapets, and lights burned in every window of the keep.

"Look, boss, it's the Black Wharf!"

Lights sparkled in the tower, and glittered on the water.

"It really looks like Castle Frankenstein."

"Hey, the lights are on!"

"Do you think they left the lights on?"

"For a hundred years?"

"Sure, they left in a hurry. And they knew how to build. The dome lights are on, right. Maybe they left the lights on."

"I'd hate to see their electric bill. The manna to run this place has got to come from Rickover."

"Then you think someone's home?"

"That was my first thought, Shotgun."

"Who, boss? A coven of witches who stew lost prospectors?"

"Hope not, I'm not in the mood to be boiled."

"Maybe it's a tribe of buxom Polynesian lasses descended from lost reality video stars."

"You wish," Jack mulled over the suggestion. "Maybe it's the Black Dwarf's lair."

"I was afraid you'd say that."

"How much do you know about the Black Wharf?"

"Not much. Galactic Studios used it in their epic, *Henry Morgan*. George Capra shot the classic *Treasure Island* here. The Black Wharf stood in for the Black Hill Cove. They say the replica of the Hispaniola is still docked there. It's the tall ship Jim sailed to Treasure Island. Below the Black Wharf is a replica of Port Royal. Laurel Pal shot *Space Frankenstein* here. The Black Wharf was Castle Frankenstein. Out back, they shot

Werewolves of Nodlon, *Night of the Lycanthrope*, and *Moonlight Armada*. Cool, hey?"

"Cool, I love vid trivia, Shotgun, but what we need now is a map. Think you can find our way around?"

"Don't know. I've never been anywhere, much less here. I don't even know if they built exact replicas for the Ninth Ring. I never thought I'd set my eyes on the real thing."

"Finally, I've never heard that before!"

"What?"

"You don't know. My encyclopedia's run out."

"So I know a lot." The dwarf blushed. "You're quite a know-it-all yourself."

"Touché, Shotgun."

"Can we go back now?"

"No, Shotgun," Jack turned towards the resort. "The lights are still on in the Black Wharf; so that's our destination."

Bora Bora

Jack turned the flyer towards the Black Wharf, and pushed the joystick forward into a shallow dive. He cruised a few hundred feet over the lagoon.

"What are you doing, boss? They may be watching!"

"Too late now, if they're watching, they've spotted us."

"Do you think you can walk up to the door and knock?"

"Better to ask forgiveness than permission. I'll land on top of that Keep. If they're friendly, no problem. If they're not, we'll find out soon enough."

"If they're not friendly, what will we do for weapons?"

"I'm ready for them. We've got shields, and they don't. And I can break things too."

"Whoa," Shotgun put his head out the window. "Hey, I can see sharks trolling the shoals."

"Good to know, Shotgun, if we go for a swim."

A flash crossed the hood. The Andromeda shuddered. The joystick shocked him, and he let go. His instrument console flickered and blacked out. Sparks exploded from his dashboard, and showered them.

"Jinkies!" Shotgun flinched, "Yow! What was that?!"

"Force shield!" Jack forced down panic. *Pilot's checklist! Do it now!*

"They know we're here now!"

"And they're not friendly!"

Smoke erupted from every crack. Jack breathed plastic fumes. "The backup's gone!"

Shotgun's gut sank and his harness bit into his shoulders. "We're falling!"

The flyer gasped and the generator screeched. The turbine let out the howl of a banshee.

He slapped the ignition but nothing happened. The Andromeda was dead.

"We're going down!" He gripped the joystick and punched

the console searching for anything that worked.

"I know that!" Shotgun snapped.

Flames burst out of the engine compartment. *Baby, don't explode!*

"Blow the chutes!"

"Yelling doesn't help!" Every mirror filled with fire and smoke. Blinded by the acrid fumes, he searched for the panic button. He pulled off a cap marked in bright, friendly letters, 'Emergency Use Only.' The cap revealed a large red button.

He pressed the red button and fired the chute. Explosives detonated on the back end of the flyer. The blast jolted the machine.

In his mirrors, bits of sheet metal, plastic and fiberglass shot into the air.

The flyer jerked and he sighed in relief.

Strands of nylon and torn cloth peeled off the back. The cloth burst into flames. A rag curled away and left behind a ring of black smoke. *It's gone! The chute's gone!*

"We've got no chutes! And we're on fire!"

"Not for long!" Shotgun grabbed the scream bars.

It's up to you! They sailed in a gentle swan dive. *Can you do it?* Momentum threw them up, and then they dropped. Their harnesses tightened. *No! I can't! She's too heavy!*

He cast a parachute and unleashed all his magic. The flyer jerked. He broke into a sweat, and his heart raced. They slowed, but the flyer kept falling. *We're falling like a brick!*

"Holy cow!"

"What Shotgun?!"

"Now I know how a cow feels when she's been abducted!"

"There's not a flying saucer in sight!" Jack waved at the Ninth Ring. "It only looks like the Bermuda Triangle!"

The Andromeda's nose dipped.

"Where's our chute?"

"No chute!" Jack pressed himself into his seat. "Hold on for the ride!"

Shields! He cast a shield. "Brace yourself!" He sucked in a deep breath.

The flyer's nose split the water. The shock slammed them into their seats.

The bubbles parted. *Magic! Renew the spells!*

Dunes of white marched across the bottom. A manta ray darted away. A cloud of sand swirled in the manta's wake. *We're going down!* His blood ran cold as ice.

He shook Shotgun, and the dwarf nodded. He pointed up through the open hole in his moon roof, and the dwarf nodded again.

Jack unclasped his harness. He grasped the roll bar, and he pulled himself out of the driver's seat. He struggled with his harness.

Water rushed past the sinking flyer. He went through the moon roof into the current. He clung to the roll bar and checked Shotgun.

Desperate, the dwarf struggled to get free. He was trapped at the lip of the moon roof. A harness strap wrapped around the dwarf's ankle held him fast. The current was too strong for the dwarf to break free.

He clung to the roll bar, and hauled until he had line of sight through the moon roof. He cast a spell and slit the harness. Undone, the strap snapped.

Shotgun's foot slipped out of moon roof. An elevator flap struck him. He flipped over and bounced off the smoldering engine compartment. The turbine glowed with an orange fire. He rolled over and his satchel dumped its contents.

Jack kicked the flyer and tried to get away. The rudder hit him in the back. His cloak caught on the rudder and spun him around. The cord flipped him upside down and strangled him. Struggling with the knot, the flyer dragged him into the deep. *She's a millstone round my neck! She's dragging me down to Davey Jones' locker!* He cast a knife again and cut the cord.

Suddenly, he was floating. Disoriented, he searched for the

surface. The blue surface of the lake shimmered in the sun. Below, the white sands marched away in all directions. *Air! I'm out of air!*

The flyer sailed to the bottom. His cloak fluttered from the rudder. The remains of the burnt parachute straggled behind.

Up! He swam for the surface and searched for the dwarf.

Spread-eagled, Shotgun floated in the water above him. The dwarf's silhouette drifted aimlessly.

Fear for Shotgun's life gripped him. *Hang in there, buddy!* A pang of regret swamped him. If he had not risked the dwarf's life, he would be home prepping lunch. *I'm sorry!* Pain returned, and his lungs screamed. *We're going to live through this!*

I can't swim fast enough! He cast magic. Telekinetic force shoved him hard. He straightened his body, and let the magic propel him up to Shotgun.

He reached under the dwarf's arms and wrapped his arms around the dwarf.

He looked up at the surface. He stopped. No reference gave him a sign of their depth. In his mind's eye, a diver writhed in pain. *We're too deep. We might die of the bends.* His chest burned in agony. They needed air. *Shotgun's drowning!*

Drown here, or die of the bends. His lungs screamed.

Bring the air to us! He cast a snorkel to the surface. Immediately, the magic pumped air down to them. *Clever beats brute force! Remember that, Jack!*

Soon a bubble surrounded them, and he took a breath. He filled his lungs. His chest burned, but the air felt good. Catching a few deep breaths, he sucked in more air.

The ease of pumping air down surprised him. *Idiot! Why didn't you think of that before?*

They floated at the bottom of his bubble of air. He expanded the bubble until it became a sizeable cave.

The dwarf was not breathing.

"Breathe Shotgun!"

He needs air!

We need a life raft. He froze the floor of his bubble cave. He thickened the bottom and created an icy raft. He levitated the dwarf and laid him on his raft.

Evacuate his lungs. He rolled Shotgun on his side.

He vacuumed water out of the dwarf's lungs. Adapting his spell, he pumped the dwarf. A noxious orange fluid rose out of his throat and spilled on the ice.

"How could I get you into this mess? Hang in there, Shotgun. No dying on this job."

Gently, he pumped the dwarf's chest and breathed for him. He completed a cycle and felt for a pulse. Nothing happened.

"Wake up, Shotgun!" He completed another cycle without results. "Breath, Shotgun, I can't do it for you!" Carefully, he repeated the operation. "No sleeping on the ice! You've got babies!" He completed another cycle. "It'll be all right, Shotgun."

Shotgun's chest rose. He coughed and spluttered.

"Yes!" Jack let go and sat back on his heels. "Thank you! Dagnabbit! Thank you!"

Too hard, Shotgun coughed again, and his arm came up.

He helped the dwarf roll over, and Shotgun upchucked.

"What is that smell?" Hacking and coughing, Shotgun struggled for a breath or two. "I'm gagging."

"Whatever you last ate, plus some seawater." Jack rubbed the dwarf's back. "I'll get rid of it."

Casting magic, he froze the noxious liquid. He scoured it off the ice, and shoved it over the side. Cleaning improved the air, and the dwarf's nausea receded.

"Feel better?"

"Yes." Shotgun sat up and leaned on an elbow. "I'll live."

He gave the dwarf a moment to collect himself. "Nothing makes you appreciate air, except trying to go without it."

The exhausted dwarf smiled, "Elementary, Sherlock." The dwarf closed his eyes, and laid on the ice.

While the dwarf rested, he propelled their raft towards a

reef. *Which way now? Reefs are near the shore. Maybe we can find a landmark.*

He risked an ascent, and he rose several feet. The magical drain was negligible. *I can do this all night.*

Shotgun sat up. He stretched. "Thanks for saving my life."

"No problem, I had to. Guilt just isn't me."

"I believe you," Shotgun smiled. "Remind me to renegotiate my contract when we get back. No more chasing criminal masterminds, magical or otherwise, without hazard pay."

"Sure," Jack nodded. "Forgot to mention part of your contract; no dying on the job."

"Thanks for reminding me. If you'll stop trying to get me killed, it would help my memory!" Shotgun relaxed as best he could on the frozen raft. "The Black Dwarf will be the death of us yet." A school of tuna swam by. "Where are we?"

"Underwater."

"And you complain about dwarves," Shotgun watched a kaleidoscope of tropical fish. "I know we're underwater."

"Technically, I created an ice raft. It's a submarine. I magically pumped air down to us. I wasn't sure how deep we were. Remaining submerged spares us from the bends. Anyway, we won't be seen in my submarine."

"Good idea."

"If they have a force shield up, they don't want visitors." He tacked to avoid a school of psychedelic fish.

"Yes, but who would guess they had a force shield."

"I didn't expect one."

A lone shark hunted on the sandy floor.

"What's our next move, boss?"

In the distance, the seafloor rose to meet a coral reef. Seaweed writhed in the current swirling over the reef. A school of rainbow fish swam by.

"Go over that reef, and see if we can reach the peninsula from there. I saw huts over there. We can circle around the lagoon and into the Black Wharf. We make our way up the peninsula, find a way into the castle, find the Black Dwarf, and clear our names."

"Great plan unless he brought lightning cannons with back up capacitors."

"Oh, ye of little faith Shotgun, when have I steered you wrong?"

Jellyfish floated nearby, and he steered away from their poisonous tentacles.

"Steering us into the Zodiac case?"

White sand lapped at the reef. Dunes marched down a gentle slope into deeper water. Starfish crawled hither and yon on their alien journeys.

"I only offered my expertise to our local flatfoot."

Steering the raft over the reef, his impromptu submarine disturbed the seaweed. Anemones and urchins added more color to the kaleidoscope. A bed of stone crabs scurried away and annoyed a rockfish. Seaweed swayed in the current.

"Next time we get an opportunity to be heroes, I don't want any hazard pay." Shotgun shivered on the ice. "On second thought, remind me I'm a coward."

Leaving the reef, they sailed past white shoals rising towards the beach. Tropical fish, eels, and crustaceans teamed over the reef. Golden fans of coral dotted an irregular ridge of russet coral.

"You're not a coward, Shotgun." Jack shook his head. "Don't confuse fear with cowardice, or foolishness with bravery. We're only doing what we can. We could, so we should."

"Is that advice for me or for you?"

"More for myself I guess." Jack shrugged, "But I was afraid, Shotgun." He looked over his shoulder at the little man. "I was afraid I'd gone and killed you."

"Well, you haven't. Not yet anyway, so watch you're driving."

They hit the top of a sand bar, and set off an avalanche of

sand. The raft jerked, and Jack tripped. He levitated to stabilize the raft. "Sorry, sailing too low! The raft draws more water than I thought." The avalanche startled a small sand shark. The predator scurried elsewhere for an unwary meal.

He allowed his raft to ascend, and the bubble broke the waves.

"Can we reach the beach undetected? I've got to get off this raft. I don't want to meet the owner of that shield just yet, but I'm freezing."

"We'll have to risk a peek to get our bearings." Jack tacked back into the lagoon, and steered the raft to deeper water. He hovered with the waves lapping over the top of his bubble.

"What we need is a periscope." Jack imagined the tool. "Two mirrors at a distance curved to magnify an image; that's all there is to a periscope." He cast the magic, and a periscope of polished ice appeared.

"Let's see where we are. Up periscope," he said, and sent the mirror up through the bubble. A quick glance at the lower mirror told him the idea had more merit in conception than execution. He saw a fuzzy image of the dunes above the beach. Waves obscured the view.

He turned all the way around. "I can see the beach. There are huts in the lagoon."

"Thank goodness, we can rest until night falls."

"Will they serve fugitives on the lam?"

He rotated slowly, and searched for any other signs. The Black Wharf glinted in the sun. "Castle Frankenstein looks dead. I don't think they're looking for us."

"Maybe they think they got us."

"Good, we may have the advantage of surprise."

Turning the periscope, an archipelago dotted the horizon.

He let the mirrors melt, and the gap in their bubble closed. He submerged their raft. "I didn't see anyone looking for us, but I don't think I can with my mirror trick. If we can reach those huts without arousing any attention, we can recuperate for a bit and continue in the dark."

"If they have thermal imaging, they'll find us for sure. If they've got any artificial intelligence security, we're done for."

An image of the children of Beslan haunted him, but he pushed back the ghosts. "So I take it we're throwing out the theory our Black Dwarf is a psychotic lone wolf murdering young dwarf girls to satisfy his inner sociopath?"

Shotgun stood up, patted his trousers, and rubbed his hands. "Head for the huts, I've got to get off your ice."

"Don't worry," he smiled. "I didn't save you from drowning to let you become a dwarf-sickle." He guided the raft along the beach. For a half mile or so, he followed the trough between the last sand bar and the beach.

The barrier reef turned unnaturally, and ran towards the beach and embedded itself into the seabed. The white shoals rippled over the reef.

"See the piers?" Shotgun pointed.

Jack steered away from the reefs, and crossed a shallow. They curled around the beach head, and sailed over a sand bar. He followed the piers to the nearest hut.

They surfaced and surveyed the hut. A deck circled the hut. The bamboo rail was tinged green. Cross ties held the beams to the piers.

"We need a ghost hunter to contact the desk clerk," said Shotgun.

"We don't need reservations."

"Checking in looks easy enough," said Shotgun. "I wonder if anyone can check out."

"Look at the bright side; we can take a shower without any visits from a psychotic concierge."

"What if the place is haunted?"

"Complain to the management."

"How do you get up there?" Shotgun kicked the water. No ladder or dock offered access to the hut.

Jack leaned over and the raft listed. "Look down."

Shotgun looked between his knees. "Oh, I see the dock. At least the water's clear."

"We'll try the next one."

The next hut was the same. At the next hut a child's row boat littered the bottom. The next was tangled in a fishing-net. They passed several more huts down the beach.

"Hey, that one's got a dock," Shotgun pointed. "Let's go for it. I'm freezing on this ice cube."

He sailed their make-shift raft up to the dock. It floated on plastic barrels. The deck was mounted on the barrels. The dock was lashed to the piers with yellow ropes. The ropes ran from rings on the deck to rings on the piers.

"Cretaceous Cruises invites passengers to disembark for a magical holiday full of fun, sun and malevolent madmen." Shotgun put a foot on the dock and hesitated. "It looks rotten."

"Those going ashore may disembark," Jack said.

"Here I go," Shotgun leapt off the ice raft. "Ah, warmth!"

The ice raft bobbed. "Shotgun!" The raft capsized. Jack slipped on the ice. He hit the water.

Water splashed on the dwarf. Shotgun jumped and the dock rocked. He danced on the bobbing dock and steadied the dock.

"An elf finds a new way to fly."

Jack swam around the dock and faced the laughing dwarf. "What's so funny?"

"You'll never make it in Venice."

"Thanks, I didn't know I was auditioning to drive a gondola."

"And no tip for taking a swim on the clock."

"No bonus for dunking your boss."

"No problem, boss," Shotgun straightened his tuxedo. "I'm charging my dry-cleaning to household expenses."

"I'm afraid you're tux is ruined," Jack smiled. "Just buy a new one when we're back to normal."

All that remained of the swimmer's ladder was a single rusty rail. Jack tried climbing out of the water. Soaking wet, it was harder than he expected.

Shotgun reached out to help fish him from the water. The dock listed and threatened to toss the dwarf into the water.

"Whoa, boss." The dwarf grabbed the deck and struggled to balance the dock.

"What? Don't you want to go for a swim?"

"No, I'm not exactly dressed for treading water."

"I'll fly," said Jack. He levitated out of the water and landed gently on the dock. He stretched out on the dock and gasped. "I was almost dry."

"Dry off magically."

"Summon up a warm breeze?" An idea struck him. "You gave me an idea." He evaporated the water off his clothes. "Whew, that's cold!" He hugged himself and shivered. "Physics!"

"What did you do, boss?"

"I evaporated the water, but now I'm freezing. I forgot. Water cools when it evaporates."

"What if you steamed it off?"

"I'd boil myself like a crawfish."

"Well, at least you're dry. You'll warm up soon enough in the sun."

"Right you are, Shotgun," he balanced on the swaying dock and looked over the hut. "What have we found?"

A deck ran around the hut several feet above the lagoon. Where a steep stair once led from the dock to the deck, only two rails hung over the dock. One rail dangled by a nail.

"No room service."

"If we can find some fishing tackle, we can catch dinner."

"If we do, it'll be as rusty as the nails in the deck." Jack poked at a nail sticking out of a pier. "I'll see what I can find."

He grabbed a rail, put a foot on a pier, and hauled. The rail snapped. His foot shot off the dock and he fell. The dock rocked upward and whacked him on the back.

"Ow!"

"Quit kicking yourself. You'd better just fly."

He rubbed his neck. "Heckling will get you nowhere."

Jack levitated up to the deck. The wood looked as rotten as drift wood. He set down on the deck keeping his weight over the joists. He tested the wood. The deck creaked but held his weight. He considered using magic on the deck, but thought better of it. *If the deck can't hold me, magic will shatter it. If I can't hold the deck together, I'll just have to walk over it.*

He cast magic stones over the treacherous deck. He walked on his stones.

At the top of the missing stairs, he found a life saver and an oar leaned against the hut. He picked up the life saver and the oar and tossed them to Shotgun. "These may come in handy. You can sit on the life saver if I have to use my ice raft again."

Shotgun put the life saver over his head, and leaned on the oar. "Anything but that raft, I think I've got frostbite."

"Your delicate tush is in perfect shape," he laughed. "I'm going in." He ducked into the hut.

Spider webs crisscrossed the corners, and entombed a ceiling fan. Bamboo paneling peeled from the walls. Dust covered collapsed heaps of furniture. Mold clung to sagging wicker. The ceiling drooped. Glass littered the floor. A bird's nest perched precariously on a window sill.

"We won't be staying here tonight."

A privacy wall shielded the bathroom from the front door. Behind the wall, Jack found a wicker chest of drawers. Bottles of perfume, tubes of ointments, and piles of hair clips, bands, and a brush sat on the top.

Curious, he opened the top drawer. The drawer stuck, and he jiggled the beauty supplies on the top. The drawer was empty save for a few scraps of paper and a card. The paper crumbled at his touch. He picked up the card. On the card, a girl danced under a palm tree. "Bora Bora," he said. "Guess we're too late for the show. The bar's closed."

Pocketing the card, he surveyed the hut again from the back

door. Amidst the clutter, rotting wicker, and decaying bamboo, he whiffed a sour smell. He sighed. He followed his magical stepping stones out the back door, around the hut, and back to the dock.

Shotgun cooled his heels in the warm water.

Taking Shotgun's lead, he sat on the dock. He removed his boots and dropped his feet into the lagoon. The warm saltwater soothed his toes. "Ah, that's good."

"Find anything?"

"No one home but ghosts." He drew the card from his pocket, "But I found a souvenir."

"The last guest left his key."

"They left more than that. It looks like a family stayed here. Children's clothes are in the closet, and cosmetics are in the bedroom. They left behind just about everything one takes on a vacation."

He took in the view. The artificial sunset bathed the beach in golden hues. Seaweed and driftwood littered the white sand. A boardwalk wound through the sand. It appeared now and then from the dunes.

Concession stands nestled under the shelter of palm trees. "Closed for business," said Jack. Most leaned impossibly far, held up by some unseen resistance. One slumped on the beach, its trusses spread over the sand and its posts scattered in all directions.

"Captains and kings you said," Shotgun frowned. "An incredible number of biots must have run this place."

"Thousands of biots, biots served for every need."

"Then why am I sad? Why do I hope that family escaped this place after the quake and survived the war?"

"Because it's right to do so, Shotgun, and you know it. The Ninth Ring is beautiful. It's a fantastic expression of what man can do. That family came here to enjoy it, and there's nothing wrong in that. Injustice justified this place. Injustice riddled its construction. The injustice done to the biots that worked here may never be repaid, but none of that justifies wishing our ghosts any harm. They came here with their kids to get away, and somehow that's all right."

"The incurable neurotic surfaces again."

"Sorry, Shotgun, I just think I understand them since I've moved from a biot's dorm to Babel Tower." Jack stared at the beach.

"Are you through preaching?"

"Yeah, yeah," Jack kicked the water and sprayed them both.

"Can we stay here?"

"No, we can't check in here. Everything's rotten," said Jack. "The hut's a mess. The floor's rotten. If we stay on the dock, we'll be discovered. We need to go for it."

"Afraid you'd say that. What will we do? Walk?" Shotgun nodded at the beach. "Dunes cover the roads."

"It's miles around the lagoon," he shook his head. "And the access roads are likely to be watched."

He pondered their dilemma. The Black Dwarf had surprised him with a lightning cannon, booby trapped a supertanker, and captured the mind of the Proconsul of Moab. He would not underestimate him again.

"We've been attacked, accused, outlawed, and brought down with a force shield. What next?"

Clouds danced in painted colors on the sky dome. Gentle waves washed on the shore, and produced a soothing noise. Waves rocked the dock, and lapped at the barrels holding up the deck with little splashes.

Curious, Jack looked over the side of the dock and saw a barnacle chasing a fleck. The dock rocked, and a wave slapped the barrels with a little splash.

"We can sail, Shotgun. The dock floats. I can propel it for miles without tiring."

"Great idea," said Shotgun. "And we won't be freezing." The dwarf gestured towards the Black Wharf. "How will we avoid detection?"

"Travel at night and hope they're not looking for us."

"If they were looking for us, they'd be here by now."

"Think about it, while I cut us loose." He tested the knots. The plastic ropes had crystallized. The shell dissolved in his hands, but the remaining material was frozen in place. The ropes held the dock fast to the rings on the deck. He cast a knife, and sliced the ropes.

The dock drifted away from the hut.

Jack sat. He took the oar, and he threaded it through one of the rings to act as a rudder. He tied a noose around the handle to keep it from slipping into the water. "Ready when you are."

Shotgun straightened the life saver and gripped the deck. "Ready."

He cast an aqua-jet, and the magic propelled their new raft into the surf.

"We'll follow the beach. I don't want to get lost in the dark."

Intruder Alert

The Black Dwarf watched the sun set from his lair. Gothic fortifications, marble gargoyles, and animatronic monsters adorned his penthouse. Complete with all the conveniences of modern living, the lair suited his taste.

Devil's Tower they called it. How appropriate! The sunset left the underworld in twilight. Lake Bali shimmered at the foot of his tower. Port Royal sprawled to the south. The replica of the pirate capital amused him.

The moon rose above the Black Wharf. The wharf began on a spit of beach, ran out to deep water, and turned to enclose a marina. A few yachts were still moored. Most had long since sunk, and a small forest of masts broke the water here and there.

A pack of wolves chased a rabbit across a playground at the foot of the castle. *When the sun sets today, werewolves come out to play.* By day, the werewolves were harmless puppies whose only interests were trespassers, rabbits and squirrels. By night, they changed into vicious hunters for the sport of the ancient game hunters.

The werewolves were a nice touch. True, their lycanthropy lacks all of the elements of traditional werewolves. Werewolves should spread their contagion by moonlight and change into guilt wracked men by day. He sighed. *Why is there no respect for the old ways?*

Close enough, I suppose, though I long for greater authenticity. When I have time, we should develop a lycanthrope virus for the biots. We can use it on these stupid dwarves. Then they'd give us good sport!

Jingling bells warned him of an approaching wench. An Amazon cradled his caster on a purple pillow. A little ditty he enjoyed blared from the caster's speakers.

"Vid on," he said.

A black dwarf wearing a baseball cap appeared on the caster's vid screen. Macaroni on his brim identified him as a captain.

"Report," he barked.

"Master Nimrod, our sensors have detected intruders."

Blast it, Sargon! Must I do everything for you? Just blow them to hell, and let the Dragon's brothers play with them. I hate interruptions when I'm enjoying my reverie.

"Intruders entered the Ninth Ring in a personal flyer. Security raised our shields, and fried their manna generator before we made a visual identification. They fell into Lake Bali. Shall we verify, my lord?"

"Have you checked the cameras and the transponders?"

"Yes, it was an old, dirty grey flyer of the kind found on used flyer lots. We can't see the driver on the cameras."

"Why can't you see the driver?"

"The camera angle, my lord. The flyer blocked our view."

"It's probably just a claim jumper," mused Nimrod.

"If he was a poacher prospecting for gold, he got lucky."

"If so, his luck has changed for the worst. What about the transponders?"

"We checked. The flyer was not sending a valid mark. His beacon was sending a standard default signal."

"Hum, he's smarter than the average golddigger." Nimrod tapped his chin. "Why wasn't he intercepted in the shaft? Don't we have alarms up there?"

"Sir, he didn't come through the shaft. We checked everything. He must have come through the dome. We think he was searching the dome's maintenance tunnels. He may have found an access shaft, or he fell through a hole corroded through the dome. The dome is almost two centuries old, sir, and the Ninth Ring has been closed since the Madrid quake. No one's done any maintenance in a century."

"Don't be insolent. I know how old the dome is Sargon. I'll overlook it this time."

Sargon blanched. "I meant no disrespect, my lord. I was only explaining he may not have known where he was."

"Perhaps," Nimrod pondered the matter, and then dismissed it with a wave, "and perhaps not."

"Of course, my lord," said Sargon.

"We have no time to waste on the rock hound," said Nimrod. "He's probably just an old sot anyway. If he turns up again, blow him to kingdom come. My motto is shoot first and don't ask any questions."

"Yes, my lord."

"In the future, Sargon, you blast interlopers. Destroy them. Whatever you have to do, just do it! Don't bother me with trivia, lest you stir my wrath. I'm busy planning the destruction of Nodlon and the conquest of Earth!"

Sargon sighed and bowed his head. "Ah, yes, my lord Nimrod."

"What news from Moab? Has the Proconsul destroyed the mage?"

"She struggled to resist, but in the end she caved. She ordered the Surete to destroy Clay on sight, but the police smelled a rat. They allowed him to escape. Our spies revealed their duplicity, but we're working out how to neutralize the opposition under the enemy's protection."

"Spare me the details. I shall make Moab pay for my crimes soon enough." He smirked as he savored the delicious irony.

Drawing himself up, he tightened his bathrobe, and stared down his nose at his caster. "Have our spies find the mage's companion. Clay can't be far from his trusty sidekick. Have my airship ready at the usual hour. Tell Helter and Skelter to meet me." He rolled his eyes. "I'll destroy this son of Phaedra myself."

"Yes my lord, as you command." Sargon saluted smartly, and the caster darkened.

"Now, where was I?" Nimrod smiled. "Oh, yes, destroying my enemies."

The Black Wharf

Applying power, Jack bowled into the oncoming waves. He propelled them away from shore and out of the surf. Beyond the first sand bar, the lake was not as choppy. Long waves slowly rocked their raft. He steered past the last hut. The beach gleamed in the sunset. Faraway, gulls called.

Powered by Jack's magic, the raft made little noise. Waves splashed against the raft as it plowed ahead.

As the sunlight faded, a bevy of stars appeared on the dome. Unfamiliar southern stars blazed with all the glory of a tropical paradise.

"Look at the stars." Shotgun enjoyed the sunset. "Can we sail by the starlight?"

"Not a problem, we have a full moon."

Shotgun twisted, and looked to the eastern sky. "Isn't it a new moon?"

"No, on the surface we just had a full moon." Jack relaxed, "Not that it matters. Every night is probably a full moon here."

"Bet it's hard on the werewolves."

"Happily," said Jack. "I'm sure we won't meet any werewolves."

The moon framed the Black Wharf. "Spooky," said Shotgun. "The Black Wharf really looks like Castle Frankenstein."

"I'm sure it's intentional. After all, it's a resort."

"Does this moon look larger than the real one?"

Jack studied the orb for a moment. "Yeah, it's a nice touch. Makes sense, a perfect night makes a perfect vacation."

Little streams interrupted the beach. A small dock or two and a few short fishing piers dotted the shore. The twilight faded, and the moon rose. Stars crawled across the dome.

They turned into a tiny cove. They passed buoys demarking a swimming beach. Beyond the beach was a wharf. A few docks clung to the wharf.

A life preserver atop a pier reflected the moonlight. Masts stood in the water next to the docks.

Jack sailed into deeper water to avoid the sunken wrecks. He steered by the gleam off the piers. A small hoist mounted on the wharf waited for a trawler that would never come.

A shop shaped like a Polynesian longhouse sat on the end of the wharf. On top of the shop was a giant octopus with a big grin. A row of surfboards leaned against one side of the hut. Large eaves cast deep shadows. A shadow within a shadow followed their approach.

As Jack rounded the last dock, he steered around the wharf. The shadow followed them. It hugged the darkness under the eave.

At the end of the wharf, they looked up at the grinning octopus.

"Need a souvenir, Shotgun?"

A four legged creature darted from the shadows. It bumped a surfboard and the boards toppled with a clatter. The creature ran to the edge of the wharf and barked.

"Whoa," yelled Shotgun. He jumped and the raft rocked.

"Yo," Jack spun their raft away from the beast. He tossed Shotgun about.

The beast barked all the more.

"What's that?" Shotgun looked back.

"A wolf, or a big dog," Jack pushed the raft as hard as he dared. Driving farther out into the lake, he put some distance between them and the wolf. The barking faded. Then, the beast howled.

A chill ran up Jack's back.

"Man that's cold," said Shotgun. The dwarf shivered.

"Now we know what it is. Howling like that? It's got to be a wolf."

Jack tacked against the waves, and turned down the beach.

"Whew, are you all right?" Jack looked back at the wharf.

"It gave me quite a fright, but I'll live." Shotgun splashed some water on his face. "Why would anyone want a beast in paradise?"

"Wolves are just wild dogs. Man's best friends. They left a few dogs behind and now they're wild."

"Yeah, dogs may be man's best friend, but that was no house pet." Shotgun wagged a finger.

"Maybe, the beast is a werewolf."

"You're kidding, boss."

"No, I'm serious. They hunt synthetic prey on the Great Station of Ur. Synthetic prey designed for extreme hunting was one of the first applications of biot technology."

"Yuck, that's disgusting."

"Why? Hunting is as old as barbecue." Jack laughed, "I'd love some grilled chicken right now."

"That thing was hunting us."

"He's just a big, wild dog defending his territory."

"Yeah, and I'm all dwarf. Dwarves might be on their menu." The shadow on the wharf howled again. "See, it's been three hundred years since it's had fresh meat. Now it wants a piece of us."

"Don't exaggerate, Shotgun. It can't possibly be that long since its last meal." He steered clear of the wharf, and propelled their raft along the beach.

The wolf bounded down the wharf. It jumped onto the beach. In the moonlight, they watched the figure. The beast paced them, and then howled again.

"It's chasing us."

"Glad we took to the water. I'd hate to meet that thing on the road in the dark."

Taking his bearings, Jack took his eyes off the wolf.

Another wolf joined the first, and another, and then more.

"Look boss! Now he's got company!"

He turned to see.

The pack bayed. The bone-chilling, haunting moan of the wolf pack filled the cove. Their howls echoed over the lagoon.

Chilled to the bone, a visceral, ancient fear stilled his hand and focused his mind.

The pack howled in renewed vigor. The second bay was no better than the first. He stepped up his speed to get away from the terrible sound. A third time, the pack bayed. Then they broke formation and ran down the beach.

"Man's best friend? If those things aren't werewolves, I'm not a dwarf!"

"Wolves run in packs and bay sometimes when they're wild," Jack calmed the excited dwarf. "I've read it somewhere."

"That's reassuring," Shotgun huffed. "Try it on late-night audio channels, boss. Just get us out of here." He kept a lookout, "They're still chasing us."

The pack raced down the beach. Moving with remarkable speed, they caught up with the raft and jumped into the surf. Jack looked back. More wolves had joined the pack. They barked, growled, and howled.

He accelerated their raft, and steered towards deeper water.

"Can werewolves swim?" Shotgun asked.

"No, they can't swim," Jack said. *I hope they can't swim.*

"What about dog paddling?" The dwarf's voice quivered.

The pack splashed in the lagoon and bayed in frustration.

"If they can paddle, we can outrun them."

"So much for the element of surprise, they're bound to hear this at the Black Wharf."

"Don't worry, they can't be heard all the way across the lagoon. Even if they can be heard, they'll think we're just a squirrel."

Jack pushed them into the surf. A wave broke over the bow and soaked them. The raft twisted and rocked. He tried to levitate the raft, and steadied it in the surf.

Shotgun looked back at the pack. A figure on two legs marched across the beach towards the pack.

"Boss!"

"Get down, Shotgun!" They flattened themselves against

the raft.

The creature gestured with incredibly long arms. It challenged the pack. The howling subsided, and the wolves ran towards the creature. It stood its ground, and the wolves surrounded him. It waded into the pack. It bobbed up and down, and the wolves milled around the creature.

"What's that?"

"Shush," snapped Jack, "unless you want to invite it to dinner." He cast a shield of shadow over their raft and hunkered down.

The creature looked out at the lagoon. It stretched to its full height and glared in their direction. Red eyes searched the water. Satisfied with its assessment, it relaxed. It patted the nearest wolf, and spoke in a garbled speech.

The creature turned and strode into the jungle. It bobbed and waddled into the palm trees and disappeared. The pack followed on its heels. One straggler howled at them, and then ran off after its companions.

Jack propelled their raft as fast as he dared without fear of capsizing. He steered them out of the cove. With the cove well behind them, he slowed to conserve his strength. Silently they continued along the beach. The lake stretched away in the distance.

~~~~~

Overhead, the Moon drenched them in an ethereal light. Stars blazed between the clouds. In the quiet, he contemplated what they had just seen.

"I think we're safe," he said. "It's behind us."

Shotgun said nothing. On the raft's bow, the dwarf had succumbed to exhaustion. His head lolled in sync with the waves.

He checked the sky and the lake for his bearings. Bora Bora was on the other side of the lagoon. Ahead stars outlined the upper towers of the Black Wharf against the artificial night. Moonlight glimmered on the lagoon. *What will we find at that castle?*

As the sky turned, he set his course and drove their raft into the night. Shotgun slept. Sleep tempted him, but he fought back.

His memory of the wolf pack and strange creature in the cove kept him going. He wove around little docks. He was incredibly tired, but he dared not put into shore after seeing the wolf pack and its master. More than once, he narrowly missed an unlit buoy.

~~~~~

Jack woke up. *Was I asleep?* He shivered.

The Black Wharf's towers were higher than he expected. The castle was silhouetted against the starry night. He was far from the safety of the beach. He took his bearings and corrected course.

After traveling a time, a spit blocked their way. He approached the spit and saw it was a causeway lined with stones. He rounded the causeway, and into a cove. He sailed along the beach, and in this way another hour passed.

The castle loomed high above the cove. The towers seemed to scrape the sky. The grey shapes of shops and inns told him they were close. The black wharf appeared out of the shadow. He squinted at first to adjust his eyes.

In the dark, he kept sailing towards the wharf. *Moonlight is tricky.* He scanned the beach for a safe place to land the raft. He steered towards the wharf. *See any werewolves? No!* Seeing no danger, he sailed ahead. *So why am I uneasy?*

The raft hit a halyard and jerked. They bounced off the rope and tipped over. The collision catapulted him backwards. He performed an ungainly back flip. His feet flew over his head. He flailed at the air and hit the water.

Shotgun rolled off the raft. The physics of improbable

results asserted itself. Free of its load, the raft fell back on its barrels with its deck up.

Jack broke the surface, and he sucked in a breath. He treaded water and called out in a hoarse whisper. "Shotgun?" From the water, he saw the ship wreck. "Shotgun?" He swam towards the spot where he thought the dwarf had fallen into the drink.

In the moonlight, a forest of masts, spars, yardarms, and halyards protruded from the lagoon. But the black wharf swallowed all light. *No wonder I didn't see the wreck! Against the wharf, it's black on black!*

"Shotgun?" He tried diving, but succeeded only in running into a slimey rope in the dark water. He surfaced for air. *No, Shotgun! I can't lose you now!* Treading water, he risked a little magical light to search. *Where is he?*

Claws and limbs pounded his back. He flinched, "Whoa!" He swirled around to see his attacker.

"Ha! Got you!" The dwarf's head popped out of the water. "Admit it, Jack, I got you!" Then, he laughed, "That was good!"

"Shotgun!" His calm returned as rapidly as it vanished. "I was worried. Are you all right?" He scolded himself. *It was funny!*

"Yes, I'm all right, but I'm revoking your rafting license." The dwarf caught his breath, and he wiped the seawater from his face.

"Sorry, I ran into a shipwreck."

Shotgun nodded and swam for their raft. Despite his heavy clothes, he bounded onto the raft like a seal. The elf levitated out of the water, and landed on the raft.

Is our journey jinxed? Their clothes had begun to dry, but now they were soaked again. *We can't sneak into an enemy stronghold dripping wet. If we're in the right place, we'll need a disguise. How can we be sure? These people aren't friendly, but maybe they're not enemies.*

"You hit a halyard." Shotgun held out a thick rope.

"A what?"

"A ship's rope; it's part of the shipwreck. Sailors use halyards to hoist sails. It's probably fake rope for a fake shipwreck though. Only synthetic rope could sit here for decades and not rot away. The shipwreck blended into the shadow under the wharf. You couldn't see it in the dark."

"Thanks, but I figured that one out." Jack took the oar, and set the raft in motion. Cautiously, he sailed through the wreck and up to the wharf. Looking back, the shipwreck was clearly visible against the stars. He stayed in the wharf's shadow and steered for shore.

He beached the raft under the wharf.

The wharf continued over the beach and buried itself in a dune. The piers were tall, thick, and black. The cross-beams were heavy. The deck was twenty feet off the water, and forty feet wide.

"Under the wharf," Jack pointed the way, "It's the only cover." They disappeared into the pitch black.

"Shotgun?"

"Here."

He risked a bit of light, and cast a dim blue ball. Shotgun was already lying on the sand. Their raft was the only man-made object on the beach between the wharf and the nearest spit.

"Shotgun, you rest, I'm going to hide our raft." A snore answered him.

He returned to the raft. He pushed it into the water, and propelled it farther under the wharf and up the beach. *Don't want it giving us away!* He took a rope and lashed the raft to a beam.

Walking back to where Shotgun slept, he saw a shadow jiggle. The shadow was a mound three or four feet long. He froze. *Is it a wolf or a giant slug?*

Alarmed, he narrowed the distance to the slug like thing. He stopped several feet away and stared at the shadow. It jiggled again. He risked a dim blue ball again. Cusped in his hand, the tiny light nearly blinded him. It hardly illuminated the mysterious creature.

He dropped the light ball and rolled it up to the slug. He guided the globe up and down the creature. The creature rippled and emitted an annoyed grunt. He sighed. It was just a miniature manatee. He doused the light.

Careful not to whack himself with a beam, he returned to Shotgun. He checked the sand with his light. Assured nothing creeping or crawling was in the vicinity, he stretched out on the sand. He checked his watch. The hour was late, but the night was still young. Satisfied, he set the alarm for the third hour and hoped for the best. Knowing not what else to do, he asked the universe for luck and fell asleep.

~~~~~

He fell and fell and he kept falling. And then he woke up.

Above Jack was the black wharf, and he remembered where he was. He gripped the sand. Every muscle in his body complained, and his back burned. He sat up and stretched.

The moon lit the beach almost as bright as day, but the shadow under the wharf was black as pitch. Fumbling with his watch, he found the light. It was not yet three.

He pondered the situation. *The Black Dwarf mesmerized the dwarves who attacked us. He controls an army of zombie dwarves. Not undead zombies, but living zombies trapped in their minds by some drug or technology. There must be many more.* He thought of the Black Wharf. *If he's there, what will we do? I can't take on an army!*

"If we wait until morning, we may never succeed," he muttered.

Shotgun was snoring. He poked his dwarf. "Wake up sleepy head."

The dwarf stirred in the dark. "I feel like a truck ran over me."

"Who needs a truck? A dragon attacked us. A force shield blew us out of the sky, and I've tried to drown you twice." He rubbed his bruises.

"At least you saved me from drowning."

"Saving your life was the least I could do, having gotten you into this mess." He stood up and stretched.

Today is different. Everything was happening too fast. *I might not see another dawn.* Gumshoe had asked him to help investigate a crime. One missing dwarf had become a crime spree. Now he was an outlaw on the lam.

Rich and famous, and with all the toys he ever wanted how could it turn out this way? *What am I thinking? I may not live to see the dawn today!*

Why was he sleeping under a wharf? *You've got a soft bed in Babel Tower! Why are you sharing a beach with toy manatees? Shut up, Jack! You haven't got time for a pity party! You were given a talent. You've enjoyed the benefits. Today you start paying the piper. As the saying goes, 'To whom much is given, much is expected.'* Now, it's time to do your duty.

"Why?" the dwarf asked. "This is a job for law enforcement."

"Magic," he answered. "The police and military have no power against the Black Dwarf's magic. The leadership can't or won't understand this danger until it seizes them by the throat. When it does, it'll be too late. I must act now or others will perish."

"There you go with that 'I' thing again. You're an entertainer, not a police officer. Don't let your advertising go to your head." The dwarf drew close. "Leave it to others. Better equipped, better prepared."

"I have no choice. If I turn back, I'll never know if I've earned my privileges, or if I was just lucky. Life is a test. Now it's time to decide if I'm a man, or if I'm just a biological entity."

"A bit early for a mid-life crisis," the dwarf snapped.

"Up at that castle is a murderer. He took the lives of innocent dwarves and molemen. Women and children died." The words fell out of him. "If no one stops him, he will kill again. Someone has to stop him. I don't know to stop him, but if I don't try, kill me now because I'll never live down the shame."

"Don't mean to interrupt your introspection," said the dwarf, with a cool tone. "But this isn't your job. You're not trained for it, and you're not responsible. We need to tell the authorities and get them down here."

"We can't trust this to authority. Not to politicians anyway. The Black Dwarf mesmerized the Proconsul. I don't know how he mesmerized her, but he did it. His technology, if it is technology, makes him immune to the law. And the police and the military are compromised." *Why are you arguing with me, Shotgun? You know all this!*

"Don't we need to find out what's going on before we go barging in? For all we know, we're not even in the right place."

"You're right there. We don't know if the Black Dwarf's here. We don't have enough evidence to convince Nodlon Yard. We need to know more anyway."

"What about NOSS? Don't you have connections?"

"What about them? I've got a friend in the secret service, but what if he's mesmerized when we get back? Then, it'll be too late. I have to go in and find out if the Black Dwarf is here. If I can stop him, I have to try. I'd rather risk trespassing than letting the Black Dwarf get away." He waved his hands as if he could be seen in the dark. "What else can I do? Knock on the front door and ask if any psychotic magicians are at home?"

"So your mind's made up?" asked the dwarf.

Under the wharf, the moonlit beach outlined the dwarf. He faced the dwarf's shadow. "I'm going up to the castle. I'll sneak in or break in. If I find the Black Dwarf, I'll bring him to justice. And if he won't go, I'll bring justice to him. If I'm wrong, I'll take responsibility."

"Now that you're pumped up," the dwarf asked, "what will

you do?"

"Go ahead. You can't go with me, it's too dangerous. Stay here and wait for me. Don't get captured though. You've seen what he does to dwarves." He reached out to shake the dwarf's hand. "Thank you Shotgun. You're a good butler, an admirable companion, and a great friend." He reached out to Shotgun. "Good-bye," he added, a bit melodramatically.

He felt only air. He stepped forward and waved his hands around. The dwarf was gone.

"Shotgun, where are you?" He heard no answer. He walked forward a few steps. "I'm trying to shake your hand." He turned around. There was no sign of the dwarf.

"Shotgun, can you say goodbye?" Irritation fought with frustration and struggled with concern. *Where is he? How can I lose my butler? Where did he go?*

"I'm sorry I upset you. Don't stalk off."

He turned to the beach and looked for the dwarf. He picked his way through the piers and dodged the cross-ties.

Then he tripped. He fell to his knees, threw out his hands, and landed on all fours. He rolled over expecting to see a manatee.

~~~~~

"Ouch! Boss!" Shotgun sat up. "What are you kicking me for?"

"Why are you lying down?"

"Oh, I feel like a truck ran over me."

"We were talking and you disappeared in the dark."

"No way, boss. I was having a great dream. Goldie and I were dancing. Jazz had the kids. My chances were good." The dwarf huffed, "And you have to go and wake me up."

"No, we talked. You think I'm having a mid-life crisis. You said this isn't my job and we need to contact the authorities before we barge in. I said I'd made up my mind, and you said I'd pumped myself up."

"Boss you're dreaming again. Sorry to break it to you, but I was sleeping over here," Shotgun patted the sand. "While you were sleepwalking, I was right here dreaming of Goldie."

"I was awake. You were awake. We were talking." *Why are you defiant?* "I don't know why you want to pretend otherwise. When I said I was going up to the castle alone, you disappeared."

"One of us was sleepwalking, boss, and it wasn't me. How could I answer you if I was asleep?"

"I woke you up. Remember? I shook you." He broke off. Shotgun sounded sincere and he never lied. Dwarves were not the type of biots to lie.

"Boss, give me a break. Now you're accusing me of sleepwalking and sleep-talking. Does that even sound like me? We're on the trail of a magician, and you're afraid to admit he's magical. He's not afraid to kill, and you've never even butchered a Thanksgiving turkey. We're exhausted. We're sleeping on a beach. You had a nightmare. It's just natural."

"It was real. It happened."

"It didn't happen. Think it through, boss. Which one of us sees ghosts? Hello?"

He leaned against a pier, and tried to blend into the shadows. He rubbed his face. "Okay, okay, I'm not sure what happened. Maybe, I'm losing it."

"Boss, lighten up" Shotgun whistled softly. "You're not losing it. I believe you. You thought we had a conversation. It's just that I wasn't there. You had a nightmare. Don't go thinking you're crazy. This happens to everyone searching for a psycho-magician with an army of mesmerized zombie dwarves who plans to kill you on sight."

The dwarf stepped into the moonlight. His eyes darted from shadow to shadow. "If you aren't having nightmares on what may be the last night of your life, then you're crazy."

In the moonlight, Shotgun resembled a zombie. His tuxedo

was torn, and his eyes were dark holes in a pallid face. He might have been going to a Halloween party.

"Shotgun, you don't have to go with me. I've got no choice. I'm the magician. If I don't go up there and find out if the Black Dwarf's here, I can't call myself a man."

"No wonder you're having nightmares." The usually steady dwarf got all worked up. "Newsflash, Jack Clay, I'm a man too. Biots are people too, remember? And if you think you're a better man than I am, you're going to have a mid-life crisis right now. This isn't all about you."

The dwarf adjusted what remained of his suit and glared at the mage. "The Black Dwarf is a psycho! Goldie is just like the dwarf girls he murdered! The mole children killed could be my children. Faith and Hope might be lying in that morgue up there! If the Black Dwarf gets away, he may kill them anyway. This guy's got big plans, and I'm planning on taking him down." Shotgun ran out of steam and settled down. He snorted and straightened his shoulders.

"I'm sorry, Shotgun," began Jack, "In my nightmare, if that's what it was, we had a similar conversation. I thanked you for your service and your friendship. Now, I'll say it again, thank you. I've got no idea what's up there at the castle. If it's the Black Dwarf, and if he has magic and if he has an army of zombies it may be our undoing. We may not survive the encounter. We may not see the dawn."

"You're a good magician, Jack. And you're a better man than most men. I'd say nothing if we just turned around, climbed up that shaft and tried to find help. But if you go up to the castle I'm going with you. He's killed girls and kids. He's messed with the minds of dwarves! Like it or not, I'm going with you."

"Shotgun, I'll not force a man on a risky mission. You're my butler; not my backup on a fool's errand." He watched the dwarf.

"Boss, where would Ollie be without Laurel, Jerry without Dean, Abbot without Costello, Batman without Robin, or the

Lone Ranger without Tonto? Besides, I've got a name to clear too."

"Your contract's no good here. This isn't an assault on Snuffie's deli aisle."

"What? You think it's easy coming up with a meal plan for an elf with discriminating tastes and a penchant for fine coffees?" Shotgun chuckled. "Next to that, challenging an army of brainwashed zombies is child's play." The dwarf crossed his arms. "This isn't about a contract. Your money's no good for this job anyway, Jack." He waved towards the pirate town replica. "You can lease me from Biot Staffing, but I'm a man – even if I am dwarf. I've got a right to defend my own, and a right to defend my home. And if you want to get in the way, you're wrong."

"You're a good man, Shotgun, and I never meant anything else. Come with me as a friend then. I'm glad you've got my back." He held out his hand, and the dwarf shook it. *If we live through this, Shotgun, I'll buy your contract.*

"Lead on Jack Clay."

Port Royal

Jack kept to the shadows and crept up the beach. He reached the deck and peered over the top.

The wharf ran a hundred yards into the lake and made a right turn to enclose the marina. Massive piers supported thick black planks. *It's black all right.* Heavy rope ran from pier to pier. Stars silhouetted a motley row of shops on the end.

Shotgun slipped up behind Jack. "I'm here, boss."

"No signs of life. The road to the castle is in front of us. I don't see any guards."

"See any werewolves?"

"No," said Jack, "no wolves of any kind."

"Thank the stars for small favors. Are we following the road then?"

"No, there's no cover on the road. The moon is so bright we can be seen from the castle, and they probably have security cameras watching the road."

"Which way will we go?"

"We're behind the dune. They can't see the beach. If we follow the dune along the beach, we can remain out of sight. We can go over the dune and go around town in the jungle."

"I don't fancy going through the jungle, boss. It'll take hours, and we might run into more wolves. Why not create an illusion? If we had a fog bank, we could walk up to the front door. They'd never know we were coming."

"I think a fog bank might get their attention. The weather isn't right, and if they check their radar they'll know it's a trick. My illusions can't be seen on radar." He thought for a moment. "Shotgun, you're a genius."

"What?"

"Disguises! I'll cast disguises. If we go as a pair of Sasquatch type things, we won't attract any attention. If they see us, they'll think we're hunting with our wolf pack."

"Sasquatch?"

"The two-legged leader of the wolf pack, remember? Those creatures are probably the natives around here." Jack cast his disguise and stepped into the moonlight. "How do I look?"

"Like a dirty ape, boss."

"Not like a man in a gorilla suit?"

"On second thought, you look exactly like a man in a cheap gorilla suit."

"Oh," Jack added a man-like face with deep, wide eyes, and thick fangs. "Now, how do I look?"

"Frightening! If we startle anyone, they'll shoot us."

"The Black Dwarf will shoot us anyway."

"Good point," said Shotgun. "Better hope no Yeti hunters are out there. I don't fancy having my hide tanned and hung up in some cowboy's living room."

"Don't worry about it. Your disguise will wear off if I get shot."

"Oh, that's comforting," muttered Shotgun.

"Besides," said Jack. "The guards will only see a couple of Sasquatch on their security cameras. They'll probably leave us alone. After we defeat the Black Dwarf, we can get his security vid footage and use it on our creature feature show. Everyone will talk about it on late-night vid for years."

"At a time like this, you've got to be kidding, boss! Our lives are on the line! And all you can think of is getting a sensational vid on late-night?"

"It's my job, Shotgun! I've entertained Nodlon for twelve years, and I've got many more to go. I have to think ahead."

"You're impossible, Jack," Shotgun shook his head. "All right, so we look like Sasquatch, but can we act like Sasquatch?"

"Hadn't thought of that," Jack scratched his chin. *Sasquatches have overly long arms and lots of hair. They walk with a weave and a bob, and their knuckles drag on the ground.*

"Just follow my lead. Walk casually like we belong here." Jack cast the dwarf's disguise. "Let's go, Shotgun."

Jack swung his arms in long, slow swings, and he weaved

and bobbed to imitate Sasquatch. He set off up the beach, and Shotgun followed. When they had gone far enough, they hopped over the rope and onto the wharf.

The sand rose into a dune in front of them. The dune ran along the beach and crossed the boardwalk. Port Royal's skyline peeked over the top. *Good, no one can see us. We'll go over the sand, and they'll assume we came up the beach.*

Shotgun followed him over the rope and they continued on their way.

Jack sidled up the dune, and Shotgun straggled behind. Their steps left a trail of little avalanches. At the crest, Jack took his bearings. The dune almost reached the corner of Port Royal. Sand spilled over the wharf, the boardwalk, and the cobblestone road. It covered the end of the wharf.

The village was a tragedy frozen in still life. It exuded an idyllic air. Pubs and shops faced the cobblestone road. A cigar pirate beckoned patrons in front of a tavern. An iron parrot sat on his shoulder. An alley slipped into the dark next to the tavern.

A cobblestone road emerged from the sand and ran from the black wharf up to the town. The road ran past the village, and veered away from the boardwalk. In the distance, it passed a merry-go-round, and then crossed an open field. A brontosaur towered over the merry-go-round.

The boardwalk circled the marina. A row of concession stands offered cotton candy and funnel cakes to a score of empty tables with tattered umbrellas. A picnic area with date palms separated the stands from the cobblestone road.

Shotgun scrambled to the crest of the dune and joined the elf.

"You make a passable Sasquatch, Shotgun." Jack chuckled, "My disguises are unusually effective by the light of the moon."

"Gee, that's good to know," muttered Shotgun. "I'm glad we look good in the moonlight before dawn. What worries me is how will we look in the light of day?"

"You're a worrywart!"

Shotgun sized up the lay of the land. "The cobblestone road is the only way up there without flying."

"We can't follow the cobblestone road. There's no cover. The wicked warlock's black dwarves might get suspicious if they see us walking straight up the road. We can't go through the picnic area either. There's nothing between the concession stands and the jungle except a few date palms."

"Won't our disguises protect us?"

"Why would two Sasquatch wander up to the castle? I can create a wolf pack illusion, but I can't explain why we're on the road. And I can't make us invisible."

Shotgun fell silent and contemplated their dilemma. "If you don't want to fly in, that doesn't leave us any options. We can go through the town, and up the ridge through the jungle. But we still have to cross that field."

Jack weighed the alternatives.

"We'll take the alleys through town," said Jack. "When we get to the other side, we'll stay behind the brontosaur. We can cross the field there. If we're not seen, we may make it.'"

"Lead on Macduff," Shotgun sighed.

Jack slid down the dune. He bobbed and rolled across the cobblestone road.

"What if they've got cameras watching the alley?" Shotgun bobbed up and down in his best impersonation of a Sasquatch.

"We'll cross that bridge when we come to it." Jack shrugged, "This way." Seeing no perils, he ambled towards the alley. "Keep up, Shotgun."

"If the elf wants the dwarf to keep up, the elf needs to slow down."

~~~~~

"Watch Captain!" A dwarf shouted, "Sir, I have activity on the wharf!"

"Keep your pants on," Sargon left his desk. "What is it,

private?"

"Sensors have picked up two creatures approaching Port Royal."

"Where did they come from?"

"Don't know, sir. They just showed up. They're entering Port Royal now."

The captain hovered over the dwarf's station. "Do we have a visual?"

"The camera on the wharf may pick them up, sir."

"What are you waiting for?" The captain slapped the control bank. "Get it up on the vid then! Now! Snappy!"

The dwarf selected a camera monitoring the wharf, and sent it to his vid screen. "Here, sir, I have them."

The captain stood over the dwarf's shoulder.

Two Sasquatch ambled up a sand dune. They stopped and gyrated as if discussing which way to go. Then they slid down the dune, and continued on their way.

"It's nothing," said the captain. "Report two Sasquatch entered Port Royal. They're just looking for their wolf pack. Alert the gate. We don't want their werewolves tearing our guards apart."

"Yes sir."

~~~~~~

Jack and Shotgun passed the cigar pirate and turned into the alley.

Boxes, barrels, and trash cluttered the alley and slowed their progress. Fishing tackle joined the mix of barrels and crates and other rubbish. They wove a path through the debris to the end of the block. Jack peeked into the street for any signs of life. All was quiet, and he stepped off the curb and into the moonlight.

A black ball of fur skittered out of a hole in the curb.

"Whoa," squealed Jack. He jumped and bumped Shotgun.

He nearly bowled the dwarf over. Shotgun stumbled into the street to keep his balance.

Chattering with displeasure, the rat scolded Jack for disturbing its nap, and it took off into the shadows.

"It's a black rat!"

"Shush, boss," Shotgun snickered. "If you squeal like a little girl again, I'll tell Jazz I have to put more starch in your panties."

"Hey," Jack complained.

"Hay is for horses," the dwarf chuckled.

"Act natural," Jack bobbed along as if Sasquatch always took nocturnal strolls.

They picked up their pace and popped into the next alley. Half-way down the block, they reached a courtyard covered by a fishing net festooned with glass buoys. Moonlight glinted off the glass.

"Did you hear something?"

Jack stopped and listened. "No, but I feel we're being watched." He led the way into the courtyard, and turned around a stack of crates. A fallen plank blocked their way, and he jumped over it. "Watch your step."

"Wait up," Shotgun skipped to pick up speed, and hopped on the plank. The rotten wood broke under his weight, and the dwarf stumbled into a stack of crates. The crates scattered over the courtyard and slammed into a fence.

Flapping and cawing roared from the fishing net, and the glass buoys clanked.

Shotgun twirled gracefully to regain his balance, and checked his fall. "That was close."

"Watch where you're going twinkle toes."

"Watch your language, boss."

A flock of birds lifted off the net and launched into the night. The flock blotted out the stars.

Jack looked up, "A flock of seagulls?"

"No boss," hissed Shotgun. "Crows!"

The birds cawed after them, and chastised them for disturbing the peace. The crows circled the courtyard three times, and then returned to their perches.

They crouched to fend off unwelcome gifts, and darted down the alley.

"Spies of the Black Dwarf?" asked Shotgun.

"No, it's Hitchcock."

The noise trailed off, and they reached the end of the second alley.

"Good thing," said Shotgun, "I've almost got my black belt."

"Why do you need a black belt? Don't you know how to stand up?"

Shotgun put a hand on his forehead, "I walked into that one."

No alley offered a way forward on the next block. Instead, an apothecary offered ice cream and elixirs for indigestion, and a wooden sidewalk ran up the street.

Jack ventured into the street with Shotgun in tow. On the wooden sidewalk, they stepped softly to avoid a racket. Their footfalls rumbled on the loose boards. They rounded a corner and discovered a pub. A list of ales dangled on a window. A sandwich board teetered on the edge of the walk. It announced the specials of the day.

"Soup, salad, and a sandwich," the dwarf read the menu. "A hundred years too late, or we could do lunch."

"Don't mention lunch, I could eat a horse."

The next shop was a gallery. The dwarf stopped and rubbed dirt off a window. "What about a unicorn?"

Jack backtracked, and he peeked through a clean spot on the gallery's window. A rocking unicorn stood amongst a sad array of dolls and bric-a-brac. A saddle straddled its back. "Lonely toys," he said. "Bet those toys can tell a story or two or three."

"It's an antique, boss."

"If we survive this, we'll come back and claim it for Faith and Hope."

"If is a big word," said Shotgun. "It stands for faith and hope. If we have faith, we can hope a better day will come."

"If you say so," Jack shrugged.

Farther along, a bench of carved driftwood awaited passersby. At their approach, a black cat snapped to attention. Whether scared or prudent, the kitty bounded away. At a safe distance, its curiosity overcame its fright and it stopped to watch them pass.

"Rats, cats, and crows," said Shotgun. "What's next? Werewolves?"

"Rats, cats and crows, oh my," Jack laughed. "It's just a coincidence, Shotgun."

"Maybe it's a warning."

"Don't get superstitious."

They rounded the corner. The next street ran caddy corner from where they stood. They turned back towards the cobblestone road, and angled across the street and into the shadows. The wooden walk ended at a bar and grill. Ads in the windows offered them seafood and Calypso dancers. The walk emptied onto a circular drive in front of the grill. Jack followed the drive and rounded the corner.

They were much closer. Across the drive, the merry-go-round stood in front of them.

The cobblestone road crossed the drive, and passed the merry-go-round. Then it passed a playground and crossed the open field. It ran directly towards the castle and plunged into the jungle.

The merry-go-round sat silently beside the cobblestone road. Ponies and carriages waited for small riders. Silent swings separated the merry-go-round from the playground. Rocking horses and other toys waited in the moonlight. Beyond them was the dinosaur.

"Follow my lead," said Jack. "But don't follow too close.

Go through the playground, and wander over to the brontosaur. Keep the dinosaur between you and the castle, and hope the guards don't get suspicious."

Jack weaved and bobbed across the drive, and Shotgun straggled behind to keep up his Sasquatch impersonation.

A tingle ran up Jack's back, and his skin crawled. He felt exposed in the open, and he suppressed an urge to run. He led them by the merry-go-round, ambled by the swings, and headed for the dinosaur. His boots sunk into the sand.

Jack passed the rocking horses. Mythical monsters mounted on springs shared the sandbox with ponies, unicorns, and a rocket. Then, he ambled towards the brontosaur. *Act casual. You're just a Sasquatch on a stroll.*

Shotgun lagged behind at a comfortable distance.

Closer now, Jack could see the brontosaur was green. It stood in the center of the playground, and it faced the lagoon. A friendly smile invited little pirates to play. It wore a silly hat that on closer inspection was a deck. It towered over the swings and the merry-go-round.

Stairs in the brontosaur's belly led to a deck along its back. The deck led to a slide on its tail. The slide circled back to a gap between its feet. Happy riders could run through the gap and back to the stairs.

Jasmine would love that dinosaur. He angled around the tip of the brontosaur's tail and under the slide. *I hope we can come back and put it to good use.*

A jet black wolf leapt from the gap. It bared its teeth and growled.

Jack froze. *It's as large as a mountain lion!* The black wolf advanced on him. It bared its fangs and growled. He backed up and tripped over the slide. He fell backwards and landed astride the slide. He rolled over it and hit the sand.

Jack pushed up on his elbows. *That's no natural wolf!*

The wolf lunged for his throat. Its teeth flashed.

He threw up his arm and blocked the attack.

The beast's jaws snapped, but it missed his throat. The wolf bit air.

The angry beast landed on him and clawed his belly. "Ow, wee!" The wolf sprang away before he could recover. He swung again, but the wolf was too quick and he missed.

Its prey was down, and it smelled fear. Fearless and confident, the wolf grinned. It sprang again.

He punched the wolf and blocked the attack.

Undeterred, the beast ground its hind claws into him.

Ow! He slugged it again, and it leapt off him.

It spun around and lunged again. Its forepaws struck him and shoved him into the sand. Its lunge was too hard and it started to slide over him. It clawed him, and its nails punctured him. *Yow, wee!*

He hit the black wolf with both fists, and it somersaulted over his head.

The beast landed on its back, rolled over, and scrambled to all fours. It turned on him, and growled.

Magic, you idiot! Use magic!

Jack rolled off the slide. He cast a telekinetic blast, and the blow knocked the black wolf back. He fired again, and the wolf rolled. Sand exploded where the beast had been. He fired and sand showered the toys. A pony mounted on a spring rocked back and forth.

The wolf evaded his shots and ducked under the brontosaur. It burst from the other side, and shot over the slide.

It sprang, and he threw up his arm to block its attack. It snapped at him, and its jaws clamped round his arm. It bowled him over, and he landed on his back. It ground its fangs into his flesh and it twisted.

"Ow!" Jack howled. He tried to flip the black wolf off, but the beast was stronger than he expected.

The wolf growled and sank its teeth into his flesh.

Ow! Jack clinched his teeth and glared at the beast.

The wolf jerked its head, and pain seared his arm. "Argh!"

Its claws tore his tunic and slashed his forearm to the wrist.

Blow its head off! He cast a kinetic ball in its mouth, and the magic jacked its jaws. Its snout twisted around and it lost its grip.

Surprise flashed in its eyes, and it backed away a step. It bared its fangs and growled. It glared at him.

He cast a ball again and struck the wolf under its chin. The blow knocked the beast back. It hit the sand with a satisfying thud. *That's better!* Jack rose to his knees.

The beast wasted no time. It coiled up and pounced again.

He cast a ball at its head. Its snout took the blow, its head spun, and the animal flipped over.

The wolf kept flying. Upside down and backwards, it slugged Jack. The blow knocked him backwards, and he fell over the slide again.

Back to square one! Shields! You forgot the shields! He cast shields on himself and Shotgun.

The wolf landed on the slide and it rang. The sound echoed across the playground. The wolf slid backwards and its tail slapped Jack in the face. It furiously clawed for purchase, but its claws slipped on the metal.

Angry, Jack fired a kinetic ball again. Magic shoved the beast up the slide. It clawed at the slide and scratched frantically at the steel. The wolf contorted to find a purchase.

Gravity had its way, and it sailed over the edge. The beast took flight and fell to the sand.

~~~~~

A grey wolf stalked Shotgun. *It's bigger than a mountain lion!* The monster charged at Shotgun, and it sprang for his throat.

The dwarf crouched to block the attack. "Hee-yah!" The dwarf spun about and kicked the wolf's head. Spittle erupted from its mouth. Its teeth hit the sand. Surprised by the sandy sandwich, the grey wolf growled.

The dwarf leapt at the wolf, and kicked it again.

The monster landed on its feet. Its eyes flashed, and it bared its teeth. It shook with demonic fury and it circled Shotgun and studied its prey.

The dwarf kept his eyes on the grey wolf and tracked the monster.

A third wolf with a white stripe down its back snuck up behind the dwarf. It stalked Shotgun from the cover of the rocking horses.

The dwarf leapt at the grey wolf and kicked. "Hee-yah!" It ducked the dwarf's attack, and he pounded sand. The dwarf feinted and attacked again.

The grey wolf evaded the dwarf's kick, and it backed off and growled.

Shotgun took a stance to attack again.

The white wolf struck with blinding speed. It landed on Shotgun's back, and drove him to the ground. He curled and rolled, and threw the white wolf off his back.

Sensing fear, the grey coiled itself to strike again and it sprang. It lashed at the dwarf and missed.

The dwarf dodged the attack, and recovered. He took a stance and sprang at the grey. "Hee-yah!" He kicked it in the belly.

The grey monster yelped. It backed off and growled in frustration.

The white beast attacked again.

Shotgun blocked the white wolf and he spun around. He sprang at the grey, "Hee-yah!" But the beast feinted to the left and leapt to the right. It dodged his kick. "Dagnabbit!" He struck sand and missed his chance to attack again.

Seeing the dwarf pound sand, the white wolf sensed an opening. It took a chance and attacked.

Shotgun heard a crunch in the sand. He twirled and kicked at the sound. "Hee-yah!" He nailed the white wolf in the belly, and sent it into the air. The white struck a rocking pony, and the toy flopped and slapped the beast to the sand. It wailed and writhed in pain.

The grey wolf sprinted passed and leapt over a pink pony. It dashed behind the swings and shot from an opening. It struck as fast as lightning.

"Hee-yah!" Shotgun twirled to block the monster's claws. A flash of grey caught his eye, and he ducked. He spun the wrong way and pounded sand.

The monster rolled in mid-air, its jaws snapped, and it caught him in its fangs.

"Jinkies!"

~~~~~

"Help!"

Free of the black wolf, Jack leapt to his feet and searched for his friend. "Where are you, little buddy?"

"Help!"

"Shotgun!" Jack spun towards the cry. *Where are you?* "Shotgun!"

A grey wolf had pinned Shotgun on the sand. "Help!" Its jaws gripped the dwarf's arm. A white striped wolf circled Shotgun and the grey wolf. The grey growled at the white and dragged the dwarf in a circle.

"Help!"

Hit it with lightning! No! I might hit Shotgun! He fired kinetic balls at the grey wolf. *Blast it Jack!*

The grey monster forgot the white wolf, and it glared at him. *Now I've got your attention!* He pummeled the grey, and his blows enraged the wolf.

Clutching Shotgun's arm in its mouth, the grey wolf shook its head. "Ow, wee!" The dwarf screamed in pain. "Kill it, Jack!"

The grey wolf faced Jack and growled, but it held the dwarf

fast.

Shotgun pounded the grey with his fist, but it ignored his blows. "Let go!"

Jack fired more kinetic balls. The monster shook off the blows and retreated under the assault. It dragged the dwarf, and growled at the elf.

Paws crushed sand. *Duck!* He cringed *Duck!* He twisted. The black wolf missed its mark. Its jaws snapped shut. Spittle covered his ear.

Jack spun to face the black beast, but it was quick.

The black wolf circled him and struck from behind. It leapt on his back, and snapped at his neck. Jack cast a shield, but the wolf simply tore into his vest and clawed his back.

Mad as a junk yard dog, Jack levitated and slammed into the sand. They smashed into the ground, and he ribbed the feral canine.

The wolf yelped and squirmed away. It rolled to its feet and bolted.

Jack popped to his feet, swung his fists, and fired at the wolf.

Aiming wildly, he fired kinetic balls and blasted the playground. Sand exploded in the air. Swings launched into the night air, and snapped at their chains.

The black beast dashed around the rocking horses, and evaded his blows.

Magic ripped the night. Telekinetic thunderbolts struck the toys. Ponies and unicorns rocked on their springs. Magic drummed the brontosaur, and the noise shook the sand.

Where are the black dwarves? I could raise the dead with this racket!

Unfazed, the black wolf dodged his attacks. Moving fast, it wove through the ponies and the unicorns, and it ducked behind a rocket.

Jack spun around and searched for the dwarf.

Shotgun pounded the grey wolf, and beat its face. The

dwarf struggled to shake the monster loose. Spittle flew from its mouth. The white wolf circled them, and its teeth flashed. The grey growled at the white. It was not going to share its prey.

Jack fired at the grey and struck it with a kinetic bolt. The blow stunned the beast, and knocked it back. It dropped the dwarf and growled at Jack.

Levitate it!

~~~~~

Jaws sank into Jack's boot, and he tripped. *What?* He fell to the sand, and the black wolf leapt for his throat. Its claws tore his breeches and gouged holes in his flesh. "Ow, wee!"

Blood drenched the sand. Red flooded his vision.

He levitated the black wolf. Its claws caught in his tunic, and the tattered cloth ripped. It slashed him one last time, and shot into the air. It soared above the brontosaur. Terrified at last, it scrambled furiously at the air. As it flew higher and higher, its fiery anger turned to icy fear. Far above their heads, the animal squealed.

The grey wolf pounced on Shotgun. Again, it sank its teeth into his arm and tried to rip off a piece of the dwarf.

Ice it! He fired an ice bolt, and struck the grey monster.

Shards of ice enveloped the grey wolf, and its face froze. It let go of the dwarf and spun to attack Jack. It tried to bare its fangs and it growled with a lisp. Its drool froze, and its fangs twitched in rage. Berserk, it growled and summoned demonic energy. Muscles rippled, it coiled into a spring and attacked.

Jack fired an ice bolt, and hit the grey wolf full in the face. Its eyes and jaws froze. The wolf struck him in the chest. He hit the sand, and the monster's paws tore blindly at his flesh.

Fly! He launched the wolf into the air. Up it went after the first.

He searched for the white wolf. Shotgun moaned on the sand, and held his bleeding arm.

The white wolf appeared on top of the brontosaur. It sprang from the deck on the dinosaur's head, and pounced on the dwarf.

Jack put his fists together, and launched the white wolf into the air. He punched the sky with his fists. *Fly foul wolves!* Magic poured out of his fists.

What would Goldilocks do? The monsters disappeared into the night sky. *No problem, she only had to handle bears! Up go the three wolves!*

Blinded by sand and tears, his arms dropped, and he slipped to his knees. Exhausted, the magic stopped pouring out of him. He struggled to get up and fought to stand. Rising from the sand, he jogged to Shotgun. He knelt beside the dwarf and placed a hand over the dwarf's heart.

The dwarf's chest rose. *Alive!* Tension broke with inward relief. *He's alive!* Magic surged and he felt it. *I've never felt magic before! Why am I feeling it? How is it possible!*

"Shotgun?" Jack lifted the dwarf's head.

"If that's the way you treat your guests," groaned the dwarf, "there'll be no tip!"

"Shotgun, are you all right?"

"I know my name, boss." The dwarf gave him a faint smile. "And no, I'm not all right. Who writes your dialogue?"

"Well, I do. It comes to me in my head."

The black wolf struck the slide. The slide rang.

"What's that?!" Shotgun gasped.

The wolf slid to the bottom. It left a trail of slime and ooze. Blood dripped on the sand.

"It's raining wolves."

The grey wolf pounded the sand. Sand erupted from the crater. The crash flattened its remains. Blood splashed over the playground.

Raise a shield! He cast a shield over their heads as a shelter. They waited breathless. *Where's the white one?* Jack looked up.

The white wolf hit his shield with a sickening splat. He

flinched and closed his eyes. The beast slid off his shield. It hit the sand with a dull thud.

Blood slipped through the shield and dripped on them.

"Yuck!" Jack whipped the shield off them, and he flung the blood across the sand.

"Get us out of here now, boss! Go for the jungle!"

Just do it! Magic surged, and he levitated the dwarf and ran. *Forget the disguises!* He plowed through the sand towing the dwarf. He ran under the slide, crossed the open field, and plunged into the jungle east of the cobblestone road.

Among the palm trees, low hanging fronds slapped them. The ground began to rise, and he tripped over a root. The undergrowth forced him to walk, and he slowed down to search for a place to rest. He laid Shotgun in the bower of a palm tree, and propped himself on a root. He shut his eyes and forced himself to calm down. *No one's coming!* He listened for pursuit. *Incredible!*

Shotgun's tuxedo was shredded from top to bottom. The dwarf resembled a castaway on a deserted island.

Jack knelt beside the dwarf and checked his friend's wounds. "Let me look at your arm." Without a word, the dwarf held out his arm. "You're bleeding, bad." He peeled back silk torn from the coat. "Can you move your hand?"

"Yeah," Shotgun winced. "It hurts." The dwarf wiggled his fingers. "It throbs and burns."

"Your arm is open. I've got to bandage it, and I'll have to take your coat off."

"No, my coat's the only thing holding me together. If you pull it off, I'll bleed to death. And we don't have any painkillers. It'll hurt so bad, I'll go into shock. And we've got no antibiotics anyway."

"Very sensible as usual, but you're still bleeding."

"Wrap it as is."

"All right, I'll do that. We'll clean the wound as soon as we can."

Shotgun agreed with a nod.

Jack took off his vest. The vest was little more than a rag, and its seams ripped as he removed it. The cloth dangled in tattered strings. Every muscle screamed. He winced as his moves opened his wounds. *A moment ago, I didn't feel a thing!* He folded the vest, sat on a root, and laid the rag over his lap.

"Those things aren't wolves," said Shotgun. "They're monsters."

Finding a loose patch of cloth, Jack ripped off a piece and tore it into strips. He wrapped it around Shotgun's arm, coat and all.

"They're werewolves," said Jack.

"Werewolves?" the dwarf winced, and moaned, "Will I become a werewolf?"

"No, Shotgun," Jack ripped more swaths of cloth from his vest. These he wrapped around the growing wad. "They're synthetic. They're biots designed for extreme hunting. No one would design a lycanthrope disease to match it. Not for a resort. It's too risky. A guest might be infected."

Shotgun's blood oozed through the makeshift bandage. Jack tore another piece from his vest and ripped it into more strips. He wrapped the bloody wound again.

"That's a cheery thought. If I'm infected, I'll probably die."

"I didn't mean it that way." He ripped strings from the fringe of his vest. These he tied around the bandage. "There you go, Robinson Crusoe. I don't have any duct tape or chewing gum, but I hope that will hold you together."

Jack touched his arm where the wolf bit him. *Look at my arm!* Pins and needles ran up his arm. He hugged his arm and rubbed it. His hands felt clammy, and his arm was damp. *Is it seawater or blood?* He wiped his hands on his breeches.

"Next time you find a pack of werewolves to attack us," the dwarf smiled, "make sure you order the small pack."

"Whatever they were, I hope we don't run into any more of them."

Jack tore more strips from his vest and wrapped them around his own arm. Unable to tie a knot with his hands, he cast a tether on one end and pulled the other end by hand. He tightened the strips, but he felt no pressure. His arm was numb. *Is it too tight?* He felt under the bandage. Satisfied he had not drawn a tourniquet around his arm, he relaxed. *Look at Shotgun! My dwarf's a mess! What will I tell Goldie? Who cares, Romeo, what will you tell Jazz?*

"Next time the universe sends you a warning," Shotgun grinned. "Heed the warning."

"I'll be sure to take that advice," said Jack. "If I'm not too busy being an idiot." He closed his eyes, and tried to regain his strength. *Who cares about the Black Dwarf? Will we survive long enough to reach the castle?*

Jack pushed himself to his feet, and helped the dwarf up. "Ready?"

"No, but we can't wait."

Jack cast his Sasquatch disguises. "Let's go." Their fur glowed in the moonlight.

"It's a good day to die," said Shotgun.

"That's inspiring?" Jack asked.

"I read it in a book."

Castle Frankenstein

Jack led them up the ridge where he hoped to find the cobblestone road. They wandered through groves of palm trees, and fought roots and branches. More than once, he stumbled over a fallen tree.

"Aha, I've found a creek." The creek was dry, and stones littered the bed. "Let's follow it. It has to run back to the road."

"Anything's better than stumbling around. I can't see my feet in these trees."

"Agreed," Jack stepped into the creek and turned downhill. "Watch your step."

In a few minutes, they reached the cobblestone road. No guards patrolled the path.

Jack turned uphill towards the castle. They stayed off the road and plowed through the grass. Their progress slowed as trees crowded the road, and branches choked their path.

"We have to take the ditch," Jack stepped into the ditch alongside the road. "Keep an eye out for patrols."

"Boss, we're exposed." Shotgun trailed him. "Sasquatch may hunt in these woods, but he doesn't follow roads."

"Got any suggestions? I'm all ears."

"No, I'm just a back-seat crime fighter bogged down in this grass." Shotgun sighed, "I need a machete."

"Great idea, Livingston," he changed their disguises to pampas grass. "How's that?"

"Walking grass?" Shotgun assessed Jack's disguise. "Not bad. If triffids are native to these parts, we'll fit right in."

"If we see anyone, we'll just stop."

"What if they have an infrared camera?"

"Then we'll deal with it." He waded ahead through the grass, and soon they covered several hundred yards.

The road curved around a bend. Jack went ahead and came upon a waterfall. A small pool shimmered in the moonlight at the foot of the waterfall. He levitated over the pool and waited for Shotgun.

Boots slapped the cobblestones. At the sound, Jack froze. He renewed their shields and took a deep breath.

Two black dwarves rounded the bend. The guards ambled by the waterfall. They might have been on a midnight stroll except for their lightning guns and turbo-packs.

Shotgun stopped next to a stand of pampas grass near the waterfall.

The patrol passed Shotgun, and he sighed in relief. The guards strolled around a bend and disappeared.

Shotgun jumped over the pool, "Black dwarves like the ones that attacked us in the Halls!"

"Black uniforms, lightning guns, and blank faces," Jack observed. "We must be in the right place."

"What do we do now?" Shotgun's disguise waved its fronds. "Do you want to go on?"

"Stay in the ditch. We've got to be close to the castle."

They walked a little farther, and the castle came into view. Venus de Milo stood in the fountain. The road circled Venus and led up to a gate large enough to accommodate any recreational vehicle. A spur dipped under the castle to a parking garage.

An ornate portcullis blocked the gate. An arch festooned with gargoyles swept over the portcullis. Revolving doors awaited guests on both sides, and a sign welcomed them to the Black Wharf.

"This place feels more like Castle Frankenstein than a five star resort." Shotgun shivered. "I'm half expecting Dracula to meet us at the door."

"We can expect the Black Dwarf to give us a warm welcome. Lightning hot in fact. If we were here on vacation," Jack chuckled, "I rather think we'd have a good time."

"No guards and no sign of surveillance?" Shotgun suggested, "Why not just walk in?"

"If they're watching the road," said Jack, "they're watching the gate."

"What will we do, boss?"

"Shush, I'm thinking."

"Disguise us as guards, boss. We can waltz right in."

"Shotgun, you're a genius. Why didn't I think of that?"

"If they spot a flaw in our disguises, we'll be in for a fire fight for sure."

"Oh, yeah, that's it." Jack snapped his fingers. "Let's back up a bit. I want to make our entrance convincing." He tried to remember what the patrol looked like, and conjured a pair of disguises. Jack touched his forehead and a black spot appeared. "Ta da, Shotgun, two black dwarves complete with lightning guns. What do you think?"

"Your illusions look great, but I'm not sure it will stand examination."

"What are you worried about?" Jack put his hands on his hips. "We look great."

"No one can see through the illusions, boss, but ..."

"But what?"

"Who ever heard of a dwarf that's six-foot four?"

"Roll with it, Shotgun!" He assumed the air of a guard on a mission, and sauntered up to the portcullis.

Shotgun jogged to keep up with the elf's long legs. "What's the plan, boss?"

"Play it by ear."

Jack circled the fountain, and strode up to the portcullis. Withered palm trees drooped in unattended pots in front of the revolving doors. Stone knights guarded the fire exits.

They veered away from the portcullis and headed towards the revolving doors. *One of these has to be the right door.*

He passed a pot, and the palm squawked at them. "Report," a tinny voice challenged him. He searched for the source of the voice and tried not to look confused. He circled the palm and strode up to a stone knight.

"Report," said the voice. He looked and found the security box. *Think of a story, Jack!* He cleared his throat to stall.

Impatience overwhelmed the unseen watchman, and he rescued Jack from the awkward silence. "Guard, why are you back so soon?"

He rubbed his tummy and moaned. "I need to powder my nose. Maybe it's something I ate."

"Too many beans," the box crackled with static. "Make it quick, the tower wants to know if we've seen an intruder. They're getting antsy. The Sergeant's called three times in the last hour."

"Please, can I go?" He danced a little jig to sell his fabrication, "I'm going to wet my pants."

A lock clicked and the fire exit door opened.

"Hurry up," the box squawked. "And next time, don't eat the beans."

Inside, the lobby was unlike anything in a medieval castle. A sea of marble tile spread in all directions. The reception desk awaited a dozen parties. The lobby opened into a lounge and a bar. The lounge opened onto a wide mall.

The mall connected the castle's towers and divided its wings. A grand staircase led up to shops and boutiques on the mall's second level. A sky bridge crossed over the gate on the second level.

Jack spied a restroom under the grand staircase and headed for it. Shotgun fell in behind hot on his heels.

The watchman appeared at the reception desk with no weapon and no cap. "Hurry up, ladies, the tower's waiting on our report."

Not daring to risk using his own voice in the guard's presence, Jack nodded and danced another jig.

The watchman taunted the retreating duo. "You two wussies even go to the bathroom together." He sniffed and returned to his business.

Jack quickened his pace. They reached the restroom and ducked under the staircase.

"Incredible, he bought it."

Jack peeked out of their hiding place. "What? No faith in my disguises?" No one was in the lobby.

"You're impossible. You were the one who was worried a minute ago."

"They're bound to catch on when the patrol returns."

"What then?"

"Don't worry. We just have to fool them long enough to find the Black Dwarf. Anyway, we can't stay here."

A clock struck three.

Feet pounded the steps above their heads. They sank into the shadows. He risked a peek into the lobby.

Three dwarves came down the grand staircase. They crossed the lobby to the reception desk.

"Shift change, boss, this may be it."

"We're in luck. If they don't catch the switch, the next shift may confuse us with the patrol."

"If they don't, we want to be as far from here as possible."

They left their cover and slipped into the lounge. Empty torches lined the pillars. Dark gothic chandeliers slung from heavy chains hovered overhead. A circular fireplace dominated an atrium in the center. Blue nightlights lit the dark, and emergency lights directed guests to the exits. They followed the nightlights and stayed in the shadows. In his disguises, they were nearly invisible.

"Early dungeon."

"Yeah, I'll have to find out who their decorator was."

Monsters of legend and literature posed about the lounge. A few leaned on rustic tables, and others reclined on the furniture. A collection of medieval weapons rested on a rack. They passed through the lounge, circled the fireplace, and headed for a long unused bar.

Lon Chaney, Jr., sipped a plastic pina colada with a cherry at the bar. The wax legend gazed wistfully at a blue parrot behind the bar.

"Werewolf of Nodlon," Jack patted the robot on the

shoulder. Lon's robotic arm dropped from the bar and dangled from its wires.

"Creepy automatons," muttered Shotgun.

They left the robotic werewolf to its plastic drink, and entered the mall. Moonlight drenched the mall from the skylights. The moonlight aided their progress. Going down the mall they put distance between themselves and the dwarves in the lobby. Hallways off the mall led to banks of lifts.

They reached an intersection, and the mall forked. Jack bounded up an escalator, and searched for a directory. Little shops encircled the balcony. He spied a salon offering face paint.

At the far end of the mall, more dwarves appeared on the grand staircase. Shotgun started, but said nothing.

Jack strolled away casually, and hoped they would not be seen.

The dwarves turned in another direction.

The walkway broadened into a food court. They sauntered across the court and passed a flower shop and a fine restaurant.

The walkway emptied onto a bridge. It soared over a courtyard and ended at the keep.

"Stay on your toes," said Jack. "That's the keep." Jack headed over the bridge.

"Thank you, Sherlock," muttered Shotgun. He hesitated and searched for booby traps. Teutonic warriors climbed the stone ivy carved into the bridge's trusses. Then he followed the mage.

A fairy tale garden filled the courtyard below the bridge. Everywhere they looked was a ruin. The garden was in disrepair and neglect. The only exception was the statue in the center. The sight stopped them both dead in their tracks.

An Olympic-sized Black Dwarf stood astride the sun and the nine planets. An unseen light illuminated the dwarf, and the sun glowed. The solar system floated in a fountain under the dwarf. The warlock's outstretched arms held a staff and a crystal ball. The twelve signs of the zodiac circled the fountain.

The forlorn garden cowered under the menacing dwarf.

"Whoa, I think we've found the Black Dwarf!" Shotgun whistled, "The madman's got a colossal ego."

"Look at what's at his feet." Jack spat.

"It's the whole solar system."

"Yeah, our nemesis plans to conquer the solar system."

"He's dreaming."

"I'm afraid he's not, Shotgun. If he can mesmerize the Proconsul of Moab, he's a real threat."

"Now we know we have to stop him."

"Let's try the keep, and see if he's home." Jack strode to the end of the bridge.

Two massive doors blocked their way. Iron hinges kept the doors in place, and iron braces held their planks together. Knockers were mounted too high for even an elf to use. Dragons wrought in iron served as handles.

Gargoyles guarded the doors. Carved pillars of fire squirreled up ribs of stone around the doors and over the entrance. The demons erupted from the fire and brandished an array of swords and maces.

"Welcome to the gates of hell," muttered Shotgun.

"Look at the motto."

"Abandon thy inhibitions, all ye who enter here," read Shotgun. "What does that mean?"

"What indeed?" Jack said, "Careful what you wish for mortal. Not all that glitters is gold."

A gargoyle carved in stone flames held out a security box. A red light flashed on the box.

"Please use your guest card," said a feminine voice. "Or enter your admission code on the keypad provided." The keypad lit up.

Jack ignored the box and tugged on a dragon. He cast a tether and pulled. The magic rocked the door, but it refused to open.

"Maybe it's locked, boss."

"Or the hinges are rusty." He cast a maypole and rammed

the door. The wood shuddered under the magic, but the door remained obstinate.

The security box repeated its message.

We're unarmed save for my magic, and there's only one way off the bridge. He looked back at the bridge. *Good place for an ambush. There's no escape unless I break the windows and levitate us out of here.*

The box repeated its message.

He broke out in a cold sweat. *Already tried that trick, got any new ideas?* He glanced at the dwarf. "Any ideas?"

"Run?" Shotgun jerked his thumb back the way they had come.

Jack rubbed his clammy hands on his breeches. He felt a square object in his pocket. *What's this? It's not my caster. That's at the bottom of the lagoon.* The box repeated its request. He pulled out the object. *Bora Bora! It's the guest card I found!*

For no good reason, he flashed the card against the reader on the security box. A diode on the box lit up in green.

"Welcome to the Black Wharf," said the box. "Please be advised, the keep is restricted to mature monsters. Exclusive pleasures await you. Enjoy."

"Thank your lucky stars, boss."

The doors spread of their own accord, and opened onto a vaulted nave. Not waiting, they crossed the threshold, and let the doors close. No black dwarves came, and no voice challenged them from the walls.

The torches in the nave were lit with projected flames, and on one side was an unmanned coat room. The architectural anomaly led to a dungeon passage. On either wall stood alcoves with hobgoblins, faeries, fauns, and other mythical creatures chained to the stone. They passed the monsters and crossed over a trap door into the inner keep.

Inside was a casino. A circular bar sat in a shallow well in the center. The bar formed the hub of rows of gaming tables. Blackjack, dice and poker tables competed with roulette wheels for space. Light flashed from the games.

Thick rafters held up the keep's roof. Hanging from an iron cap was Bacchus. The mythical monarch sported a jolly grin, and he swung on a wrought iron vine above a cornucopia. Fruit and treasures showered on the bar from the cornucopia. Bacchus and the grapes glowed.

The dwarf craned his neck and took in the sight. "The ancients knew how to live."

"While others perished," said Jack.

"Yes, it makes one wonder what would happen if they had left everyone alone."

Undaunted by the size of the keep's floor, eight balconies choked with more games circled the keep. A forest of bar stools crowded each table and the whole packed the keep. Against the walls, empty restaurants offered every cuisine Jack had heard of and a few he could not identify.

"Nine rings, Shotgun."

"What?"

"Eight balconies and the center: The nine rings of Casino Bacchus."

Shotgun counted the balconies, "Yeah, you're right boss; nine rings."

"Nine rings of hell, Shotgun. The masters of the universe played here while biots fought wars to pay for it all."

"True enough boss, but it's history. Let's stay focused all right?"

"Is it history? I wonder Shotgun. What if it's connected?"

"What if it's connected? Oh, I'm sure you're right. I'm a dwarf, you're a half-elf, and we live it Nodlon." Shotgun sighed, "But we have immediate problems. We've got to stop the Black Dwarf."

"But how, Shotgun?" said Jack. "How is it connected? I'm missing a clue there somewhere."

"Boss, remember the solar system? This guy's a megalomaniac, and he's open for business." Shotgun flicked

Jack. "Those lights aren't for show." He pointed to the top floor. "Someone's up there."

"Yeah, let's go."

A bank of lifts waited for riders. As an alternative, a flight of stairs curled up the keep.

"Stairs, Shotgun."

"Do we need the exercise?"

"We need space if it comes to a fight. I don't want to be trapped in a lift."

"Can we fly?"

"No, I want to know what we're up against before they find out we're here." They climbed a few flights without seeing anyone.

A pair of dwarves appeared. They slung their lightning guns slung over their shoulders, circled the balcony, and headed down the stairs.

Jack poked Shotgun. He held up a finger to his lips, and gestured up the stairs. The dwarf nodded. He checked their disguises and upgraded their lightning guns to blasters. *As long I'm creating illusions, we could carry Mach 5's, but it might attract attention.*

They kept climbing. Only a flight away, he renewed their shields.

The dwarves descended without speaking. They watched their feet.

As Jack passed the dwarves, he noted their blank faces. One bore a red chip, and the other had a black chip. Neither dwarf looked up as they passed, and they said nothing. Jack sighed with relief.

"Hey," said the red dwarf.

Jack froze. He half-turned and looked over his shoulder. The dwarves looked up at them.

The red dwarf pointed at the carpet.

What? Jack searched the carpet. Scarlet splotches marred the motley pattern. The spots led down the staircase and around the landing.

"What's that?" the dwarf asked.

Not for the first time, Jack wondered if biotic intelligence was a cruel disease. *Dwarves are terribly clever, but intelligence is wasted on them. Always ready to serve, but it rarely benefits anyone especially the one who possesses it.*

He deliberately lifted his feet one at a time and examined the soles of his boots. "Must have stepped in something," he ground his boots against the steps. He wiped his boots and watched the dwarves in the corner of his eye.

The dwarves went on their way. He waited for the dwarves to go and snuck a peek over the rail. They were going down.

He lowered the illusion on his arm and searched his bandages. He found a damp patch of water and blood and swallowed hard. *Why is it moist? Is it seawater? Am I bleeding?*

Jack and Shotgun resumed their climb. At the top, windows circled the keep. Curtains covered all but one large window. He strolled up to the window and peeked inside. He doubled back and bumped into Shotgun.

"It's a control room," said Jack. His wound tingled. "Maybe it's ground zero."

"The watchman said the tower was waiting. He called it a tower, boss. We're in the keep."

"What is this place then? Banks of monitors are in there, and it's crawling with black dwarves. It's got to be something."

"The keep is the center of this theme park. I bet it's the operations center. Before I was busted for hacking, I worked on a data acquisition system for the military. We were on thin layers hardwired to the system, and they had us working out of an office near an operations center. The center monitored all of Nodlon's data flow. Once, I had to repair a cable tray in there, and I watched the operators. Too much data was flowing through, and the operators couldn't follow it all. They didn't really control anything though. They just used it to get the big picture and then they reported to the Octagon."

"Even better then, maybe we can locate their headquarters tower from here without alerting anyone. We've gotten this far. We just need some proof we can get back to the Crown, and we can get some backup to stop it."

"Boss, are you naïve? The Crown isn't coming down here. This is bigger than anything we thought of. We're being invaded, and their leader is a magician who can control minds. If we don't sabotage this place and defeat the Black Dwarf, we're never getting out of here."

"Invasion? How can this be an invasion? These are our dwarves. They may be brainwashed, but it's some kind of techno-wizardry. The Black Dwarf may be crazy, but he's just a terrorist."

"What about the victims? If this is a Martian invasion, why not kill dwarf maidens and leave a trail of bodies?" Shotgun shrugged. "Maybe he is trying to start a panic. Nodlon's in an uproar. It's worse than you imagine. Living in Babel Tower, you literally have your head in the clouds."

"Maybe you're right," Jack nodded. "I am out of touch. But I have eyes, and everyone's evacuating. Support for war must be high as a kite. Leaving bodies around only increases the support for a war with Mars. It just makes no sense though. If you're recruiting dwarves to fight Nodlon, why murder the dwarves?"

"Maybe they only kill the ones they can't turn into zombies? How should I know?" As if remembering where they were, Shotgun glanced around looking for dwarves.

"We have one advantage, Shotgun. If we stun the dwarves, we can deprogram them. If we rescue the dwarves, maybe they can help us stop the invasion."

"Good idea, boss." The dwarf lowered his voice, "Company."

"You two!"

The cry startled Jack, and he turned around without thinking. The door of the operations center stood open. A black dwarf held the door open with his foot. He sported a captain's cap with golden macaroni embossed on its brim.

Macaroni! He's an officer! Flattery will appease his suspicions. Jack straightened up and saluted Nodlon style. Beside him, Shotgun followed suit.

"Have you forgotten how to salute?" The captain's fist shot into the air demonstrating the proper salute. "Try it again!"

They imitated Macaroni's salute and punched the air with their fists.

Macaroni stuck his nose in the air and assumed a smug look. He smirked. "Now drop and give me twenty."

From his days as a conscript, Jack recalled the discipline. He levitated to the floor and completed a half push-up. He winced as the pain shot up his arm and threatened to overwhelm him. *Shotgun can't do this, but we've got to keep up appearances.* He levitated Shotgun, and let their disguises sham the humiliating motions.

Despite the magic holding him up, pain stabbed him. It ran up his wounded arm and down his back. He fought not to faint. He concentrated on their disguises and made them as impenetrable as possible. *Spying isn't glamorous!*

Macaroni stepped onto the balcony. "Why are you lollygagging out here?" All he could see was the captain's boots.

"Lunch break, sir," Jack choked.

"Get your chow out of the break room, and get back to your posts. And if I see you loitering outside the watch room again, I'll personally escort you to Master Nimrod, and let him dine on your brains."

"Yes sir."

Macaroni retreated to the control room, but he watched them from the window. Their disguises bobbed up and down on the balcony. Satisfied, the captain left the window and resumed his duties.

He levitated them both, but he struggled to stand. His wound sent out waves of pain, and they backed away from the watch room window and rested.

"Grumpy pinhead," said Shotgun.

"Odd though, he certainly wasn't one of the brain dead zombies."

"Curiouser and curiouser."

Jack tried the next door, but it was locked. Quickly, he tried the next and found it locked. They retraced their steps to the top of the stairs. He expected the next door to be locked, but it swung open easily.

The door revealed a break room and a kitchenette with a fridge and dual zappers. Another pair of dwarves sat at a table mindlessly chewing their food. On the wall was a blank vid screen. Plain doors led to the adjacent offices.

Jack spotted trays of food on the counter, and pangs of hunger hit him. He was famished. They had not eaten in two days. He was not used to missing a meal, and he briefly pondered how the ancients survived.

Rice and beans shared the trays with meatloaf mush. A few lonely onions swam in a puddle of brown goo. A dispenser with yellow and pink liquids sat next to a thermos of coffee.

He took a disposable plate and some utensils. He took a cup and poured a coffee. He loaded the plate and sat down and ate. Shotgun followed his lead and joined him. The food was cold and bland, but hunger made the best appetizer. Soon they devoured a considerable quantity.

Their presence finally registered in the dwarves' addled brains or triggered some forgotten sense of etiquette. Either way, one of the dwarves spoke, "You're nearly too late. We've got to be at the airfield at dawn for the invasion of Nodlon."

Jack stuffed his mouth to disguise his voice. "Yes, let us eat. We have to hurry."

The dwarves bussed their table, washed their hands, and covered the food as if going to war was an everyday occurrence for black dwarves. Finished, the dwarves left.

Jack started to raise his hand, but Shotgun held it down. "They're mesmerized. It's like they're sleepwalking. They don't know what they're doing."

"Right," Jack checked himself.

He took a second helping, and scarfed down another portion. He felt his strength and equilibrium return.

"Master Nimrod," said Jack. "Macaroni said he'd take us to Master Nimrod."

"Could he be the Black Dwarf?"

"Yes, you're thinking what I'm thinking, Shotgun," Jack pushed his plate away. "Master Nimrod may the Black Dwarf."

"He might be a lieutenant." Shotgun leaned back in his chair. "Then again, dim Bob may only be the Black Dwarf's right hand man."

"Nimrod, dim Bob, or whatever he's called," said Jack. "He's big cheese."

Thinking ahead, he searched the kitchenette for a means to take some food. He found a paper bag with a handle and appropriated the aluminum foil covering the food. He wrapped as much food as possible in the foil and put the impromptu pouches into the bag.

"What's that for?"

"Now we have another meal, if we survive long enough to eat it."

"Optimist," Shotgun scoffed.

He handed the bag to his dwarf. "Can you get the handle over your head?"

"No sooner said than done," said Shotgun. He slipped the bag's handle around his neck. "It's a good morning to save Nodlon from the Black Dwarf, no matter who he's working for."

"Yes, and again, I'm glad you're here."

"Can't let you save Nodlon and have all the fun without me."

"Let's try the back door," Jack put a hand on a door knob. He hesitated, "When we reach the watch room, Macaroni won't be so cool while we sabotage his operations center. Any suggestions?"

"Yes, give yourself a promotion now, and grab a couple of real lightning guns."

"Good ideas. We can set the guns to stun, and the dwarves will snap out of the zombie state." He altered his disguise to mimic Macaroni's uniform. "How do I look?"

"Nice cap."

"Here we go." Jack cast shields and turned the knob.

~~~~~

They walked into a dimly lit room. Jack allowed his eyes to adjust. Nightlights lit row upon row of sleeping dwarves. Dozens of cots occupied the bay, but not all of the cots were occupied. A small chest sat beside each cot in military order. *The unoccupied bunks must belong to the dwarves on duty.*

An aisle ran to a door where a guard sat with a lightning gun.

Jack sauntered towards the guard. He paused occasionally, and affected an air of a superior officer inspecting the troops.

The guard stared at him as he approached. He stopped before he got too close, and he added a layer of shadow to his illusion.

Fear of offending an officer was greater than fear of an intruder. *Ha! One weakness of military decorum!* Confident the dwarf could not make out his rank or face in the gloom, he challenged the dwarf. "Stand at attention in the presence of a superior officer." He spoke firmly but quietly.

The door guard shot to his feet in response to his chutzpah. "Sorry, sir, I didn't recognize you."

At attention, the door guard could not get a good luck at his disguise.

"Keep your voice down." Jack swept the room with a theatrical flourish. "No need to wake these troops due to your incompetence. They'll need to prepare for the invasion soon enough." He crossed his arms and looked down his nose. "Have you seen any sign of an intruder?"

"No, sir," the door guard answered. "But we've been alert. Nothing unusual has happened."

"Good, everything seems to be in order this morning," Jack reassured the dwarf. "I just have a brief errand." Jack walked up to the door, and reached out for the knob.

"Halt, sir." The door guard twitched nervously, but remained at attention. "I'm not to let anyone enter the watch room without the password."

"Master Nimrod has sent me with a high security message," he ad-libbed. "And no one mentioned a password. Would you delay Master Nimrod's battle plans while I return to the tower for the password?"

Thinking furiously, the dwarf's eyes rolled in his head. "Sir, please don't make me disobey orders." He rocked side to side on his feet. "I don't want my brains eaten." His hands tightened on his lightning gun. He grimaced as he struggled with an inner conflict.

Inspiration struck Jack, and he improvised. He cast a spell on the door and opened it a crack. He added a vocal to his illusion, and the door spoke. "Oh, there you are Captain, Master Nimrod's asking for you."

"Sorry," Jack said to the door. "I forgot to get the password and this sharp young dwarf is doing his duty."

Still at attention, the dwarf sweated.

"Let him pass," said the door, "I'll take full responsibility."

Relieved, the dwarf immediately relaxed, "Go ahead, sir."

They stepped through the door into a short corridor. Fans hummed and a deep metallic whine came from a nearby room.

He let the door close, "Watch for company."

Shotgun watched the corridor. "Brilliant, you should add ventriloquism to your act."

"Necessity is the mother of invention." Jack summoned a thermal fire and welded the lock and hinges shut. He hoped the universe favored Nodlon tonight.

He peeked into the noisy room. Servers filled several racks. Cooling fans whirred loudly. Rows of servers hummed. Indicator lights flashed in rainbow colors, mindlessly signaling their status to no one in particular. Against the wall, a rack of battery packs hunkered under a condenser covered with frost.

Shotgun poked him urgently. He pulled his head out of the server room and straightened up. Spinning smartly, he resumed the air of a haughty inspector.

Macaroni strutted up to them and sneered. "May I help you?"

"Master Nimrod wants to know if everything is in order."

Macaroni frowned and suspicion crossed his face, but he backed away. "Why wasn't I told of this? There are protocols and procedures." He led them to the watch room.

The corridor ended in the control room. Banks of operator stations faced a swath of windows overlooking the castle. The setting moon silhouetted the massive tower on the castle's western end. *The night's almost over! Dawn will come soon!* The luminous orb reflected off Lake Bali.

New and used electronics cluttered the watch room. *Shotgun was right. It's an operations center.*

Only a skeleton crew maintained the night watch. Busy monitors, fluttering gauges, and flashing diodes cast a creepy aura on the dwarves manning their stations. Vids, casters, microphones, keyboards, joysticks, trackballs, motion sensors, and gesture recognition gloves competed for space at every station.

The center's windows commanded a panoramic view. The view spanned Port Royal and the black wharf, the fore-tower overlooking the lagoon, and an amusement park with a bodacious waterslide. The southern tower obstructed the view of the park where the wolf pack had attacked them. *Thank my lucky stars! The playground in Port Royal is the only spot they can't see.*

Operating manuals and training disks ran along the

consoles above the vid screens. Large vid screens displayed rotating scenes from cameras across the resort.

One vid displayed an airport. Terminals and hangers jammed into the spaces around landing pads. Spotlights pierced the dark, and lights lit the pads. The airships and transports bore the insignia of the Martian War Maker. *No Martians here. Are these dwarves really working for Mars?*

Macaroni went to a master console overlooking the casino. He bent over the console and rummaged about. Satisfied with whatever he found, he picked up a desk caster.

"Boss," Shotgun tugged his elbow.

He followed Shotgun's gaze to the captain's console.

Macaroni eyed Jack with suspicion and spoke into the caster. The electronic din drowned his words, and Jack heard only susurruses through the buzzing and humming. A long frown told Jack the whole story.

"We're up," said Jack. "He's summoned the cavalry. He'll be over here to delay us."

The watch captain circled his console and straightened his cap. He wove a path towards them through the operator stations.

Jack smiled and prepared to make light of whatever the captain said. He grabbed Shotgun's elbow and hurried to meet him half-way.

Macaroni confronted Jack with a haughty air. He drew himself up to his full height. "Captain, state your name and your command, and be quick."

Jack replied without missing a beat. "I'm Captain Hastings, and I'm responsible for special operations."

Taken aback by the confidence of his reply, Macaroni hesitated. "Wait here, while I verify your story." Keeping an eye on them, the captain crab walked back to his desk caster. He glanced at the caster and punched the console, "Tower."

Here it comes. We're surrounded by dwarves with lethal weapons. Giving Shotgun a gentle nudge, he shoved Shotgun into the corridor. *Get your shields up!*

Hastily, he cast the magic, and his shield smacked the nearest bank of operator stations with an audible whack. The bank shuddered.

Piles of operating manuals teetered atop the bank. The first stack wobbled. It careened into the next stack and set off a domino effect. Manuals toppled over. Binders broke apart and paper joined the flurry of disks and books flying off the bank. Manuals and papers smothered the operator's stations. Electronics slid off the busy console. The avalanche crashed to the floor.

The falling bric-a-brac flipped an open water bottle over. Upside down, the bottle poured its contents into a cable gap. Sparks shot from the station's console, and a puff of smoke rolled out of the back.

Macaroni forgot his call and advanced on Jack. The watch captain flushed in anger. He drew his lightning pistol and high stepped over the mess. He kicked a chair, shoved aside the debris, and closed the distance.

"Who are you?" Macaroni pointed the lightning pistol at Jack.

Jack cast a telekinetic blow and knocked Macaroni back. Surprised, Macaroni fired a wild shot. Jack pounded the watch room with telekinetic balls. Everything that was not pinned down flew into the air as if hurled by a poltergeist. Dwarves popped out of their chairs and stared.

"Attack!" Macaroni ducked behind a bank of consoles. He aimed wildly from behind the console and fired at Jack.

Lightning bolts cracked the air. Bolts bounced off Jack's shield and struck other banks. Sparks showered from the controls. Banks of consoles squealed. Operator stations sizzled and the consoles hissed. A column of greasy smoke rose from the cabinets.

Anger clarified his mind and he cast a tether on the pistol. The pistol flipped out of the captain's hand, and flung itself at Jack. He grabbed at it, but it bounced off his shield.

He fired a telekinetic blast and knocked Macaroni back. He fired again and ducked for cover.

The fight confused the dwarves. They watched the visiting captain attack their leader, and then exchanged glances. One shrugged and another shook his head unable to figure out what to do.

Macaroni snatched a lightning gun from a baffled dwarf. "Give me that!" The watch captain ripped the gun from the dwarf's hands, and pushed the dwarf. The startled dwarf toppled over his station and rolled off the console.

The watch captain laid down fire where Jack had been. The dwarves simply watched their captain attack the visitor. They stood by as if it was a spectator sport.

"Attack!" Macaroni advanced. "Help me, you fools! Attack!" He darted between operator banks to flank Jack.

The dwarves exchanged blank looks and turned back to their duty stations. A couple pulled fire extinguishers and they fought the flames bursting from the consoles.

Shotgun waved at Jack and brandished the watch captain's pistol.

"Here!" The dwarf tossed him the lightning pistol. He caught it and switched the power to stun.

Unsure of what to do, the dwarves advanced clumsily.

Jack stunned an approaching dwarf. The dwarf bounced off a controller's counter and dropped his weapon. The other dwarves watched their comrade fall and made no move to find cover. He resisted an eye roll. They were mesmerized, but they were still armed with lethal weapons.

Jack fired again. The bolt cracked, and the air stank of ozone. Quickly, he stunned another dwarf.

Macaroni darted from one bank to another.

Jack fired at the watch captain. His pistol clicked and nothing happened. The firing meter read low charge. He ducked around the bank and hoped to confuse the watch captain. He low crawled to another bank, and spotted a dwarf. He checked his pistol, and its meter read ready.

He stood up. Several dwarves turned to look at him. He stunned the one farthest away, and the remaining dwarves turned to watch him fall.

"Idiots," shouted Macaroni. He broke cover and fired at Jack. The bolt ricocheted off Jack's shield.

Jack fired at Macaroni, but the pistol only clicked.

The captain ducked for cover. The remaining dwarves watched Macaroni crawl away.

Jack followed the dwarves' gaze. He moved down the bank of control stations and searched for a shot. *One shot left.* He passed a bank and fired at Macaroni.

The bolt hit the watch captain and singed his shirt. Unfazed, the captain's eyes narrowed. "Intruder alert!" he growled.

What? Why didn't he go down?

"Didn't you hear me?" The dwarves stood dumbfounded. "Sound the alarm," yelled the watch captain. Macaroni stomped towards Jack, raised his lightning gun, and shot him.

The bolt struck Jack's shield and knocked him back. The bolt bounced off his shield and another bank erupted in sparks. A short burst of flames erupted from the console and smoke poured out of the bank.

Jack tripped on a mound of fallen manuals and fell backwards. Near him was a fallen dwarf. He felt the young man for a pulse, and he was relieved when he found it. He searched for the dwarf's weapon and found a charred lightning gun. The dwarf's utility belt held a full set of power packs.

Jack took the power packs. He dropped the dead pack out of his pistol, and shoved a fresh pack into his weapon. He pocketed a spare just in case. He peered around looking for the mad watch captain. *That shot was good, but Macaroni wasn't stunned.*

The watch captain paced the aisle between the banks of consoles. "Where is he?" Macaroni stood in the shambles of his watch room. He shook his fist at the dwarves manning the operator stations. "Have any of you zombies seen our visitor?" A chorus of denial came from the dwarves still standing.

He scrambled to lap Macaroni and attack him from behind. Instead, he slipped on a stack of manuals and slid under a counter and banged his head.

The watch captain heard him fall and pounced. He bounded down the aisle, and cleared the distance with demonic speed. He sent chairs spinning and electronics flying. His eyes bulged and he bared his teeth. He rounded the bank and stood over Jack.

Macaroni smirked. He straddled his quarry, and laughed maniacally, "Goodbye, spy!" He fired his gun point blank at Jack.

The bolt flashed, and ricocheted off Jack's shield. The thunderclap exploded in the tight space under the counter. His ears rang. Macaroni dropped on top of him, and slid off his magical shield.

Burn marks splashed across Macaroni's uniform from a crater in his chest. The hate-filled smirk was still frozen on his face.

Jack grabbed the countertop, found solid footing, and stood up.

The watch captain sprawled over a pile of electronic bric-a-brac. His eyes stared into empty space.

Dead as a doornail – and he doesn't look any different!

The remaining dwarf stood dumbly in the middle of the watch room holding a fire extinguisher. Jack kept an eye on the dwarf, and stepped away from the fallen captain. He posed with an air of authority.

"Soldier," he said.

The dwarf saluted, "Sir."

"The watch captain is dead." Jack returned the salute.

Ever industrious, Shotgun surveyed the mess. He searched the stunned dwarves and acquired a lightning gun and swung it over his shoulder. He stuffed his pockets with power packs.

The door guard rushed into the watch room.

"Look out!" yelled Shotgun.

The door guard stared at the mess with a slack jaw. The station monitors were black. Wires and circuit boards protruded from the ruins. An occasional spittle of sparks popped at the operator stations and smoke trickled from the consoles. More dwarves ran up the balcony and into the watch room. They all stood dumbfounded at the mess.

"Finally!" Jack pretended to straighten his uniform, and he feigned annoyance. "I'm glad you ladies decided to show up. Where were you? Can't you respond to an intruder alert?"

The door guard looked confused. "Sir, the door wouldn't open." He surveyed the debris and the fallen dwarves. Smoke still rose from several banks of consoles.

"Sir, what happened?"

"The watch captain lost his mind," said Jack with empathy. "When I confronted the watch captain, fear drove him berserk. He's committed suicide. Sad really, these things happen on the eve of battle. Now, clean up this mess."

"What should we do, sir?" The door guard looked to Jack for directions.

A thought popped into Jack's head, and he hatched a plan.

"Spies have infiltrated. The spies mesmerized their accomplices, and ordered them to take the watch room. They think they are serving Master Nimrod, but they're not. Any dwarves who assault the watch room are accomplices. Nimrod ordered us to hold our position and prevent the accomplices from taking this room. Nimrod wants the dwarves alive, so set your weapons to stun. We need to capture the spies and their accomplices."

All the dwarves dutifully set their weapons to stun.

"Sir, how will we recognize the accomplices?" The door guard shot a confused look at his fellow dwarves and his brow furrowed.

"Stun any dwarf who believes he serves Master Nimrod. After you stun the accomplices, they will be confused. When they wake up. Set all their weapons to stun. When the confused dwarves have recovered, tell them to stun any accomplices they run into. Send the confused dwarves to the airport to look for me. I will arrange their evacuation."

"Yes sir."

"Right, Master Nimrod expects my report, and he will not be pleased. He'll have to call off the invasion. We will have to evacuate the dwarves. Handle this job well, and your conduct will appear favorably in my report. When the evacuation begins, go to the airport and find me. I am the only captain Master Nimrod can trust now. Understood?"

"Yes sir."

"What are your orders?" He asked the befuddled door guard to confirm that he got the message.

"Set all weapons to stun, hold the watch room, stun the accomplices, and go to the airport when the evacuation begins."

"Good soldier."

"Sir, you're injured." The door guard pointed at a scarlet puddle by Jack's feet.

"Probably just coffee soldier," he glanced at the puddle. "I'll attend to it later. Now, carry on, chop, chop."

"Yes, sir," the dwarf thrust out his fist.

Jack returned the salute and parted the greasy smoke with his fist. He stuffed Macaroni's pistol in his breeches, and waved a come hither to Shotgun. He stepped over fallen junk and wove around toppled chairs.

As he stepped onto the balcony, he heard a faint voice. "Report, watch captain!" it called. In the commotion, the captain's console had toppled and spilled its contents on the floor. The desk caster dangled from its cord.

A stunned dwarf woke up and moaned. Guards helped wobbly dwarves stand.

The squeaky caster chattered. A voice squeaked, "Report! Hello? Report!" None of the dwarves paid any attention.

He backed out of the dwarves' sight and glanced back. No

one else was on the balcony except Shotgun. He shot a magical bolt at the caster. Sparks exploded from the device, and the caster sizzled and plastic melted. A cloud of smoke billowed from the fried caster. *I need to learn how to stun people! I can't rely on weapons as a non-lethal choice.* The blast distracted the dwarves.

Jack sauntered towards the stairs, and Shotgun fell in behind. He watched their reflection in the window glass, and admired his handiwork. In their smart black uniforms, they oozed with ominous authority. *Oops!* Shotgun had two weapons. His guard carried a real lightning gun and an illusion of one. He updated Shotgun's disguise and erased the extra gun.

Dwarves streamed into the keep from the west wing. Spreading through the casino, several dwarves ran up the stairs. The dwarves passed Jack and Shotgun with hardly a glance. They headed west and passed a bank of lifts.

A sergeant saluted him, and he returned the salute, "Report!"

"Sir, we're here to secure the watch room."

"Good," said Jack. He spoke with authority. "Spies mesmerized our dwarves, and forced them to be accomplices. The accomplices control the watch room. They think they are serving Master Nimrod, but they are working for the spies. Set all weapons to stun, and retake control of the watch room. All stunned dwarves will be confused when they awake. Send them to the airport for evacuation when they recover." He demanded verification. "What are your orders?"

"Set all weapons to stun. Take control of the watch room. Send all stunned dwarves to the airport for evacuation when they recover."

"Carry on, sergeant. I must deliver a top secret message to the tower. Perform well, and your conduct will be featured favorably in my report."

"Yes sir," the sergeant saluted, "thank you, sir."

Stragglers jogged out of the nave, and ran past the lifts.

Jack returned their salutes and sauntered into the nave.

"The truth can be a very effective weapon," said Jack, "if your timing is right."

"Don't get cocky, boss. We're not out of the woods yet." Shotgun patted his weapon. "We still have to find the Black Dwarf and give him a taste of his own medicine."

Two dwarves guarded the open doors. A wooden bridge ran west over the courtyard. The Black Dwarf's statue loomed over the bridge.

Banners clung to the ceiling in each corner. Runs ran through the coat of arms, and fringe dangled to the stone. The army's footprints went through the fresh dust coating the nave's floor.

A neon pink golf cart with a candy-striped roof was parked on the bridge. Pink tassels trimmed the roof and the rear bench faced backwards. A red dragon on the cart's nose bit its own tail. Jack veered towards the cart and stirred up little clouds of dust.

"Sir," called one of the guards.

Jack resisted an impulse to flinch. He spun on his heel and clasped his hands against his back. He took a couple of paces towards the dwarf with an aggressive air. He maintained a military posture. The guards stared at the floor.

"What is it, soldier? Master Nimrod awaits my report."

The dwarf saluted, and he responded in kind.

"Are you bleeding sir?" The dwarf pointed. A fresh path of splattered drops matched his every footfall in the dust.

"Yes, I know. I will attend to it later." He made an about face and made for the cart. "Carry on," he called over his back. He handed his pistol to Shotgun, "Hold this."

Shotgun hopped into the rear seat and covered their back with his lightning gun.

Jack climbed into the driver's seat and grabbed the wheel. Assessing the controls, he twisted a key on the dash. Nothing happened. He pressed a red button and the dashboard lights came on. A stick shift sprouted from the dashboard. He shifted the stick and pressed the foot pedal.

The cart rolled backward. He shifted the stick again, and the cart jerked. The cart lurched forward. He threw them a couple of times before he got the hang of driving it.

He pressed the foot pedal and headed over the bridge. The cart hummed. He pressed the pedal to the metal, and they picked up speed. The tires slapped the stones. They jumped over an expansion joint and launched into the air. The cart bobbed up and down on the tired springs. Their seats squeaked. He tapped the brakes. He drove off the bridge and entered the mall on the west wing.

The bridge landed on a walkway which separated down the middle. He veered to one side and raced along at top speed. They zipped past dark and empty shops. Art, fast food outlets, and knick-knack purveyors blurred together. He dodged benches, and flower pots, and navigated past kiosks.

They reached the end in minutes. Two more dwarves guarded a bank of lifts at the end of the mall. He steered the cart up to a petrified palm and parked near the guards.

He reversed his maneuvers to climb out. He winced as pain shot up his arm. He turned his back on the guards and tightened his bandages.

"Are you all right?" whispered Shotgun.

"Fine, as long as I don't sit, stand, walk, or breathe," he forced a grin. He retrieved his pistol from Shotgun and recast their shields. He shammed a sense of urgency and marched up to the dwarves.

"Attention," he yelled before the guards had a chance to challenge him. "Don't you know to salute in the presence of a superior officer?" Jack stopped before he entered their line of sight.

"Yes, sir," they said in unison and saluted.

He returned their salute and left them at attention. "I will let your inefficiency pass this time, but next time it will be noted." He stuck his nose in the air and stepped between the guards.

The guards looked at each other and turned to look at him. "Sir? We need a password, sir."

"Oh, yes of course."

Not waiting for a reply, Shotgun stunned the querulous dwarf. True to form, the silent dwarf watched his partner crumple to the floor. Baffled by the inexplicable collapse of his partner, the dwarf made no move to use the deadly weapon at his side.

The dwarf came to his wits, and asked, "Hey, what happened?"

"Hay is for horses," Shotgun replied, and he shrugged.

Baffled the dwarf tried to think but nothing happened.

Jack stunned the dwarf. He stepped forward and caught the fellow. He let the guard slump to the floor. "You read my mind."

"The lights were on," said Shotgun, "but no one was home."

"I hope we can rescue them all. I'm sure their wits will be restored when they come to."

"Catch the name of this tower," Shotgun poked Jack in the ribs and pointed to the lifts.

"Devils Tower, how apropos?" Jack spied a stairwell. "We don't want to be trapped in a lift." They rushed to the stairwell, threw open the door, and looked up.

The stairs wound around the stairwell up several stories.

"Good grief, boss, I'm tired already. How are we going to fight after climbing these stairs?"

"Let's fly. It's a tight squeeze. Give me a hug."

He and Shotgun levitated. Despite his caution, they both sported more than a few extra bruises by the time they reached the topmost landing.

"Remind me to tell you to jump in a lake the next time you want to levitate me. If biots were meant to levitate magically, the ancients would not have invented anti-gravity."

"When the ancients meant for biots to fly, they designed them with wings. My magic is natural, so apparently nature meant for me to fly."

"Do you expect me to believe that?"

"No, but it sounds as good as anything else." All of his muscles ached and his belly complained. He was tired as he had never felt before. "Do you still have our packed lunch?"

"Oh, brother, all you can think of is your belly?" He pulled the satchel from his neck, "Remember Caesar, thou art mortal." He sat on the landing, and spread out the food.

"Yum, yum," muttered Jack. "Never expected cold rice and beans would be our last meal."

"We may be glad of it before the day is over." Shotgun broke off a clump beans and popped the gooey bits into his mouth.

Ravenous, he scarfed the food down. His jaws tightened and his belly grumbled. "I was simply observing, one of us received the gift of flight."

"When they passed out the gifts, you weren't overly burdened with insight, oh, introverted one." Shotgun licked his fingers.

"Too true, you cut me to the quick. I'm not burdened with a scrupulous conscience and an unhealthy compulsion to self-reflection."

A tinge of regret came over him. *Who am I to complain? Hungry children live in the wild beyond the Pale.* As an overnight success at the age of sixteen, he had only known celebrity. *I didn't enjoy two years as a conscript, but Nodlon fed me like a king.* If he fasted once in a while, he might empathize with the hungry. *When we get back to Nodlon, I've got to help.*

He sighed, *Am I a good man?* He believed in life and he had risked his life to save others. He consoled his conscience. He wanted to be a good man, but he hated his moods. *Moody, angry people never help.* He brushed aside the downer filling his head.

Shotgun crushed the foil and tossed it off the landing. He wiped his hands on his pants and patted his belly. He stretched.

Jack tried standing, but felt a twinge in his back.

"Be careful," warned Shotgun.

"This isn't the time, Shotgun, but I have to ask you a question." He hauled himself up by the landing's rail.

"Sorry, boss, but I'm spoken for."

Jack snorted and he felt a magical surge. "If we get out of this, I want you to be my best man." Humor invigorated him.

"I've already agreed to be Jazz's maid of honor."

"Shotgun you can't wear a gown," he scoffed. "Chintz isn't your style."

"Have to," the dwarf shrugged. "Jazz agreed to be Goldie's maid of honor."

Jack lifted his index finger to the sky, "Then I'm going as Goldie's maid of honor."

"No way, boss, evening gowns aren't your style."

"Let's split the difference, I'll be your best man if you'll be mine."

"It's a deal." The dwarf reached out and Jack pulled him to his feet.

He breathed deeply, focused his magic, and cast shields. "I've shielded us with magic, but take cover when you can. Don't assume I'm protecting you. If I'm stunned, you won't have a shield."

"Don't get hurt. I left all our meds at home."

"We're safe as long as I pay attention."

"Don't develop attention deficit disorder then."

Jack grinned at the dwarf's barb. "If anything happens to me, save yourself."

Can I take on the zombies beyond that door? He pulled on the door handle. It was locked. *Blast it. I'll huff and I'll puff and I'll blow your door down.*

He waved Shotgun away and stepped back. "I'll blast it off." He conjured a battering ram in the shape of a maypole. The maypole slammed the door and it shuddered with a boom.

"So much for the element of surprise," Shotgun raised an

eyebrow. "If they weren't waiting for us before, they will be now."

"Thanks," he reset his maypole spell.

"Hey, how about trying a mass effect gun? If you sharpen your ram to a point, maybe you can bust the latch."

"Sure, why not?" Jack conjured a needle-point and sharpened his maypole.

The latch turned.

Jack and Shotgun froze.

Blondie

The door opened, and a dwarf maiden in a black uniform stepped through. Her blond bangs were neatly tucked under her baseball cap. The cap sported a pink "BD." Her blond pony-tail dutifully bobbed with her every motion.

"All you have to do is knock," she huffed. She scolded them in a schoolmarm's tone.

"Who are you?" He thrust his nose in the air.

"Sergeant Blondie at your service, sir," said the blonde. "I'm in charge of the Amazon detail here at the lair."

"I'm Captain Hastings," he sauntered past the blonde. "I have an urgent message for Master Nimrod."

Two strides put them into a posh lobby that reminded Jack of happy days at the Circus. Another blonde dwarf guarded the lobby with a lightning pistol on her hip and a dumb expression on her face. A golden dragon attended by Chinese damsels overlooked the lobby. A fountain gurgled atop a jade bowl.

"I must see Master Nimrod immediately." He kept an eye on the blondes.

Blondie's high heels clicked on the marble. "Sir, are you bleeding?" She touched his arm.

Pain shot up his arm, and he bit his lip. He glanced at the floor. Rainbows drizzled on the marble tricked his eye for a moment, and then he saw it. Blood drops trailed back to the stairwell.

"Yes, but it is imperative I report now. Spies have infiltrated the Black Wharf. They mesmerized the black dwarves and forced them to be their accomplices. The poor devils think they are serving Master Nimrod but they are really helping the spies." He gestured at the lifts and pitched another whopper. "They stunned the tower guards, so we climbed the stairs. Send help to them at once."

Oblivious to the incongruity of the meaningless explanation, Blondie agreed at once. "Yes sir." She saluted and jiggled in a manner more becoming than Jack expected. He exerted a manly effort to maintain eye contact and returned her salute.

She drew a caster from her utility belt, and requested a detail to secure the tower's lifts. She repeated his instructions, and stowed the caster.

She smiled, and her eyes glazed over. For a second, she stared at some mirage only she could see. "Nimrod's Ninja Nightwalkers are always ready!" she sang in a bright sing-song. Her eyes rolled around the lobby and came to rest again on Jack. Something reset in her head and she blinked.

"We have to bandage your wound before you see Master Nimrod. All of us will be punished if we let blood stain his carpet." She shuddered emphasizing the point.

She waved for Jack to follow and stalked off. Going down the hall, they passed more blondes marching towards the lobby. He took larger strides than Blondie, so he slowed to let the guards pass. They stared ahead with the same blank expressions. He peeked at their weapons and assessed their assets. Blasters were slung over their shoulders and pistols bounced on their hips.

Blondie halted in front of a tastefully appointed door. Not paying attention, he almost bowled her over. She entered a security code into the keypad. He took note of the code and suppressed a smirk.

Inside, the servant's quarters had been converted to a barracks. A common room with tables and soft chairs adjoined a set of small bedrooms. A kitchenette occupied one corner. Twilight dawned through a window.

"Sit," said Blondie.

Obediently, he and Shotgun sat.

In the kitchenette, she picked out a clean washrag and rinsed it in the sink. She stood on her tip-toes and searched the cabinets. She pulled out a first-aid kit. Opening the kit, she fumbled with the contents, and selected a bandage and an antiseptic spray.

"Let's see that wound, soldier."

Jack splayed his arm on the table. Concentrating carefully, he melted his disguise. He let his illusion dissolve off the wound. His shredded tunic appeared soaked in blood. Mud coated the wound and blood oozed from his makeshift bandage.

She frowned and shook her head. "Wow, I must be a blonde if I missed that." She retrieved a waste basket from the kitchen.

Untying his impromptu bandage, Blondie dropped the dripping rags into the waste basket.

Bells rang in the back of his mind. "Maybe you can cut the sleeve off." He tried to help. "Master Nimrod will be angry if he has to wait any longer." The wound throbbed.

"Umm, yeah," she said. She sliced into his sleeve and cut away the makeshift bandage. Tentatively, she pulled the cloth off the wound, and dropped the gooey mess in the trash. Tooth marks ran around his arm.

Seeing the bite, she moaned, "Icky."

She took the washrag and gently wiped the mud and blood from his arm. She set aside the filthy rag and sprayed his arm with antiseptic. The aerosol tingled on his cuts. The pain vanished. She unfolded the bandage and bound the top half of the bite. She applied another bandage and taped it to seal the wound.

"Good as new," she admired her handiwork. She poured him a glass of water and offered him a few pain pills.

"Thanks," he swallowed the pills.

The door opened and a red dwarf entered the common room. She saw Blondie tending Jack, and gushed, "An officer and a gentleman, Blondie you have all the luck."

"Yes, Delilah. He's here to see the master. Can you help me clean up?"

"Delighted," she bent at the waist and retrieved a kit and a towel from a lower drawer.

Shotgun clutched his temples and rolled his eyes. "I've got a headache."

"Sergeant Blondie, please tend to my shotgun." He modified his illusion on Shotgun's arm and revealed his makeshift bandage. "Can you bandage his arm?"

"Oh, dear, how did I miss that?" Blondie asked. She promptly ministered to Shotgun and bandaged his arm. "Take these, soldier," she said and handed him pain pills and water. She fussed with the first-aid kit and put everything away.

Delilah soaked a towel in hot water and advanced on Jack. Her heels clicked and her pistol bounced in time with her walk. She pressed the hot towel on his face, and massaged his face and temples. "Never wipe your face, it only spreads the oils. Always let the towel soak up the grit and grime." She produced a tiny spray bottle and spritzed him. She styled his hair with the skill of a pro, and then peeled the towel from his face.

She produced a tube of lipstick, sensuously dolled her own lips, and before he could protest, she applied a thick wad to his lips. "Spread it, darling." She rolled her lips and blew him a kiss.

Not bad. He rolled his lips and tasted strawberry wax. *Note to self. Hire her for my make-up team.*

She pulled out a sanding bar, and started manicuring his fingernails.

"That's enough Delilah," said Blondie. "We don't have time for the full treatment."

She smacked her lips, and her face puckered into a pout, "Oh, pooh." She packed her things. She put away her cosmetic kit and cleared the table. "Later then, sweetheart," she cooed.

"What about me?" Both girls glared at Shotgun.

"Flaunt it if you got it." Jack shrugged.

"Keep your feet on the ground and your knees together, Cyrano de Bergerac," said Shotgun. "You've got a girl waiting for you."

"Ah, true," said Jack, "but I'm an officer and a gentleman, and I'm tall."

"Just one girl, handsome?" Delilah swayed. "Blondie and I are available when you want to go quadrophonic."

"Ugh," Shotgun slapped his cheek. "Can we go now?" He interrupted Delilah's act. "Master Nimrod needs your report, Captain Hastings."

"In a hurry to have your brains eaten?" Jack winked.

Shotgun huffed, puffed, and shook his head.

"Sir, we're ready now," said Blondie. "Let's go."

The Emperor's Clothes

Blondie led them up the hall. They stopped at a Chinese Zodiac carved into an oversized double door. "Master Nimrod," she said. "An officer, and a gentleman, requests an audience."

"Who are these guys?" crackled an intercom.

"Captain Hastings wants to see you," said Blondie. "He's an officer and a gentleman."

"An officer and a gentleman?" Nimrod asked. "Who is this insolent who wants an audience?" Palpable irritation singed the air. "State your business!" Nimrod growled.

"Sir," said Blondie. "The captain said spies have infiltrated."

"Blondie, what do you know about the spies?"

"Nothing, sir," Blondie said.

"Then cork it!" shouted Nimrod. "Speak captain, before I turn your giblets into a Jackson Pollock!"

He briefly imagined his giblets hanging on a canvas in an art gallery for the admiration of onlookers. *Why? Why would a bemused elite unable to discern the difference between art and an insult to their intelligence find my giblets of interest?*

"Sir," said Jack, "Captain Hastings here. Spies mesmerized our guards in the watch room. We believe the spies are headed to the airport."

The Chinese Zodiac parted and the doors swung wide.

Blondie ushered Jack and Shotgun into the suite. "Good luck, Captain Hastings," she whispered. She stopped at the threshold. The doors closed when the intrepid duo cleared the threshold.

A recliner mounted on a turntable dominated the suite. The villain basked beneath a sun lamp dangling from the ceiling. Strategically stationed blondes awaited his beck and call. One protected Nimrod's face from unwanted rays. Another held the magician's robe and staff. A third held a crystal ball, and several more fussed over him. They carried trays of appetizers and offered him grapes, cheese, and wine.

The turntable wheeled around and jerked to a halt. Once again, Jack beheld the Black Dwarf. He wore swimming trunks and his logo dangled from his neck. A sickly pallor colored his skin and a cruel expression twisted his face. On his forehead was a black microchip. The chip was the tell-tale mark of Nodlon's ubiquitous and loyal servants.

The shock of recognition startled Jack. *Evan Labe!* His pallid cheeks and blue lips suited a vampire more than the missing black dwarf.

"Battle has erupted in the keep, captain! My zombies are fighting each other! My watch captain won't answer my calls! Can you explain, captain?"

"Spies penetrated the watch room and hypnotized the dwarves." Jack saluted and stalled for time. *Think of a plan!* "Now the dwarves are their accomplices." Jack spluttered, "Many are confused?"

"Confused?" Nimrod barked, "Confused how?"

"They have forgotten where they are," he said and added a touch of truth. "They remember who they were."

The warlock popped out of his recliner. He pushed aside the blonde manicuring his nails and kicked his pedicurist. He donned his robe and tied the sash. Signs of the Zodiac embroidered in silver filigree covered his robe. He snatched his staff and advanced on Jack.

He tensed. *You said too much Jack!* Filled with foreboding, he refreshed his shields, and focused on their disguises. *Thank my lucky stars. I've fooled him! He can't penetrate our disguises!* He fingered his pistol. *Will it work on Nimrod? It didn't stun the watch captain! Use magic.* He recalled the ambush in the Halls of Industry. *No Jack, the blondes are too close. Lightning bolts may ricochet and kill them!*

The warlock sidled up to Jack. and studied his face. He looked Jack up and down and scratched his chin.

Up close, Nimrod was the malevolent warlock from central

casting. A smarmy expression hinted of perverse desires. Black sockets encircled the dwarf's blue eyes. Pale and wan, the Black Dwarf resembled a zombie more than any of his dwarves. Only his eyes showed signs of life.

The warlock swayed side to side. He held up his staff. Arcane runes traced in filigree covered the shaft. A white stone mounted atop the staff glowed under Jack's nose. He sought something in Jack's face he could not find in Jack's answers.

Jack shivered as a force tried to penetrate his illusion.

"They remembered who they were?" The warlock wheezed with a slow steady hiss, "Cap … tain? And who were they, captain? Who were they?"

"Themselves, I suppose, sir. I didn't think to ask them."

"You didn't think, captain?" The warlock hissed. He drew out his syllables in a serpentine sizzle. "Who are you? I don't remember seeing your face before?"

"Captain Hastings," replied Jack.

"Who sent you?" The warlock snapped, "When did you arrive?"

"The watch captain ordered me to see you this morning."

"Are you playing games with me?" Nimrod growled through clinched teeth. "Sargon has no authority to order anyone to see me!"

Jack smelled a hint of paranoia, and tossed out an idea. "Perhaps, my Lord, I am misinformed. Could others be playing against you?"

"Yes, Captain!" Nimrod straightened to his full height, and his finger went to his dimple. "But, the question is: Whose side are you on?"

The warlock flashed a grin and his eyes flared. He swept a hand through his hair and it fell in a perfect wave. He gazed down his nose at Jack.

"Look into my eyes," hissed Nimrod. All the blondes trembled. They cringed as if recalling some torment.

Jack met the warlock's gaze. Fire burned in Nimrod's eyes.

A warrior stood in a pit of coals. Flames gushed from his red-hot armor. Goose pimples prickled Jack. Fear tickled him, and he shivered. He blinked, and broke Nimrod's gaze. "Is this a staring contest?"

The warlock glared at Jack, and stepped back. His eyes narrowed, and he shot a glance at Shotgun.

Shotgun set his face in a look of grim determination. A bead of sweat betrayed his fear. He ground his teeth. Yielding to an invisible pressure, Shotgun looked the warlock in the eye.

Thwart his magic! Jack cast contact lenses over Shotgun's eyes. *Nimrod's got to Shotgun!* Eye to eye with the warlock, his friend's eyes turned black. Shotgun broke eye contact and glanced at Jack.

"What magic allows you to resist my gaze?" Nimrod twirled his staff, and thrust it at Jack and Shotgun.

Not knowing what to say, he held his breath. *What's the warlock's next move?*

"Aha! I get it," Nimrod shouted. "You're Phaedra's son!"

Chaos broke loose. A whirlwind threw him across the suite. Jack struck the wet bar. He somersaulted over the sink and kicked a hutch full of steins, goblets and wine glasses. Bottles, glassware, and ceramics crashed to the floor. He slipped between the counters and fell. The liquor cabinet buckled and dumped its contents on top of him.

Frightened blondes dropped their trays and styling tools.

Shotgun slammed into a wine rack. Dowels collapsed and bottles shattered. The nectar of the gods spread in a purple pool. Unbroken bottles rolled off the rack. He recovered his wits and fired his lightning gun at the warlock. He unleashed a volley of stun bolts. The plush pile crackled. The bolts bounced off Nimrod. The dwarf jumped to his feet and took aim. Glass crunched under his boots.

Nimrod fired a lightning bolt at Shotgun. The bolt ricocheted off his shield and struck the billiard table. Wooden shrapnel exploded. Splinters pierced pillows, cushions, and the unlucky blondes.

Amazons squealed and ran for the doors to escape the melee. The wounded clutched their scratches and pulled at the splinters embedded in their tender flesh. One blonde threw open the doors and yelled for help.

The warlock fired again at Shotgun. Billiard balls pummeled the fleeing blondes. One ball cracked a window and left a spider web of cracks. Shotgun staggered under the force of the blow and his bolts went wild.

Jack's head spun. *Only my shield saved my life.* He strengthened their shields. He cast magic and batted away the shelves. He sat up and peeked over the bar.

Lightning flashed. Thunder shook the bar. The dwarf maidens screamed.

"Leave the blondes alone!" Jack clinched his fists.

Nimrod advanced on Shotgun and surveyed the hapless hacker's handiwork.

"You dare fire on Nimrod, a servant of the Dragon Lord?!" Nimrod contorted with rage, his timber rose, and he screamed, "Die worm! Dust you were, and dust you will be!"

Clearly this dwarf won't listen to reason! Jack spotted his lightning pistol in the bar's sink. He snatched it up and stuffed it in his breeches. *Use magic lightning you fool! The blondes are safe!*

Nimrod aimed his staff at Shotgun and gestured. The staff glowed and fired a beam of blue flame. A blinding flash filled the suite. Fire splashed off Shotgun's shield. Flames scorched the furniture and seared the carpet. Smoke wafted from the billiard table's remains.

"Dimrod!" Jack taunted the warlock. He rounded the bar, aimed his fist, and fired a lethal bolt.

Nimrod's cloak flashed. Lightning singed the cloth, and ran through the filigree. The metallic threads popped and the warlock flinched. He twirled his staff and conjured a whirlwind.

The wind threw Jack over a poker table. He bowled over

the table and fell into a couch. The table flipped over and batted his shield.

"Full power, Shotgun, use full power!"

Shotgun switched his gun to full power and fired again.

Sparks burst from Nimrod's cloak and the filigree split the cloth. The warlock whipped his staff around and fired a whirlwind at the hacker.

The whirlwind blasted the wet bar and the cabinetry exploded. A shock wave shot across the suite and showered the dwarf with glass and wood.

Shotgun stepped on an unbroken bottle. Spinning on the bottle, the room blurred. The bottle tossed the dwarf away from the bar, and he stumbled on shards of glass. His feet shot out from under him. He bounced off his shield and dropped his gun. The broken glass narrowly missed impaling him. *Wow, that was close!* Scrambling for cover, he jumped behind the shattered billiard table.

"Master, what shall we do?" Blondie ran into the suite and stood in front of the Chinese Zodiac. Delilah and the other blondes huddled behind her. The blondes clutched their weapons.

"Blondie! Delilah!" Jack called out. "Master Nimrod has gone mad! Get the blondes out of here!" He dove behind a fallen couch.

Outraged, the warlock gestured at the couch. It flew off Jack, flipped onto the four-poster bed and smashed the canopy. Not content to remain there, the couch bounced off the bed, and rolled across the floor. The melee forced Blondie to retreat.

"Kill him," Nimrod yelled. He pointed at Jack and his fingers trembled.

Confused, the blondes hesitated in the doorway. Their affection for Jack's handsome figure fought their programming.

"Run," shouted Jack. The Amazons just stood there. "Run girls! Spies have hypnotized Master Nimrod. Stun the accomplices!" He fired lightning bolts to draw the warlock's attention.

The warlock turned, and Jack jumped and levitated. He fired at the warlock. He flew across the suite and tried to flank his opponent.

Jack cast a telekinetic wall and shoved the blondes into the hallway. Then he cast the doors shut. The Chinese doors slammed, and he blocked them with the bed.

The warlock gestured, and the couch flew at him. It hit him, and the blow shoved him against a bookcase. He bashed the case wide open, and split the shelves. The shelves tipped, and the books cascaded onto Jack. Books bounced off his shield and slapped the walls. Books exploded and loosed pages fluttered through the air.

Finding his wits, Jack tightened his fists. *Nimrod's shields deflect my fire! But Nimrod's not immune to inertia and momentum!* He mustered his magic, and tossed a couch at the warlock.

The couch caught Nimrod off-guard and bowled him over. He tripped over his turntable and splayed his arms to catch himself. His staff caught on his recliner, and he lost his grip. The staff skittered towards the fireplace. He landed on appetizers and fingernail files abandoned by the Amazons.

Jack spotted the loose staff, and cast a spell on it. It flew into a window. The window cracked, and the staff rebounded back into the lair.

~~~~~~

Nimrod's staff bounced off the window and spun out of sight.

Shotgun broke cover. He crawled through the debris field gingerly avoiding the glass. The staff was embedded in a bean bag. *Come to me, Excalibur!* Shotgun drew the staff from the bag and quickly examined it.

At close quarters, he made out intricate details. Fine

engraving filled the spaces between the filigree. Valkyries held the white stone.

Can't let Nimrod have this back! Not in one piece anyway! He spied the eight ball in the pocket of the pool table. He picked up the ball and hammered the stone with it. The ball bounced off the stone without scratching it. The eight ball was not so lucky, and a distinct hole marred the surface. He tossed the ball.

If the stone won't break, maybe I can melt the staff. Shotgun shot it. The lightning bolt burst on the stone. It singed the carpet. He shot the staff again, and the Valkyries' arms curled away from the stone. The hacker pried the stone out of the Valkyries' arms.

The stone was cool, and unharmed, but the staff was hot, and he burned his fingers. He pocketed the stone and licked his fingers to cool his burns.

He crawled to the patio. He slid the door aside and crawled out on the penthouse deck. He dragged the staff to the rail. Rising on his knees, he reared back and threw the staff over the side.

~~~~~

The warlock was under the couch. *Keep him there!*

Jack levitated over the fallen chairs and scattered debris. He dodged the warlock's bolts and the legs of overturned tables. He landed on the couch and pinned the warlock to the floor. Straddling the couch, he once again gazed into the sickly visage of Evan Labe. He aimed his fist at the warlock.

"Give up, or so help me, I'll blast you!"

"Who is your master?" Nimrod yelled with the air of one used to power. "Answer me, and I may yet allow you to serve me!"

"Who are you? Why are you luring dwarves into your little death cult? How are you brainwashing them?"

"So many questions and so many answers you have given

me."

"Are you Evan Labe?"

The warlock smiled. He flicked his hand the way one flicks at an annoying gnat.

The couch catapulted across the room throwing Jack backwards head over heels. He crashed into an end table. *Ouch! I've got to think of a better spell for shields.*

Jack levitated. A bolt flew past him, and the end table exploded. *Magic!* He thrust out a fist, and fired a lightning bolt. The bolt struck an appetizer tray and ricocheted.

A desk struck him and he slammed into a wall. He landed behind the bed and the table dropped on top of him. He cast the table off, and it crashed into a wall. He rolled away and crouched. He fired a bolt at the warlock and renewed his shields. He took cover behind the headboard and fired three more lightning bolts in rapid succession.

The flashes blinded the warlock. Thunderclaps made it difficult to follow his prey. "Keep moving!" Nimrod shouted, "I love playing whack a mage!"

Is he immune to my lightning bolts? Jack fired at the warlock.

The warlock returned a volley at Jack. His gaze flitted over the turntable, the carpet, and the fireplace searching for his staff. "I'll hit you yet, Clay!" He fired another round.

"Where is Evan Labe?" Jack yelled.

The warlock whirled on Jack. His robe revealed swim trunks and knock knees. Nimrod loosed a bolt, and the headboard exploded.

Jack rolled over the bed.

"Evan Labe rots in hell!" The warlock thrust his fist at Jack and fired a kinetic bolt.

The blow struck Jack in the breast. He was tossed backwards and lost his breathe. Fighting for air, he summoned magic and inhaled. His chest burned as air flowed back into his lungs. Fear and anger accelerated his pulse. He renewed his shield and deflected the warlock's next thrust.

The warlock pounded the air with his fists. Bolts pummeled Jack.

The warlock struck again, and his bolts went wild. The blasts smashed the windows and drummed the walls.

Jack fired again and leapt into the flash. He steadied himself and fired again.

The warlock withered under Jack's bolts. His cloak spat electric sparks as the threads snapped. The bolts singed and frayed the sash. The cloak fell open, and a bolt struck the warlock in the belly.

"You are outmatched!" The warlock snatched at his robe and screamed, "You cannot defeat me!" He waved at his turntable and levitated the trays, tools, knives, forks, and shattered glass. He flicked his wrist, and launched the sharps and flatware at Jack.

Jack ducked under a Mediterranean coffee table. Junk flew over his head. The breeze made his neck prickle. Junk crashed into a window. Knives shot holes in the window. Trays bounced off and rolled away. A bottle of wine struck the window and it burst. Glass shards showered Jack. He flinched and covered his face, but the glass bounced off his shield.

Looking up, he peeked over the top. He searched for the warlock. A barstool propped up his hiding place, but the warlock was nowhere to be seen. The suite was ransacked. Windows were shattered. The recliner had toppled off the turntable. Furniture was overturned, and the bar was smashed. The billiard table was a ruin.

"Dimrod!" Jack tried to provoke the warlock. "Dimrod!"

"Shotgun!"

Feathers fluttered over the bean bag.

"Shotgun? Are you all right?"

Shotgun emerged from behind the billiard table and pointed out a window. The dwarf seemed composed, but his face was ashen. "He flew away, boss."

"Flew? How?"

"He didn't use a jetpack, if that's what you're asking." Shotgun waved his arms. "Hate to break this to you boss, but he levitated the way you do. Magic, it has to be magic."

"All right, Nimrod is magical. So he can use telekinetic magic to fly. If Evan's a mutant, why become a monster? I've never met Evan, but I can't believe he's a serial killer auditioning for the role of global despot."

"Boss, why ask about Evan Labe? When we catch up to the Black Dwarf, let him have it."

Jack looked pained. "He mesmerized the dwarves. He tried to mesmerize us. I don't know why we were immune to his gaze, but I am sure that's how he turned the dwarves into zombies. Maybe Evan's possessed. I can't kill Nimrod if Evan's still inside! If Evan's possessed by magic or technology, can we exorcise Nimrod and save Evan?"

"Face it boss, that thing's not Evan Labe. I don't know anything about demons, and I don't know why Nimrod resembles Evan. I can't explain it, but that thing not Evan Labe. I never met Evan, but I'm a black dwarf. I'm even a criminal black dwarf. I'm as bad as they get, and all I wanted was my genealogy. Evan was a mild mannered geek. He was a nice kid with a lonely heart and an interest in computers. He's not a sociopathic warlock with awesome magical powers! I don't know what Nimrod is, but I do know that thing we fought is not Evan Labe. He's a monster."

Shotgun's right. Jack sighed. "I want to save Evan if I can."

"I'm sorry about Evan, but I know what happened. He went to New Gem. Just like the girls, he hoped the chop shop would make him irresistible and give him a new life. They slipped him a mickey the way they did me, and he blacked out. They didn't mesmerize him, and they didn't kill him. They turned him into that thing!" Shotgun grimaced. "I know you don't believe in it, but I'm sure Evan's on the other side."

"The other side of what, Shotgun?" sighed Jack. "The

afterlife?" he shook his head. "Is there an afterlife? And if there is, is Evan in heaven or hell? Nimrod said he's rotting in hell."

"Don't believe what Nimrod says," Shotgun looked around nervously. "Nimrod's a murderer. He's probably a liar too. I don't know anything about an afterlife, but I can't believe this is all there is. What jerk would do this people? I can't believe Evan is just gone. And I don't think he'd go to hell for making a mistake."

"Good reasoning, Shotgun. You're a good man among you're other talents. I would remind you though that I've never shot anyone before with the intent to murder them."

"Nimrod's not under a spell, boss. What he used on Evan isn't the same. It can't be. Nimrod has magic like yours. His dwarves aren't volunteers and this is no cult. They fight without motivation or inspiration. He's turned them into zombies somehow. Whatever he used on them, it's some kind of magic. Get that through your head, Jack."

Pounding interrupted them. "We're going to have company soon." Shotgun glanced at the Chinese doors. "What about the blondes?" Shotgun hooked a thumb at the doors. "We have to rescue all of those dwarves. What if this Nimrod guy makes it to the airport? What if he mesmerizes all of the dwarves we've stunned? He'll attack Nodlon and start a war with Mars. Think of the dwarves. Think of Nodlon. Think of Mars. Murder is taking a life for no reason. Taking Nimrod's life will save many others. I wish you'd get over it before he kill's again."

"Black dwarves, Shotgun, you're a genius."

"Yeah, I know." Shotgun sighed, "But what did I say?"

"The staff!" said Jack. "Nimrod summoned whirlwinds with it. He's formidable without his staff, but he didn't muster a whirlwind after he lost it. If we can find the staff, maybe I can use it. It might be the advantage we need."

"I tossed it off the tower, boss." Shotgun's shoulders drooped. "You tried to throw it out the window, so I threw it over the rail."

"Let's go after it. We can't let him find it."

"If he finds it, I don't think it will work too well." Shotgun held out the stone, "I took the stone out of it, just in case."

"Good thinking, you've just earned your bonus for the week."

"Oh, thanks." Shotgun brightened. "What if he has a spare though?"

"We'll cross that bridge when we get to it."

Jack navigated through the debris. He checked the patio. Not seeing the warlock, he stepped out and peered over the rail.

"Sorry boss, I threw the staff pretty hard. It's probably in the lagoon."

The lake glittered in the setting moon. The boardwalk circled the base of the tower, and continued along the beach to the north. A deck overlooked the lake.

"Shotgun, we're in luck. Look!"

"What? I don't see anything."

"See! A thin line on the deck?"

"No."

"We're about to find out what it is." He cast a tether on the line. It leapt off the deck and flew into the air. After a second, he caught it.

"Nimrod's staff!" The head of the staff was shattered. The arms of the Valkyries were smashed, and the rod itself was bent slightly just below the head.

"Look there, we can reset the stone and see if it works." He held out a hand. "Let me have the stone, and I'll repair it."

Shotgun tossed him the stone, and he slipped it into the Valkyries' arms. "Don't look." He cast a lightning bolt and smelted the arms. He cast an ice bolt and chilled the arms. He alternated magic until the lovely warriors enfolded the stone. "Hardly worse for the wear, Shotgun. Now to try it."

"What if it doesn't work?"

"For what I have in mind right now, it doesn't need to work."

Jack walked back to the patio door, "Stay here in case this doesn't work."

Taking advantage of the suite's high ceiling, he levitated over the debris field and landed near the shattered bed.

Jack twirled the staff, and the rod glowed. "It's working all right! It's a manna booster, Shotgun, I can feel the energy." He blasted the bed. It flipped off the door, flew across the suite, and smashed a window with a satisfying crash. He marveled at the ease with which it flew.

"It's an amplifier, Shotgun! I don't know how it works, but the energy level is incredible!"

"Maybe this is the break we hoped for?" Hope buoyed the dwarf's spirits, and he bounced on his toes. "If Nimrod doesn't have a spare staff, we can stop him now!"

"We'll try, Shotgun!" He faced the Chinese Zodiac. "Starting now!" He thrust the staff at the doors and flung them open.

Orpheus

Blondes mingled in the hall. Their weapons were slung over their shoulders. Many held their heads in their hands, a few cried, and others wept and moaned. Blondie treated the wounded, and Delilah tried to comfort them.

All of them started when Jack threw open the doors. Many flinched, and several yelped. One nervous blonde buried her head between her knees. They stared at him. None raised a weapon, and they all looked to him for direction.

Jack held up the staff, and cast an illusion of a Chinese dragon. The dragon sailed down the hall and all the blondes looked up. One gasped, "It's the Dragon Lord!"

"Master Nimrod has lost his mind and turned traitor," Jack pitched a whopper. "Now I am in charge.

"Blondie, Delilah, come here." Unquestioningly obedient, the two blondes stopped working. They hopped over their compatriots and jogged up to him, and saluted.

"We haven't got time for formalities. Set all weapons to stun, and lead all the blondes to the airport, and keep them safe. The invasion is off, and we must stop Nimrod from mesmerizing any dwarves and starting a war. Any dwarves who serve Nimrod are accomplices to the spies and must be stunned. Do you understand?"

Compliantly the dwarves nodded. *Under Nimrod's spell, they lack the will to resist my commands!* They readily accepted new orders.

"Nimrod fled up the side of the tower. Where is he going? I thought we were on the top?"

"Captain," said Blondie. "Above us is the laboratory, and above that is the roof deck. That's where Master Nimrod docks his ornithopter."

"A lab? What's a lab doing above a penthouse?" Jack raised an eyebrow.

"It's a restaurant, sir, or it was. It's a lab now. After we restored power to the castle, we converted it into the lab."

"Why would he go there?"

"I don't know, sir." Blondie withdrew, and she trembled. "The lab is Master Nimrod's inner sanctum. I've never seen the inside."

Suspicious, Jack probed the pretty little dwarf. "Why haven't you been in there? What's he up to?"

Blondie shook her head. Her pony tail bounced. "Sergeants go in sometimes, but only officers come out." She looked at him puzzled. "Now that you mention it, sir, the dwarves who come out are always different."

"Different?" Jack glanced at Shotgun. "Blondie, does any officer remember you after going into the lab?"

"No, sir," she shook her head. "They're officers and they don't speak to us."

"Now I understand," Jack nodded. "I think I do anyway. Is there any way we can get up there?"

"The lab has its own lift." Blondie frowned, "You can only get up there from the lobby."

"Is there any way in from the roof deck?"

"I don't know, but I think so."

"Got it," Jack swung the staff. "Thank you girls. Now get all of the dwarves out of here. If any resist, stun them. They may be confused, but take them with you. They've been mesmerized by the spies. Whatever happens, don't let Nimrod look anyone in the eye. Don't fail me. Got that?"

"Yes sir," they said in unison.

He dismissed them and turned away.

"Sir," said Blondie.

Jack looked over his shoulder.

An expression of concern drew itself on Blondie. She gave him the googly eyes. He had seen it before many times on love struck groupies.

"Blondie, we haven't got time for this," said Jack. "Get out of here now!"

"Watch out, sir! They say there's a monster up there. I've heard it steals your soul."

"All right, Sergeant! Now, go!" *What now? Is there a monster? Should I believe her?*

"Do be careful!" She dropped her gaze and turned away.

"I will Blondie, now go!" Without another word, he ran through the Chinese doors, flew over the debris, and rejoined Shotgun on the patio.

"Blondie and Delilah are taking the dwarves to the airport."

"Good, they can handle it." Shotgun stuck his index finger up to the sky. "If we can handle Nimrod, they may have a chance. We can't let him escape! What are we going to do?"

"Fly," Jack gripped the damaged staff. "Hang on. He's got an ornithopter on the roof if he hasn't taken it." Jack levitated the dwarf and up they flew. "Don't look down!"

They soared off the penthouse patio and over the boardwalk several floors below. "Too late, boss," Shotgun felt sick. "Don't run out of magic, I'm too young to die."

Above the penthouse, windows interrupted the tower's gothic architecture. Heavy curtains covered the windows.

They passed the windows and the tower opened onto a deck. Rough cut beams supported a roof that soared up to a crow's nest topped with a flag. Tables and chairs were shoved aside to clear a landing space. An ornithopter perched on the lip of the deck.

"Nimrod's ornithopter!" said Jack. "We're in luck, he hasn't got away yet."

"Oh, lucky, a psychotic warlock gets another chance to kill us." Shotgun rolled his eyes.

Jack landed near the ornithopter. The aircraft was a creamy white with silver and black stripes. She had the sleek lines of a bird of prey. He studied the cleverly folding wings and feathered ailerons. The Black Dwarf's logo was stenciled on the wings.

"She's a Fedayeen model, I think." The retractable boarding ladder was extended. He looked at the plate on the bottom rung. It read, "Frank Flight Sales and Service." He handed Shotgun the staff, "Hold this and keep an eye out." He climbed up the ladder to look in the cockpit.

"That's why I'm here."

The convertible was open. The roof was stowed in the boot behind the back seat.

"She's a beauty," Jack whistled. The little hot rod was the latest in aeronautical engineering. A quick glance told him she afforded all the amenities desired by a connoisseur of personal aircraft. The dash sported a concealed wet-bar for the well-to-do playboy, and the back seats provided individual vids for the kids.

"How can this guy afford an ornithopter?" Shotgun huffed, "Aren't they a wee bit rare?"

"Simply stole her, I'd say." He admired the instrument panel, communications, and power controls. Thinking back to his instrument flight training, he recognized most of the navigation instruments. The joystick and the pedals, though, were all but unrecognizable.

"Almost all pilots take an anti-gravity rating," he said. "Anyone can fly machines equipped with levitators. A small core of purists and hobbyists prefer real aircraft. A few even believe levitrons emitted by gravity waves from the levitator cores cause cancer, psychotic transition," he paused and grinned at Shotgun. "And falling home values."

Jack smiled and shook his head. *Why do people believe such nonsense?* He lacked any obsession with non-existent waves, or any interest in obsolete technologies. He had not bothered to learn how to fly any of the many niche market aircraft. Nonetheless, he admired brilliant engineering and fine craftsmanship when he saw it.

"Very funny Jack, but Nimrod's coming back and he won't be very happy."

Jack did a fireman's slide, and dropped to the deck. "She's a beauty, but I can't fly her. Fortunately, we can fly magically."

"Can you sabotage her?"

Jack looked back at the ornithopter and felt a tinge of regret. "No, I didn't think it was necessary." *You know it is!* "It's like destroying a stain glass window."

"Jack, think of Nodlon, and blast this baby off the deck."

Heaving a sigh, Jack stepped away from the ornithopter. The flying machine was tethered to the deck, and she faced a newly cut gap in the railing. *I'll blast the anchors and let her roll off the deck.* He found an anchor, but it was a simple buckle clipped to a recessed bolt.

"Unbuckle the anchors, and I'll push her off."

He released the anchors on his side, and Shotgun released the anchors on the other side.

Silently, he apologized to the spirit of Saint Louis and summoned his magic. He twirled the warlock's staff, and blasted the ornithopter with a whirlwind. The magical wind lifted the ornithopter.

Designed for flight, she almost flipped over, but she slammed into the deck's roof first. A few rafters snapped and dropped to the deck. Her front wheels missed the edge, and she slid off the deck. Her nosed dipped, and her tail flipped off the deck. She tipped over and her tail slapped the roof. The impact gouged a bite out of a beam, and she fell.

They ran to the edge and watched. She clipped the tower and flipped over. Her tail smashed into the tower's lower roof and she stopped. She poised on the roof as if considering whether to perch on the roof or allow gravity to do its will. Slowly, she bowed towards the freakish statue of the Black Dwarf, and her nose hit the roof. She slid off the roof, flipped upside down, and dropped out of sight.

She left behind a gaping hole in the roof.

"Good enough?" Jack rubbed his hands together.

"Sure, boss. Never destroy tomorrow, what you can destroy today."

"Ha, yes. Nothing like creating an old chestnut to set the mood before facing one's doom."

"What's our next move?"

"Into the belly of the beast!"

He made for a wrought iron railing in the middle of the deck. He used the staff to part a path. He gave it a thrust and blew the wicker and tables out of the way.

The rails led to a staircase. Rustic beams and brick reflected the faux gothic theme.

They tried to descend quietly, but their footfalls echoed against the brickwork. The stair took them to a hall. The hall divided the floor into a lounge and a restaurant.

The lounge faced the courtyard, and the Black Dwarf's statue. An image of a red dragon floated inside his crystal ball.

A pair of lifts faced an unmanned podium flanked by archways leading into the restaurant. Ogres in shining armor guarded the arches from alcoves. Above the arches, a sign read, "The Black Wharf."

Plank doors with dragon handles and iron straps blocked the arches.

Jack motioned to an alcove, and Shotgun took shelter with an ogre holding a pike. The dwarf unslung his lightning gun and checked its power settings.

He faced a door and concentrated. He thought of a set of spells which might be effective weapons. *Mortal combat! That's not what magic's for! Yes, it is today! I've got whirlwinds, levitation, ice balls, and lightning bolts. I can use my kinetic cannon to avoid killing anyone.* He patted the pistol in his breeches. *You can stun them if it's got any power left.*

Try a whirlwind! Jack thrust the staff at the arches and blasted the doors. The iron cooping cracked and the whirlwind sundered the doors. The hinges burst. The planking collided with devastating effect. The shock split cooping and the planks rattled on the rivets. The whirlwind peeled planks off the cooping and propelled them into the lab. Planks struck machines and dwarves alike.

Jack levitated through the doors, and quickly assessed the

battlefield. A mad scientist's dream sprawled across what once was an elegant restaurant. Tools, chemicals, lab benches, robots, and racks of electronic gear jammed the one-time dining room. Magnetos, transformers, and dynamos sparked and hissed.

In the center of the lab, a monstrous contraption of otherworldly design stood upon a stage. It towered over everything in the lab. Electronic eyes covered its head, and antennae sprouted from its crown. *Super, just what I need! A goliath class robot! An iron man from the days of yore!*

Cables and tubes ran from the giant to racks of machines and smaller robots. The robots encircled the giant robot and formed a high-tech Stonehenge. Columns of wire and cables ran up its core and ended in arms and wings festooned with clamps and probes.

The mechanical monster loomed over a pair of operating tables. *What kind of gruesome experiments are going on here?*

Stunned dwarves sprawled in an open circle about the robot. The rest ran for cover. *They're all captains and sergeants!*

Dwarves broke cover and fired their blasters. Lightning bounced off his shield and struck the machines. Robots squealed as the voltage fried their mechanical brains.

He aimed for the racks and fired a whirlwind again. Racks fell into each other, and instruments flew willy-nilly.

Stricken dwarves hit the floor. Others dove for cover.

A gangly dwarf snatched up a pair of lighting blasters. He tossed these to a burly dwarf, and the fat one jumped behind a tesla generator.

Jack twirled the staff and fired a lightning bolt at the generator. Sparks flew. He twirled it again, and cast a telekinetic blast. He ripped the machine off its pad, and dashed it against a wall.

Cables snapped. Flames and sparks exploded from the racks. Smoke filled the demonic lab with an acrid stench. A magneto whined and showered the dwarves with sparks. Dwarves scrambled for safety behind the robots.

A few fled out the archways.

In the hall, Shotgun's weapon crackled as quickly as the dwarves ran from the lab. Stunned sergeants fell. The captains took to the stairs and fled for their lives.

A red dwarf caught his foot in a cable and struggled to escape. Jack cut it with a snap. The dwarf staggered out of the lab, and Shotgun stunned him.

Jack advanced to find more targets. He entered the ring of robots. Several brandished tools and tried to bludgeon him. He twirled the staff, and a whirlwind whipped around the room and blasted robots apart. The giant stood silently above the operating tables unmoved and unfazed by the melee. He checked the giant, but it appeared to be off.

He examined the operating tables. They were bolted to platforms suspended from hoists. The hoists were mounted on the ceiling vault. The tables had a roll bar to strike the kick plates on trap doors in the ceiling. Each hoist was ready to lift its table through its trap door.

The burly dwarf leapt over an operating table. He leveled the two lightning blasters at Jack and blazed away. Bolts ricocheted off Jack's shield, striking dwarves, robots, and machines alike. Electric thunder ripped the air. Flames shot from the electrocuted machines. Greasy smoke billowed into the vault. The acrid stench of ozone and burnt plastic filled the theatre. Robots squealed and their animatronics jerked as the bolts struck.

Shotgun returned fire from the archway. He aimed at the source of the bolts and fired into the smoke.

Jack twirled the staff and thrust it at the burly dwarf. The fat dwarf blew into a roll bar and back flipped. He dropped his blasters and slammed into the goliath with a death defying crash. The robot sparked and spat the dwarf back onto the roll bar. He bounced off the bar like a jelly mold and his legs went under the bar. He landed flat on the operating table. The table knelt on its springs and launched the burly fellow into the air. He back flipped again and landed face down onto the floor.

"Ouch! Bet that hurt!" Jack spotted a live robot in the smoke.

It tried to whack him with something like a dentist's drill. He threw a whirlwind at it. Mounting bolts popped and the robot toppled over. It slammed into another robot which let out a high pitched whine. The machines fell into a cabinet. Glass smashed. Acids poured over the robots sent up a fume. The cabinet toppled into an instrument shelf and tools rolled off. Drills, scales, and screwdrivers cascaded over the dwarves cowering behind the cabinet.

Dwarves screamed in terror, and not a few broke into a rant of curses. Around the lab, cries went up as they called to Nimrod. Alarmed robots clicked and buzzed for attention.

Jack spun the staff and launched a whirlwind. It struck at a bench loaded with arcane experiments. Gurgling pots, boiling up troubles flew into the air. The whirlwind tossed instruments and chemicals into the machines. Bubbling liquids spewed over dwarves and machines.

Fallen robots beeped and whirred. Calculators hissed and sizzled. Computers hummed and tried to complete their assigned tasks.

More dwarves darted for the exits only to be stunned by Shotgun. Dwarves yelled, and fired their weapons in wild fear. Bolts struck friend and foe alike. Those that found their mark, bounced off Jack's shields and shattered upon the smoldering ruins.

The trap doors flew open and a wind extracted the smoke. The rush of fresh air enflamed the smoldering machines and flames burst from the fallen robots.

Startled, Jack gripped the staff and prepared for a counter attack.

The smoke cleared and a figure stood on an operating table. *Nimrod's here!*

As cool as a cucumber, Nimrod casually flipped his new

cloak over his shoulder. Silver fire glowed from his cloak. He put his hands on his hips and rested an immaculate boot on the goliath in the center of the lab. He struck a cocky pose and peered down his nose at Jack.

Nimrod looks like he stepped out of a make-up trailer! Nimrod's appearance bewildered Jack. *Where did he go? A day spa?!*

From his perch, Nimrod commanded the lab. Dwarves called to him for aid. Fires burned and warning lights flashed, but he ignored these distractions.

"Back again?" Nimrod sneered. He gestured at the suddenly quiescent lab and smirked. "What death wish drives you to this madness?"

"It's over Nimrod," yelled Jack. *You sound a bit nervous old fellow. Confidence! Overwhelm him with confidence!*

"Is it?" Nimrod lifted his nose.

"I've got your staff and I know how to use it!"

"Do you, Phaedra's son?" He gave Jack a coy leer. "Do you really? You don't sound too confident."

"I think I've got the hang of it."

"I'll give you one more chance, Jack Clay!" Nimrod smirked again. "Join me and together we can rule the Solar System." On top of the table he loomed over Jack. "And if not, I'll have to send you to hell."

"Never! I'll never join a snake like you! You're a baby killer!"

"Oh, I wouldn't be so sure if I were you!" He winked at Jack. "You're brother already has."

"What?" Jack blinked. "I haven't got a brother."

"Oh, but you have."

"You said, 'brother.' What brother?"

"Oh, too late now Jack," Nimrod laughed. "You should know by now I'm just a tease."

"Murderer! Liar!"

"Now, Jack, patience," Nimrod waved at the goliath. The

machine tilted at a dizzying angle but it was still standing. "Here's someone I'd like you to meet. An iron man from the early wars. We found him here and I took a fondness to him. We've patched him up, but he's not ready yet. Still, I'd like to show you what he can do." Nimrod spread his arms and beamed.

"Orpheus!"

The goliath sparked into life. A lever flipped upwards and stopped with a clack. An inner fire illuminated the machine's tubular trunk. Pulses ran up and down the inner column. A psychedelic iridescence illuminated the lab. The robot groaned and its lights flickered.

Dwarves bolted for the doors.

Jack heard the sound of stun bolts popping. *Good man, Shotgun!*

Nimrod put a hand to his forehead, "I'm surrounded by idiots." He gestured at the robot. "Now, Jack, you will pay for wrecking my playroom!"

Atop Orpheus, an accordion of mirrored lenses mounted in metallic rings on its back twisted around to focus on Jack. The lenses flared and the rings telescoped into a barrel. The goliath twisted and the barrel bore down on Jack.

A light flashed through the smoke. A steam pipe burst with an angry hiss. Deep within the bowels of the resort's electronic brains, the fire suppression system suddenly recalled its function.

Sprinklers popped from concealed compartments. The heads unleashed a torrent from the rafters, and in moments water covered the lab.

Water drowned the fires, sparks, chemicals, and combatants. Flares and steam exploded as chemicals and water reacted violently.

The cold roused the burly dwarf. He snatched up a blaster and rounded the operating table. Oblivious to physics, he leveled the lightning blaster at Jack.

"No!" yelled Nimrod.

The burly dwarf fired into the rain. The bolt exploded in a ball of steam. The blast backfired and threw the stricken dwarf into the rising water. His splash covered the warlock. Already soaked from head to toe, the splash merely added insult to injury.

Nimrod threw out his arms melodramatically and rolled his eyes. "It's hard to find good help these days."

Jack gripped the staff and redoubled his shield. He splashed in the pool on the floor seeking clear air. He jumped into the air, and levitated into the vault. Water rained from his shield.

"Orpheus, destroy the elf!"

Jack jumped, but the robot tracked him with an uncanny precision. He jerked to evade a blow. The goliath fired. Bricks and mortar exploded from the ceiling. The shrapnel pelted his shield and he fought to remain air borne. *Shields! Keep up the shields!* He leapt again. Water covered his shield in a sheet. *Which way am I going?*

The goliath tracked him and fired. A beam of pure energy shot from the rings and struck his shield. Water exploded into steam. The blast threw him against the ceiling.

Stunned, Jack lost his concentration and his shield dropped. He fell onto a robot. Frozen in electronic death, the robot's arms cradled the mage in a mechanical bough.

Energy burst from the goliath. Lightning surged through the water. It electrocuted everything in its path.

Unlucky dwarves lying in the water shivered in an electric dance. The blow stunned those dwarves who cowered in the recesses. They dropped into the water.

The surge hit the giant robot, and the goliath squealed, "Oh no, not again!" Its appendages extended straight out and it shook spastically. The core brightened, and then its tube flashed. The accordion collapsed and the mirrors shattered in quick succession.

"What a jerk!" Orpheus wheezed, "What a jerk!" The iron man let out a death rattle.

The lab quaked. The sprinklers shut down and the downpour stopped.

The force shook the operating tables on the stage. The warlock wobbled. He flailed the air and tried to maintain his balance.

Unconscious, Jack rolled off his perch and into a puddle. The cold shocked him back to consciousness. Stars filled his eyes. He shook his head to clear the fog. Firewater soaked him to the skin. He cast his shields, and pushed off the floor. He bounced on his shield, and surfed across the wet floor. He propelled himself back to the lab's stage where the warlock stood.

A ramp ran up the side of the stage to allow a gurney to roll up to the operating table.

The warlock fired a blast and the water behind Jack exploded.

He surfed up the ramp and struck the table bearing the warlock. The table wobbled wildly.

The unexpected jolt knocked Nimrod off the table and he fell into the shallow pool of firewater. Nimrod stood up in the ankle deep pool and glared at Jack.

"Thy end is near, Jack."

Water swished as Nimrod plowed through the pool. He pulled back his hood and patted his cloak. He muttered something, and rolled up his sleeves. He approached his foe and reached for his staff. "I think that's mine."

"Not so fast," Jack propelled himself away. He slid off the stage and bowled Nimrod over.

The blow knocked the warlock back. Nimrod landed on his butt in the firewater.

Jack levitated to his feet, and summoned a telekinetic blast. He twisted the staff for good measure.

The blow flattened Nimrod. Firewater splashed in all directions.

Jack twirled the staff, and fired ice bolts at the warlock. A volley of ice bolts immobilized the warlock in a block of ice.

"Why?"

"Why what, Jack?"

This time he advanced on the warlock. "Why this?" Jack broke off. Shaking with anger, words failed him. He stuttered speechless for a second. "Why are you murdering dwarves? Why are you fomenting a war with Mars? Why did you kill the mole boys?"

"Oh, all the excitement?" said Nimrod casually. "Our plans are divulged only on a need to know basis. Minions of the Dragon Lord need to know, and those who are not one of us have to die." Nimrod smirked, "You're not one of us." He held out his palms, "You can see my position."

"Why murder dwarf maidens? Why murder children?"

The warlock lifted an eyebrow. Thawing slush slid off his hairdo and hit the water with a plop. "I'm afraid you wouldn't understand." He lectured the benighted magician in a pedantic tone. "You have no god save your petty passions. You can't understand the attraction of absolute power."

Frustrated, Jack struggled to understand the incomprehensible. "Power? Over children? Over biots? What kind of power is that? You're a bully!"

"Ah, how I enjoy your emotional distress," Nimrod chuckled. "So you think your magic comes from the genetic technology running through your veins." His eyes narrowed and he smirked, "Souls fuel our magic. It's a concept quite beyond your grasp." More slush dropped.

Alert to a trick, Jack fire a few more ice bolts and locked the warlock in the ice.

What does he mean? Bet he won't give me a coherent answer, but I won't know unless I try! "What's a soul?"

"Clueless Captain Jack," Nimrod winked. "You've missed your chance, and now you will never find out." The warlock twitched his nose, and his eyes flickered.

The ice detonated. Ice blasted the room. The ice prison

shattered. It left only a crater.

The force blew Jack back, and his feet sailed out from under him. His shield parted the water and broke his fall. Stars filled his eyes, and he blinked.

The warlock leapt with supernatural power. He flew up to the operating table. He grabbed a switch hanging from the hoist, and pressed the up button. Gears ground, and the table lifted off. Water drained from the table as it emerged from the pool.

Jack tried not to pass out. Inside, his primal instincts flared, and his pulse raced. He blinked and his vision returned. He pushed himself out of the water and recovered. He gripped the staff and renewed his shields. His quarry was missing. The warlock was nowhere to be seen.

He twisted the staff, and launched himself into the air. He surveyed the lab and saw Shotgun pointing up. "He's getting away!"

The warlock's table cleared the rafters, and the roll bar struck its trap door.

Shotgun brought up his lightning gun and blasted the hoist. The hoist froze, and the platform stopped. "Kill him, Jack!"

Nimrod gestured at Shotgun. A telekinetic blow tossed the dwarf away from the door. Shotgun flew out of sight.

"No!" Jack twirled the staff and fired a whirlwind at the warlock.

Nimrod looked down upon him with disdain. He held up his palm, and deflected the wind with ease.

The blast reversed direction and slammed Jack into a wall.

Again, his concentration wavered. He felt a sickening drop in the pit of his stomach. *Levitate!* He recovered and redoubled his shields.

"Jack!" Nimrod shouted. "You're out of fashion."

Hearing his name, Jack checked himself. His illusion was gone. Once again, he was dressed in his shredded tunic, breeches and boots. Without his cape and vest, he looked every bit a pauper having a bad day.

The warlock leapt out the trap door. On the roof, he fired a nuclear jet at Jack. Then he waved a friendly wave and darted off.

The jet ricocheted off his shield. A wall exploded and bricks dropped on him and bounced off his shield. Bricks and stones buried him. The wall collapsed and drove him to the floor.

Coughing, he spat out the dust. The weight of the debris pinned him to the floor. Frantic, he twisted the staff and cast a telekinetic blast. The force blew the debris off.

Jack emerged from the crater and looked up. The warlock was gone.

Dwarves littered the lab's floor. Some rested in the water, and others were draped over the robots and the machines. In the center of the lab, Orpheus was dark. No one struggled for life.

He levitated over the lab to the archway.

"Shotgun?" He looked for the dwarf, "Shotgun?" In the lounge, his butler's boots hung from the back of a divan. "Shotgun!"

Jack ran to the fallen dwarf. Without his illusion, Shotgun's tuxedo was as torn as a hobo's jacket. His head lolled over the seat cushions. His arms were splayed out but he still clutched his lightning gun.

Jack shoved aside a coffee table, and knelt over the dwarf. He searched the dwarf's face for signs of life. He laid a hand on the dwarf's chest and held his head, "Come on, Shotgun, no dying on the job."

"If you ask that guy one more question, Jack, I will kill you myself!"

"Shotgun!" Jack gave the dwarf a hug. "Man, am I glad you're still with me!"

"Little room here, Jack, I'm trying to breathe." The dwarf opened one eye, and blew a breath. "How many times will he try killing you before you let him have it?"

Jack forced a wry grin. "All right, all right, the next time we see him, I will let him have everything I can think of."

The tower shuddered and groaned.

"Earthquake?" Shotgun's eyes widened.

An angry voice rumbled through the tower. "Jack Clay!" Shouts reverberated over the courtyard and beat the windows in the lounge. "Where's my ride?"

The vault in the lab collapsed. The blow jettisoned debris from the lab. Trash billowed through the arches. It flew into the hall and fluttered over the lounge.

The lounge trembled. Jack crouched and shielded Shotgun.

"Time to go," Jack helped Shotgun to his feet. "Can you walk?"

"Yes sir."

The tower shook again.

They staggered on the shaking floor.

"My head is spinning!"

"I don't think it's you, Shotgun!" The floor bucked and threw them to their knees. "Too late, the tower's going down! We've got to get out of here now!"

Jack searched for a way out. The Black Dwarf statue mocked him through the windows overlooking the courtyard. Anger welled in his craw. He twirled the staff and cast a whirlwind. The glass burst.

They staggered to the windowsill and looked down. They were several stories above the courtyard. The statue of the Black Dwarf stood between the tower and the keep. Below them was a hole in the roof where the ornithopter had smashed into it.

"Let's fly," he grabbed the dwarf and jumped.

Shotgun put a hand to his mouth.

"Hang on! No barf bags on this flight." They sailed out the window, and away from the tower. The tower emitted an unnatural noise, and Jack accelerated.

"Up there," Shotgun yelled and pointed into the sun.

The warlock flew east into the morning. His cloak fluttered as he soared through the air without any visible means of support.

"He's levitating!" Jack cried in unbelief.

"Bring him down," yelled his dwarf. "If he reaches the airport, he'll mesmerize the dwarves or kill them!"

He summoned all his strength. They zipped away from the tower and chased the escaping warlock.

They closed on the warlock. *Pay attention, Jack!* He concentrated on their shields and levitation. *You lost your concentration during the battle. Nimrod nearly killed Shotgun! He nearly killed you!*

Shotgun raised his lightning gun and fired a volley. The sun blinded him, and his shots flew wild. The bolts sailed harmlessly into the sky.

Nimrod whirled on them. "If none will rid me of these troublemakers, then I shall rid myself of them."

The warlock attacked with the sun at his back. He fired a bolt. Lightning flashed and a thunderclap exploded in the courtyard. The blast slapped his enemies.

Stunned, Jack's heart skipped a beat. *Pay attention!* He hovered. *Fly!* He searched the sky for the warlock.

Nimrod circled his prey.

Jack led his target, twirled the staff, and fired ice bolts.

The warlock evaded Jack's bolts and whipped around to attack again.

Lightning! Reflect it back at him! Jack strengthened their shields and cast a mirror of water.

The warlock thrust out his fist and fired a bolt. The flash snapped. The thunderclap struck and the bolt struck the mirror.

The mirror shattered. The blast knocked them back, and Jack blinked.

Shock flitted across Nimrod's face, and he hovered. "Clever Jack, but what will you do when you run out of tricks?" He hurtled at Jack with both fists outthrust.

Jack thrust the staff at his oncoming enemy. He fired a volley of lightning blasts.

Shotgun raised his gun and fired. A few bolts struck the warlock and bounced off.

A tornado burst from the warlock's angry fists. The wind engulfed them and spun them around. Spinning in the whirlwind, they were trapped.

They tumbled in the eye of the storm. Jack struggled to orient himself and get a shot at the warlock. He cast ice balls, fire bolts, and lightning bolts into the eye of the storm. His spells had no effect. The tornado spun them around, and they bounced off the inner wall of wind.

"Devil's Tower!" shouted Shotgun. "We're going to hit it!"

Caught in the tornado, the warlock drove them into the tower. Nimrod's magic offered them no escape.

"There's the hole made by the ornithopter!" Shotgun called out. "He's pushing us into it!"

They slammed into the hole. Nimrod dropped them and the tornado vanished.

Jack hit a broken roof section spread-eagled. Stunned, he fought to focus. He renewed their shields. *I can't see him! Don't fall!* He levitated Shotgun. *Work darn it! Do something right for once!*

Jack looked up. He was splayed on a damaged section. The roof sloped steeply, and it wobbled up and down. The sun shone down from the dome of the sky.

Nimrod circled overhead. Then the warlock sailed east and disappeared into the morning glare.

"Runaway, Nimrod!" Dizziness and nausea welled up inside him, and Jack struggled not to be sick. "We'll catch you! We're not finished with you yet!"

Lying on the steep roof, he looked for Shotgun. The dwarf lay on the precipice of another section. Fear for his friend's life gripped him, and he focused on their shields. He tried to levitate the dwarf, but the effort only made his stomach turn. *Magic! I need manna!*

A jet of fire struck the tower. The blow shattered the top of the tower. Shockwaves shook the tower, and the structure groaned. The tower moaned, and the sound floated out of the hole as if a dying beast called for help.

"Shotgun!"

A fireball shot from the lab and enveloped the roof. Smoke billowed from the former restaurant. The explosion sundered the gothic façade. The blast sent debris into the morning sky.

"We've got to go, buddy! Can't stay here!"

Stones dropped from the sky and began pelting the roof. He threw up his hands instinctively to protect himself. The roof tiles shifted under him and the roof split with a crack.

Their unstable ledge shook and Shotgun teetered on the edge. He reached for the dwarf and slipped. And they slid off.

Flight of the Black Dwarf

Nimrod drove the tornado into the tower. The elf and his dwarf struck the hole and disappeared. *Gone! I've done it! Jack Clay and his meddling dwarf are gone!* He cut the whirlwind and sped to the hole to see the results.

His ornithopter sat in a heap on the courtyard floor. *Dagnabbit! No appreciation for craftsmanship, Jack!* Nothing for it, the ornithopter's destruction had forced him to levitate on magic alone. *And without my staff, I may run out of manna at any time. If the Black Dwarf was meant to fly, I'd have chosen a bird to possess instead of a dwarf!*

Goodbye, Jack Clay, and good riddance! He sighed. *That was too close! He was difficult to handle, and now I need a new staff. If he knew our secrets, he might have beaten me.*

He circled over the hole. *No sign of them! Where are they?* He cursed his luck.

In a fit of rage, he put his fists together and fired a plasma ray. Plasma ripped the sky. Plasma struck Devil's Tower. His lab burst into a fireball. Windows shuddered. Flames erupted. Black smoke roiled over the roof. A mushroom cloud swallowed the crow's nest. The tower trembled. He struck again. The ray blasted the walls apart. Stones fell from the tower walls. Unsupported, the burning tower dropped, and crushed his lair. The walls burst asunder, and the tower collapsed.

Thunder rolled over the courtyard. Amazons and soldiers ran for their lives in the courtyard below. They ducked under the patio furniture. Dwarves swarmed around his statue like ants. *Die! Fools!* He fired lightning at them. *I decide if you live or die!* He slaughtered them as they dove for cover.

One blonde dragged fallen dwarves to cover while another tended the wounded.

See how they run! See how they help each other? He chortled, "How noble? Here, let me help!" He blasted a few more dwarves before tiring of the sport.

Time to go! He turned east. *We'll have to scrub the attack on Nodlon, but the delay won't trouble us. The next step of my plan falls into place.*

He sailed for the airport. He passed over the keep. He left the castle behind and turned at the water slides. He flew over the golf course and the airport came in sight.

All seemed in order: Transports stood ready at the terminals, and a few dwarves milled about servicing those craft. Momentarily forgotten, his black airship sat in its hanger at the opposite end of the field. He enjoyed the airship, but it was time to step up to a higher class of machine.

Ashur's Revenge dwarfed his airship. He admired her wicked design. She was his personal spacecraft, and she waited alone on the tarmac. She was a merchantman, but she bristled with weapons. A dual-barreled blaster was mounted under her nose. Missile tubes lined her keel. Plasma cannon sprouted from her wings, and she sported a number of less obvious machines of war. Shield nodes ran her length. Stealth mesh made her invisible to radar, and an electromagnetic pulse projector was buried in her cargo bay. She also sported a solid manna generator and an artificial gravity projector. She could make Mars in six weeks, and Pluto in as many months.

An observation deck on her aft served to host dignitaries and negotiate deals. *Keep your friends close and your enemies closer!* He grinned. Once she sailed to the out-worlds where weapons represented the long armament of the law. *Now, she serves the man who will rule the Solar System!*

He landed at *Ashur's Revenge,* stretched his legs, and shook out the tension. Levitation was a useful spell, but he preferred solid ground. Better yet he preferred a horse.

The levitators glowed in preparation for flight. *These new machines destroy more efficiently, but they sanitize killing.* He savored the memory of his victims dying. *Give me a horse and a sword! I want to smell the fear! I want to see the terror in their eyes as my enemies die!*

Two dwarves guarded a ramp to the passenger deck. The dwarves saluted. "Did you have a good trip, sir?" said one.

"No you idiot! Clay destroyed my ornithopter and took my staff. I had to levitate on pure magic. It's like gambling. I might have fallen out of the sky!"

The hatch opened, and he strode between the dwarves and mounted the ramp.

The dwarves made an about face. They raised their weapons.

For a split second, he hesitated. *Why aren't they following me?* He spun on the dwarves.

They shot Nimrod. A volley of lightning bolts ripped the air. Thunder rolled over the tarmac.

Sparks showered from the silver threads. Flames sprang up from his cloak.

"Are you out of your minds?" He snapped his fingers and doused the fire.

The dwarves pelted him with bolts.

He deflected the deadly charges. Bolts ricocheted off the tarmac.

Nimrod thrust out a fist and shot a dwarf with a bolt. The force flung the young man on his back. The other abandoned the effort and ran.

He fired a bolt. The dwarf rolled and flames exploded from the tarmac. The dwarf swerved towards a baggage tram.

Nimrod struck the tram. The machine's batteries popped, and an acid cloud spewed from the hood.

The dwarf changed direction and sprinted for his life.

Nimrod fired again and hit the dwarf in the back.

The dwarf flew into the air. His blaster hit the tarmac and skittered away. The dwarf bounced on the pavement and collapsed spread-eagled.

What's happened to my zombies? They're mesmerized! Mesmerization doesn't wear off!

Sennacherib and a few of his lieutenants stood in the hatch.

They stared open mouthed and slack-jawed. *Tremble my lackeys! I should fry you where you stand!*

All of his lieutenants saluted. Sennacherib bowed, "My lord." He glanced at Nimrod's singed cloak. "What happened, sir?"

"Are you blind?! Idiot! My own guard attacked me from behind!" He strode up the remaining stairs and into the craft. He glanced up and down the cabin. "Can anyone tell me what's going on here?"

"Revolt, sir," Sennacherib glanced at the fallen dwarves on the tarmac. "Someone's reprogrammed the dwarves. We've got a mutiny on our hands. They're clever. They feign loyalty. And we can't read their minds until they fall asleep."

"Mutiny of the black dwarves," said Nimrod. "How poetic? What else can go wrong? I'm surrounded by incompetents!"

"My lord, we've tried to get a handle on it all morning." A bead of sweat rolled down the pilot's brow.

"Get us in the air, Senna. Destroy the airport and the transports. Leave the dwarves here. We can't trust any of this lot. By the time they discover where they are, it will be too late."

"Aye, my lord," the pilot bowed. He heaved a sigh of relief and retreated to the cockpit.

The warlock relaxed in his recliner.

The terminals shrank in his window as they lifted off.

Sennacherib circled the airport. Destruction rained from the spacecraft's arsenal. Black dwarves scurried to and fro seeking cover from the hail of death.

Fire bombs dropped on the hangers. Sennacherib blasted the flyers and the airships. A volley of missiles incinerated the transports. Plasma cannon set the terminals ablaze. A firestorm rose from the airport.

"My lord," said a blonde Amazon. "May I get you a drink?"

"Merlot," he said. "Are you feeling all right, Barb?"

"Why yes, sir! Why do you ask, my lord?"

He gazed into her eyes and sensed his spell. "Nothing, Barb. Get my drink."

Barb smiled and twisted salaciously. She shook her skirt and tapped her boots. The pretty thing winked at him. She turned and sashayed to his bar. The blonde deftly juggled a bottle and a goblet. Soon she returned with a generous portion of a rare vintage.

Nimrod swirled the goblet and tested the bouquet. *Time to move my headquarters, anyway.* He consoled himself. *Jack's meddling is a minor setback. It's an inconvenience and nothing more. The wheels are in motion. Mars will declare war with or without an attack. If war comes before we destroy Nodlon, it makes no difference.*

The spacecraft circled over the airport again. They avoided the thick, greasy smoke rising from the ruins. A thunderstorm rose on the sky dome as the fire system responded to the blaze. Nimrod relished the firestorm.

Sennacherib appeared on his intercom. "Sir is the damage satisfactory?"

"Good enough, Senna, get us out of here."

Sennacherib turned the ship west, and they sailed over the castle.

Nimrod caught one last glimpse of Devil's Tower. *So long, Cretaceous Clay. You've met your doom, and now you lie in your tomb.*

They flew over Lake Bali. Dolphins played in the atolls, and sharks hunted on the reefs. Rainbow fish danced over white shoals.

"Bah humbug," Nimrod said. He stood and handed his goblet to his Amazon. "Fill her up, Barb."

Barb took the goblet, "Yes sir." She went to the bar, and fussed with the bottles.

He watched the blonde open another bottle. Satisfied, he turned to his observation deck. *Time to enjoy the fireworks.* The castle smoldered, and the airport burned. Manna tanks exploded with satisfying concussions. Fireballs rolled up from the tanks and licked the dome. The ghost in the machine projected a thunderstorm over the airport. Lightning cracked on the sky dome. Rain erupted from the sprinklers. The fire extinguishers worked to douse the fires and the ruins smoked. The mess pleased him.

My little lair was comfy while it lasted, but the hour grows late. He glowered. *Next, Jack we shall unleash the power of the Yellow Stone. And there will be nothing you can do about it while your corpse rots under Devil's Tower.* He chuckled. *I can't wait to see you in Gehenna at the mercy of my trolls.*

The soft clomp of high heels disturbed him. "My lord," said Barb.

He turned. His Amazons held their blasters at the ready. "Barb, Ella, what are you doing?"

They fired, and the window blew out.

Wind whipped the deck with hurricane force. It threw him into the air, and he cast a tether to hang onto the spaceship.

The blondes trained their blasters on him. Plasma ripped his cloak apart.

He held up his hand and cast a shield. The blondes fired again. He swirled his palm and deflected their plasma jets.

The plasma narrowly missed the blondes, and they dodged their own fire. Barb signaled Ella, and she fired at the deck. Ella switched settings and began cutting up the deck. Plate peeled from the deck. Wire lashed at the warlock and the debris shielded the Amazons.

Clever! Pieces of the spacecraft pelted Nimrod. *Are they no longer mesmerized?* He threw a fist and fired a plasma bolt. A plate flew at him and intercepted his shot. He ducked and the metal missed him. It sailed into the air.

The blondes fired a volley of plasma bolts.

He deflected the bolts and fired again.

A bolt hit Barb, and she dropped her blaster.

The blaster sailed at Nimrod, and he ducked.

She slammed into the deck. The wind picked her up, and threw her at the warlock.

He flinched and dodged the blonde's broken body.

Her safety line went taut and her harness caught her. She stopped short of flying off the deck.

Ella charged. Her blaster blazed. Plasma struck the warlock's shields and ricocheted in all directions.

Furious he deflected the bolts. Sparks shot from the walls. Plates melted. He leapt out of the nuclear fire. He cast a line and seized her blaster. Magic snatched the weapon out of her hands.

He caught her eye. She was unafraid. *No fear? No anger? No disgust?* Heeding her expression no mind, he fired a plasma jet with his fist. "Die traitor!"

The jet struck her breast. She folded. Blood sprayed over him. Her body hit the deck and she slid to the edge. Her safety harness caught her and she stopped next to Barb.

He steadied himself with magic and marched back to the deck hatch.

Senna shouted at the hatch door. He punched the key box and pried on the hatch lock. The hatch groaned and slid open.

His lieutenants fell back and bowed.

He shot through the hatch and glared at his remaining lieutenants. "There will be hell to pay for this!"

"My lord, the hatch was locked from the other side," said Senna.

"Are there any more zombies aboard the ship?"

"No, my lord," his pilot looked down and shook his head. "Forgive us, my lord, we can't recognize the zombies who are loyal from the ones who have turned."

"Yes, for that reason, I shall not punish you as severely as you deserve." Nimrod spoke a word from the old tongue, and his servants fell to their knees and clutched their bellies. They rolled on the floor in agony before he released them. "Let that be a lesson for your incompetence. I'd let you have a full measure, but it would greatly inconvenience me. I shall not be so forgiving next time."

"Thank you, my lord," one cried. They all took up a chorus of flattery.

"Senna!"

"Yes my lord." The pilot dared not look up, and he kept his gaze on the floor.

"The observation deck has been compromised," he hissed slowly. "Kick in the deck gravity. Raise the shields, and try not to screw up!"

"Aye, my lord," the pilot jogged to the cockpit.

"Go to the emergency manna shaft and hover. We will seal the access behind us." Nimrod shouted, "Got that? Or do I need to draw you a picture?"

"Aye, my lord," called Senna.

"Good! Don't forget to breathe in and breathe out while you're at it!"

His lieutenants glanced at each other. "What are you idiots waiting for? Skelter get me a drink. Helter start dinner. The rest of you find something to do before I find out I don't need you!"

He looked out the hatch. The observation deck was a shambles.

In the distance, the Devil's Tower smoldered. A dark cloud hovered over the Black Wharf and the airport. The rainstorm had doused the fires.

They passed over an atoll, a reef, and then left Lake Bali behind. They flew over a peninsula lined with white beaches. Piers ran from empty boardwalks lined with palm trees. They soared over cottages, pavilions, and water slides.

Then *Ashur's Revenge* plunged into his access tunnel. The great earthquake had sealed the Holloway and closed the main entrance. No one had suspected the Ninth Ring survived, and the Ring was lost.

But the Dragon Lord had not forgotten the Ring. His spies were everywhere. Serpents and snakes, wolves and weasels, cats and rats, and even birds answered to him. What they knew, the

Dragon knew. And his spies knew where the Ninth Ring was.

They had waited for the stars to align and finally their time had come. *Our time! My time! I made the jump between the worlds. I found this place and I made it my lair.*

He had driven an access tunnel from the emergency manna dump shaft to the Ninth Ring. Now, *Ashur's Revenge* tore through his tunnel at a ridiculous speed.

Fools! Frightened of their own technology, it never occurred to them to look under Rickover Station. They could have reached the Ninth Ring and cleared the Holloway decades ago. They had no idea how close they were.

The ship slowed to a halt. They hovered in the manna dump shaft. The shaft ran at an angle nearly straight up back to Blueberry Lake.

If the Ninth Ring was the perfect place to stage an invasion of Nodlon, the shaft was the perfect highway through which to attack. "Life is what happens," he sighed, "while evil plans." *I will return to this place!*

"Is this satisfactory, my lord?" asked Senna.

"Hold here, captain."

"Yes, my lord."

He opened the hatch and stepped back onto the observation deck. He summoned magic and cut the blondes' tethers with a flick of his hand. He levitated their remains and flung them into his access tunnel.

The girls flew into the tunnel and fell to the dirt.

"To Gehenna with you traitors!" he cursed. "How dare you betray me?"

He cast a plasma jet and a few rocks fell. *Dagnabbit!* Without his staff, he lacked the magic to drop the shaft's roof in one fell blow. He set to work. He gouged out the ceiling and slowly filled the shaft with rock. He broke into a sweat, and his arms wearied with the exertion. Finally, the last of the roof fell and the shaft closed.

"Senna," he croaked.

"What are your orders, my lord?"

"Go," he huffed and puffed. "Leave Nodlon, take us to Yellow Stone. We have a nation to crush, and a world to conquer."

"Yes my lord, as you command."

Bouncy Balls

Jack tumbled off the roof and a truss whacked him in the back. He flipped head over heels.

"Help!" cried Shotgun. "Jack, I'm falling!"

Jack levitated him, "Got you!"

"Get us out of here, boss."

"We'll surf out." He cast an ice board.

"Hang on!" He pushed Shotgun to the front of the board. He balanced the magical surfboard and looked for an escape. The broken roof had gone clean through the floor to the mall below.

Jack dove into the hole. "Get down!" He crouched and shot the barrel. They blew into the mall. He cross-stepped back and forced the board into the bottom turn. He pinned Shotgun to the board with magic and levitated the nose. Jack rolled the board and sailed over the balcony. *Can't do that on a wave!*

"Whoa!" Shotgun flattened on the board and yelled. "Watch out!"

He glimpsed the lobby. The golf cart and the dwarves were gone. *Good! Blondie got them out! That's a relief!*

The board lifted off over the balcony rails. He let the board take the pressure of the lift, and he pushed for more speed. They ripped down the mall. Thunder echoed. He pressed the ice board for more speed.

"Keep your head down!"

He carved the air around the chandeliers, and the chandeliers rocked in their wake.

Ahead the mall divided into an intersection. *Safety!* "That's the way out!" *Go Jack!*

"We're gonna make it!" He was stoked. *Come on baby! We can make it!*

"Great!" Shotgun shouted, "I wish I shared your confidence!"

"What, no faith?" He glanced back.

A wall of dust chased them. He twisted Nimrod's staff and willed the manna into the board. He punched it and the board burst forward.

The shockwave hit them. The board jiggled. It launched them into the dust cloud. He levitated the board and let the wobble roll out.

Stones and rocks pelted his back. *We'll be buried alive!*

The cloud plunged them into a grey twilight. The Black Wharf's blue emergency lights came on and the cloud glowed.

Jack flew by memory. He carved the dust cloud and wove to avoid the chandeliers. One struck his shield and rocked the board. *Don't strike the ceiling!*

A rail flashed out of the dust. *Up!* He levitated to find air to clear the rail. *Go up!* The board slammed into the rail. The rail clanged, and glass shattered. The board flipped and they were airborne.

They slid off the board as fast as pancakes off a hot griddle. Shotgun went head over heels, and Jack flew over the rail.

His foot struck the rail and he bowled over. He hit Shotgun and their shields bounced.

"Ouch," shouted Shotgun.

His board whacked him. *Thank the stars for shields!* He levitated, but he lost all sense of direction.

He flew through the intersection and hit the rail on the other side. Glass shattered and broke his concentration. He fell. *Shields!*

He landed on a pile of soft balls. He bounced on the balls. He swam in the balls and searched for a floor. *Stop! You're not getting anywhere!* He rolled onto his back and floated on the balls.

"Shotgun! Shotgun, where are you?!"

The tower rumbled, and the rumble became a roar. The shockwave roared overhead. A concrete wall snapped in the lobby and the blocks burst. The walls around him exploded. Rocks, stones, studs and nails showered him. Dust billowed around him, and the cloud thickened. Rocks struck his shield and bounced off.

The thunder faded to a rumble and quiet gradually settled over the bouncy balls. *Where's Shotgun?* As the dust settled, a few more small stones dropped on him.

~~~~~

"Shotgun?"

"I'm over here, boss!"

"Are you all right?"

"We're alive?"

"Yeah, I think so."

"Good, remind me not to fly Jack Air again. As soon as we get out of this I want to take a flyer. I think you owe me some frequent flyer miles."

"Beggars can't be choosers."

"I'm not begging. As I recall you're the criminal and you got me into this."

"Thanks, Shotgun," he relaxed. "Does that mean I don't get a mint?"

"Boss, at this point I'm thinking you can do your own laundry."

"That bad, hey?"

Shotgun swam through the balls.

"Let's just say, I could use some inspiration. We're trapped in the Black Wharf two miles below Nodlon. We're so deep; we're halfway to hell already. Any deeper and we'd be knocking on the gates of hell."

"I think you're exaggerating, Shotgun." He chuckled. "I'm guessing hell is up there somewhere. Maybe it's in the direction of Capricorn."

"Boss, we're so deep, it gives new meaning to the phrase, 'As lost as the Ninth Ring.' Oh, wait, that can't be right!" Shotgun rolled in the bouncy balls. He threw balls at Jack. "No,

I forgot. We're so lost; we are in the Ninth Ring." The dwarf pummeled the elf with bouncy balls.

"Hey," Jack shook his head. He let the bouncy balls pummel him. "We know where we are! We just have to get out of here!"

"We're trapped! If we can get out of here, how are we going to get out of the Ninth Ring? Nimrod will take all the airships and destroy the rest!"

"Oh, ye of little faith, Shotgun! We'll get to the airport, stop Nimrod, and rescue the dwarves! We'll find a flyer there."

"Stop Nimrod? That wacko is already mesmerizing everybody again. By the time we get there, he's going to be invading Nodlon."

"Look Shotgun," he cheered the dwarf. "We're not finished. We've done pretty well so far."

"Done well, Jack? He nearly killed us! How many times are we going to let him have a go?"

"Don't get bent out of shape. Let's tick off our progress so far." Jack held up an index finger. "We found the Black Dwarf, and discovered his name. We don't know exactly who Nimrod is, but we can give Gumshoe his name when we can get back to Nodlon, and let Nodlon Yard work on it."

"Great boss!" Shotgun scoffed, "Why do I have a feeling Nodlon Yard doesn't have a rap sheet on this guy? Nimrod's not your garden variety psychopath."

"All right," said Jack. "Good point! But that's not all we've done." Jack held up another finger. "We found the Black Dwarf's lair and destroyed his headquarters. We've fomented a mutiny of the black dwarves. We've stopped his army, and I bet he'll have to call off his invasion of Nodlon. When we get out of here, we can rescue the missing dwarves. We've made a good start."

"Nimrod is a mad-man! He's headed back to Nodlon! He's a child killer, and he means to destroy more of us or I'm not a hacker." The dwarf sighed. "I'm thinking of Goldie, Faith, and

Hope. Think of Jazz!"

"I'm thinking of Jazz!"

"We've got to stop Nimrod before he destroys any more lives! We have to find a way."

"Chin up Shotgun, we'll find a way."

"Speaking of finding a way, boss, we've got to find our way out of this pile of bouncy balls."

"Yep, you're right, but I'm not too worried." Jack picked up a squishy, pink ball. "Pick a direction and start swimming. There's bound to be an end to the bouncy balls."

"Fancy falling into a bouncy ball pit; that's incredibly lucky."

"Good thing, too! We hit a rail, and it broke my concentration. I lost the shields for a moment. If we hadn't landed in the bouncy balls, we could've been killed!"

"You're saying these bouncy balls have sat here for a hundred years or so until along we come to fall into them? What are the chances of that?"

"It's impossible, Shotgun. Maybe the universe is on our side."

"If the universe is on our side, why not arrange for that Nimrod fellow to blow a gasket and save us the trouble."

"Oh, I don't know Shotgun. Maybe it's up to us to stop him. Maybe that's why we landed in the bouncy balls." *Maybe that's why I have magic.*

"Starting to have an open mind are we, boss?"

"No Shotgun. I'm just wondering if we're alone or if we've got any help."

"Are you going soft on me, boss? What's so special about us? You're not starting to believe your own advertising? Are you?" Shotgun pelted the mage with bouncy balls.

"Maybe I'm just going soft." Jack chucked a few balls at Shotgun.

"Let the universe sort it out then."

"Come on Shotgun, let's get out of here."

"Give me a minute." Shotgun snuggled in the bouncy balls and closed his eyes.

"What do you need a minute for? Our quarry is getting away."

"I need to let my stomach catch up with the rest of me before we give the Black Dwarf another chance to end our corporeal existence."

"You don't need any time for that. If we catch up with him, the chances are good you won't have to worry about your stomach ever again."

The dwarf closed his eyes and moaned.

"Contemplating the rings of Saturn, Shotgun?"

"No, just searching for the courage to try again."

The dwarf closed his eyes, and everything went black.

~~~~~

The End

Epilogue: On the Beach

Waves washed over her. They were warm and pleasant. She was not alone, but she was not frightened. Somehow she knew her fellow swimmers were friends. She did not know how she knew, but she did.

She was close now, very close to the shore. The bottom was rising up to greet her. *Where have I been all this time? Was she floating over an ocean? What if she sank and the water had swallowed her up?*

It won't you know, said a voice in her head. *You're not pure enough to fly, but the abyss can't take you if it tried.*

Who are you?

Stony silence answered her question. The waves rocked her back and forth, as gently as a baby. She remembered her first nanny, a little hobgoblin named Harriet. When she fell off a swing, nanny rocked her just like this.

It's just you Angela. It's just part of you talking in your head.

No, said the voice. *I wouldn't go as far as to say that. Grasshopper!*

I told you I'd never leave you, Angela.

Oh, it's only you grasshopper. So you made it here too.

We can't be parted, he said.

Where have I heard that before?

I love you, said the voice.

Somehow, I thought if I died, I'd be free of you.

You are free, love, he said. *Remember what they said at Tollmerak; they gave up the control programs. It was too cruel, and biots killed themselves to stop the nagging. I told you, I'm not a stability program.*

Like I'm supposed to believe that?

Your chip is gone.

Now we know the answer. Wish I'd known that before.

Her head bumped on the sand. The waves tossed her upon

the beach. For a while she enjoyed the warm sand before she realized she was breathing again.

Where am I grasshopper?

Don't know. Open your eyes and find out. It can't be too bad, can it?

So I take it I have to open my eyes? Very well then I will. She forced her eyes open, and the light nearly blinded her. She blinked and rolled over. She hid her face from the sun.

The beach ran up to some dunes. Driftwood littered the near ones. Tufts of sandy grass topped the far ones. Golden light bathed the sand. Not far away was a crab. She gave it a stare, and it skittered down the beach and into the water.

"Where am I?" she asked aloud. "I'm going to sunburn."

She crossed her legs and looked out to the sea. The ocean was blue, and the sand was yellow. The clouds were pure white, and the morning sun trimmed the edges in gold. Surf broke over a reef, and porpoises played beyond the breakers.

I'm sorry grasshopper. I should have listened to you. If I hadn't gone to that chop shop, I wouldn't be here now, would I?

It's all right angel, he said. *I'm sorry too. If I'd done my job right, you would have listened."*

What will we do now? Tears ran down her cheeks, and she wept. *I don't even know where I am.*

"You're on the beach," said a boy.

She started. *I was alone!* She half turned and saw a young dwarf in a white robe. She covered herself with her hands.

"Don't worry," he said. "I've brought you a robe." He held up a bundle of white cloth.

"Can you read my mind?"

"Sort of," he smiled. "No, I can't read your mind, but it's not hard to guess what you're thinking."

"Who are you?"

"I'm a friend, and I don't tell lies. Not that you can lie here anyway. So stop fretting. Here, take this." He handed her the robe and turned his back. "Put it on. I won't look."

Warm and as soft as down, it felt good. It had no label.

She slipped it on and tied the sash. *I feel like a guest at the Ritz.*

"My name's Angela, what's yours?"

"I know your name."

"You didn't tell me your name," she said. "How do you know mine?"

"I'm Evan." He held out his hand and she took it. "Come on."

"Where am I?"

"Don't you know? Surely you have some idea."

"I remember going to a chop shop. Then the lights went out. That's all."

"I see. No idea whatsoever?"

"No."

They walked slowly up the beach.

"Am I?"

"Are you what?"

"Am I dead?"

"Do you feel dead?"

"No, but I've never been dead before. It's awfully strange."

"Then, can we assume you're not dead? You're certainly not at home."

She felt weak and her knees buckled. She dropped to the sand. The young man caught her and broke her fall.

"What's happening to me?"

"You nearly fainted."

"I'm dead is that it?"

"We covered that Angela. You're not dead. You're just not home yet. Don't worry. I've been sent to greet you. We're going to go up that dune over there." He pointed to where the dunes parted and a little stack of drift wood marked a path. "You'll learn, and in time, you'll know."

"Where are you taking me?"

"Don't worry, I said."

"It's not?"

"What? No of course not. You landed in the sea, and you made it to the beach. So you'll do. You've got too much to learn to explain it on the beach in your bathrobe. Just stop worrying, and know you're going the right way now."

"Hug?" she tugged at his robe.

His arms opened, and she hugged him. She was so grateful, but she was not sure if it was proper to hug him.

Told you I'd find you a boyfriend.

Shut up, grasshopper!

"Are you an angel?" she asked.

"No, if I were an angel I would have been here on time and not let you worry yourself. I'm just a dwarf like you, though I've been here awhile longer than you."

"How long have you been here?"

"That would be telling." Evan grinned, "Stop it please. I'll answer all your questions eventually. It's not a big mystery, but there's no rush. Trust me; you'll have lots of questions."

He squeezed her hand and led her up the beach.

~~~~~

The Adventure Continues
Cretaceous Clay
& the
Yellow Stone

Coming Soon!

~~~~~

"Welcome to the book trailer for ***Cretaceous Clay & The Yellow Stone***." A dragon sunbathed under the stage lights. He occupied a fair portion of the stage. He curled around a black dwarf in a camp chair marked with a large gold star.

"It's called a trailer since it trails the book." The dragon chuckled.

"Kevin, it wasn't funny the first time, and it still isn't funny." The dwarf looked apologetic. "Kevin is one of those guys you know." He shook his head. "You'd rather not invite him to the company picnic, but you can't say no because you'd feel like a heel. When he shows up though, he turns out to be the life of the party." The dwarf patted one of the dragon's claws. "Kevin comes in handy at a barbeque."

"Hey, Evan, I resemble that remark!" Kevin missed his mark and the joke fell flat. "You guys are jealous! Breathing fire takes talent. Too little and I ruin the shot. Too much and I'll barbecue the stunt men."

"Kevin, get on with it. Introduce yourself. Everyone's waiting."

"Oh, yeah, I suppose I should get this show on the road." Kevin let smoke rise from his nostrils. "Hi, folks! I'm Kevin the Clever, and I portray the Dragon Lord in the ***Chronicles of Cretaceous Clay***. I'm the real power behind the Black Dwarf."

"All right, Kevin," the dwarf stood up on cue. "If it's not

too much trouble, can you introduce a real star?"

"Don't let that star on your chair go to your head Evan." Kevin's eye twinkled. "Evan portrays the Black Dwarf. He thinks he's smoked Jack in the Ninth Ring, but we know Nimrod can't do anything right."

"Have you checked the script?" asked Evan. "Maybe Nimrod's got a trick up his sleeve?"

"Jack's name is in the title, Evan. I think we can assume he wins."

"So? Nimrod's made progress. Jack's an outlaw, and he's lost his flyer. I'd appreciate it if you don't attack my illusions."

"Delusions, Evan. Nimrod's got nothing. Jack's destroyed his lair in the Black Wharf and driven him out of the Ninth Ring. He's got Nimrod's staff and he's picked up more clues to what makes Nimrod tick."

"Kevin," The dwarf sighed. "What's next on our agenda?"

The dragon loomed over the dwarf and grinned. "Before we tell our Gentle Readers more about Yellow Stone, we have to answer some questions from the peanut gallery don't we?"

"Yep, Kevin, that's right. Several fans have asked us the same questions. We've gotten in touch with the author and she's authorized us to share some of the background details."

"So who is the author, Evan?"

"As most of us know, Jack Clay is the legendary hero of the Gap. Like Robin Hood, authors have told and retold his story again and again since the incredible events during the Gap changed the world. Jack has appeared as an incurable romantic, a vigilante, a comedian, and in the controversial version, 'Interview with Jack,' he even became a conflicted vampire.

"The author of our series is Kathryn Ann Dayna. Twenty five years ago, Kathryn retired on a hobgoblin's stipend. She decided to write a version for young adults to make ends meet.

"We caught up with Kathryn on the moon where she is currently a writing instructor at Doxos Luna. She gave us her best answers."

"One of the most common questions from fans is when. When does the story take place? In a sci-fi story, why would anyone care?"

"They're fans, Evan," said Kathryn. "And they want to know! I left many questions unanswered because I didn't want to bog down the story, but fans want to know these things.

"Everyone knows the story opens in the spring of 364 A.A. Four centuries of the Age of Aquarius had left Earth a wreck. Peace and understanding may guide the stars, but most people didn't get the memo.

"In the first century, biotechnology effectively replaced mankind and men no longer needed one another for much of anything. The era of man ended when their population collapsed and biots replaced them. Unfortunately, the first biots were cruelly mistreated and certain violent elements took advantage of their plight to start the Regressive Wars. Some say there was only one war – the biot war, but others claim to identify over thirty distinct conflicts. Everyone agrees though that the era of Regressive Wars ended when Colonel Justin won the Aftershock War and sent the warlords of Ur packing.

"The Aftershock War left Nodlon as the sole superpower on Earth. It was a simple case of the last man standing."

"Another common question: How did Nodlon come to be?"

"Nodlon began as a mine. Most of us forget our Thornmocker is Daniel Donald Thornmocker the sixth. His grandfather's grandfather started Thornmocker Industries, and it was his grandfather who started Nodlon.

"T. I. was a global mining firm in the first century. Ironically, Nodlon owes its existence to coal and the invention of anti-gravity technology by Marconi Blaze.

"Thornmocker started mining where Nodlon is today to supply complex hydrocarbons for the construction of the Great Space Station of Ur. No one would haul carbon out of Earth's gravity well on hydrogen perchlorate or any other chemical fuel, but the anti-gravity solved that problem.

"We forget the great space stations required air, water, and complex hydrocarbons. Before they established the space lines from the Oort Cloud and built the refineries on Mars, Earth was the nearest source of carbon.

"They started Ur just prior to the first Regressive War, and it took the vast majority of Thornmocker's hydrocarbons. After they finished Ur, the mine fell on hard times. The Regressive Wars had all but shut down Earth's economy and the demand for raw natural resources had fallen to an all-time low.

"With the family business threatened, Thornmocker started Nodlon. He turned the mine into a resort for the elite of the Solar System. Nodlon sits in a spectacular valley in Wyoming, and it was easy to throw a shield over the surface and construct a paradise. The mines served as a city under the city.

"Nodlon's resemblance to *The Time Machine* was no accident. Thornmocker modeled Nodlon's society after H. G. Well's novel. He named the city Nodlon after London, and he deliberately fashioned a community after the Victorian era. He got the idea from a trip to London in the late second century. He wanted everyone to remember the city before it was nuked.

"To his credit, Thornmocker wanted to make sure the biots were not abused – at least not in his opinion. Biots weren't treated quite as poorly as one might expect. If the biots weren't happy, at least they tolerated their lives and were never pushed to the point of revolt.

"History records that free biots voluntarily moved to Nodlon even before the Aftershock War. The decision had long term consequences since revolts and bloodshed prevented other powers from arising during the dark days when no one else on Earth dared hand a biot anything more lethal than a popsicle stick.

"After Colonel Justin won the Aftershock War, he emancipated all the biots who served Nodlon during the war. Dwarves were not left out, but there are very few free dwarves living in Nodlon today. Most dwarves are not free – or 'under contract' in Nodlon's society – because they were a new model when the war started. Very few dwarves were able to serve and so very few received manumission.

"Nodlon rose as a superpower in the Solar System because she had three things no one else had: The manna generators of Rickover Station, space yards to build interplanetary supertankers and warcraft, and a highly educated, trained, and loyal staff of free biots.

"No one else had the labor base after the war. Other populations living on the surface perished in acts of war, but Nodlon's biots lived underground and her elite moved to the Ninth Ring. When other kingdoms had no skilled labor, Nodlon counted on its free elves, goblins and molemen to serve as craftsmen, tradesmen, and working stiffs.

"Offworld ne'er do wells focus on Nodlon because all the other terrestrial powers were blasted back to the stone age and are still recovering. No one wants to tangle with Nodlon's navy however. Nodlon is the world's sole superpower and the only surviving nuclear power on the planet."

~~~~~

"What are biots?

"Biots are 'biological robots.' Despite the label, they are synthetic people created from human, animal, and synthetic DNA. The tie that binds them all is the contract system. Social contracts force many of them into slavery with too many necessaries to justify an open rebellion. Without the emancipation granted by Colonel Justin, most of them would not be free. Thanks to the Colonel, most biots are free in Nodlon.

"Biots come in many kinds. Elves, goblins, molemen, and dwarves are the most common in Nodlon by far, but there are many other kinds.

"Noddie is a good example. She's a synthetic leviathan – a sea serpent. Noddie, of course, is one of the most beloved characters in the original legend, and she had to be included. Her father was possessed by the dragon, and she has played many roles in the various tales of Jack Clay."

~~~~~

"What is the difference between dwarves of different colors?

"Short answer: None.

"Bio-Soft Interstellar invented dwarves. Bio-Soft Unlimited is their successor, and the largest manufacturer of dwarves. They chipped the dwarves to reassure buyers. What with biot rebellions underway in many corners of the planet and the solar system, few customers wanted the risk of free biots. They chose black as the color of authority and control. It had nothing to do with *Treasure Island* – so they said.

"Cybernetics Corporation introduced the white dwarf line simply to distinguish their dwarves from Bio-Soft's black chipped dwarves. Then they offered red dwarves with a series of upgrades. Other manufacturers offered other colors, but social pressure caused humans and free biots to desist from using more colors. Owners were simply too embarrassed to personalize or customize their dwarves. They preferred to pretend dwarves were either machines or humans, and not ask questions.

"Nodlon's legal system is quite peculiar. Free men and biots live under one system, but biots under contract live under an entirely different set of rules.

"Dwarf children born to parents under contract are also under contract. They are chipped after birth. Synthetic children born artificially are also chipped. Agencies purchase synthetically born biots and collect the interest on their contracts.

"Biots born of free parents are free in Nodlon, and are not subject to the indignity of the chip. Save for the biots descended from those emancipated by Colonel Justin, few biots would be free. Only a handful of biots born under contract earn their freedom. Due to the interest on their contracts, very few biots can escape servitude.

"Either way, naturally born biots usually enjoy the benefit of having parents. They are not raised by an agency in a nursery. Albeit some agencies, such as Big Bee, have incredible success rates with their children and some parents fail to raise good children, biots tend to be remarkably stable and peaceable. Most psychiatrists believe this is due to the elimination of genetic disorders."

"In the book, dwarves rebel under the Black Dwarf's leadership. But they are mesmerized, and they are not acting of their own accord."

~~~~~

"What are chips for?

"In the late fourth century, when our story unfolds, chips were used solely for tracking. The chips don't work outside the city unless the dwarf is in a vehicle connected to the com-grid.

"This may seem odd, but the 'control' offered by the chips led to a number of abuses and unintentional tragedies caused by the software - reality interface. Certainly an abusive person can take advantage of someone with a remote control device in his forehead. What really led to undoing the control chips was the inability to make basic human decisions. A dwarf child might not escape from a fire or an adult dwarf may be unable to run into a fire to save his child or his owner's child.

"Although fire is almost unknown in Nodlon, it only took a few instances of such horrific errors to force Bio-Soft to delete the control software from their chips. Nonetheless, the chip alone is a sufficient sign of the dwarf's servile status to remind the bearer of his place in Nodlon society."

~~~~~

"Thank you, Evan for interviewing Kathryn." Kevin winked. "Now that we've answered a few of everyone's favorite frequently asked questions, can you tell us what happens in ***Cretaceous Clay & the Yellow Stone*?"

"Yes, Kevin. After Jack and Shotgun recover their wits, they return to Nodlon in disguise. Constable Wiggles cannot bring our intrepid duo in out of the cold, and the heroes have to plow on as outlaws. Like Robin Hood, our heroes press forward. Their friends and fans remain loyal, though.

"No one believes the Proconsul of Moab is in her right mind with a chip in her forehead. With a little help from his friends, Jack picks up the Black Dwarf's trail again and hunts him down to the Yellow Stone."

"Yellow Stone? Isn't that spelled Yellowstone? And what's it got to do with Tambora? Isn't that a barbecue?"

"No, Kevin! Yellow Stone is a new geothermal energy project. The Ministry of Manna is developing the potential of Yellowstone's magma chamber. They named their new station 'Yellow Stone' after a gigantic block of sulfur they found during the initial excavation."

"Funny, Evan, I thought Rickover Station had plenty of power. Why does the Ministry need more power?"

"Why indeed, Kevin? Objects in motion tend to remain in motion, and powerful bureaucracies seeking power always seek more power. It seems the Ministry is not above this simple law despite the oversight of King Justin and his idealistic daughter, Princess Virginia."

"What about Nimrod, Evan? Will Jack defeat you again and bring you to justice? Or will you escape to fight again in a fourth episode?"

"Kevin, Jack did not defeat my character. The real question is will Jack fail again?"

"Jack didn't fail, Evan. He drove you out of Nodlon. He destroyed your lair in the Ninth Ring, and he stopped your invasion of Nodlon. You can paint lipstick on that pig if you like, but Nimrod's had to retreat twice."

"Kevin, do you have to make it sound that way? I may be a black dwarf, but I'm not the Black Dwarf. Nimrod and I have nothing in common."

"Come on, Evan, I thought you were a method actor."

"Arrgh, Kevin, you are impossible!"

"Oh, well that explains a lot," Kevin grinned, "but what about the barbecue?"

"Kevin, the Black Dwarf's plot is called Tambora not tandoori. Tambora is a volcano. You're thinking of that tandoori chicken we had last week at Maharajah's Indian Buffet."

"Yeah, yeah, that place is great! You wanna get some take out."

"After work, Kevin! Can you focus? We've got to finish up here first."

"Right, right, so what can you tell us about Tambora?"

"Nothing will I dare say. That would be telling! It's a spoiler."

"Warlocks, volcanoes, and dwarves, oh, my!" cried Kevin. "What will you do next?"

"Good question, Kevin. What will the wicked warlock do next? Does it have anything to do with the Yellow Stone?"

"Oh no!" cried Kevin in a silly tone. "What about the war with Mars? Can Jack and Shotgun stop it?"

"Kevin, will Shotgun see Goldie and his little girls again?!"

"Evan, will Jack marry Jazz or become a hero sandwich?"

"Not if the Black Dwarf can help it. Nimrod will grind Jack into Swiss cheese and deliver him in a robo-cab." Evan intoned melodramatically.

"What about the subplots? What happened to Virginia? And will the biots ever be free?"

"Find out in ***Cretaceous Clay & The Yellow Stone***, the next exciting adventure in the Chronicles of Cretaceous Clay!"

"Cut," yelled the potbellied man in the fishing hat.

~~~~~

Biots Are People Too!

Made in the USA
Charleston, SC
30 December 2013